Conversations with
St. Bernard

Other Abingdon Books by Jim Kraus

The Dog That Talked to God
The Cat That God Sent

Conversations
with Saint
Bernard

A NOVEL

JIM KRAUS

Abingdon fiction
a novel approach to faith

Nashville

Conversations with St. Bernard

Copyright © 2015 by Jim Kraus

ISBN-13: 978-1-63088-927-2

Published by Abingdon Press, P.O. Box 801, Nashville, TN 37202

www.abingdonpress.com

Macro Editor: Teri Wilhelms

Published in association with MacGregor Literary Agency

Library of Congress Cataloging-in-Publication Data has been
requested.

Printed in the United States of America

1 2 3 4 5 6 7 8 9 10 / 20 19 18 17 16 15

To Terese and Elliot—
who are my source of daily inspiration

Prologue

Lewis snorted loudly as George let the RV rumble to a gradual stop.

"Too windy?" he asked. "Sorry."

George glanced at the GPS system on the dash and scowled. Then he pulled out a map—a real paper and print map—carefully sliced out of a large road atlas and folded into sixths, so it would fit neatly under the visor on the driver's side. He looked at the first fold, scowled again, then flipped it over.

He glanced in the rearview mirror. The road behind the RV remained empty. He had time to survey his options. There had been little traffic on Route 6 as he navigated his not-so-large RV through the north central portion of Pennsylvania. He looked at the GPS again. An arrow, which George found annoying, pointed to the left. It also flashed every five seconds.

"Stupid GPS."

George brought the map close to his face. At sixty-eight, his visual acuity was not what it had once been.

But then . . . nothing is as it was once, he thought, and his scowl was briefly replaced by a more curious expression, an almost smile, but not truly a smile, just a degree or two distant from a smile. When he almost smiled, from a distance, one might think of an aging Jimmy Stewart. Handsome, but unaware of the depth of his own appearance. Someone recently mentioned his cogent look, most of the time, aware, trim, and well-maintained.

Might be talking about shrubbery . . .

George looked up and tapped at the compass he had glued to the ceiling of the RV, next to the rearview mirror. Evaluating both the map and the compass, he realized the GPS unit was pointing in the right direction.

"Rats," he whispered to himself.

George had hoped he'd caught the electronic gizmo in a mistake. He had not.

For the past three days, since departing from Massachusetts, he had not once proved the GPS wrong.

"There is always a first time, isn't there, Lewis?"

Lewis, in the passenger seat, did not reply. He had most of his head and right shoulder out the window, leaning heavily to the right side, breathing deeply. It was obvious Lewis had thought he had seen a squirrel in the tree next to the stop sign, but it must have been a leaf quaking in the breeze.

Lewis, like most dogs, appeared to be fascinated by squirrels. However, if the truth be told, he was more aggravated than fascinated. Scampering and chattering, with their scolding, imperious attitude, a squirrel could simply disappear from a dog in the blink of an eye. And Lewis, like all dogs, found it both perplexing and exasperating. That was the truth of squirrels and dogs. And Lewis was a dog who had great regard for the truth. Everyone who met him soon discovered Lewis was a dog who had a supreme reverence for the truth, and he appeared to tolerate nothing less from those circling his life.

The large dog wore a sturdy nylon harness attached to the seat belt, and which gave him mobility in the seat, yet would keep him mostly protected in the event of any traffic mishap. Lewis pulled his head back inside and looked over at George, his traveling companion. George tried not to smile at the dog's naturally wise, avuncular expression. It was clearly apparent Lewis loved traveling—or at least riding in the RV, or perhaps in any sort of vehicle. Obviously, George imagined the dog's fondest dreams had come true as they began to make their way across America.

The pair of them, as odd as they were at the moment, were headed toward Towanda, Pennsylvania, and Riverside Acres, an RV park on the south side of the Susquehanna River, just across from Towanda, their planned stop on the third day of their trans-continental journey.

But Lewis's journey began just a year prior to this day. And George's journey started many, many years before—more than a lifetime, it seemed.

PART ONE

1

Lewis had not been the largest of his litter. St. Bernard puppies are never small, yet Lewis was "smallish." Lewis's mother had been on the smaller side of the breed, as well, weighing in at no more than 125 pounds or so.

Lewis earned the name Lewis because of the Burden family—the family who had adopted him.

Alex Burden, the singular offspring of Trudy and Lyle Burden, sat on an old, modestly shabby couch in the basement of the breeder's house, the upholstery covered with a thin veneer of dog hair. A slight boy, of average height, with a shock of brown hair with a mind of its own, Alex also had brown eyes, penetrating brown eyes, making him look older and wiser than his years.

Alex's parents remained at the doorway, watching their son watch the puppies. Alex was a deliberate and careful child, observant to a fault. Six yelping, growling, jumping, tussling, happy puppies were among his choices. The Burdens had been promised the first pick. And his parents had declared Alex, and Alex alone, would make this decision, this puppy choice.

"After all," they said quietly to each other the night before, "they are all St. Bernard puppies with a good bloodline. Alex can't make a bad choice."

So they agreed.

Alex had been a child with more than his share of troubles in his first eight years of life. There had been open-heart surgery, almost as a newborn. There had been a repaired heart valve at age three. There was the coarctation—a serious narrowing of the aorta—at age five. Other maladies had plagued his childhood. Surgeries and doctor visits had pocked his first years of existence.

But for the past three years, his health had improved, and his doctors claimed the most obvious dangers had passed and happily declared Alex to be a normal, healthy child, with no limitations on his activities. Mostly.

Just be careful. And observant, the doctors said. *Once burned, you know . . .*

"Normal kids have dogs," his father stated. "I had a dog. We have twenty acres of woods behind us. Our house is big. We can handle a big dog. Alex would like a full-sized dog."

So the three of them came to Clairvaux Kennels just west of the port of Gloucester. The breeder, Penny McAlister, a kindly woman of scattered attention, hovered behind the Burdens. She swatted at an errant strand of hair. Most of her hair was in strands, and most were errant. A personal style, but it fit her like a cold hand in a warm mitten.

"I know which one he'll pick," she whispered.

Trudy turned her head, just a bit.

"Which one?" she whispered back.

One puppy, the smallish one, the smallest of the litter, not actually called a runt, for no St. Bernard can truly be called a runt, the one who stood at the edge of the enclosure, his front paws at the top of the small solid partition, his eyes showing a fierce determination to scale the wall, to explore what none of his brothers and sisters had yet explored—or wanted to, apparently. The remaining members of his litter had been content to squirrel about in a large furry ball near their sleeping mother.

"Him," Penny said with finality. "He will want the one who will try to do all the things he couldn't do as a small child. He'll pick it."

Penny had been advised of the rudiments of Alex's extensive medical history.

Trudy, wearing her most sensible sweater and Danish clogs, did not think he would pick the one at the edge.

A dog who likes to explore, his mother thought, *and it could be dangerous. And Alex knows too much about danger.*

"This one," Alex said, pointing to the puppy who now had his rear leg almost to the edge of the partition, almost gaining a foothold, then slipping back and falling in a heap, only to scramble to his feet and try climbing the fence one more time.

Penny arched her eyebrows in celebration as she passed Trudy and retrieved the adventuresome puppy, then placed it in Alex's arms.

The puppy did not squeal or squirm or attempt to get away. He seemed most content to stare at Alex, stare hard, as if he were memorizing his face, and sniffing hard, to memorize his scent. Alex stared back. He did not speak. He did not introduce himself or tell the puppy he was a good puppy.

There was no giggling. There was no whimpering. There was no nipping and no petting—not yet, at least. None of it occurred. The puppy and the boy just absorbed each other, silent, and nearly still.

After a long serious moment, Alex finally spoke.

"His name is Lewis," he said.

"Lewis?" his mother asked. "Why Lewis? Do you know anyone named Lewis?"

She had read somewhere, in a newspaper, perhaps, young boys of Alex's age would often try to name a pet after a friend in school. The experts said it was the equivalent of awarding a high honor.

"No," Alex replied. "Other than . . . like in Lewis and Clark. You know, those guys I read about who explored America. Seems like a good name for an explorer. And there's a Clark in my class. He wouldn't like it if I named a dog after him."

And what do the experts know? his mother thought, smiling.

This is how Lewis was named Lewis.

His more unusual abilities showed up later. Much more unusual than simply being adventuresome.

Lewis expected the truth.

And often got it.

Not always, but often.

2

George locked the front door and stepped back. He looked at the house, trying to see it as dispassionately as he could. There were memories inside—some good and, during the last years, not so good.

And now . . . maybe I'll be able to get a good night's sleep . . . away from here . . . and the memories.

The house had been completely empty for nearly two weeks. George had sold much of the contents in an estate sale, run by a quartet of too-chatty ladies who had bustled about the house for over a month in preparation. What did not sell in the estate sale, and was in good condition and usable, went to a local church charity resale store. What George felt guilty about donating to charity went unceremoniously into a trash bin. Old metal shelving, still serviceable, perhaps, a little dented and rusty—those went to the trash bin. A stack of *National Geographic* magazines. (George felt more than a little guilty when he threw them into the trash bin.) Box after box of cheap—inexpensive—paperback books George read while waiting. In the span of a year or two, the pages had already turned yellow and brittle. Even the local used bookstore had turned them down. An upholstered sofa that had seen better days. Odds and ends. Broken things. A ten-year-old computer. Two old analog TVs.

And now the house stood empty and broom-swept and ready to have the next family occupy it and make a life within its walls.

For George, his time was over.

It had been three years since Hazel had . . .

George did not like thinking about the last decade. Life's final descent, for Hazel, had been a long and arduous and painful path.

No one should have to spend so much time and energy dying.

George knew it was coming, her ultimate end, and so had everyone else in their small circle of family and friends. He had waited almost two years before putting the house on the market. It had sold in two months, and for his asking price. He had rented a small apartment in Gloucester and installed the bare minimum of necessities.

His one major purchase since Hazel died had been a used RV—a recreational vehicle.

We always wanted to travel. And for the last ten years or so, we couldn't. So I will go in her stead. Recreation? Maybe. Honoring a promise is more like it. A promise. A plan fulfilled.

Their one daughter, George's only daughter, only child, Tess, lived in Phoenix with her husband, Gary. She called once a week, but with her mother gone, his wife gone, they had less to talk about than before.

She had been enthusiastic about her father's plans for a trip across country.

"It will do you good to be busy and meet people."

She sounded relieved. No decisions to make regarding his care. If he was able to drive across America, he was more than capable of taking care of himself.

George walked to his car and did not look back as he drove away.

"One chapter closed," he said to himself. "And one chapter begins."

He came to the stop sign at the end of Sumner Street, the street where he and Hazel lived for forty-five years. His heart hurt, just for the moment, upon realizing some chapters are more final than others.

Ain't it the truth, he thought to himself.

If he had any idea of how the concept of truth would change his life in a few short months, he gave no indication. He simply nodded to himself, agreeing with his own sage comment, and turning left, he headed to the west side of Gloucester and his new home on the second floor of the far west building in the Gloucester Arms Apartments and Condominiums complex.

3

The newly named Lewis sat quietly in the pet carrier next to Alex in the backseat of the Burden's SUV. Alex slipped his small fingers through the wire bars in the front of the carrier. Lewis sniffed at them, making sure whose fingers they were, then laid down staring straight ahead. The small blue blanket had once been Alex's, and it had been kicked to the rear of the crate.

Lewis did not whimper or whine. The breeder had cautioned them to expect it.

"They are leaving their families, after all," she explained. "For some puppies, it can be quite traumatic."

Alex knew Lewis would be fine. Lewis was leaving a family, of course, but he was entering into a new family. In truth, he was already in his new family. Perhaps dogs, over the centuries, have learned they are most often destined to be part of a human pack, rather than a canine pack. A human pack would offer more love, Alex thought to himself. And maybe a better place to sleep. And food at regular times.

Alex had read multiple books about dogs—especially the St. Bernard breed in the weeks prior to this day. He knew all about instinct and tendencies of certain breeds. A St. Bernard was supposed to be noble and unflappable. Alex was not sure what *unflappable* meant, but he imagined it was a dog who would not get too excited about things it did not understand. Alex felt much the same way. He didn't under-stand all the intricacies about his illnesses and conditions, but he had accepted them as his fate. He had seldom cried. He had seldom reacted with panic.

Alex's mother turned around in her seat in the front to make sure everything was normal and upright during their forty-five-minute trip home. Each time she looked, she saw Alex, with a beatific smile on his face, and Lewis, lying prone in the carrier, his soon-to-be-massive head resting on his soon-to-be-immense front paws.

She whispered to her husband, "I think Alex has a new best friend."

"We can totally hear you, Mom," Alex called out. "Sheesh."

"See," she said, whispering again. "He said 'we.'"

"Mo-o-o-m," Alex said, in an almost melodic whine of a sort. Lewis, the dog, wasn't complaining, and as Alex sort of complained, he almost felt guilty for doing so. It was obvious this might have been a first time for Alex, a first time of hearing what he sounded like to others. Lewis, the dog, was the echo chamber, as it were, a recorder and a furry instrument playing-back-at-true-volume. Not simply a dog, but a mirror.

Alex did not want to be a petulant child—the kind you sometimes see on Nickelodeon shows and cartoons.

Alex had learned *petulant* last week in his advanced reading group.

"Sorry, Mom," he added. "It's okay if you whisper."

His mother did not respond, but her eyes, wide open in surprise, met her husband's surprised glance back to her. Alex had been a well-behaved boy, but not one who would often lead with an apology.

His mother had read not-saying-they-were-sorry behavior was typical of only children. They had no one to shift blame to, and "children are loath to accept it on themselves," the childhood expert reported.

When they arrived home, Alex carried Lewis around the house and showed him where every room was. He carried him upstairs to show him his bedroom. Even though St. Bernard puppies are large, Lewis was not quite large enough to master step-climbing—not just yet.

Lewis appeared to be content with a short visit in each room, sniffing and looking, as Alex explained what each room was. They spent the most time in Alex's bedroom. Alex's parents had not yet decided on sleeping arrangements. A large dog crate had been erected in the laundry room on the main floor, with a custom hypoallergenic dog mattress inside. But Alex had made alternative plans and placed his old sleeping bag at the foot of the bed.

"What if he cries at night, Alex?" his mother asked. "Won't it keep you up?"

"He won't cry, Mom," Alex replied. "He's not one of those dogs. He needs to be with me. Or near me."

His parents acquiesced to their son's request. He was not a child who demanded much. And since his medical troubles, his parents were reluctant to say no to simple requests.

Pick your battles carefully.

"If it doesn't work or if the dog cries all night, he'll have to go to the crate. Okay?"

"Sure, Mom."

During the first week, Lewis never once cried or whined at night. Apparently, Lewis curled up on the old sleeping bag and slept when Alex slept. On the eighth night, well after dark and well past Alex's bedtime, Alex's mother heard a loud whine coming from Alex's room. She hurried to investigate.

Lewis sat, forlorn, on the floor at the foot of the bed, his head lowered, his eyes staring at the ground, a thin, lonely cry coming from his small throat. At first, Trudy thought he might be in pain. Alex remained asleep and had not stirred.

Then Lewis looked up at Trudy with those eyes, those wide, imploring, deeper-than-the-ocean eyes.

And then Trudy realized she had moved the tattered sleeping bag to vacuum in the afternoon and had forgotten to replace it. She had stuffed it into a closet just to get it out of the way. She quickly retrieved the bag and folded it twice, and laid it at the foot of the bed. Lewis obediently stepped out of the way to allow her to place the bag in the precise spot it had been for the past seven days. Lewis waited until it was down and straightened flat. Then he sniffed at it once, climbed on top, circled three times, and laid down, facing the door, his head nestled between his paws. He blinked twice and then closed his eyes.

Trudy could scarce hold the entirety of the scene in her heart and quietly slipped out of the bedroom, closing the door most of the way, allowing the hall light to provide some illumination to her son and his dog, walking away before her emotions brought a tear or two of happiness.

⸻

Up until this point in his life, Alex had not demonstrated much in the way of dedication to a single task. Again, his myriad illnesses had made it difficult for his parents to stay strict, and insisting Alex stay with a task until it was finished. He had tried soccer and claimed he didn't like it. The following spring, he had tried baseball. Alex enjoyed playing with his teammates but never appeared comfortable, either at bat or attempting to catch a fly ball. He did not repeat in either sport.

So when Alex spent hour upon hour with Lewis, teaching him to stop and sit and come and walk at heel, both Trudy and Lyle exchanged glances at first, then conversations about how a dog seemed to have changed their son into a better person—or at least a person with more gumption to see things through to their conclusion.

Alex and Lewis would walk along the sidewalk in front of their house, Alex calling out, "Heel, Lewis. Heel."

And Lewis kept up, walking at Alex's right side, his head just about even with Alex's right kneecap, not darting off, not chasing an errant bird or leaf, but keeping pace. The truth be told, St. Bernard dogs, even puppies, are not known as "darters." Their movements are larger and appear to be deliberate, always considered. Small dogs, terriers, poodles, and the like—well, they dart and weave and charge and jump and yelp and chase. Not so with Lewis. There was a certain large, hefty dignity as he walked beside his human companion.

Lewis accomplished the walk-to-heel training with flying colors. Alex could walk him down the block, cross the street, even encounter a yappy, pocketbook dog on the way, and Lewis would not once break stride. He knew his place was to always remain at the side of Alex.

Of course, Alex kept a pocketful of small dog biscuits in his right pocket as well—the size made for toy-sized dogs. For Lewis, a single biscuit would be one chew, maybe two, and a swallow. Lewis did love dog biscuits. In order to keep the biscuits coming, Lewis behaved himself and tried to follow every command Alex gave him.

When Alex smiled and said, "Good boy," Lewis smiled in return.

It was obvious even if he did not get a biscuit, he would have been happy.

But the biscuits helped.

Lewis knew the truth about learning and following and being true, even as a puppy. Biscuits lubricated the process, but Alex's smile would be reward enough.

4

George spent weeks upon months after Hazel had . . . well, after Hazel was gone, researching RVs, visiting RV sales lots, checking prices, making long lists of pros and cons. After all, he had trained as an engineer, and engineers are nothing if not methodical and precise.

Besides being methodical, he was also frugal.

His wife often teased him about being "cheap," saying he tossed nickels around like they were manhole covers. George took all of it in a good-natured way. He considered himself thrifty.

When it came to his wife's medical needs, however, George had spared no expense. They had gone for second and third opinions. If the doctors suggested it, there would be no treatment beyond their reach. When the time came, he brought in the best hospital bed on the market. He had arranged for nurses to come in frequently and, at the end, for nearly six months, to be there twenty-four hours a day. His being frugal—or cheap—offered George the freedom to spend money when it had been necessary.

Alone now, George had more than enough. There would be no financial worries or sleepless nights over the thoughts of outliving his resources.

Running out of money as a possibility simply never entered his thoughts and considerations. It was as if George knew what would happen in the future, of when his end was due. He did not worry, not now, and would not worry into the future.

After a long period of careful, and sometimes, agonizing consideration of RVs, George pulled the trigger. It felt good to have finally ended his quest.

He had purchased a three-year-old, nineteen-foot MVP Tahoe, cab-over RV. Easy to drive, comparatively speaking, with good gas mileage, also comparatively speaking of course, with a shower, toilet, small kitchen, couch, TV, A/C, heater, Wi-Fi accessibility, and a full bed over the cab area.

George said it looked like a truck camper on steroids.

And he had no plans on being electronically connected during his travels, but the Wi-Fi was not a costly item, and he had no reason to remove the required wiring and whatnot.

Even as a young man, George was not the most comfortable and intuitive driver, so an easy-to-handle RV had been a critical component of his decision. A month prior to his purchase, he took a bus-type RV for a test drive—a forty-foot monstrosity with multiple beds and with a kitchen bigger than the one he had at home—and being in traffic had terrified George every minute he was behind the massive steering wheel. While he didn't actually love driving the compact RV, it handled almost like a car—not quite, but almost. George imagined he would eventually get accustomed to the bulk of the new vehicle.

"The former owner only used this one for three summers," the RV salesman, "Call-me-Chuck," had told George as they sat at his small desk at Jerry's RV Sales Depot to discuss the deal. "It's a problem with a lot of buyers in the mobile recreational vehicle market. They don't do their research. They don't think things out fully."

Call-me-Chuck had complimented George on his clipboard with pages and pages of questions and requirements. "You're a man who knows what he wants, am I right? Am I right?"

"I'm driving across country. I want something easy to drive, easy to service, big enough to feel comfortable in, since I plan on being on the road for twelve months."

George had looked at several compact RVs before settling. A three-year-old model would have lost some of its original value, at least on paper (better for George), while not losing much of its mechanical integrity and longevity.

"A good choice, my friend," Call-me-Chuck had stated. "You will be one happy camper with this model." Then Call-me-Chuck nearly doubled over in laughter. George did not think it was the first time he had used the joke.

First off, as the new owner, George had his new RV painted. He liked black cars. He had always owned black cars. So he had the RV painted black with just a bit of white pin-striping.

"I hate all those swoops and flourishes on most RVs," George told the body shop. "And they all seem to be beige. I don't like beige. I just want it painted black."

There was a truck-and-auto repair shop in Gloucester offering RV "refreshment." George had the refrigerator replaced, a new mattress installed in the bed area, a new couch, a new gas stove, and a new toilet system.

"I don't want anything to break while I'm traveling."

The shop's mechanic poked and prodded, tested and tightened, and declared the motor and transmission to be in almost-new condition.

When George had brought the RV home, back to his condominium, he'd placed a decal on the back of the unit—a white outline of the continental United States, each state outlined individually. Then, using a white paint pen, he'd filled in the area of Massachusetts, his starting state. He thought it made perfect sense, since it is, by definition, a state he had been in when he started driving his RV.

An armful of road atlases and travel guides were stacked on the dining room table in George's small apartment. He had made pages of notes, working on a tentative itinerary, looking for RV parks in the areas and locations he planned to visit.

I have ten months until I leave. In ten months, I can be totally ready. I want everything settled as well—all the legal matters to be signed, sealed, and delivered. I don't want my daughter to have to deal with anything unexpected or unpleasant. She won't know what to do about estates and wills and every-thing—so I'll have it all taken care of. It's the least I can do.

George, methodical as ever, wanted everything to be as normal and as usual as possible—even if it wasn't.

"It is what an engineer does. Plans for every eventuality."

George looked out the window to the darkening western sky.

Even death.

5

"Will you be home for dinner tonight, Lyle?" Trudy called out from behind the open refrigerator door. She could hear Lyle rushing about, always in a hurry to leave for work, almost always forgetting something—briefcase, car keys, lunch, wallet, whatever. Today was no exception. Trudy tried to view this hurry-hustle-bustle-lost-and-found-and-agitated as a charming quirk of her husband's—and not simply a habitual passive-aggressive form of forgetfulness.

"Probably. Have you seen my wallet? Did Alex move it? Or did Lewis take it out in the backyard and bury it?"

Lewis also stood by the open refrigerator, patiently waiting for some sort of food to tumble out, food he would gratefully snatch and eat. When he heard his name, he looked up at Trudy. Trudy would have sworn there was a hurt look in his eyes from being falsely accused.

"It wasn't you, Lewis," she whispered to him. "He was just kidding." Lewis responded by looking relieved.

"It's up on the dresser in our bedroom. Where you left it."

She heard the fast clumping as her husband ran upstairs and the fast clumping as he hurried back down a moment later. She heard him muttering, "I didn't put it there."

Of course you did, Trudy thought and shook her head.

"How about chicken tonight?"

"Sure. Fine. Chicken."

She heard the back door open.

"Have a good day, honey. You too, Lewis."

The two of them looked at each other with a knowing look. At least, Trudy imagined Lewis to have a knowing look.

She found a package of frozen chicken breasts and put it into the refrigerator to start to thaw. She noted the packages of frozen corn and lima beans—Alex loved corn and lima beans. There were potatoes in the pantry closet.

"Dinner is set, Lewis. One less thing to worry about."

She nudged Lewis to back up. Lewis liked the refrigerator, especially when it was open, and didn't want to back up—not without getting some food out of it—but he did so, a little grudgingly, perhaps.

Alex had boarded the school bus a few minutes earlier, with Mom and Lewis at the door, Mom waving, Lewis wuffing in farewell. And now with Lyle gone, the big house grew still and quiet.

Trudy set about making herself toast and coffee for breakfast. She seldom ate before her crew departed. Too often, she would come back to cold toast and tepid coffee after searching for homework or the right color sock or the yellow necktie or the disappearing briefcase or helping a semi-frantic Alex with his unfinished homework from the night before.

She had learned, over time, it was best to wait a few minutes until after the morning squall had passed over.

Lewis seemed to like these quiet moments with Trudy as well. He would sit near his food bowls and watch her butter and add jam to the toast, add the cream to the coffee, and then, after she sat down at the table, he would rise and slowly, deliberately, make his way to her side.

Apparently, Lewis had learned Trudy was a soft touch—especially when Lewis put his deep-set eyes on their I'm-still-hungry setting, his head nearly at table height.

Lewis shambled over to the table, sniffing in deeply. He was a dog who loved the way food smelled. She could hear him, after she put his breakfast in his bowl: instead of eating it immediately, he would stand there, his nose inches away from the kibbles—inhaling deep breaths, as if he was truly savoring the scent of his first cup of food of the day. Only then would he eat. He was a careful eater, not a dog to wolf down his food like a hungry . . . wolf. He chewed with thought, slowly, enjoying each morsel. She could hear him eating as she prepared Alex's bagged lunch for school. She would hear him as she made the coffee for her husband. She could hear him as she returned from the front of the house carrying the morning paper.

And as always, Lewis would watch Trudy as she ate, studying each move with devotion, bordering on passion, watching each bite and each swallow with undisguised envy.

"Lewis, they say bread isn't good for dogs," she explained, perhaps for the fiftieth time. And every time, Lewis would snort in reply, as if to say "they" had no idea of what a dog needs to eat.

Trudy's resolve softened by the second slice, and she handed Lewis a corner of the toasted bread, thick with butter, carrying a thin smattering of peach jam as well.

Lewis, like a surgeon, carefully took the treat and chewed it slowly, enjoying the human tastes.

After he ate and realized all Trudy had remaining was the warm liquid in the cup—a liquid Lewis wrinkled his nose at—he simply sat back on his haunches and watched Trudy sip and read the papers.

After a moment, Trudy looked down at Lewis.

"I can see why Alex loves you, Lewis. You think I'm the most interesting person in the world, don't you?"

Lewis wuffed in response, his shoulder moving up and down with the sound. It was not a bark. It was not a whine. It was a ruffling sound, like he was clearing his throat, like he was agreeing with what she had said. When Lewis disagreed—with the food in his bowl, with a piece of broccoli offered to him—he would snort loudly and shake his head. Wuff meant yes, as far as Trudy could tell, and a snort meant no.

Most of the time.

"You know, Lewis, I like you a lot, too. You are one easy dog to talk to. I like that in a dog."

Wuff.

"I hear Alex talking to you at night. After you go to bed. I hear him whispering to you."

Wuff.

"I'm glad. You know Alex is an only child. And I worried about him being lonely. Or I did. Since you're here, not so much."

Wuff.

Trudy took another sip of coffee. She found herself talking to Lewis a lot. And the oddest thing was that Lewis always appeared to listen intently.

It's not the oddest thing . . .

Lewis listened, but the person doing the talking felt compelled . . . compelled might be too strong of a word . . . perhaps felt some manner of instinctual urge or a silent encouragement or a canine version of exhortation . . . to speak the truth.

A canine who desires honesty.

"Tell the truth," Lewis appeared to say, "and all will be well. If not, I will be ever so disappointed."

At least it is what Trudy imagined.

Something about his eyes . . . or his face. Hard to lie to his sweet, sweet face. He would be crushed if I lied to him.

And Trudy did not lie to Lewis. She often found herself unburdening herself to the noble and steady Lewis.

I bet Alex feels the same way.

"Alex was such a shy child, Lewis. I thought it was because he was so sick when he was small. So many operations and hospitals and doctors. I was so afraid for him. Lewis. You couldn't know. So many scars on such a small little body."

Wuff.

"And the truth is, Lewis, I still worry about Alex. A lot. I worry about every little thing. I worry so much. When he gets a cold or cough, I panic, Lewis. I do. We came so close to losing him when he was a baby. I couldn't take it if something happened. So, now I worry. Lyle doesn't seem to worry at all. He says he cares, but he doesn't worry. So I have to worry for both of us, Lewis. It's a lot of worrying."

Wuff.

I'm talking to a dog, she thought. *Like he understands.*

"I just could not bear to lose him, Lewis. I just couldn't bear it. I would simply die. And I'm not just saying it. I would cease to want to live. Honestly."

Lewis did not speak but stood instead and walked to Trudy and placed his large head in her lap. He had never done it before. And then, moving only his eyes, he looked up into Trudy's face, and he stared. It was a penetrating stare, a stare seeming to be more X-ray than normal vision.

And Trudy stared back and stroked his head . . .

And then the thought just erupted into my thoughts . . . like it came from somewhere else . . . I heard . . . "You have to trust, Trudy." It's exactly what I heard. It wasn't me doing the thinking. It's not something I would think of—it just isn't. Trust? It's not something coming from me. It was from someone else. Or from somewhere else. And then . . . in just the same way—another voice, another thought just entered my head, clear and almost as loud as gunshot, "God knows what He's doing."

Trudy stiffened a little and sat back and looked around the kitchen—as if looking for the source of the voice, the thought from somewhere else.

There was no one, no one except for her and for Lewis.

After another long moment, Lewis lifted his head from her lap and leaned back, just a little, and looked hard into her eyes. And just then, Trudy did feel a sense of peace, as if Lewis was telling her everything would be all right—no matter what was about to happen.

Trudy tried to talk, had trouble finding her voice, and then whispered, "Are you sure, Lewis? Are you sure?"

Wuff.

At 1:30, Trudy went to the pantry to get the potatoes out for tonight's dinner.

"This is funny," she said to herself, moving boxes around, peering up and down. "I could have sworn there was a bag of potatoes in here."

She got down on her hands and knees and looked under the bottom shelf.

Nothing.

"Well, looks like we have to go to the store. Want to go for a ride, Lewis?"

After Trudy uttered the words "go for a . . ." Lewis had taken off like a rocket, albeit a slow rocket gradually gathering momentum, but once going, was simply a blur. He slid on the shiny wooden kitchen floor and shouldered into the back door with a furry thud, smiling, wuffing, practically prancing in a state of preride delirium.

Lewis loved going for rides.

No, it was more than love. Lewis was passionate about going for rides. Next to being with Alex, going for a ride was the absolute best, most wondrous, most thrilling thing Lewis could imagine. He literally bounced to the large and well-traveled SUV in the driveway, panting, juggling from paw to paw, looking like a smallish, furry circus elephant trying to do the fox trot.

She opened the door, and Lewis, agile for his size, launched himself into the front seat.

Once she got in and buckled, he wuffed, then looked at the closed window.

"Okay, Lewis."

She switched the button, the window rolled down, and Lewis stuck his head out and greeted the outside with a huge St. Bernard grin, his tongue already lolling to one side, his nose wet with anticipation, his nostrils wide and eagerly sucking in as many scents as he could.

Lewis loved going for rides. Loved, loved, loved.

Trudy navigated the three miles to the market and pulled into the lot. Lewis looked disappointed. His face showed he considered the three miles as much too brief an excursion. She got out of the vehicle and locked the doors, leaving Lewis's window open.

"You won't let anyone steal you, will you, Lewis?"

Wuff. Wuff.

"Protect the car. I'll only be a potato minute, okay?"

Wuff.

Within five minutes, Trudy had returned with a carton of sour cream, chives, bacon bits, and a five-pound bag of Idaho potatoes.

They all looked so good.

She could see Lewis's head. A small crowd—well, two people—stood by the car. Trudy recognized one of them—an acquaintance who lived a few blocks away who Trudy sort of remembered meeting at a charity function.

Helen? Ellen? Helga?

"You have a wonderful dog here, Mrs. Burden. Alex brings Lewis by every so often. Such a sweet boy. And such a sweet dog."

Trudy tossed the groceries into the backseat.

"Thank you. He is a good boy. They both are, I guess. I mean, both Alex and Lewis."

Helen-Ellen-Helga smiled in response.

"What I would give for a dog such as this. But Myron here, well, he wouldn't hear of it, would you?"

Myron shrugged.

"We're retired, Mrs. Burden. A dog this size? Too big for a retired person. Helen is just dreaming. But for Alex, just right. Am I right?"

"You are indeed, Myron."

She waved to them as she backed out, and Lewis wuffed at them twice, a smile on his face.

"You are just right, Lewis. Just right."

6

Alex moved slowly across the freshly mown backyard, the rich, salad odor of cut grass near intoxicating, making his each step as soundless as he could, carefully placing his heel and rocking slowly forward.

His target, his intended victim, was his noble St. Bernard, Lewis. Lewis, at nine months, would keep growing for almost another year, but in height and length, he was within 80 percent of his full potential.

Lewis was big, but not truly huge. It became apparent he took after his mother, a St. Bernard of almost delicate proportions—as St. Bernards go—as if any 120-pound animal who tries to sit in your lap could be called delicate. And he was a dog who got semi-offended when the owner of said lap took umbrage with a 120-pound toddler climbing on top of his or her thighs. With fur. And nails. And often a severe case of dog breath.

From his first day with his new family, Lewis appeared to love basking in the sun, which is what he was doing as Alex slowly crept closer.

Alex had never once truly surprised Lewis. Every time he got close, Lewis would roll over or look up or simply wuff to let Alex know he knew where he was and was aware of his plans.

But not today, Alex thought. I think he's asleep.

Alex took one more small step, then stepped big, almost a jump, and before anyone could blink, he had launched himself into the air, a sort of suburban, dog-attacking, self-taught ninja. His broad smile gave him away—there was not a hint of malice in his expression, just joy and abandon. Midway through Alex's flight to Lewis, Lewis sniffed once, and in less than a heartbeat, the dog quickly lumbered over to his left side.

Alex clumped down hard on solid ground, missing Lewis by nearly a foot, and his breath escaped him with a wuff, a wuff to do a dog proud. Lewis shook his head, wuffed back at Alex, and grinned, as if to say no one sneaks up on a St. Bernard—not even when they are napping in the warm sun of a New England afternoon in late summer.

No one.

Alex knew he would try again. Just as he knew he would probably never be successful.

Can't sneak up on a St. Bernard. Can't do it.

Alex rolled to his side and draped his arm around Lewis's shoulders. Lewis obviously liked being cuddled and leaned back against his young charge, wuffing almost silently, the sounds rolling deep in his throat, as if the sound was just for Alex and no one else, like heavy machinery operating somewhere in the distance, a thick, rolling wuffing sound.

"Good dog, Lewis," Alex said.

And Lewis appeared to agree with Alex and smiled, a saintly smile.

It was then Alex felt something in his chest.

It sort of moved . . . or something.

As a four-peat operation survivor, Alex knew how to self-diagnose, even at his early age. He didn't need to go on the Internet to type in curious symptoms. He paid close attention to what the doctors had told him. He knew what they looked for when they listened to his heart and his lungs and tapped at his chest. He had scars to remind him.

But this wasn't like those. This was more like a hard tickle.

Lewis looked up and seemed to narrow his eyes at Alex.

Alex stared back.

After a long moment of silence between the two, Alex turned his head to the side and looked toward the house and the kitchen windows.

I know what you want, Lewis. But I can't tell Mom yet. Tomorrow. Maybe something happened when I hit the ground. Maybe I just hurt a muscle or something. If it still hurts tomorrow, then I'll tell her.

Lewis kept staring. His rolled wuffs sounded a bit louder.

"I know, Lewis. I know. I'll tell her. Tomorrow, okay?"

Alex stood up and rubbed his chest.

"Okay, okay. Tomorrow. Sheesh."

And then Alex brushed off his knees and his chest, the grass clippings snowing green, catching the sun like thin, fluttery emeralds.

Lewis stood as well. His eyes seemed to pierce Alex. And Alex did not look back at Lewis.

I can wait to tell her until tomorrow. Maybe it's just a muscle or something. But it feels more like a tickle. It's all it was. A tickle.

Lewis caught up with Alex as he walked toward the house. His head was now at Alex's waist, and he bumped his hip with the side of his head, just to let Alex know he was there and would always be there.

And it was the truth.

Trudy and Lyle sat in the kitchen, after dinner, after cleaning up, after all the matters of the day were settled, and the house had drawn quiet. Trudy lifted her head and listened. She heard the water running in the upstairs bathroom. Alex often showered at night.

Then they both heard the now familiar clump-clump-clump—the sound of a large animal making his way down the steps, one step at a time, but two feet at a time, bouncing, as it were, down the carpeted steps.

It was a hesitant Lewis who descended, as if he might be afraid of tipping over headfirst. Trudy often watched as the dog paid careful attention to the placement of his feet just so and the bounce in his shoulders as he made his way to the main floor.

Then came the soft scratching of nails on wooden floors.

Trudy had insisted on rough planking for the main rooms, so even if Lewis managed to scratch the floor, no one would care—or notice.

Lewis made his way into the kitchen, sniffing, walking slowly. The only food in the room was the two cups of coffee on the table between the upholstered chairs in the alcove of the bay window, overlooking the garden and garage.

"Sorry, Lewis, no snacks tonight."

Lewis remained standing, then stepped to Lyle, stopping when he reached Lyle's knees. He looked up. He was not smiling. If Lyle had been asked, he would have said Lewis was staring as if he were expecting something—a word, a cookie . . . something.

Lewis was Alex's dog first, then Trudy's, and finally, Lyle's. Lyle knew and understood the pecking order in Lewis's life and was fine with it.

Dogs need an alpha male—and it's Alex. No need to try and share the position with him.

But tonight felt different.

Lewis stood at Lyle's knees. Lyle put his hand out and stroked the big dog's head. Lewis tolerated it for a moment but then stepped back. This was uncharacteristic. Lewis never stopped anyone from petting him.

"It will be all right, Lewis. Don't worry," Lyle said as he leaned forward, almost whispering.

Trudy appeared surprised.

"What?"

"I told Lewis not to worry," Lyle said, now feeling a little foolish for having said it.

Trudy tilted her head. "Why did you say it?"

Lyle shrugged. "I don't know . . . exactly. Lewis looked like he needed a word of encouragement."

Trudy stared at the dog. Lewis did not look at her, just stared at Lyle.

"It will be okay, Lewis. You shouldn't worry," Lyle repeated.

And then, Lewis seemed to nod, retreated a few steps, circled the braided rug by the chairs three times, and lay down, his head facing the staircase in the next room, just visible through the open archway of the living room.

"How odd," Trudy said. "Usually Lewis is the one who offers encouragement."

"I know," Lyle replied. "But it's what he needed."

Trudy looked at her husband, not sure if was simply trying to be funny, or if he meant it.

Lyle watched the dog and watched as his chest expanded and contracted, watched his eyes focused on the stairs, and wondered what in the world Lewis had to be worried about.

7

George closed the door of the small pantry in his refurbished RV. The pantry had rails on each shelf to prevent cans from sliding back and forth as the vehicle navigated sharp corners. George filled the first cabinet with canned stews, single-serving cans of soup, cans of tuna fish and chicken, instant coffee, powdered coffee creamer, a few cans of baked beans, a jar of strawberry jam, and two cans of fruit cocktail.

He looked over his accumulation of foodstuffs—all designed to remain fresh—or at least edible, probably forever, George thought.

The cabinet door latched shut with a solid click.

The evening before his maiden voyage, his first test overnight in his RV, George planned to purchase half-and-half, butter, bread, and orange juice.

His doctor, "the good doctor Beth" as he called her, said to stay away from fruit juices—"They're just liquid sugar, George"—but George did not think he could face the morning without at least a small glass of juice, plus three cups of coffee. George never asked the doctor about coffee.

She never asked me about coffee, either. No sense in worrying her.

He selected Colonial Mast Campground and RV Park as his destination for the first trip. The campground was due north of Portland, Maine, no more 125 miles distant and most of them were freeway miles.

He pulled out a road map of Maine from a box marked "Maps" he'd brought with him from the old house. The map was given to him, courtesy of Fred . . . "you now, the Fred who owned Fred's Esso Station on

Manchester Road"—which was now a fourteen-pump gas station and twenty-four-hour mini-mart with sixteen kinds of coffee and an entire wall of soft drinks nestling in a long bank of coolers.

George had been reminded of it when he bumped into Fred—from the no-longer-existing Esso station—while grocery shopping for his trip. Fred was ensconced in one of those electric shopping carts that stores have for those unable to make a walking circuit around the cavernous store.

"Hey, George," Fred called as George slowly made his way down the soup and Hispanic food aisle.

George looked up and stared, not yet sure of who it was who had called him.

I don't know anyone in a wheelchair, do I?

"It's me. Fred. From the Esso station. I used to fix your car. You had a 1963 Buick LeSabre. Black, wasn't it? Had trouble with the transmission."

"Hey, Fred, how are you?" George replied. "It was indeed a Buick. A lemon, it was. Nothing but headaches."

"Bad for you, good for me," Fred replied, grinning, then coughing fitfully.

"Uhh . . . sorry you're . . . you know . . . being in a wheelchair and all," George answered, never quite sure of how to handle these interactions. His wife, Hazel . . . well, she always knew what to say and how to make people feel special. George did not have her ability, not at all.

Should I have said I'm sorry? Hazel would always know what to do.

George waited.

I miss her, he thought, then quickly banished the idea from his head.

Fred hesitated a minute, thinking, then finally grinned. "You mean this," he said, sweeping his hand in an arc, obviously referring to his motorized shopping cart.

George shrugged in reply.

What do I say now?

"Oh, I ain't crippled, George. Not me. I'm slow but not crippled. Bad knees, but not so bad. Too many days spent kneeling on cold concrete, changing tires. It was years before we got the hydraulic lift at the station. So, no, I can still walk. Slow, but I can get around."

Fred motioned with his finger for George to come closer.

George did so and leaned forward.

"Don't tell anyone here at the store, but I just like driving this thing around the aisles. I lost my license two years ago. Too many accidents, my son said. The police said it, too, along with my insurance agent. So, the only driving I can do now is taking this around the store. I can do about ten laps before the battery runs out. I drive around until the bus from the senior center comes back and takes us home."

George had to smile in reply.

"Your name came up a few days ago," George said. "Well, sort of, anyhow. I'm planning a trip and used one of the old road maps you gave away for free—back then."

Fred's expression sort of puckered up, prunelike.

"You got to be careful using it. Might not have all the new freeways on it. The bypass around Gloucester wouldn't be on it."

"I noticed. But the interstate was on it. It will be good enough for this trip."

"Where you headed?"

"Just up to Portland. A little north of the city. I'm taking the RV out for the first time. Want to make sure everything works."

"You got an RV?"

George nodded and told him all the specifics—make, model, engine, and interior accoutrements—all the while, Fred's smile waxed and waned.

"Always wanted to travel in one," Fred said, obviously wistful. "Your wife all hepped up to travel in a RV? Most women say they don't want to travel in a house—they still have to cook and clean and sweep and all."

"Well . . . I'm traveling alone. My wife . . . she . . . three or four years ago . . ."

Fred's smile vanished.

"I am sorry, George. You know, I knew it. These days, I read the obituaries before I read the comics. I remember now, I did read she passed on. I forgot. Sorry for your loss."

George never knew how to respond to this comment either.

"Thanks."

"But still . . . I envy you, George. Being able to travel like a gypsy. I wish I still could. But time caught up with me. So I'm stuck driving a scooter around a grocery store. Don't it beat all?"

George smiled again.

"Nice seeing you again, Fred. The new gas station just isn't like it was in the old days."

"Nothing is, George. Nothing ever is."

Fred offered a dispirited half wave of farewell and twisted the handle on the scooter, the motor produced a tired whirr, and slowly, Fred rolled down the aisle and away. He extended a stiff right arm, then made a sharp right turn.

8

Alex called out his good nights to his mom and dad, then climbed into his bed.

Tomorrow is Saturday, and I can stay up and read tonight.

He grabbed his latest book and pushed the pillows against the headboard. All the while, Lewis had been watching him, more closely than ever before, Alex thought.

"I know I should have told her, but it did not feel as bad today," Alex whispered. "I almost felt normal, Lewis. I did."

Lewis stood on his smooshed-down sleeping bag and appeared to think for a moment, then walked to the head of the bed. He turned and sat down, in a most deliberate manner. He shook his head, his ears audibly flapping and slapping against the top of his head. Then he shook his whole body, ruffling his fur and himself, and then sat still, staring straight at Alex.

Alex heard him breath, deep breaths, almost deeper than the breath Alex drew.

Instead of paying attention to Lewis, Alex opened his book and made it look like he was reading, engrossed in the story of renegade owls and hawks involved in all manner of avian intrigue.

Of all characteristics of a St. Bernard, Lewis embodied patience most of all. At least most of the time. At least this evening. Lewis sat, still, quiet, his only movements the expansion of his chest as he drew in breath after breath. And the occasional blink.

Alex chose to attempt to ignore his canine companion, turning the pages of the book in a more relaxed manner than usual. He thought of turning on his side, facing away from Lewis, but knew the dog would just stand and make his way to the other side of the bed. Besides, if he did, the lamp would then be on the wrong side, and Lewis would see through his ruse immediately.

After fifteen minutes of pretending to read, and pretending Lewis was not staring, Alex sighed deeply, folded a page corner over to mark his place, and faced his friend.

"Okay, Lewis, you win," he whispered. "I promise I will tell Mom tomorrow."

Lewis wuffed in response. The wuff was not exactly accusatory, but close to it.

"But it's better than it was. I don't think it's what I had before. You know, it's not something wrong with my heart. It's not like it at all. It's different. Sort of tight, is all. Like my lungs are smaller than they used to be."

Lewis stepped closer and put his chin on the side of the mattress, inches from Alex's face.

"I know I have to tell her, Lewis. But she worries so much. I know she does. You know. You're at home with her when I go to school. She used to call my teacher during the day and ask if I was feeling okay, if I was sick, if I took my medicine."

Wuff.

"I know I should tell the truth, Lewis. I guess the truth is I'm worried this time. You know, every time I got sick before or had to go to the hospital, I never worried. But this time, it's different. Maybe I was too little back then to worry. I guess I didn't know what might happen. I guess knowing more stuff makes you more worried."

Lewis pushed his wet nose against Alex's forehead, then backed away.

"What happens, Lewis . . . if I get real sick? What will you do? I worry they'll have to get rid of you or something real stupid."

Lewis stepped back. A serious look appeared on his face.

Wuff.

Lewis pushed up on his front paws and in an awkward, near clumsy manner, pushed his head onto Alex's shoulder, like a shy girl on a first date.

Alex put his arm around the gentle dog. The slow, steady thump of Lewis's heart was nearly loud enough to be heard from several feet away.

Alex held on tight.

"I know, Lewis, I know everything will work out for the best. I know it. I mean, if God helped me through all the operations before . . ."

Wuff.

"He did. My teacher at church said so. I don't think Mom believes it. But my teacher did. She said God kept me safe for a reason."

Alex shut his eyes. He had not thought of Mrs. Woloshun for a long time. But he did remember her saying it.

Wuff.

"I know it will all be okay, Lewis. I know I have to tell her the truth. I know. I know."

Then Lewis backed up, slowly, and returned to all fours paws on the floor.

Wuff.

And then, Lewis appeared to smile and nod, almost imperceptibly. Then he walked to his sleeping bag, circled three times, lowered his head to his paws, and closed his eyes.

9

George felt the tension in his shoulders begin to dissipate when he saw the sign for the Colonial Mast Campground and RV Park on the horizon.

Intellectually, George knew he would find the campground. But emotionally . . . well, George admitted he could be a worrywart at times. He had visions of driving about on dark roads, narrow, meandering back roads with no markings, searching in vain for a place to spend the night.

He pulled into the front drive and rolled up to the small two-person gatehouse. A young man came out with a wave.

"Nice paint, sir," he said. "Don't see many black ones. Sharp."

"Thanks."

George handed him a copy of his reservation.

"Space 128. Here's a map. Take a left at the stop sign and follow the road around the lake. All the spots are marked. You can't miss it."

"Thanks."

"You need any firewood?"

George blinked, surprised at the question.

"Uhh . . . no. I have a stove and all I need inside."

"No, I mean, like for making s'mores. Like a campfire. Or whatever."

George tried to remember if he ever ate a s'more. Maybe when Tess was a small child. Maybe.

"No. No firewood this time. But thanks."

George put the RV in gear and slowly made his way around the lake.

The young man had been correct. The spaces were easily located, and spaced well apart. It was one reason George selected this campground. "Wide open and spacious. You'll think you're the only camper within miles," the guide book extolled.

It's not wide open—or empty, George thought as he pulled onto the concrete pad numbered Space 128. The sun reflecting off the water glistered against the RV, and George squinted.

It is close to the water. It's nice.

He set the emergency brake, as the owner's manual recommended. The spot was already level, so there was no need to set the leveling jacks at the corners of the unit.

George got out of the RV and walked around, making sure everything looked to be in good order. A stubby telephone pole stood at one corner of the parking spot. A thick black electrical cord snaked down the pole into a junction box, skewed at an odd angle.

Why couldn't they just install it straight?

He plugged his electrical connector into the box.

I paid for their electrical service. Might as well use it.

He walked to the door, flipped a light switch to make sure he had a connection, then switched it off again.

Still have an hour or two of daylight.

He walked down to the water's edge and stared out. Small wavelets danced and gurgled on the rocks. The water looked cold, but clear. He thought of getting the one folding chair he brought with him to sit for a while. But he didn't.

I can see just as well from the RV.

He watched a small sailboat tack into the evening breeze. Two young men crewed the vessel. He watched as they switched sides when the boat turned into the wind, leaning out over the dark water, holding onto lines attached to the decking.

I should have learned to sail, George thought. *We lived so close to the ocean.*

Hazel did not like being on the water, not even a small lake.

No sense in just me sailing alone.

After a few minutes, George returned to the camper. He opened the cupboard door and pondered his choices. He removed a can of "New and Improved" Dinty Moore Beef Stew—*Now with more Beef!*

He tested the gas stove. Ignition and a bright blue flame—a textbook response. He selected an appropriate pan, emptied the stew into it, turned the heat to medium, and slowly stirred his evening meal until he could see wisps of steam coming off the dish.

He took a soup bowl out of the cupboard, emptied the stew into it, got a spoon, and sat at the small dining room table. He took a bottle of water out of the doll-house-size refrigerator.

Before he sat down, he switched the radio on from a panel behind the driver's cockpit/seat. He fiddled with the dial until he heard the familiar chatter of a baseball game announcer. George did not know who was playing, but it didn't matter. It would be a soft, pleasant noise to fill up the silence.

He ate the stew, not in a hurry to finish. He drank most of the water, capping the bottle after each drink. When he was finished, he leaned to one side and placed the bowl into the sink. He had filled the thirty-gallon water tank before he had left. He washed the bowl out and the pan, dried it, and put them back into the cupboard.

The sun was still an hour away from setting.

George thought about making coffee.

This late and I'll be up all night. And I would have to climb down from the bunk area. In the dark. And I would like to sleep through the night. I've had enough of interrupted sleep these past few years. Maybe the change of venue will keep those dreams at bay. I hope so.

Instead, he gathered up the Gloucester newspaper and began to read about the recent city council meeting where they discussed the merits of increasing the parking meter fees in downtown Gloucester from twenty-five cents an hour to fifty cents.

"Double the rate? And they think it's okay? No wonder America is in trouble," George muttered.

By the time darkness fell, George had read through all three sections. He stood up and flexed his back. He stepped outside. A chill had come upon the area. George thought he could almost see his breath as he exhaled. At night, he could see campfires on either side of his spot. He could see families and faces illuminated by the flickering fires. He could hear laughter floating in the darkness. The smell of burning pine and oak thickened the night, lightened with the scents of chocolate and of burnt sugar.

Must be those s'mores.

On his left, beside their fire, in the window of the large RV, he saw a blue flickering, the unmistakable light of a TV.

And he looked up, staring into the star-filled space of the heavens. He stared for a long time, then took a deep breath and let it out slowly.

I said I was going to do this and I am. Plan your work and work your plan.

10

Alex woke up Saturday and blinked his eyes. He tried to take a deep breath but felt a sharp tightness, a constriction in his lungs. He coughed, trying to keep quiet, holding his arms around his rib cage.

This isn't a cold. I've had colds. This isn't one of those.

Lewis was already awake and gave every appearance of having been awake for some time. He stood by Alex's nightstand, staring, as if keeping guard.

Alex coughed several times, wincing a little after each cough.

Lewis moved closer and stuck his face a few inches from Alex's.

"I'll tell Mom this morning. I promise."

Lewis wuffed, acknowledging Alex's promise, and stepped back and allowed the young boy to climb out of bed but did give him a nudge with his head as he walked past, almost like a friendly reminder Lewis planned to hold him to his word.

A few minutes later, after Alex described his symptoms, his mother scooped him up in her arms, feeling his forehead for any slight signs of a fever.

"It's not a cold, Mom. I don't have a fever."

Trudy quickly wrapped the boy in one of a half dozen afghans scattered about the main floor, then ran upstairs to get the new, and expensive, thermometer guaranteeing "accurate readings from a quick swipe of the forehead."

Trudy swiped Alex's forehead three times, looking more and more worried with each normal reading.

"A cold I understand," she said between readings two and three. "This . . . I don't know. What else hurts?"

"Nothing, Mom. Just when I take a breath. It's sort of tight is all."

"Tight?" she replied, her voice rising, the tension apparent.

"Lyle, get dressed. We're going to the hospital!" she shouted upstairs.

"The hospital?" Alex complained. "Can't I just go see Dr. Larson?"

"No. You cannot. We are going to the hospital. Now!"

Trudy ran upstairs and was back down, dressed, in all of four minutes. Her husband clumped down a moment later, holding a pair of sneakers.

"I'll start the car," she said.

"What about Lewis?"

Trudy looked incredulous. "He can't go with us! What are you thinking?"

"No, I mean, has he gone outside yet?"

Trudy had her hand on the doorknob.

"No, I don't know. I don't think so. I don't have time to think about it right now."

Lyle grabbed the leash. "Come on, Lewis, you only have a minute. Get busy."

It was obvious Trudy was doing her best to keep her panic at bay, closing her eyes for a moment, taking deep breaths, clenching her fists. But it was also obvious she was not going to maintain control for much longer.

"Can I put on jeans?" Alex asked and then coughed once more. "I don't want to go in my pajamas."

Trudy looked relieved she had something inconsequential to do.

"Sure. Okay. You stay here. I'll get them," she said as she ran up the stairs to Alex's bedroom.

She returned with jeans and a T-shirt and a pair of slippers.

"Okay?"

Alex nodded. "Thanks."

Lewis came back inside and hurried to Alex's side.

"I'll be back in a little bit, Lewis."

Wuff.

"I told you I would tell her—and I did."

Trudy, now on hyperalert status, heard her son's confession.

"When did this start? How long has this been going on?"

Alex stepped backward, as Lewis stepped forward.

"Just a couple of days. I fell. I thought it was just a muscle. Out on the lawn. I tripped."

He heard his mother whisper something, something sounding like an oath or a curse or something he was not supposed to hear.

Alex's father broke the tension.

"Let's go. The car's running."

The intern on duty did not look old enough to buy a beer, let alone prescribe medicine or diagnose any illness more complex than a scraped knee.

"Mr. Burden, Mrs. Burden," he said as he sat on an arm of a chair in the waiting room, "There's nothing serious going on. I saw Alex's charts so I knew what to look and listen for—but his heart sounds strong and regular. Nothing seems to be out of range. His lungs are a little congested. It's probably what he felt."

Trudy did not appear to be relieved, not at all.

"He said his lungs felt too small for his chest. It does not sound normal to me."

"I know. He said the same thing to me. And trust me, we are looking for any damage or deterioration of the heart. We've got him prepped for a quick CAT scan, just to be sure, but I am positive it will be normal. I don't want to over test—but given his history, a CAT scan is called for."

"Of course, of course," Mrs. Burden replied. "But what is it then? What's wrong?"

Trudy's voice edged up in volume and pitch, her words tight, loud, and reedy.

"Mrs. Burden, let me ask you a question . . ."

She leaned forward.

"Have you introduced anything new to the environment. A new laundry soap. New carpeting perhaps?"

"No. Nothing like that. Everything is the same as it has always been."

The doctor rubbed his chin and then tilted his head.

"Nothing new? Nothing at all?"

Trudy turned to her husband, her eyes wide, almost with shock.

"Lewis. Could it be . . .?"

11

A television in the far corner of the waiting room droned on, set to an all-news-all-the-time station, the volume turned down low, so all was just a low mumble. The commercials came in with more volume. No one seemed to be paying attention to the flickering blue light this morning.

Other than the Burdens and the young doctor, there were only two other people in the waiting area: an elderly woman who was rearranging her purse and had a small stack of loose paper beside her, and a young Hispanic man, in a too-tight T-shirt, dozing in the morning sunlight.

The doctor looked at both of Alex's parents using his best, serious, I'm-a-real-doctor gaze. "It could be a reaction to dog hair or dander. Some patients with Alex's condition are more prone to allergies and adverse reactions to changes in their environments."

Trudy now stood, her hands clasped tightly together, the fingertips almost white from the pressure, her face tight, her lips pursed.

"I can't believe we didn't think of it before we got the dog. How stupid can we be?"

Lyle, Alex's father, did not speak and appeared to be trying not to look guilty.

The intern, the young-looking Dr. Jason Bell, who had grown up on a pine tree farm just west of Gloucester, almost stood to remain at eye level with Mrs. Burden. But Mr. Burden had remained seated, so Dr.

Bell was torn between the two parents and remained perched on the arm of the chair.

"But I can't say for sure. We'll have to have an allergy specialist come in for an evaluation."

"We'll have to get rid of . . . the dog," Trudy said, softly, almost as if she were speaking to herself and not wanting her words to be heard by anyone. And she did not mention Lewis's name. It would have been too hard.

Dr. Bell held up his hand, palm out.

"You shouldn't do anything until Alex is tested. It might be the dog. But it might be something else entirely."

Trudy turned back to the young doctor, almost too quickly. It was obvious she was in no mood for equivocations and "perhaps." She glared at him.

He did not wither. Perhaps, this early into his residency, he had already learned how to stand up to withering stares and guilt-inducing, wide-eyed, fixed looks.

"Mrs. Burden, I know you have every right to be worried about Alex . . ."

This time, Trudy's glare did work, and the young doctor stammered.

"But let's wait until we get an accurate diagnosis. Sometimes young children get this reaction from something as common as tree pollen or ragweed. Or even grass. And the condition is not life-threatening."

Trudy closed her eyes and took a series of deep breaths.

"When can we see the allergy specialist?"

The doctor replied, "Well, there's Dr. Rogers, he's an otolaryngologist—but he might be too specialized—and I don't think he sees many young children. If I were you, I would make an appointment with Dr. Kang—he's a good pediatric allergist-immunologist."

"Who's on call today? Is this Dr. Kang here? Can we see him now?"

This time, Dr. Bell did rise.

"Mrs. Burden, your son might have, probably has allergies. It could be to the dog. But it could also be something else. I can write out a prescription for medicine to help his breathing and keep the symptoms under control. Like I said, it's not life-threatening. There's no need to see any allergist today."

Trudy stared at Dr. Bell for a long, tense moment.

"Are you sure?"

"I am," the doctor immediately replied. "I am sure the CT scan will confirm it. I'm sure. His heart is good. His lungs are fine. A little congestion, but no more than comes with a cold. If you've had the dog for some time . . . then maybe it's something else."

Trudy took another deep breath, then, after a moment, replied.

"Thank you, doctor."

And just how am I going to tell Alex we have to get rid of Lewis? And where will he go?

She blinked.

Would we have to put him . . . ?

And with this thought, she stopped thinking about Lewis and began to worry anew about Alex.

12

George puttered around his small apartment in the morning, cleaning and straightening what few things needed cleaning or had been left crooked.

He seldom left dishes in the sink, so the wire dish rack for drying was empty save for his coffee cup and a single spoon in the small corner holder. He had been eating his toast off paper towels recently, so there was no dish to wash after breakfast—just a spoon, a knife, a small tumbler for his juice, and his coffee cup.

George had an entire cabinet filled with formal coffee cups and less formal coffee mugs—but he only used one cup. It was a nondescript white cup, on the smallish side, with CUTTER'S APPLIANCES printed on the side. It held just the right amount of coffee. A bigger mug meant the last of the coffee would get cold before he could drink it all; a more formal cup simply never felt comfortable to George, too fussy and proper. And if the Cutter cup broke—well, no matter—since it was a free giveaway. As George rinsed it, he tried to remember what appliance the cup was given away with.

"Might have been the microwave. It would have been . . . 1995. Or '96."

I've gotten over a decade and a half of use from a free item. A good cost/ benefit analysis, I would say.

On the three-stool breakfast bar, George had neatly stacked his travel books, his RV park guides, and a series of out-of-date tour books purchased for $1.00 at the last book sale at the public library. He knew admission prices would have changed and perhaps the hours of operation—but what else could they change at Mt. Rushmore? And since he did not need hotel information and planned to cook most of his meals in the RV, if a restaurant or hotel listed in the old book closed, it would be no problem for George.

He did anticipate staying in a hotel on occasion—perhaps as often as once a week. He thought a full-size shower would be something he might miss—and having more room at night to walk around in.

But maybe I'll get used to living in a hobbit-sized environment. People in prison get used to being in a cell. No reason I can't adapt to a new reality.

He had not yet decided if he would take any of the guidebooks with him. They were large and cumbersome.

Maybe I'll get one of those electronic tablets or something. Then I could have all the books I need in one spot.

He mentally added it to his internal checklist: evaluation of the new tablet gizmos.

There was another package on the four-person dining room table. George could see it from where he stood, holding his now clean and dry coffee cup.

He had purchased it three weeks ago and waited a full week before even taking it out of its locked traveling case.

Inside the black matte case lay a Glock 9x19mm Parabellum pistol. The salesman at New Hampshire Firearms in Exeter said it was the exact same model as the ones used by the West German border agents . . . "Back when they had The Wall."

George had done his research as well—all confirmed by the salesman.

"Glocks are easy to use, reliable, and effective. Can't buy a better weapon for the money. Compact with great stopping power."

When George first held the pistol, he was surprised at how sturdy it felt, solid and precise, and how cold the metal was against the palm of his hand. He hefted it, as if he knew what to do when evaluating a handgun.

The salesman did not talk a lot.

"Glocks sell themselves," he said. "Most of our state troopers use a Glock as their personal handgun. It should tell you all you need to know."

George paid for it with a check.

"It will take three days for the sale to clear the state. As long as you don't have any felonies on your record, you'll be good to go."

George assured the clerk his record should be immaculate.

"Not even a speeding ticket. Maybe a parking ticket. My wife never carried change with her."

The salesman offered a weak smile in return.

"Come back on Friday. If you want, you can test fire it at our range. Free for all customers. Just buy the ammo."

George did so. On Friday, he shot twenty-five rounds with the gun at a paper target with a swarthy-looking criminal pointing a gun back at him.

He did not like the noise, and the recoil of the weapon surprised him at first, but by the twenty-fifth bullet, George became nearly comfortable. And he hit the target with some frequency.

He purchased the locking traveling case and a single box of twenty-five shells, the smallest quantity of boxed bullets.

It will be more than enough. Much more than enough.

The case lay on one corner of the table, just where George had placed it when he arrived back at his apartment.

He spent much of the following day preparing a hiding place in the RV. Above the cabinets in the kitchen, above the mini-refrigerator, there was a small hollow area behind the crown molding. When he placed another thin piece of wood over the case, it all but disappeared. The only way someone might find it was if they knew where it was to begin with.

No one will ever look up there.

George was certain.

I can hide it there and forget about it until the time comes.

George took the locked case and placed it in the bottom drawer of the bedroom dresser—*just for the time being. Until I'm ready to leave.*

Plan your work and work your plan.

13

Alex sat in the family room, on the large couch, an afghan over his lap, Lewis at his feet, watching cartoons. Usually, Trudy did not like Alex just sitting and watching some mindless TV show, but today, Trudy felt as drained and empty as she had ever felt and could not possibly have summoned up the energy to make her son do something more productive with his time.

Just let him enjoy himself . . .

Trudy and Lyle sat in the kitchen, the drone of the chattering animated voices audible in the background. Two cups of coffee sat on the table. Trudy had her hands wrapped about hers, as if she were trying to draw warmth from the mug.

Alex had taken the medicine Dr. Bell had prescribed. The pharmacist claimed they could make do with a cheaper medicine available over the counter. Trudy averred and insisted on the prescription-strength pills. Within fifteen minutes of taking the pills, Alex said he thought he was breathing better and the tightness in his chest was lessening.

Trudy looked at him carefully. He was of an age now to bring about situational responses.

He might claim to feel better just to put me off being so protective.

She leaned closer to Lyle and kept her voice soft.

"What will we do about Lewis? He can't stay here. Not if he's making Alex sick. I looked it up on the Internet on the way home on my phone. One website said allergies can be serious with young people with heart conditions. We both know what Alex had—and how terrible the time was. We can't take any chances, Lyle. We just can't."

Lyle wanted to reach out and take Trudy's hand, but he hesitated. There was something in the soft, urgent shrillness of her voice keeping his hand still.

"We have to wait until he's tested. Maybe it's the grass. Or the laundry detergent. You heard the doctor. It could be anything."

Trudy's face drew tighter, obviously indicating Trudy was not buying his argument.

"It's the dog, Lyle. We both know it. I can't let our little boy stay sick for the sake of a dog. A pet is discretionary, Lyle. I'm not risking the life of my only child for an animal."

Trudy's shrillness had given way to a metallic, hard firmness.

Lyle nodded. He had heard her firm tone before and knew there was little he could do to change it.

"Well, whatever it is," Lyle replied, "we say nothing to Alex until we get a report from the allergy doctor. And we make no plans. I'm not jumping the gun, here, Trudy. We can wait a few days. He loves Lewis."

They sat in silence.

A jingle for a chocolate-covered breakfast cereal spilled out from the family room.

"A few days," Lyle repeated.

Trudy's face did not soften at all.

"Okay. But if it's the dog, the dog goes."

And at the moment, Trudy's mouth tightened.

How am I going to lie to Lewis?

At night, after the lights were out and the house grew silent, and Alex heard the sounds of rhythmic breathing from his parents' room, he sat up in bed. Then he crawled so his head was just above the reclining Lewis at the foot of the bed.

Lewis was up. Anytime Alex stirred for more than a moment, Lewis woke. Sometimes he simply opened his eyes and listened. Sometimes he stood up and looked at Alex, worried he might be in pain or having a bad dream.

This night, Lewis simply rolled and twisted so he could look up and see Alex's face by the reflected moonlight.

Alex did not like shades on his windows—so if the moon was full, the room was bright.

"Lewis," he whispered. "I heard them talking. I heard what they said about me and you."

Lewis did not smile like he normally did when Alex talked to him but stared at him, as if he understood everything being said.

"They think little kids can't hear stuff. But I heard, Lewis."

Alex tried his best not to sniffle. The few times he cried were always preceded by a sudden onset of sniffles. He worried his mother would hear him and come running. He did not want her to come. And he did not want her to hear what he had to say to Lewis. This was a private talk between a young boy and his dog and moms shouldn't overhear.

"Lewis, you have to promise me something. Okay?"

Lewis looked like he tried to nod in agreement. Alex knew he would have wuffed if it were in the day and no one was around, but he heard Alex whispering and Alex knew Lewis would be whispering, too, in his own way.

"You might have to go to some other family. You know I might be getting sick from your fur."

Lewis looked down at the floor, as if he was feeling guilty and a little ashamed.

"It's not your fault, Lewis," Alex whispered and put his hand over the bed and stroked Lewis's head. "It's me. I'm allergic to you, I think."

Lewis glanced up, a hopeful look on his face.

"If I'm allergic, and you have to go to another family, you have to promise me you will never forget about me, okay? Because I won't ever forget about you."

At this, Lewis stood up and placed his front paws up on the foot of the bed. His head was even with Alex's head.

"You have to remember what I told you about Mrs. Woloshun. Okay? All of this is part of God's plan. Like maybe you have to go with someone who needs you more than I do."

And then Lewis did something he had never done before. He clambered up onto Alex's bed, climbing carefully and slowly, unwilling to step on a foot or leg hidden under the covers. He then waited for Alex to turn and put his head back on his pillow. Then Lewis carefully lowered himself and lay next to the young boy.

"An operation, I can understand, Lewis," Alex whispered in his ear. "But I don't understand this at all. I love you, Lewis. And I don't want you to go."

Lewis pushed his head against Alex's shoulder and almost silently wuffed back in the boy's ear.

"I don't understand why believing in God has to be so hard sometimes, Lewis."

Lewis wuffed again.

"I believe and I don't understand. It just hurts and I don't understand why."

14

George had not expected his daughter and son-in-law to make the long trek from Phoenix to Gloucester—just under three thousand miles—merely to visit him. Tess had flown in at least every six months toward the end, and during the last month, she simply stayed. But now the necessity was gone, George did not imagine he would get many out-of-town visitors.

But Trudy had a high school reunion to attend and notified her father several months in advance of their plans.

We'll get a hotel room. I know your apartment is small. And we both like our own space, don't we, Dad?

Gary and Tess arrived at George's apartment with a box full of pastries from Virgilio's.

"We come bearing gifts," Tess said with great cheer and offered her father a quick peck on the cheek. George was not the most demonstrative of men but enjoyed having his daughter in the area for a few days. Gary shook his hand. Neither of the men were native to hugging.

"You do have a coffeepot, right, Dad?" Tess asked. "You're not still making the horrible discount instant coffee?"

He was, but it was a battle not worth fighting. He nodded.

"On the counter. And I just bought a new can of Maxwell House coffee."

Tess tilted her head in suspicion.

"You bought it for us, didn't you? You haven't used the coffeemaker since Mom died, have you?"

Tess used the word *died*, and it provided a little jolt to George's heart. He tended not to even use *death* or *died* in his thoughts. It was as if he simply closed the door on part of his life and seldom even went near it. To hear *death* brought the door closer—and even opened it a bit.

"Not often," George said after a moment.

Not worth telling a lie over. I haven't used it since Hazel . . .

"It's okay, Dad," Trudy said as she used an ancient can opener on the Maxwell House blend. "I just want you to be happy. And I like good coffee. I think you should have good coffee, too."

"I like instant. It tastes exactly like instant coffee should taste."

Tess shook her head, as if giving up the debate before it even began.

"Well, at least Mr. Coffee is an improvement over instant. You do have half-and-half, right?"

George smiled. "Of course. I'm not a complete Neanderthal. I have some standards."

The three of them sat at the small table and ate their way through most of what Tess had purchased.

"No decent Italian bakeries in Phoenix. Actually, other than supermarkets, no bakeries at all."

"Too hot," George said. "People don't eat donuts when it's 110 degrees outside."

Tess smiled and patted her father's hand. "I know you think we moved to the first circle of hell—in Phoenix. But it's not too bad."

Gary cleared his throat. He had not spoken much since he arrived. He never spoke a lot. Some people claim women marry an image of their father. Tess might have made the claim ring truer. Both men were taciturn . . . closer to being phlegmatic, if the truth be told.

"There's a computer store over by the mall, isn't there?"

George shrugged.

"Don't know. Don't shop there."

Tess patted her father's hand.

"We know you don't, Dad. You would use smoke signals if you still could. And yes, Gary. Just north of the mall. There's a store called Tiny Planet Computers, I think. They make their own."

"You mind?" he asked, his eyes alive and a smile on his face.

"Go. Have a good time."

As he got up to go, George stopped him.

"If they have any brochures on some of those new tablet gizmos, pick them up, would you?"

"Brochures?" Gary looked confused. Tess appeared shocked.

"Dad, no one gives out brochures for computers. It's all online," Tess said and noticed her father's obvious disappointment. She turned to her husband. "But check anyhow, Gary. Maybe out here . . ."

Gary shrugged.

"Will do," he said, picking up the keys to the rental car and slipping out.

They both watched him leave.

George turned to his daughter.

"They don't have brochures?"

His daughter waited a moment, smiled broadly, and hugged her father for the longest time, neither of them saying a word. They didn't need to.

Tess gathered up the cups and wiped the crumbs from the table into the empty paper bag. George washed the cups as she did so. In a moment, the kitchen was clean and back to tidy and neat.

Tess watched her father methodically dry each cup. He had used the good ones this morning. She knew he would have normally used the Cutter Appliance cup but instead used a thinner, more elegant cup. Those cups were reserved for company.

Tess was sure they had not been used more than five times in the last decade.

"You still going to church, Dad?"

George shrugged.

"Sometimes."

Tess almost scowled.

"Dad, don't lie. You told me to always tell the truth."

George nodded.

"I guess I did. And no, I don't go often these days."

"Why not? Mom loved going to church."

"She did."

"Doesn't your faith help? When you get lonely?"

George did not look at his daughter, but instead out the large window in the living area of the apartment. If you had a pair of binoculars, you might see a sliver of the ocean between the buildings to the east.

"Did it help your mother live? Going to church? Praying? Didn't seem to make a difference."

Tess folded her arms over her chest. It appeared she wanted to go to her father and perhaps put an arm around his shoulder, but she did not.

"But she was positive and joyful to the end. She had peace. It was because of God."

George shrugged. "If you say so."

"I do. God was in this, Dad. He was."

He waited to reply and then spoke in a soft voice, almost a whisper. "If you say so."

She may have had peace, but I didn't. And still don't.

Tess put the half-and-half back in the refrigerator. Everything in there, and it was not much, was set most precisely: the milk jug at right angles, the eggs in the small nesting tray on the door, the ketchup, the mustard, the olives, all equidistant from one another and apparently deliberately placed.

That's my father, Tess thought with some degree of fondness, but with an equal amount of exasperation as well. *Always careful. Always thorough.*

"So, Dad, tell me about your grand tour of America. You'll have to show us the RV when Gary gets back."

George spread out a table-size map of the United States. He had carefully drawn a yellow line along his intended route—with a yellow highlighter.

"If I have to change the plan, I'll use a pink highlighter. And if it goes to a third routing, I'll switch to green."

Tess simply smiled.

"Always careful and methodical, aren't you, Dad?"

George appeared to be puzzled.

"It's just normal planning, Tess. Everyone should do it this way."

He began to trace the route.

"The circles are stops, so far. I may add a few more. After all, I'm planning on this lasting a full year. So I have the luxury of seeing some things off the beaten path."

"Like?"

"Well . . . see down here?" George pointed to an area south and east of Pittsburgh.

"It's where Falling Water is. The Frank Lloyd Wright house. The one he built over a stream for the Kaufman family. Big department store moguls at one time. The family still uses it occasionally, from what I've read."

"I think they do. And I've seen pictures, Dad."

"I don't think Wright was a particularly good engineer—but I would like to see it. See how a bad engineer builds a house. It's sort of off the beaten path a little bit and will take at least a full day to get there and back from Pittsburgh. But I have the time, so it's okay."

"And this yellow line will take you a full year?"

"Sure. See the big yellow circle around Pittsburgh? Did you know Pittsburgh has more bridges than Venice? I always wanted to design a bridge. But it never happened. I can spend three or four days looking at them and studying them. It will be fun."

Tess put her arm around his shoulder and hugged him.

"Dad, you and I have difference definitions of the word *fun*."

George looked hurt—for a moment—then smiled back at his daughter.

"I know."

He stared at the map.

"Your mother wouldn't like spending four days looking at bridges, either."

Tess hugged him again.

"I know," she said. "It is sad she never got to travel like you two wanted to."

It was obvious George did not enjoy speaking of his wife. His face tightened, and he looked away from his daughter.

"It would be nice to have someone to go with you on this trip."

George shook his head and shuddered.

"You mean, like some sort of old-age traveling companion? A senior for a senior? No. I've thought about it. I'm sure I could find someone who wouldn't mind a free trip. But no. I couldn't. Too much complaining. Too many 'Why are we stopping here?' questions. And you know, Tess, I am not the easiest person to get along with."

Tess stood back and had a look of mock surprise on her face.

"No! You? It's simply not true," she exclaimed, laughing.

"It is true," he replied. "And the RV I bought is a one-person unit. Or perhaps two small people."

"Well, still, it would be nice for you to have a companion on this trip. One who wouldn't complain."

He shrugged.

"Good luck on finding someone. And who would be crazy enough to want to live in a small RV for a year?"

Sighing, Tess said, "You're probably right, Dad. But maybe. Things have a way of working out, you know?"

"Not likely."

"God has a way of surprising us, Dad."

George sort of huffed in response.

"I don't think I want any more divine surprises, if you don't mind, okay?"

Tess went for a walk after breakfast and their talk. Her father sat at the small desk in a corner of the living area.

"Bills," he said.

She took it as his desire to be alone. Too many people, even family, for too long a time, even a couple of hours—well, it would be stressful.

And he's getting used to being alone. We're making him a little nervous. Asking questions. He's not used to it.

She walked, without having a destination in mind.

He seems to be shrinking. He seems to be getting bitter. He seems to be folding in on himself, like the rest of the world doesn't matter anymore.

She turned a corner and caught the distinct, acrid scent of saltwater and fish.

How I miss the smell. All I get in Phoenix is sand. And sand doesn't smell at all. And hot doesn't smell either.

She stood and refused to let any tears form.

But what can I do to save him from where he's going? I guess I need to pray that he finds a way to see the truth. Somehow.

15

Trudy had not paid attention to where she was walking. She started off heading in the direction of downtown Gloucester, but paid scant consideration to her route or ultimate destination. Lewis happily walked along side, sniffing, snorting, and staring up after the occasional squirrel.

Lewis loved walks, the longer the better, apparently.

Trudy simply needed time outside to think.

Alex and his father left earlier in the day to go to the Salem Witch Museum. Trudy thought the whole idea of witches and heretics being burned at the stake was most upsetting, but Alex had pestered them both for nearly a year to visit. Lyle had relented. Trudy had not.

Instead of sitting inside and worrying about what was going to happen and what fate would require her to do, Trudy decided to walk instead—and worry outside and wonder what fate would have her do. At least she would be in the sunshine while she worried.

"What am I going to do, Lewis? What if the doctor says Alex is allergic to dog hair?" Trudy was pretty certain that Lewis did not really understand what she was saying, nor did he grasp what was going on—but she thought that Lewis was more subdued these last few days, more pensive, more deliberate. Maybe he didn't understand. But maybe he did. Trudy was never sure. She knew that dogs don't understand English, but she knew that Stewart understood emotions—better than any human she had ever met.

The pills had helped Alex. His cough had improved—not completely gone, but it was better. His lungs sounded clearer—not totally clear, but better. Trudy imagined with the right medication, perhaps Alex and Lewis could coexist.

"It's all because of the Internet," Trudy added. "I hate it sometimes. So I find out medication for allergies can affect Alex's condition. There's a higher risk of complications, Lewis. They're not 'indicated for prolonged use.'"

Lewis looked up at Trudy with those eyes of his and snorted.

"I know, but it's true, Lewis. If Alex has to stay on medication, it could hurt his heart."

Lewis listened to Trudy, then shook his head and resumed sniffing at the sidewalk.

They walked for nearly a half hour. Trudy looked around to gain her bearings.

"Oh . . . we've gone this far?"

They stood beside a small park midway between their house and downtown. The park may have had a name, but Trudy did not know it, even though she passed the park hundreds of times over the last few years. A small cement path led to a cluster of benches.

"Lewis, time for a break, okay?"

Lewis happily followed her to the bench and sat down on the grass next to the bench with a happy "wuff." He tilted his head back and breathed in deeply. The thick scent of salt water and fish was stronger now, and Lewis, after a few full sniffs, sneezed mightily. He looked back at Trudy with a lopsided, jowly smile.

After five minutes of sitting, Trudy took a deep breath and let it out slowly. She unclenched her hands. She didn't realize she had made fists with them until she opened her eyes and looked at her hands. She took another cleansing breath.

"So what are we going to do, Lewis? I can't turn the clock back. I can't make Alex forget about you."

Trudy had been sure, since the day in the hospital, Lewis was the cause of Alex's distress. After a full day of Internet research, she became more positive. Everything pointed to an allergy to dog hair. Allergies took a while, especially in children, to make themselves manifest. A year, a little more, was all it took for Alex to start showing symptoms. Severe symptoms. Not just a runny nose and itchy eyes. His CAT scan was normal, but the intern did say to make the appointment with the allergy doctor as soon as they could get in to see him. And the symptoms would get worse, Trudy was sure.

Why did I ever say yes to getting a dog? This is going to be so hard. Alex won't ever forgive us if Lewis has to go. I know he won't.

Lewis shambled to his feet, as if Trudy had been talking aloud to him—which she had not done. He blinked in the bright sunshine. Then he sneezed.

Maybe they're allergic to each other.

Trudy tried to keep the tears away.

Wouldn't this be rich? Just what I needed. Not only do I feel guilty for Alex's illnesses, but now I'm going to be responsible for taking away his best friend.

She closed her eyes, more tightly.

She felt the bulk of Lewis edge toward her, his large head nudging against her thigh. He could tell she was upset, and Trudy was sure he was trying to make things better.

"You can't, Lewis. Not this time. This isn't going to get any better. It's just going to get bad and then horrible."

Lewis was not deterred. He placed his large front paws on the bench and edged closer to Trudy. She had no alternative except to take his head in her hands and stare into his wide, innocent eyes.

"I know you don't want anything bad to happen to Alex. I know you love him, Lewis. But what am I supposed to do? Something has to happen. And no matter what it is, it will be horribly painful."

Lewis shut his eyes and laid his head on Trudy's lap. He did not look comfortable at all, sort of bent and twisted in a non-St. Bernardian fashion, but it was all he could do at the moment to get as close to Alex's mother as possible, short of wrestling up onto the bench itself and climbing into her lap.

She bent to him and held him around his large, muscular shoulders and allowed herself a moment to weep silently.

67

Tess had forgotten how wonderful Saturday mornings could be in her hometown. Not hot, a breeze coming in off the ocean, people outside, actually walking on the sidewalk, no one sweating or coming close to sunstroke or heat prostration. She wondered why she wanted to leave Gloucester so badly after college.

Get away from the known and familiar, I guess. Strike out in a new direction. Totally separate from your parents.

Up ahead was a small park, trees, shrubs, a small fountain in the center, and a cluster of benches. Tess thought it would be wonderful way to spend an hour or two, watching people pass by, thinking about the past.

When she reached the corner is when she saw Lewis—although, at the time, she did not know his name. The large dog appeared to be unlimbering from half-lying on the bench, the woman with him, helping him navigate down.

She doesn't look happy.

Tess's mother had the gift—to know when people needed a kind word or a hug or a simple, cheery hello. Tess always thought she took more after her father, reserved, quiet, analytical, rather than a person who got involved with others and who intuitively understood their emotional needs.

Mom did. I don't think I do. Or at least I never used to think I did.

But after her mother died, Tess felt a difference, as if she needed to carry on the family tradition of empathy, as if the specific trait, the gift, had been somehow passed down from mother to daughter, in those precious few weeks when Tess was at her bedside every waking moment.

Maybe something happened to us both. I guess I'm the only one left in the family to keep the tradition alive—and actually care for people. And pray for people. I don't think my father will be doing any serious praying anymore.

Less than a half block away, Tess saw the dog look up and in her direction, as if he was expecting her to come.

My mother often said to help people in need, to pray for them, is the highest calling.

She smiled to herself.

And dad? Well, he said the most important thing in life was to keep an organized house—and change the oil in the car every two thousand miles.

Lewis watched carefully as Tess approached.

"What a big dog," she said as she came close.

Trudy sniffed. "Although, the experts say for a St. Bernard, he's on the small side."

"Wow," Tess replied. "But he's beautiful."

Lewis began to rock from side to side, an expression of impending joy, Tess imagined. The dog offered his best lopsided, jowly grin.

"Can I pet him?"

Trudy offered a short, controlled laugh.

"He would be offended if you didn't. His name is Lewis."

Tess bent to her knee, and Lewis came up to her, gentle as an old, tired bear, and stopped a foot away. She could pet him, but Tess was sure he stopped because he did not want to intimidate her by drawing too close, too soon.

Tess stroked his head. Lewis closed his eyes in pleasure. Then she scratched behind his ears, and he looked at her, those deep, deep eyes, as he took tiny dog steps closer to her.

I know my mother would have stopped here today. She would have noticed one of these two needed to talk.

Tess looked up to Trudy. She saw a slight tremble in the woman's lower lip.

It's a beautiful day. I need to listen.

She smiled at Trudy, offering the most inviting, welcoming, beatific smile she could muster.

I wonder which one needs to talk the most?

16

Alex could barely sit still on the way home from the witch museum. While the displays were not overly graphic with flesh and bones being burned at the stake and the rest of the lurid historical details, it was enough to inflame Alex's taste for the macabre.

Lyle remembered being just as fascinated by the same manner of bizarre and unusual that seemed to fascinate his son.

Must be a male sort of thing. Or an age sort of thing. I remember being taken in by vampires and werewolves when I was his age.

"This was totally cool, Dad. Thanks for taking me."

"My pleasure. We don't seem to get away—just the boys—too often."

Alex nodded.

"You feeling okay?"

Obviously, Alex expected the question at least a few times every day. Especially since his most recent scare.

"I am. The pills help a lot."

"Good."

"When do I see the allergy guy?"

"This Tuesday."

The drove along in silence for a few miles.

"And he'll be able to tell what makes me sneeze and all?"

"It's the plan. Then we'll be able to make changes. New laundry soap or new furnace filters or adding air purifiers—whatever is needed."

Alex looked out the window for a stretch of a few miles.

"It's probably Lewis, isn't it?"

Lyle had expected Alex to ask that question. He was a young boy who knew his way around a hospital and around a diagnosis. Alex had access to the Internet as well and probably researched the situation.

"Maybe. We won't know for sure until we see the doctor."

"I'll bet it's Lewis."

"Well, it could be."

"I would guess it is. Sort of obvious, when you think about it."

Lyle glanced over at his son, expecting to see pain or sadness or anger on his face. But he did not. Alex looked . . . normal. Almost happy. Or perhaps reconciled to the truth. Placid. At peace.

"Mrs. Woloshun would say it all happened for a reason."

"Mrs. Woloshun?"

"My Sunday school teacher."

Lyle tried to hide his surprise.

"You remember her? It was . . . four years ago. You were little."

"I remember her. She was real nice. And I trusted her. I still do, I guess."

Lyle thought for a moment.

"Good, son. She sounds like a smart woman."

Alex nodded.

"She would say all of this has happened for a reason. She said it about me being so sick when I was little. She said it would all work out—and it did. And we need to learn from the things God puts in our life. I don't know . . . but maybe I did learn some stuff from being sick."

Lyle wanted to remember every word of this conversation. Alex did not share like this often, and even less often with his mother—so Lyle wanted to make sure he caught every nuance.

Trudy will start to cry when I tell her.

"She would say it would all work out—just like it was planned. She said God always has a plan. She's right, Dad. It will all work out."

"I hope so."

"It will, Dad. I know it will."

Two miles later, Alex piped up.

"Can we stop at McDonald's? And not tell Mom?"

Lyle did not smile though he wanted to. He wanted to hug his son, tousle his hair, and tell him he was the most important thing in Lyle's life and he would do anything to keep him close, to protect him, to keep him from harm for the rest of his life.

Instead of doing it, he simply replied, "Sure. And we'll keep it a secret."

Alex waited two more miles until a McDonald's came into view.

"Thanks, Dad. I know it will all work out."

As they pulled into the lot, he added softly, "Somehow."

17

Hi, I'm Tess Bardle. From Phoenix."

"I'm Trudy Burden. And you've met Lewis."

Lewis was mooshing his head into Tess's shoulder, wuffing quietly, demanding more pets from this kind stranger.

"The only thing Lewis likes better than being petted is going for walks and rides in the car," Trudy said. "So what are you doing in Gloucester? It's a long way from the desert."

"I'm here for a high school reunion. Gloucester High. Don't ask what year."

"I wouldn't dream of it."

"And I'm visiting my father. He still lives here."

Trudy found it calming to be speaking to another adult without having to discuss allergies or illnesses or displacing dogs.

"What do you do in Phoenix? I mean, if you don't mind me asking."

She needs to talk.

"I'm a nurse."

"You are?" Trudy exclaimed.

"I am," Tess replied. "I work at a family clinic in Phoenix."

Trudy drew in a deep breath.

"Do you know anything about allergies in children?"

"Some. At the clinic, we have a couple of allergy doctors on staff. The dryness and the heat keeps the pollen at bay—but it does a nasty job on sinuses. They're always busy."

Tess watched as Trudy's shoulders visibly relaxed. Even the muscles in her face seemed to loosen, to soften. Tess thought she saw the words *thank you* form on Trudy's lips, but she wasn't sure.

She does need to talk.

"You have time? Can I ask you a question?"

"I have time. I'm free all morning."

Trudy laid out the basics of Alex's condition, a rough sketch of his medical history, and the moment of introduction of Lewis into the house.

When she mentioned the name "Lewis," Lewis looked up and wuffed.

"He's too smart for his own good," Trudy said as she patted his large head.

"Sounds like dog hair and dander might be causing it," Tess said. "But you need to see a specialist. Given what your son has gone through. I'm sure you will, right?"

"Of course," Trudy said quickly. "Tuesday is his appointment."

Tess saw the tension in Trudy's eyes.

Maybe I am more like my mother than I realize.

"But your son loves Lewis, doesn't he?"

Trudy just nodded.

"And you're worried about . . . what happens to the dog . . . if he is making Alex sick."

Trudy nodded and did not speak.

"Well, here's one thing you need to do when you get to the doctor. They may not suggest it—since doctors are just well-trained mechanics. If it is dog hair, they'll tell you the dog has to go. Simple. But there might be another way."

"What?"

"Patients can get a series of weekly injections—over the course of a year. It will drastically desensitize the allergy symptoms."

"I read about it on the Internet."

"So all you have to do is find a temporary home for Lewis for a year—until Alex gets a full series of shots."

"A year?"

"It will be easier for your son to be separated for a year—rather than forever."

Trudy took in a deep breath.

"So where am I going to find someone willing to take a very large dog for a year?"

Tess smiled.

Now I know why I stopped. Now I see.

"You know, I think I might know someone who would be a perfect candidate."

18

Tess did not speak about Lewis until dinner. She had wanted to see the inside of the RV—to judge if it was roomy enough for both her father and a St. Bernard.

It was.

While not exactly spacious, it would offer more than ample room for a man and a dog.

Even a man and a large dog.

"And it has a built-in Wi-Fi connector," Gary exclaimed. "George, this is so cool."

Tess remarked on the ingenious use of space inside—room enough for a kitchen and a bathroom and a living area and a dining area. Of course, the living area and the dining area were the same area—with a few foldouts and put-aways involved in switching their purpose.

"This is so nice, Dad," she said, sitting on the couch. "I can see how you could make this work for a long trip."

George appeared happy his daughter and son-in-law approved of his choice, and they both seemed genuinely impressed with the interior furnishing and the RV's accoutrements. Gary sat in the small above-cab alcove holding a queen-sized bed, and George and his daughter sat on the couch in the middle of the RV. Of course, this couch offered seat belts, but as couches go, Trudy declared, it was "more than adequately comfortable."

"I could have gone bigger," George stated, "but there is only me. And there's more than enough room for me in here. And all the things I need. And the bigger it gets, the harder it is to drive."

Trudy offered an odd smile at her father.

"Speaking of traveling solo . . . and traveling companions, Dad . . ."

Even Gary perked up at this opening. Tess had not spoken to him about Lewis either.

"I think I have found you a traveling partner."

"Alex," Trudy said, after sitting both him and Lewis down on the good couch in the real family room—the one no one used except when people Alex didn't know came over—"what would you say to Lewis taking a trip for a while? Not forever. Just for a while."

Alex did not reply, not right away. He first looked at Lewis, and Lewis looked back at him, and then both of them looked at Trudy.

"How long?"

"Until you get the shots to make you not allergic to dogs. If the doctor says the shots will work and all."

"How long?"

Trudy shrugged.

"Maybe six months."

Lewis cleared his throat, then snorted.

Come on, Lewis. You can't do this. I'm not lying. I'm not.

"Maybe a year. Depending on your sensitivity. We'll have to wait until we see the doctor."

"Where would he go?"

Trudy tried to smile, earnest and open.

"All over America, Alex. Wouldn't it be the best thing?"

"A St. Bernard? Are you crazy, Tess?" And this remark was from Gary, who had so far stayed out of the discussion. "They're big dogs."

George nodded sagely.

"Real big dogs, Tess. I don't think it would work. This is a small RV, after all."

Tess tried to remember what her mother did in situations like this.

Act firm. As if the decision has already been made. All you have to do is fill in the details. And do not put up with any negative thoughts.

Tess smiled.

And Mom smiled. A lot. Like you smile at a small child when you're trying to explain something complicated.

"Dad, you like dogs. You liked Mitzi, remember?"

George responded with a scowl.

"It was your mother's dog. And it was a small dog. Not some gargantuan beast of a dog."

"Dad, I remember you crying when you had to put her down. You loved the dog. And now . . . there's an opportunity to show the same love to a dog and a little boy and, well, to an entire family. You'll have someone to talk with while you drive. And he'll be good protection. You do realize you're . . . well, you're an older person, traveling alone. I would be worried sick. But if Lewis were along . . . well it would be different."

"Lewis," George snorted, "what sort of name is that? They named a dog Lewis?"

He's coming around.

"Trudy said he was named after the explorer. It's fate, Dad. You'll both be exploring. And he's the sweetest, most calm dog you'll ever meet."

Gary looked as if he was about to speak, and Tess glared at him, just for a moment.

Gary shrugged instead of speaking and looked down at his hands instead.

"Listen, Dad, I don't want you to decide today. And maybe the doctor will find it's something else altogether. But I just want you to think about it. We're here for a week."

George looked at his daughter with some suspicion.

"Remember this, Dad. You will be helping out a family—and a sick young boy. This could prove . . . providential to them. Seriously. It would be an answer to prayer."

Don't layer it on too thickly. He'll see through it.

"Sleep on it, Dad. I know you don't like to rush into decisions. Just promise me you'll keep an open mind. Okay? Please say okay."

George looked as if he were going to scowl, then didn't.

"Okay," he replied. "I promise to think about it."

"Maybe we'll get to meet him this weekend. He's older. Sort of like a grandfather."

Alex had not responded to this unexpected solution with any great deal of anxiety or trepidation.

"And he likes dogs?"

"It's what his daughter said. And he would be alone for the whole trip. So Lewis could keep him company. I think this could work out for both of us."

"Or all three of us. Me, Lewis, and this guy."

"Right. The three of you," Trudy quickly replied.

"What do you think?"

Alex's face tightened up, like it always did when he was puzzled or confounded by a problem. Then he brightened.

"If Lewis likes him, then it's okay with me."

And Trudy, for the first time in days and days and days, felt a glimmer of hope, flickering off in the future.

"Okay," she replied. "Then it's a plan."

19

After dinner, after the "Lewis" discussion, after watching too much news on TV, Tess walked into the kitchen to make her last cup of coffee for the day.

Too late for a full pot. And Mr. Coffee doesn't do well with single servings. I guess I'll have to use Dad's instant . . . coffee, if you can call it coffee.

She removed the jar from the cabinet, measured out a serving into an empty cup, and filled the electric kettle with water. From the living room, she heard the sound of a baseball game. Or it might have been a football game. They all sounded the same to her. She listened. No one was speaking. She glanced out around the corner. Her father and her husband were sitting on the couch, staring straight ahead at the flickering images, not saying a word, each apparently lost in their own world.

It's a baseball game.

She watched them for a moment.

They can sit for hours and never say anything to each other and they will say they had a good time together. I don't get it. I don't.

The water was boiling, and she poured it out into her cup and added half-and-half. She made sure the coffee and creamer were returned to nearly the exact place where they had been placed.

I'm doing what my father does. Making sure everything is exactly like it was. Being precise and orderly.

She sat at the kitchen table and read over the *Gloucester Times*. A stack of advertising and catalogues and other unopened mail solicitations were piled on the corner of the table. She was certain her father placed them there in preparation to put them in the apartment complex's recycling receptacle down by the parking lot.

She slid the stack over and flipped through them. An L.L. Bean catalogue. Three envelopes offering "low-cost insurance for seniors." A solicitation for RV insurance. A thick booklet of local businesses with coupons for "buy one dinner and get the second at half price."

I can see why he doesn't go through these carefully.

She stopped halfway through the small stack. A large postcard, addressed to her father, using his name and not "or current resident," had been sent from the New Hampshire Firearms in Exeter.

She flipped it over. "Huge customer appreciation sale. Get a free New Hampshire Firearms T-shirt with the purchase of a new Double Tap 9mm or .45cal Tactical Pistol." There were lists of other rifles and guns with a list the hours of operation and website.

Why would he have gotten this flyer? He's never owned a gun. Unless . . . he bought a gun.

Tess turned the card over. It was his correct address and the preferred spelling of his name—with the middle initial.

Why would he need a gun? Protection?

She felt a cold jolt in her heart. She stopped thinking, trying hard to stop making connections in her mind.

I have to do something.

Slipping the card back into the stack, she tidied it up, squared the corners, and slid it back to the edge of the table.

I can't imagine . . .

She closed her eyes.

He has to have something to live for. It's all there is to it.

Three days after Tess found the advertisement for the gun shop, the Burdens drove past the New Hampshire Firearms store in Exeter on their way back from the allergist. No one paid any attention to it.

"We could have waited for an appointment at his Gloucester office," Lyle said as he navigated the heavy traffic on Interstate 95.

Trudy did not answer. And Lyle, obviously, did not expect an answer. The doctor in question came highly recommended, and the

Tuesday appointment in his Exeter office was the only time available for the next several weeks.

Other than Lyle's comment, no one had spoken on the trip back to Gloucester. Alex stared out the window. He did not appear sad or apprehensive, just bored.

Dr. Casario had given them the news they had all expected.

"We did the scratch tests. Nothing on pollen or dust or grass or mold. But the dog dander swelled up almost immediately. Alex is very sensitive and allergic."

Trudy nodded as he spoke.

"And when can we start the shots?"

"The shots?" the doctor asked.

"The desensitivity shots."

"I don't always recommend the shots, Mrs. Burden. With severe cases, they might not work as well. It's a lot simpler just to get rid of the offending allergen."

"I know. But the 'offending allergen' is my son's dog. So when can we start the shots?"

"Mrs. Burden . . .," the doctor replied and looked clearly like he was about to launch into a long discussion of why removal would be better and cheaper and more convenient than a year-long series of shots. But then he looked again at Mrs. Burden's face.

"Mrs. Burden, I take it you have researched this?"

"I have."

"And all of you are set on this course of action?"

"We are. So when can Alex get started?"

"Well, this week, I suppose. You'll be at the Gloucester office, correct?"

"We will," Trudy said firmly.

The doctor stood up to leave.

"You know getting rid of the dog would be easier and would solve a lot of his problems."

"We do. The dog will be gone for a while. Maybe a year. But he'll be coming back. So we want the shots to start as soon as possible."

The doctor shrugged, as if he had been used to hearing the same sort of determination from other pet owners over the years.

"If the dog was gone forever, we could employ other treatments. No weekly injections."

"No."

The doctor looked over to Alex.

"You don't mind getting shots, young man?"

Alex almost grinned.

"No. I mean, I'm okay with them. I've had shots before."

"I know. I could tell it from your medical history. I just want to make sure you don't mind going through the treatments."

Alex remained resolute.

"No. I'm okay with it, Dr. Casario. I am."

Before he left the room, the doctor turned back.

"I had a dog when I was your age. I understand. He must be a special dog, right?"

"He is, doctor. He is."

<hr />

George and his daughter stood by the Burdens' front door.

"I'm still not sure about this," George said, a new glumness added to his normally placid tone.

"Please, Dad. We've been over this. Today is only a meeting. No one has promised to do anything."

The door swung open to expose the smiling face of Lewis, with Trudy's hand on the doorknob.

"Come in, come in," she said, happier than she had been in weeks.

Lewis and George did not move right away. Instead they stared at each other, like they both knew what was going on, even though George was pretty sure he was the one who did and the dog simply looked inquisitive—and maybe a bit guarded.

"Hey. Lewis," George said.

Lewis turned his head to the side. He waited another long moment, then took the two steps to him and sniffed loudly.

"He's never this cautious," Trudy said, as she stepped backward into the foyer. "Looks like he's buying a car or something."

"Hi, Lewis," Tess said brightly, and Lewis wuffed in reply and went to her, pushing his snout into her thigh, all the while, never taking his eyes off of George.

"He doesn't like me?" George asked.

"No, it's not the reason," Trudy said. "Come on in for coffee. Alex will be home in a few minutes. I think Lewis has an idea something is brewing—other than coffee. And he's been sort of cautious these last few days. Dog intuition, maybe."

They sat around the kitchen table. Trudy had a carafe of coffee—the "good stuff" according to Tess—and a plate of thick shortbread cookies.

"Lewis loves shortbread cookies," Trudy said.

"So do you, don't you, Dad? See—you already have something in common."

The two of them—George and Lewis—kept their staring game up. Lewis finally broke and offered his lopsided St. Bernard grin and stepped to George and allowed him to pet his large head.

"Look, he's come around," Trudy said, relieved.

Tess watched and then spoke up.

"How is Alex with all this? He does know Lewis would be gone for a while, doesn't he?"

"He does," Trudy replied. "And he seems more than fine with it. Like he almost expected something like this to happen. He said as long as Lewis is happy, he would be okay with him taking this trip."

George cleared his throat.

"I haven't decided if this is all going to work out, you know."

Both women quickly agreed with him.

"Only a meeting."

"We'll play it by ear."

"No promises."

"If it works—fine. If not—it's okay, too."

But George had been married for a long time and had raised one daughter. He knew when matters had already been decided and when they hadn't. This matter felt decided.

George figured when Lewis lumbered his front paws up on George's thighs and went in for a delicate slurp on the face, the matter was truly and totally settled.

"Will I get to see your camper?" Alex asked as he sat at the table munching on a cookie, after sharing a large corner of it with Lewis.

"Sure. I was planning a short trip next weekend. Up to the L.L. Bean outlet store in Freeport. I figured I would spend the night there and then come back. Maybe I could take Lewis with me to see if he likes the RV."

"He would love it," Alex confirmed. "He loves going for rides."

"Good. He doesn't get carsick, does he?"

Mitzi used to get carsick. It was awful.

"No," Alex said firmly, almost offended. "Do you drive funny?"

"Funny?"

"Starts and stops and jerky stuff. It could make him carsick."

George shook his head.

"No. I think I am a pretty smooth driver. Just right."

"Good. And you'll bring the RV here so I can see it?"

"Sure."

"And it has a bed over the front seat?"

"And a kitchen and a bathroom, too."

"Cool. I wish we could get an RV, Mom."

Trudy rolled her eyes.

"Maybe someday, Alex. Maybe."

20

As George stood in the parking lot of his apartment complex waving good-bye to Tess and Gary, he was making a mental checklist of everything he needed to accomplish before taking his second RV trip—to Maine.

With a dog.

He took in a deep breath.

A St. Bernard.

He turned back to the building.

What have I gotten myself into?

On the kitchen table, lay a parting gift from Tess and Gary—a new, state-of-the-art tablet, complete with all the features George might need: a reader for books and magazines and newspapers, an e-mail service feature, an Internet browser, and even a way to watch movies.

"I don't watch movies now. Why would I want to watch a movie on this tiny screen?"

"This way we can stay in touch while you're traveling. You could even Skype us," Tess said, bubbling with possibilities.

"Skype?"

Gary shook his head. "If you need it, stop in at the computer store to ask how it's done. Or ask Alex when you get back from your weekend."

"Skype? Do I need to know how?"

As he climbed the steps back to his small apartment, his now nearly empty apartment, his list of to-do's now stood at seventeen—without yet adding groceries to his list.

And this is only for a two-night stay.

George drove up to the Burdens' on a Thursday morning.

"Alex will be in school," Trudy explained. "But since Lewis is only leaving for a couple of nights, I think it will be fine."

George carefully navigated the RV into the driveway. He could see Lewis's head in the dining room window. Once he stopped, Lewis started jumping, or almost jumping, in excitement. His head bobbed up and down like he was in a boat in choppy water.

He recognized me.

Lewis greeted George with the full Lewis fanfare: a series of pleasant wuffs, including circling George several times, pushing his head against his thigh, bouncing as only a St. Bernard can bounce—with gravity and dignity. Finally, Lewis sat, front paws wide, grinning, tongue lolling, smiling up at George—with the certain expectation George would have brought with him some sort of delicious St. Bernard treat.

George did. He had one large-size Milk Bone in his pocket, which Lewis received with canine gusto, running around the kitchen island with it, tossing it up in the air and catching it again, before he stopped near the refrigerator and chewed it noisily.

"You now have a friend for life, Mr. Gibson."

"George. Just George. Please."

"George."

"I think I have everything I need. Except for Lewis's food and bowls."

"I have them in a shopping bag. Two cups of the food every day. He may not eat it all at once. Just leave it out."

"Will do."

"And he does . . . you know . . . have to go out every few hours during the day."

"So do I," George said. "We'll do fine."

Trudy nodded and handed him a heavy shopping bag with Lewis essentials packed inside.

"Well . . . we will see you on Saturday, right?"

"Right."

Lewis came over to Trudy and nudged against her. She bent down and hugged him. "You be good, Lewis. You be good. Be on your best behavior."

Wuff. Wuff.

"Come on, Lewis."

Lewis looked carefully at Trudy and seemed to nod in agreement with her, as if telling her he would be well-behaved and this was just a short trip and he would be back soon.

And after their silent good-bye, Lewis climbed into the RV, slowly and somewhat tentatively. But once he reached the passenger seat—which looked much like the passenger seat in the family's SUV, he sighed deeply and settled down, smiling, with his head tilting out the window.

"We'll be back Saturday. I'll call you tonight to let you know how things are going."

George did not let the good-bye take any longer. To George, even after all his years of marriage and fatherhood to a daughter, he would admit, readily, women could still be a great mystery. He knew long, weepy good-byes served no one well, and since he saw tears forming in Trudy's eyes, he felt it most expedient to leave before the scene turned more dramatic.

Lewis wuffed twice more as George backed down the drive and pulled away, heading north.

"He's going to Maine? Forever?"

"No," Alex replied. "Just until Saturday. This time."

"Not forever?"

Alex shook his head. He and Stacey Williamson and Herbert W. Trimble and Clint Bowers sat at their favorite lunch table, sandwiches and cookies and bananas and grapes and carrot sticks and Rice Krispies treats spread out before them like an adolescent buffet.

"No. Mr. Gibson won't leave for the big trip for a week or two. I think. Then Lewis will be gone."

Stacey nibbled at her carrot sticks like a small, red-haired bunny.

"Will you be sad when he goes? I would be sad."

Alex shrugged. It was obvious he would not admit to any great weakness, not in front of his friends.

"Maybe a little. But he'll be back. After I get all my shots."

"Do the shots hurt?" Clint asked. He seemed most interested in the painful parts of any medical treatment. "Do you bleed?"

Alex shook his head. "No. It's just a regular shot. It doesn't hurt much. A little. Not much."

Herbert managed to stuff an entire Rice Krispie square into his mouth at one time, chewing noisily, but still managing to talk.

"Do you think Lewis knows he'll be gone?"

"Maybe. But I think Mr. Gibson needs a friend. Especially on a long trip. Otherwise, he would be by himself. And you know how Lewis is. He gets you to tell the truth."

The three lunch friends considered the statement, then all nodded, as sagely as they could, the noise of the cafeteria rising as lunch was coming to end, and recess just about to begin.

"He does, doesn't he?" Stacey added. "I'll miss Lewis a lot. Can I write him letters?"

"E-mails," Alex said. "Mr. Gibson got a new tablet and he'll be able to get e-mails. You can write him e-mails."

"Then I'll do it. To tell Lewis we won't forget about him."

The plane rumbled down the runway, building up speed, then lifted off the ground in a noisy rush. Tess never liked takeoffs . . . or landings. She held onto Gary's hand as the plane banked sharply to the right and set a course for Chicago, their stopover location.

As the plane leveled off and the noise decreased, Tess relaxed.

"Do you think Dad will be okay? You were alone with him a lot this week. How did he seem to you?"

Gary appeared startled by the question.

"What do you mean? He looked like he's always looked. Like he doesn't like me."

Tess scowled.

"It's not you. It's just he doesn't like anyone. After Mom died, he's gotten more cantankerous. More of a curmudgeon."

Gary shrugged.

"I didn't notice any difference. He did seem a little more involved when he was showing us the RV. It seemed to perk him up."

"It did. Do you think he'll be able to pull off a year's drive across America?"

"I don't know," Gary replied. "He seems to like routine. Stopping in a different place every few days . . . I don't know."

"I know. I worry about it, too," Tess admitted.

"And now . . . you've wrangled him in to taking a dog with him. It seems so out of character."

Tess wanted to tell her husband about the gun shop flyer she saw, wanted to tell him she was worried about her father, wanted to tell him she had a bad feeling about what he planned on doing . . . but she had no proof. Other than the flyer, and a sense of . . . something wrong, Tess had no way of being more specific.

"But maybe the dog will cheer him up," Gary said. "Maybe it's just what he needs."

Maybe. At least it's what I'm praying for, Tess thought.

Lewis began to wuff and dance in his seat as George turned the RV into the Burdens' driveway. The dog looked over to George, a smile on his big face, as if to say, "See, I told you we would come home . . . eventually."

The dog bounded out of the RV, wuffing louder, dancing, and bouncing.

Alex met him in the driveway, both of them immediately lost in a tackle of young boy and St. Bernard, happy hellos and wuffs abounding.

Trudy came out, drying her hands on a dishtowel.

"Hello, George. Everything go well?"

"It did," he said, almost as if he were surprised.

"I am just about to serve dinner. It's only meatloaf. Please, you have to stay and eat. And tell us all about how Lewis handled the trip."

"Yeah, stay, stay," Alex called out from under Lewis.

"If it's not too much trouble . . ."

On the way back from the Burdens', George replayed some of the last few days.

Lewis proved to be an exceptionally easy passenger. He rode in the passenger seat most of the way. For a portion, he simply laid down on the carpeted floor of the kitchen/dining room, snoring audibly as George cruised north.

The first night, at the Freeport campgrounds, Lewis finished his dinner, then sat patiently while George ate a dinner of canned stew.

"It didn't look like he wanted any," George said. "He just sat and watched."

"He doesn't like stew," Alex confirmed. "Even if Mom makes it. He doesn't like it."

Afterward, after dinner, the two of them walked around the campground. Lewis was on his leash, of course, but George imagined that he would not even need a leash. The only time Lewis left his side was to answer the call of nature.

"He saw other dogs and squirrels and a lot of people, but he stayed by my side. Unless I told him it was okay to meet somebody. You trained him well, Alex."

The part of the journey George did not mention was the effect Lewis seemed to have on people. Or at least on one person. Maybe it was a fluke. That's why George thought it best to keep this one to himself.

After George shopped at the outlet store—he was after a few specific items—and only spent twelve minutes in the store, he came out and took Lewis for a walk.

People seemed to gravitate to Lewis, perhaps due to his size or his dignity or his deliberateness. He did not appear to be your standard sniff and bark sort of dog.

No, this one is different.

A woman came up to Lewis and George and bent down to talk to Lewis and, after only a moment or two, began to tell George of her family life and her troubles and the pain she was having with her youngest son.

I'm not the one you should be talking to, George thought as she kept on. *You should talk to a friend or a counselor . . . or a priest or something.*

It was what she said as she stood to leave.

"This dog . . . Lewis, you said? He's a special one, all right. Like he's listening to you. I think Lewis would want me to go home and tell my son how I feel. I think it's what Lewis wants me to do."

My wife could have handled this. I'm not sure I'm good at this. Telling the truth.

"Maybe you should do it," George offered, unsure.

Lewis just wuffed.

Twice.

George pulled into the parking lot of his apartment and turned off the engine.

He sat for a while, thinking.

I said I was going to do this, and I am.

21

George had not made more of his date of departure—his departure to see America—than he had about any other date. His birthday would have slipped past, unobserved and mostly unnoticed, save for the birthday card and telephone call from his daughter.

There were no family members left in George's immediate family to wish him birthday greetings. He was an only child of only children.

And to the few friends he maintained in Gloucester, he had made it abundantly clear he disliked any manner of birthday fuss.

The two weeks before his leaving, he had emptied his apartment of all perishables. He cleaned the refrigerator thoroughly and left it unplugged. The few canned and unopened boxed foods remaining that he did not want to take with him, he delivered to the local food pantry.

Well before his departure, he had decided to keep the apartment—and had just signed the lease for next year and paid the rent in full.

"It's not expensive—and who knows?—maybe I'll want to come back early. I would need a place to stay."

I won't, but if I were to give up the lease . . . there are people who might worry about it.

He didn't think they would, but George did not like to take chances.

Maybe Tess would find out. I don't want her to worry. I have made up my mind. It will be better this way. Whatever is left here, can all go to charity.

George even sold his car.

I've got the RV now. It will get me to where I'm going.

93

George pulled into the Burdens' driveway to collect his passenger.

I'm not sold on this whole take-the-dog-along thing. But if it doesn't work out, I can ship Lewis back. Mrs. Burden said, "If you have to, you have to." While I know he will be sort of a problem, it will also be sort of nice to have someone to talk to while I'm driving. And he does seem to enjoy riding in cars. Or RVs.

He put the emergency brake on and stepped out. Trudy and Lyle were already outside. They both looked apprehensive. Nervous. And a little sad.

"All we all set?"

Trudy wiped at her eyes, which were red from either crying or allergies.

"We are. Alex is packing Lewis's bag."

George walked closer to them and lowered his voice.

"Is Alex okay? I mean, it is his dog and all. He's okay with him leaving like this?"

Trudy shrugged.

"I don't know, Mr. Gibson . . . George. He says he is. But he loves the dog. He hasn't cried at all. I don't know what to believe. He's the one who should be all emotional about this—and instead, it's me."

George was just about to tell Trudy he understood, it was the same way with his wife. When she passed he hardly felt anything, and the people who were farthest from the pain and suffering were the ones who cried and wailed the most. George wanted to tell her, but he did not.

It's not my place.

The door opened, and Alex and Lewis walked out. They did not seem upset or angry or sad.

Lewis grinned at George as if he was greeting an old friend.

Alex extended his hand.

"Hello, Mr. Gibson," Alex said as George shook his small hand.

"Hello, Alex."

Alex looked up at him.

"We talked it over, Mr. Gibson."

George tilted his head and looked over at Trudy.

"No, me and Lewis . . . we talked it over."

"Oh. Okay."

"And Lewis wants to go with you."

George tried not to appear surprised.

"Did he tell you so?" George asked.

"Sort of. I said it out loud," Alex explained. "If it was a lie, Lewis would have known and he would have let me know. He knows he's going away for a while. But it's okay."

Alex wiped at his nose with his sleeve. If he was trying not to cry, he was doing an excellent job of it. His eyes were just a bit watery, but they were the same way the last time George visited.

"It's the allergies," Alex said. "And the shots will make it better."

But today, Alex motioned George closer.

George leaned over and then sort of went to one knee.

"I have to tell you a secret," Alex said.

"What sort of secret?" George asked.

"I'm not sure if my mom knows this. But you can't lie to Lewis. He doesn't like it."

George nodded as if this quality were standard issue in dogs.

"Will he bite me if I lie?"

Alex almost laughed, but it sounded like a stifled giggle.

"No. Lewis does not bite. Ever," Alex declared. "Never ever. It's just he will . . . well, he will just be . . . disappointed. You'll know."

"I will?"

"Yes. Lewis can tell when someone lies, and you'll know right away when Lewis is disappointed. You will see it in his eyes. Maybe his whole face."

"Really?" George asked.

From the corner of his eye, he could see Lewis watching, and George could have sworn he was nodding the whole time Alex explained about Lewis and the truth.

"I don't know why Lewis is this way, but it's the truth."

"Okay," George said. "I won't lie."

Alex looked over at his dog. "Maybe it is just me. But I think it's Lewis."

George nodded, then felt nearly compelled to put his hand on Alex's shoulder.

"Will you be sad we are leaving? Are you sad?"

Alex nodded this time.

"I am. But just a little. Lewis will have a good time."

Alex leaned in closer to George.

"Here's the real secret, Mr. Gibson. I think Lewis is supposed to go on this trip. We talked about it last night, and I am pretty sure Lewis thinks he has to go with you. Like there's a reason for it. I don't know what it is. I don't think Lewis knows either. But . . . you know, we're okay with him going."

George did not have a reply.

Alex brightened a little. "And he'll be back. It's kind of like Lewis is going to summer camp . . . and it lasts a year. He'll be back. And I'll be here. And he'll have a good time."

As the two of them talked, as Alex shared his secret, Lewis bounded off, back into the house. In a moment, he came back outside, dragging a ragged satchel.

"He's got his toys in there, Mr. Gibson. We packed it last night. He's got his squirrel and his porcupine and a bag of crunchies and a big chew bone."

George stood.

"Good. And I bought him a bowl for his food and water made just for an RV—it doesn't slide around on the floor or spill. And I got Lewis a seat belt adapter. So he'll be safer."

It took a few minutes to put the harness around Lewis. He pranced around proudly once it was secure. Alex gave the interior of the RV a last-minute inspection.

Trudy watched her son and tried to keep her fears at bay, her fear this will be the last time Alex would see Lewis.

Alex bent down to Lewis and hugged him tightly.

"He needs someone to talk to, Lewis. You keep him company. You make him tell the truth, okay?"

Lewis answered with a series of heartfelt wuffs, and then he climbed into the passenger seat and allowed George to attach his harness to the seat belt.

"Well, time to go. I will call you tonight. And Alex, thanks for helping me figure out how to do the Skype stuff."

"Bye, Mr. Gibson. And Lewis, take good care of Mr. Gibson."

As George pulled out of the driveway, the three Burdens stood in a tight group, waving, and Alex called out, "Don't forget me, Lewis. And behave."

As the RV gathered speed and the Burdens disappeared in the background, George had an odd feeling, a feeling things would change.

"I don't know what will change, Lewis. I'm too old for too much change, you know."

Lewis wuffed in reply.

After a few minutes on the road, George glanced over at Lewis who was staring at him, not in an anxious way, nor angry, nor sad, but in a just curious manner, as if he was trying to decipher just who this person was who sat next to him and was piloting the RV.

"Lewis, what are you staring at?"

Lewis did not speak.

"Do I have something in my teeth?"

No response.

"Do you not want to leave Alex? Are you sad?"

No response.

George thought, just for a second, mentioning the name of Alex might cause a reaction. But it did not. Lewis remained implacable.

Then he wuffed once, and then once again, and then looked straight out the front window.

"I know it will be a long trip, Lewis. I know."

Wuff.

"We'll take it slow. And I know I like routine . . . but I can get used to driving and staying in different places. I can. Yes. I can."

Wuff.

"Lewis," George said and stretched out the sound of his name. "I said I was going to do this, and I am, Lewis. I am."

This is something I have to do. I promised her.

Wuff.

"Well, I can't say more now. Not now. Maybe not ever."

PART TWO

22

George had laid out his itinerary with military precision.

"This is the way things should be planned—so you know where you'll be and when you'll be. It's important. Have a plan. Stay on schedule. Work your plan."

If I knew how to needlepoint, I would needlepoint it—"STAY ON SCHEDULE."

From Gloucester, George headed west. Rolled up in a cardboard tube, in a cabinet above the sink, was his "master map"—a four-by-three-foot map of the United States—with his intended route outlined in yellow highlighter. Many months prior, he had purchased two copies of the map. His first plotting, his initial stab at the best and most efficient cross-country route, had included a number of stops he no longer wanted to make and a series of stops he had added. "Too many dead ends." This led to a hodgepodge of different routes on the first copy, with different colored markers and a plethora of confusing notes concerning stops and no-longer stops. The price of the second copy of the map was insignificant when compared to the neatness and precision of the final version.

When unrolled, George could follow the yellow line as he left the East Coast and moved westward. He could mark his stops with a red marker and chart his progress as he headed toward the Pacific.

He knew what lay in store. It offered him cold comfort—yet it was part of the plan, and staying on the plan was part of who George was.

"Stay on schedule. Have a plan."

Since he and his wife had spent so much of their lives in or near Gloucester, they had also seen or visited most of the region's highlights. Everything George wanted to see within a three-hundred-mile radius of Gloucester had already been seen. Some, many times.

"How often can you walk Boston's Freedom Trail? When you were little, we must have gone to Boston a dozen times. You loved it." George remarked to his daughter as he'd planned his trip. "I need to travel a ways until I run into something I haven't seen before."

It's why his first real stop was Towanda, Pennsylvania.

He measured out the distance on his road map using a ruler.

"Right around four hundred miles. And in the RV, I can average fifty miles an hour, so the trip would take all day. Probably be too much for the first leg of a long trip."

On the second day of the journey, having spent the previous night in an RV park right off the freeway, George was on a two-lane road coming up on the town from the south.

"You see, Lewis," George explained as he made the turn the GPS system had recommended, "Towanda is an old city with lots of old buildings. I told you I was an engineer, didn't I?"

Lewis glanced over at George and offered a polite wuff.

"The guidebooks said they have over four hundred buildings in their historic district—you know, in the Greek Revival and Queen Anne styles: banks and churches and even an opera house."

Lewis looked over. George thought he offered a bored, semi-amused look, but then again, George thought he might be projecting too much human response onto his traveling companion.

"It's why we're going to stop here for a few days. I want to explore a bit. Maybe draw some of the buildings. Always wanted to have a sketchbook filled with interesting things. It would be something I could leave to my daughter. So she would know what was important to me. I don't think I talked much about it when she was growing up. It was Hazel's department. You know, what life was all about. How to live. What's important. Those things. Things a parent teaches a child. I guess I didn't do as much of it as she did. Hazel . . . she was the teacher."

George stared ahead and concentrated on the road. When his wife's name was mentioned, or even brought to mind—even now—he felt a coldness, an emptiness in his heart. He wondered if that emptiness would ever leave him, would ever be filled with something warm again.

"Did you know Towanda means 'burial ground' in the Algonquian language, Lewis? They were Indians . . . I guess, Native Americans is the more correct term."

Lewis tilted his head at the words "burial ground," almost as if he knew what the words meant and was a bit disturbed by them.

Of course, he doesn't know what it means, George thought. *And if I'm not careful, I'm going to start believing he understands what I'm saying. Instead of becoming one of those crazy cat ladies with fifty cats, I'll become a crazy dog man, who insists that his precious dog understands every word spoken to him.*

But the truth of the matter was, Lewis did appear to grasp certain words, or thoughts, or perhaps emotions. He nodded at the correct times, he wuffed at the right times, as if he was holding up his end of the conversation.

"Right, Lewis. Native Americans. They lived all around here."

Lewis shook his head with great vigor, his jowls making small, wet, slapping sounds as he did. He then snorted twice and stared hard at George. He whimpered, just a note above silence, as if the dog wanted something but did not want anyone else to know about it.

"You need to stop?"

Wuff.

It was a soft, quiet wuff, sort of a sandpapery wuff, like the sound of fine grit sandpaper drawn against a flat wood surface.

"Okay. I'll find a place."

George realized, from the outset, that he needed to respect any request from Lewis for a break. Lewis, after all, was a large dog, and George's RV was not.

George piloted the RV to a small, flat patch of grass and gravel on the side of the road. He unbuckled himself, then Lewis, and clambered over the center console and opened the side door. Lewis carefully stepped down.

George had the leash in hand, but Lewis looked back over his shoulder, with an expression clearly meaning, "Don't bother. I'll be quick."

George shrugged.

"Well, if you say so. But stay on the grass, okay?"

Lewis was ready to come back in just a short moment.

Buckled back in, George said, "Okay, on to Towanda."

Wuff.

This was louder and more comfortable, as if to say, "I'm ready now."

Riverside Acres RV Park lived up to the implied promise of the name. George's space was a stone's throw from the Susquehanna River. Lewis did not appear to like the river.

Upon descending from the RV, Lewis stared hard at the glistering waters, lit by the afternoon sun—hissing, burbling, rushing south—and barked at it, loudly, at least a dozen times. Then he looked back to George as if he were expecting some sort of explanation for this curious phenomenon.

"It's a river, Lewis. It's just water. A lot of water, but still . . ."

Lewis looked back at the river, then to George, then to the river, barked twice more, to be sure, to let this "river" know Lewis was on guard, then thoroughly sniffed his way around the RV and back to George who was sitting in the open side door, stretching his legs. Lewis sat down as well, positioning himself so he could see both George and the threatening waters at the same time, without having to move his head.

"Alex trained you well, didn't he, Lewis?"

Wuff.

His wuff at Alex's name always seemed happy and confident.

Lewis seldom walked more than a few feet away from George and never took off at a gallop, chasing some real or imagined prey. Lewis appeared to be a most civilized animal, and one who understood the dangers lurking out there when he walked with George, away from the RV. When they walked, George would attach a retractable leash, but Lewis never strayed more than an arm's length or two away.

George looked up at the sun and yawned. He knew it was too early for dinner.

"Lewis, you want to know why old people eat early?" George asked as the pair of them walked along the paved road in the RV park. "It's because 'seniors' don't have anything else to do. We've run out of things to occupy ourselves by three in the afternoon, so we start looking for early-bird specials. We've gone through the mail—all three pieces of it—read the newspaper, done the crossword puzzle and the Jumble, read the want ads, if the paper still has want ads, and then the obituaries, although some of us get to those first, and then we putter about looking for something broken or something to break. It's sad, isn't it, Lewis?"

Lewis looked over at George and appeared to grin slightly.

"If I get that way, please bite me," George said, sounding serious.

Lewis pulled up and stopped as if he were shocked by George's suggestion. Lewis shook his head rapidly and snorted loudly.

"I was kidding, Lewis," George replied when it appeared the poor dog had taken him at his word. "I don't want you to bite me. Or anyone. Unless you have to, okay? For something serious. Or dangerous."

Lewis turned his head, with a quizzical look on his face.

"I don't know what it would be. It would have to be dangerous, right, Lewis? I can't say what it might be at the moment."

But I do know. I could say, but I don't want to lie to the poor animal.

"You'll know if you have to do something like bite someone when the time comes. You're a smart dog, right?"

Wuff.

Lewis had not turned his head back to vertical.

"You'll know. But don't worry about it now. We've got a walk to accomplish this afternoon."

Lewis started back up, always leaving a good bit of slack in the leash.

"And we've got to kill some time before dinner. It's only half past three, and we have at least a few hours before we can eat, right?"

Wuff.

"Eat like normal people."

Wuff.

And not like an old person who doesn't know what to do with his freedom.

23

The following morning promised a delightful day: sunny, cool, and perfect for walking and drawing.

George considered walking downtown. It was only a few miles, but he thought about the return walk, when he would be a bit more tired. He knew the distance would not bother Lewis in the least, and the weather wouldn't wear him out.

It is a mile or two . . . maybe even more to the historic district.

He sat and considered his options.

Lewis could do it easy. I could do one way, easy. I'm not sure about the return trip.

George offered a half smile.

Just like real life. Halfway is easy. All the way back is hard.

The pair of them were taking their morning constitutional; Lewis after all, did not have the luxury of indoor facilities. A few streets down, rounding the corner in the RV park, came a blue and white, battered, noisy, small bus tilting a few degrees to the left. The destination lamp on the bus simply read "Town."

Other than the driver, it was empty.

George flagged him down.

"You do mean Towanda, right?" he asked.

The driver, probably ten years older than George, nodded. His camouflaged baseball hat was tilted to the right side, most likely unintentional and not meant as a fashion statement.

"It's a service we offer. Town and back. Five times a day. You tell me when to pick you up. I'll be there. Not many people here today. Early in the season. Come summer, this bus will be full. And we'll hold to a schedule."

"Can I get my sketchbook back at the RV?"

"I'll take you there."

As they boarded the bus, Lewis looked askance at the rickety door and steps and climbed in with some deserved hesitation. The bus driver looked over and laughed, "The dog has to pay full fare. He's a big one, ain't he?"

George was halfway to reaching for his wallet until he realized the driver was simply making a joke—at Lewis's expense. Lewis responded with a wuff and let the driver pet his head before making his way to the second seat.

"Good looking pup, there. He like to travel?"

"Seems to," George replied. "We've only been on the road for a few days. Maybe it'll change."

The bus started with a lurch and a rattle.

"Oh, I don't know, people are the way they are. I 'spect animals be the same way. Back when I was working—working for real, and not driving this bus—my boss would go to meetings all the time. Training, he said. Seminars and the like. Said they were for making him a better boss. You know what? He never changed. He stayed exactly the same. Scatterbrained, sloppy, and disorganized. Always wanted to tell my boss's boss somebody was wasting their money. But it weren't my place to tell the truth 'bout things."

The bus groaned as it leaned into a sharp turn.

"You're in the black one, right? Snazzy. I like the way your unit looks. Not the usual boring colors."

George hurried inside to gather his things, including a small folding stool with a shoulder strap. He had already organized his sketchpad and pens in an artist's shoulder bag, each pen in its own small holder.

Need the stool. Have to sit down to draw.

Lewis stood in the aisle of the bus waiting for George to return.

I would swear he had a nervous look in his eyes.

"Lewis, I would never leave you. Never."

Lewis was about to respond with a wuff but then stopped himself and stared hard at George as he sat down.

"You don't believe me?"

Lewis hesitated, then responded.

Wuff.

Towanda proved to be a worthy stop, chock-full of all sorts of old buildings, most of them meticulously maintained and still in use. The two of them, George and Lewis, walked along the streets in the historic district for a while, and George took mental notes of the buildings he wanted to sketch.

He found a spot in the shade of an old bank building, erected in 1895, and unfolded his stool and sat down. It gave him a perfect view of the building across the street.

Lewis watched him carefully, then sat down as well, grinning slightly, just a foot or two away.

"You enjoying this, Lewis?"

Wuff.

"Good. My daughter, Tess, you met her . . ."

Wuff. Wuff.

"She said I should just take pictures. She said it would be so much easier. And they would be in color. She said I could use a digital camera or something. I could even use the tablet thing they bought me."

George opened his sketchbook to the first page.

"I don't know, Lewis. Anyone can take a picture. Drawing something makes you see what you're looking at—in detail. You have to pay attention. Pictures would be too easy. And if I were taking pictures, we would be done now, and then what would we do?"

Wuff.

"Like I said, I don't want to start trying to decide on which early-bird special I want to have. Not just yet anyhow."

Wuff.

The pair of them sat opposite of the Keystone Theater, formerly Hale's Opera House. George took out a black Copic Multinier SP pen, expressly designed for rendering and detailing sketches. George had researched the market before buying the pen, as he did with virtually all new purchases. The pens came in various colors and point sizes, all would produce a fine line, with no bleeding. All boasted waterproof pigment in the ink.

George liked precision. He liked control.

George uncapped a black ink pen. Lewis sat just in the sunshine, his head titled back, his eyes closed, and a slight canine smile on his face, his body radiating contentment. His nose quivered a little as he sniffed, obviously enjoying the scents of this town.

George drew a precise straight vertical line, marking one side of the building, then another horizontal line for the foundation. He looked back up at his subject and then drew again. In the span of only a few minutes and a few dozen pen strokes, he had the building framed in, roofline to sidewalk, windows positioned, even the newer theatrical marquee over the entrance was drafted in with elegant clarity. He leaned closer to the paper as he drew the individual bulbs framing the marquee—a feature no doubt added when the building was transformed from an opera house to a movie house in the 1930s.

He straightened up and looked down, then back at the building.

"Not bad, so far."

Lewis opened his eyes and looked over. George tilted the pad to him. Lewis wuffed softly, appreciatively.

George returned to drawing, adding in more and more detail, hints of the brickwork. He drew a small patch of individual bricks in the bottom corner. It would take too long to draw all the bricks, so this was a reference point. He drew in the windows, the sills, the cornices. He added the keystone bearing the date of construction: 1888.

He stopped, stretched his back, and smiled.

A voice from behind startled both George and Lewis.

"Man, this is cool. Are you like an artist or something?"

George and Lewis both turned at the same time to see a young man, a tad scruffy, a few day's growth of whiskers, or more depending on his ability to produce whiskers, wearing a dark zippered hooded sweatshirt and frayed jeans. Underneath his sweatshirt was a white shirt, both collar buttons unbuttoned.

It could stand to be ironed, George thought, *but I guess it's the way young people wear them these days.*

The young man was smiling broadly.

"No. Not an artist. This is sort of a . . ."

What is it? Something to leave behind so I can let my daughter know where I've been and what I thought was important? A promise I made to . . .

". . . it's sort of a hobby. Drawing old buildings."

"Wow. You get paid for this, or what? You should. It's cool . . . I mean good. Like something you would buy in some fancy store or something."

George nodded in appreciation.

"Well, thank you. But it's just a hobby."

The young man apparently just noticed Lewis, hidden in plain sight.

"Wow, it's some dog you got. Is he, like, for protection?"

Puzzled, George replied, "Protection? From what?"

"I dunno. Like maybe it keeps people from stealing your stuff. Like your drawings or something? I wouldn't steal anything with him around, for sure."

"No, no protection. Although I admit his size can be intimidating. But Lewis is just along for the ride. He likes to get out and meet people."

George glanced over to Lewis, who appeared to be smiling with a beatific sort of serene smile.

So this is how it is going to be with you around? George thought to himself.

George thought he noticed Lewis nod, nearly imperceptibly. Maybe not, but there it was.

The young man hesitated a minute, looking deeply at Lewis who was staring back at him.

"Is he friendly?"

"Extremely."

The young man slowly went to one knee and waited for Lewis to take a step toward him. Then he carefully patted him on the head and scratched at the fur on his neck.

"Used to have a dog. Then my parents split up, and they said the dog went to live on some farm. I think they dumped him, actually."

Lewis wuffed and snorted at the same time, a sort of almost angry snorf.

"Yeah, it was a rotten thing to do. And I was just a little kid back then."

George wondered if he should keep on drawing.

Have a plan. Stick to the schedule.

He pivoted back and continued to add details to the drawing, framing in the doors on the street level, shading the glass nearly black.

"You like an architect or something? It's good—what you're drawing, I mean."

George kept on working.

"No. I was an engineer."

"Like an engineer who builds buildings?"

George offered a slight laugh. "No. I designed pumps for plastic sheet extrusion machines—they're for making plastic trays for food. No buildings. But I always wanted to design a building. Something big."

"You, like, made the trays for Oreo cookies?"

"I don't think Nabisco used our machines, but we did make equipment to make products like that."

"Well, it's still pretty cool," the young man replied. "And your dog is pretty cool. What's his name again?"

"Lewis."

"It's a cool name. Lewis. Like the explorer, right?"

George was about to tell him the story of Alex and allergies and how he reluctantly became the dog's traveling companion and all the rest but knew it would be too long and complicated.

"Yes, like the explorer."

"Cool. I like history and other old stuff, too."

The young man watched a moment more as George added another layer of detail to his drawing.

"By the way, I'm Parker. I guess the name's not after anyone. Well, maybe it is. Parker Stevenson, my mom told me once, but I'm not even sure who he was. Nobody famous like Lewis, for sure. My girlfriend said he was on some TV show. The Parker guy, I mean."

"And I'm George. And you have met Lewis."

The sketch was nearing completion. Somewhere George read knowing where to stop was as critical as knowing where to begin. He pulled the pen back and looked at the building again, then back to the drawing. He added a few curved lines above the building to suggest clouds—but just a few.

Enough.

He capped the pen and put it back in the sleeve in the bag.

"You done? You're good. And fast."

"Thank you, Parker. You were a good audience."

Parker nodded.

"Hey, George, you have lunch yet?"

George turned in his chair.

What an odd question from a stranger.

"I mean . . . well, why I'm asking is I'm sort of a waiter. Not sort of. I am a waiter. At least for the time being. So I get a free lunch before my shift starts. I could split it with you and all. Maybe you might want to draw the place where I work."

Again . . . odd.

"Parker, it's kind of you . . . but I have Lewis with me. Most restaurants probably would not believe he was a Seeing Eye dog."

Parker's face showed a flash of incredulity, as if he thought, if only for a second, George was actually blind and needed a Seeing Eye dog. Then his face brightened, realizing George was not being literal.

"Oh, yeah, well, taking Lewis would be okay. We can eat outside on the back deck. People bring dogs there all the time."

24

Five minutes later, the three of them were sitting at a picnic table behind the Firehouse Restaurant and Bar, housed in, of all places, a former firehouse with two brick turrets framing the front of the structure and the two doors once used to house the fire trucks. As they walked there, Parker talked more with Lewis than George, explaining to the dog he's a waiter, he dropped out of the local community college, and he's not sure what to do with his life in general.

Lewis kept up his end of the conversation by wuffing and snorting at what seemed to be the most appropriate moments.

"I usually get a burger and fries. They're tasty, but maybe you want something else . . .?"

"Parker, please get your free meal. I'll get my own burger . . . or whatever," he said, and then whispered, "Lewis will probably want to taste mine and he's got a big appetite. So we don't have to share, okay?"

"It's okay by me, George."

When the hamburgers were served, Lewis stood, sniffing deeply. The waiter, another scruffy young man in a white shirt, looking much like Parker, brought out a separate plastic basket with a fully cooked hamburger patty in it.

"The cook dropped it on the floor. I thought it was clean enough to serve, but the cook is all worried about the health department and stuff. So, he was going to throw it out. I thought Lewis might like it."

Parker had introduced the new waiter to Lewis and George.

Lewis visibly smiled, or at least George thought he did.

George divided the dropped burger into sixths and fed Lewis a section every few minutes. Lewis would have wolfed down the entire burger in under three seconds if George had let him. George imagined eating slowly would be healthier and better for the digestion, and inhaling food was purely an instinctual remnant from the eons dogs had spent in the wild, chowing down on moose or mastodon, or whatever, making sure they had eaten enough before an even bigger dog came along and took the carcass away from them.

Lewis was grinning his St. Bernard grin, content, satisfied, aware, happy, at peace.

It was then, as he looked at the calm face of Lewis, George felt a sudden jolt of awareness—an awareness . . . no, a need, a need to ask Parker questions.

Just questions for now. He wants to talk. He wants to have a father.

George looked over at Lewis whose tongue was busy making sure all the good hamburger grease was off his whiskers and face.

So where did the thought come from? A father? Lewis—was it you? Or maybe it was Hazel nudging me . . .

George did not like to think about Hazel—not when it was simply a passing thought, a glancing image. To George, the brevity felt disrespectful of her memory. And George was not the sort of man who could believe in spirits and nudges from the great beyond. And he also did not believe in nudges from a large, furry, contented, and full St. Bernard.

Even more ridiculous. But it's sort of what it felt like. A little nudge.

He watched Parker watch him. There was an air of hopefulness in his eyes, of wanting something he did not know he wanted.

Regardless of who it was . . . I heard it. Or felt it.

George took a deep breath.

And I might as well go along with it. After all, I'm babysitting a St. Bernard. How much more ridiculous can my life and this journey get?

"So, what did you study in college . . . when you were going?" George asked, trying not to stammer.

I'm not used to asking questions and pretending to be interested in people.

"Nothing much in particular. Just the intro courses everybody has to take. Intro to writing. Some stupid humanities course no one liked or understood. A math thing as well. And other stuff."

George chewed his hamburger slowly, Lewis watching him, and Parker ever so carefully.

"But where were you going with it? Is there anything you wanted to do?"

I don't like this, George thought to himself as he asked the young man questions. *Hazel would have loved it. She would have known his favorite color by now and his grandmother's maiden name. I'm just not good at it. Being empathetic isn't in my genes, I guess.*

Parker shrugged and dragged a thicket of French fries through a puddle of ketchup in his basket. He chewed, looking thoughtful, then shrugged again.

"Don't know. Like . . . why did you become an engineer and all?"

George used to have a practiced answer to the question, though it had not been asked of him for decades now.

"I was good at math. I liked precision. Engineering is a steady job. And I wanted to get married and have a family."

It's what I used to say—and meant it. Now, I'm not so sure. The way it worked out, the way my life wound up—well, it isn't what I had signed up for at the beginning.

"See," Parker said, gesturing with another thicket of fries, "it's why you guys back then had it easy. You knew what you wanted. You knew how to get there. I don't know any of this stuff. Back then, everyone knew stuff. Everyone knew where to go."

George gave another section of the burger to Lewis, who made it disappear almost without bothering to chew it.

"You said you had a girlfriend. What about her?" George asked, and he tried to hide the fact that he really did not care about Parker's girlfriend, but it seemed like the right question to ask.

Lewis wuffed in response and looked over to George and offered him a slightly greasy, hamburger-pattified smile.

"It may be the problem. I dunno. Like she just decided she wants to go to some beautician school over in Erie. It's like two hundred miles away. She says it's only for a year. She says she wants to open her own place when she's done. Already has a name for it: Carol's Cute Cut, Color, and Dye. I said it was stupid because color and dye are sort of the same thing. She says I'm being stupid and it's a cute name."

George took a napkin and wiped at his hands.

"You don't want her to go?"

"What am I going to do here all by myself? For like a year. I dunno."

Lewis turned to Parker and snorted, loudly, shook his head, and snorted again.

Parker looked at Lewis.

"He doesn't like it when people lie, does he?"

Lewis wuffed.

"You were lying?" George asked. "I couldn't tell, but Lewis does have this effect on people sometimes."

The young man leaned back.

"I don't know. Maybe. Maybe. I want to leave, too. But I don't want to go to Erie. It ain't much better than here, you know? It's on the lake and all, that's about it. But here's the big thing: she says we should move in together and save money."

"Move in together?"

Lewis snorted, even louder than before.

"I guess. I mean, getting married is like a real big step. Moving in together would sort of be halfway, right?"

George felt a wave of despair wash over him.

If this is what Hazel had to deal with . . .

"What do your parents say about it?"

Parker shrugged. It was obvious shrugging was an answer to many of the questions he faced.

"My dad ain't been around for a long time. And my Mom has been living with this guy for a long time . . . he's sort of like my stepdad, but they never got married or anything. I don't think she would much care, you know. One way or the other, she would probably be okay with it."

Lewis shook his head and looked over to George, an odd look on his face. George would have said it was despair as well, but he was pretty sure dogs don't feel despair.

Maybe Lewis does.

"Listen, Parker," George said with surprising firmness. "Do not move in together. It will never work."

"Why?"

"Get married or don't get married. Living together is not halfway."

Now where did this come from? Why do I care about what he does with his life?

George almost grimaced but changed it at the last minute to a more serious, perhaps stern expression. "But just because a decision is hard is no reason to not face it."

Parker made a face like he was considering the advice.

"Living together to save on rent money is a pretty anemic reason to 'almost marry' another person, if you ask me," George said. "But then again, you probably think I'm a dinosaur."

"No. I don't. I'm not sure what anemic means, but you're sort of against it, right?"

"I am. Marriage is . . . well, sacred. You need to be sure. And I think you need to figure out what you want to do with your life. You're young. You have lots of options."

"Naw. Young, sure, but I'm not like a genius or anything. I don't think I could be an engineer."

"Do you want to become an engineer?"

Parker screwed up his face into a tight lemon.

"No. I can't say I do."

"Then what?"

"You know what I might like to do? I never told anyone 'cuz I figured they would laugh." Parker looked down at his hands, as if almost ashamed.

"What?"

"I read this book back when I was in high school about the merchant marines. They're not marines or anything. I mean, they don't shoot anybody, but they go to this school out in New York or someplace. On the ocean, I think. They learn how to work on big boats. Like in the ocean. I think it would be so cool. Like going all over the world and getting paid for it."

Lewis wuffed several times.

"Lewis thinks it's a good idea, Parker."

"You know, I looked into a while ago. I was at the library and used their computer. You can send an application to their sailor school online. Do you think I should do it?"

"What would your girlfriend say?"

"She would think it's stupid. She says I should, like, find a job here. Work at the Pep Boys place like my stepdad. Fix tires. I'm good at it, but I dunno . . . think I want more, you know."

Wuff. Wuff.

"Traveling the world is easier when you're young, Parker. I had to wait till now to travel."

"What about your wife, George? She like to travel?"

George would not let the question cause his face to scrunch up.

"She passed on a few years ago. We wanted to travel, but then she got sick. So now it's just me and Lewis."

Parker looked like he wanted to say something sympathetic, but it was also obvious he had no idea of what it might be. Instead, he sort of nodded and bowed his head a bit, for a moment, anyhow.

George knew not knowing what to say was endemic. Knowing the right words was not native to many people. And being at a loss for those words of comfort was typical of old men with dogs—and young men with wrinkled shirts.

"Lewis thinks you made a good choice, Parker. A good decision. And thanks a lot for inviting me to lunch. Never would have tried this place by myself."

Parker brightened.

"Hey, man, you're welcome. And thank you. You, too, Lewis."

They all stood.

"I think I'll head on over to the library after work today. Maybe see what I have to do to apply. I think it'll be my plan."

"A good plan, indeed."

Wuff.

Just before shaking hands, George had one more question for Parker.

"Would you have stopped to watch me draw if Lewis hadn't been with me?"

Parker pursed up his face considering the question.

"Don't think so, George. People with dogs . . . dogs like Lewis, 'specially, you can trust them, you know? 'Cuz they have a dog. You have to be normal to take care of a big dog."

George smiled. "So you stopped because I'm with a dog."

Parker smiled back. "No offense . . . but sort of. Sure."

Lewis looked up, grinned, and wuffed softly, several times.

I told you so.

25

Later in the afternoon, the small blue bus from the RV park dropped George and Lewis off in front of their RV. Lewis bounced out, sniffing and wuffing. George stepped down carefully. As he looked to the left, in the RV place next to his, almost hidden by a row of evergreens, was a VW bus—well-worn, red and white, with music playing. George thought he recognized the tune: a ditty a few decades old.

And no one says ditty *anymore, do they? I think my daughter listened to the song.*

He unlocked his door. He waited a moment, Lewis at his side looking up.

Then he decided it was a good time to rest for a while, maybe have a cup of coffee, and maybe even stretch out and take a short nap. And Lewis wanted fresh water as well.

I'm retired, he told himself as he closed the door, *and I can set my own schedule.*

Lewis climbed up onto one side of the couch. It was apparent he would have liked to circle two or three times, matting down imaginary, instinctual grasses, but the couch was a little too narrow for an elegant, sweeping turn. Instead, Lewis compromised his instinctual behaviors a bit and walked back and forth, without turning around, like a small furry car being piloted by an inexperienced driver, attempting for the first time to parallel park.

Four back-and-forth repetitions seemed to satisfy Lewis. Then he lay down, rolled to his side, his back to the back of the couch, his feet overhanging the seat just a little. He looked at George once more as George busied himself with making coffee. Then he lowered his head to the cushion and closed his eyes.

George took to the other side of the couch, placed his coffee on the small windowsill, quietly unfolded the day's copy of *The Daily Review* newspaper, with "offices in Towanda, Sayre, and Troy." By the time he got to the second section and into articles about the historic Stevensville Church and a piece about "Grandmother Squires" moving out of Towanda, his coffee was gone and his eyes had grown heavy.

He folded the newspaper, leaned back, and listened to the raspy snoring of Lewis and wondered again, as he had wondered every day for the last several months, if he had made the right decision in taking this trip.

I will never tell Lewis I feel lost.

He closed his eyes.

Lost and alone.

And scared of the night.

—⚬⚬⚬—

George thought he was dreaming, and in his dream, music from the radio waxed and waned, and he wanted to reach over and turn it off but couldn't find the knob to control the sound.

He awoke with a start, with Lewis standing on the couch, staring out the window, wuffing loudly, rocking back and forth on his front paws as he did when he was excited and wanted to go in or out and was prevented by a closed door—or in this case, a closed window.

George shook his head to clear the dream from his thoughts. Outside, on the other side of the hedge of evergreens separating the parking spaces, was an older woman—within a few years of George's age, plus or minus a year or two . . . or three. George had never been good at guessing ages. But she appeared . . . spritely. And she walked with purpose. George imagined she was older because of her short white hair.

Sharp features. That's what Hazel would say. Sharp. Focused . . . somehow.

She may have been old, but she wasn't walking old. She took firm, purposeful steps, like she was on a mission. She walked from one end of the VW bus to the other. George thought she might be talking to someone, seeing her raise an arm, gesturing. But he did not see anyone else.

Maybe she's dancing to the ditty.

Lewis began to whine and wuff at the same time, then jumped down from the couch and positioned himself by the door, looking back at George, a worried look on his face.

"Okay. We can go out. But no bothering the neighbors. Got it?"

Wuff.

Lewis bounced down to the pavement, rocking the RV slightly as he jumped. He took a few steps toward the next campsite, sniffing loudly. He looked back at George again.

"You heard me. No bothering the neighbors."

Lewis looked back at the hedge and wuffed loudly this time.

In a moment, the woman peered through the hedge.

"Good Lord, you're traveling with a bear?"

George would have described her tone as lilting, but he was pretty sure no one said *lilting* anymore.

She sounds amused. It's kind of like lilting, I guess.

"He only thinks he's a bear. His name is Lewis."

At the sound of his name, Lewis bounced, starting with his front paws, much like an elephant bounces. George was not sure elephants could actually bounce, but he imagined Lewis and a pachyderm shared some common athletic limitations.

And no one says pachyderm *anymore either, do they?*

"And my name is Irene," the woman said and pushed her way through the hedge. "He won't try to eat me, will he? Lewis, you won't eat me, will you? I'd be pretty tough, if you tried."

She did not wait for George to assure her the large dog was indeed friendly. Instead, she went right to him and knelt down and grabbed his face in her two hands, smiling. "Lewis, glad to meet you. Are you a good dog?"

Wuff.

Lewis pushed into her shoulder, forcing her to hug him back to avoid being knocked over.

"You are a good dog."

Wuff.

She released Lewis, stood up, and offered an extended hand to George.

Blue eyes. And a firm grip. Assured is how I would describe it.

"And you are?"

"Uh . . . George. George Gibson. From Gloucester. That's in Massachusetts."

"Well, George from Gloucester, it is nice to meet you. Where's the little woman? Men always call their wives 'little women' even when they're not. Men of a certain age, anyway. And you're probably of the age."

If George was taken aback by her forward nature, he did not show it.

"I'm traveling alone. My wife . . . a few years ago . . ."

Irene's wide smile disappeared in a blink.

"Oh, I am sorry, George. I just assumed—you know. I've been doing this for a while and I can count on the fingers of one hand the times I have met a man traveling by himself in an RV. Always seem to be a couple. All the single men are at home sitting in their recliners watching *The Price is Right*."

Hey, I like The Price is Right. *Except the new host. Him, not so much. I liked Bob Barker better.*

Irene continued, "So . . . sorry for being presumptuous. No harm intended."

The apology, or explanation, sounded heartfelt.

"It's okay. It's been a few years. And I suppose being on the road as a single is a bit unusual. Especially an older single. So where's your husband?"

Irene offered a semi-smile.

"Now we're even, George. I lost my last husband a few years back. I decided not to wait for another one—and I'm here alone as well. Ain't this a coincidence? The only two single RV'ers in America parked next to each other."

Lewis sat next to Irene and looked up and smiled his crooked St. Bernard smile.

"You like traveling with this big bag of fur? Sort of like having another person with you, isn't it? A furry one."

Lewis wuffed twice, as if replying to Irene. Then he stood and nudged against her thigh. "I guess I should have asked Lewis first. He seems like he's following the conversation, doesn't he?"

George nodded. "Sometimes I think he understands English. He is a good listener, for sure."

Sitting, Lewis's head came up to Irene's waist, and then some. Without looking, she reached down and stroked the crown of his head. Lewis's tongue lolled out as she did.

"Likes attention, doesn't he?"

A large, beige RV rambled past, and even with the windows closed, the twang of country and western music spilled out.

"I hope they don't park near us. Can't take adenoidal music."

The RV rumbled on to the end of the lane and turned away from them.

"Good. People go camping to get away from all the racket—and then it follows you around. Doesn't make sense to me, am I right, George?"

George did not answer, but Lewis wuffed.

"So, Lewis, am I right?"

Wuff.

"Well, George, Lewis, it was nice meeting you both. How long are you staying?"

"Two more nights."

"Same here. We'll see each other again. Have a good evening."

Lewis followed the small woman as she walked around the ever-greens this time, instead of through them, stopping at the edge of their campsite. Lewis turned his head back to George, almost as if he were asking permission to extend his visit.

"No, Lewis, not now. We'll see her again. I promise."

Lewis walked back slowly, his head lowered.

"We'll see her again. We will."

Lewis looked up as if he didn't believe him.

"I mean it, Lewis."

Lewis offered a dispirited wuff in response.

"Let's start dinner, then," George said, hoping to cheer up his sad traveling companion.

Come on, Lewis. It'll be okay. This has been a good day.

Lewis lumbered up into the RV and climbed onto the couch and arranged himself so he could look outside and into the adjoining campsite. George saw an odd, wavering distance in his expression, as if he were thinking of some other place, and of some other people.

Maybe Lewis is just missing Mrs. Burden. And Alex.

George put a kettle on for coffee.

Maybe he's just lonely for what he's left behind.

He measured out the instant coffee.

I know I am.

26

George tuned the radio in the RV to the local news station—something called "The Bridge—We play all the oldies, all the time." As he measured out the kibbles for Lewis and heated water for his morning coffee, he paid attention to the radio, hoping to catch the local weather report.

"Weather on the Ones!" shouted an overly enthusiastic announcer.

Good. Same as yesterday. Sunny and cool. I could have looked it up on my new tablet thing, but listening to the radio is easier. Sort of.

George had noted two other Towanda buildings he thought were sketch worthy.

As Lewis sniffed at his food, and delicately nibbled each thumb-sized kibble, George finished making himself toast and coffee.

"I've picked out what buildings to draw today, Lewis."

Lewis looked up, licked his face, wuffed politely, making inconsequential conversation, and then promptly returned to his breakfast.

"Actually, I could draw probably a few dozen buildings here, but these two caught my eye. I said before I left I would only draw things I liked. So it's what I'm going to do. Three drawings for a small town. It should be plenty. I want to take the time to see things clearly. That's what I want to do. They all don't have to be historically worthwhile, you know, Lewis. I might even draw an abandoned building or two. I like those, too. They tell a story, Lewis, you know what I mean? Someone had big dreams when they built it—and now all of it is gone. What they once worked so hard for—what they loved—is now just abandoned.

Or derelict. You know, I think an old building tells a more compelling story than does one still in use, Lewis. Broken dreams, you know?"

Doing something I always wanted to . . . I haven't done what I wanted to do in so long I'm not sure what it feels like. I couldn't do what I wanted to with Hazel . . . and I'm not sure what it was I wanted, exactly.

He had circled the two structures on the walking tour pamphlet he'd found in a rack in the RV park office.

Maybe this is what I always wanted to do. Maybe.

One of his intended subjects was a three-story retail structure, currently housing the *Daily Review* newspaper. The building was constructed in 1896, he read in the brochure, in the Italianate style. The other place was the Stanley Little house, erected in 1874, in what the brochure called the Second Empire style.

"I haven't even heard of the First Empire style, Lewis, let alone the Second. Whatever style they are, I like them."

The only sound George heard was Lewis's methodical chewing.

He sat at the small breakfast table he kept folded away when not in use. He opened yesterday's newspaper and read through the classified ads, looking at merchandise for sale, even though he had no real wants, looking at rental property listings, even though he had no interest in renting, and looking through the surprising large section of help wanted ads, even though he'd not thought of work for months and months now.

"Hey, Lewis. Pizzaland in Towanda is looking for a delivery person. It says 'retired people with a dependable car OK.' It's something I could do. Feel useful, you know."

It feels like a long time since I felt useful.

At this, Lewis looked up from his bowl and eyed George carefully. Then he snorted. And then returned to his food.

"You wolf down a hamburger, but you spend all morning on two cups of kibble."

Lewis did not look up but wuffed into his bowl. His wuff sounded a bit offended.

George folded the newspaper into a neat rectangle, smoothed the edges, and took Lewis's leash from a hook by the door.

"Ready?"

Lewis shook his head, as if clearing his breakfast thoughts, and stood, showing an almost grin, a half grin, or grinette, as it were.

He looks better this morning. More chipper.

George fastened the leash.

And no one says chipper *anymore, do they? I am a dinosaur.*

The two of them walked along the narrow lane, away from the river. Lewis was not the sort of dog to take an inordinate amount of time in settling nature's demands. George had expected worse.

Mitzi would take what seemed like forever to find just the right spot. I hated this aspect of owning a dog. Standing there, looking like a fool, watching. Maybe it's why she took so long—because I was watching.

Lewis wuffed loudly, breaking George's drift into an old memory. The dog pushed against George's side, against the pocket holding the handful of dog treats.

"Give me a minute, Lewis. I'll get you one."

Lewis bounced a bit, rocking from left to right, nodding his head enthusiastically. He gobbled the treat down in one happy bite and then looked up, as if expecting more.

"Mrs. Burden said one, Lewis. It's all you get."

Lewis looked dismayed. Then he shook his head and wuffed loudly, as if calling Mrs. Burden a pernicious liar, a prevaricator of the first order.

"Okay, just one more," George said, acquiescing to the plaintive look on the dog's face.

I bet she gave him two or three each time.

Back at the RV, he gathered up his supplies and bag and chair once more and waited for the blue and white bus to wheeze down the road.

He said 9 o'clock.

George looked at his watch.

8:55.

"It's good to be early, Lewis. A few minutes early to everything. No one is kept waiting, then."

Lewis did not pay attention. He was looking back toward the VW van. He sniffed loudly, then rocked back and forth, as he did whenever he was excited.

"Hey, George, Lewis. What are you doing—waiting for a bus?" Irene kept a straight face for only a moment, then began laughing at her own remark. "He did say 9:00, right? The bus driver, I mean."

And as if answering her, the bus rattled around the corner.

"Speak of the devil," Irene said. "You going on a picnic, or what, George? Hardly enough food in your bag for the both of you."

George and Lewis stood to the side as Irene hopped up the steps, as if in a hurry to get moving. Lewis lumbered up, taking each step carefully, as if he still did not trust the road-worthiness of this rattling machine. George followed, a little slower than Irene.

Okay, a lot slower. But I have a bad knee. And hip. And another knee.

Lewis backed himself into the opening between the seats, the only thing missing from him looking like a truck was the "beep-beep-beep" of the warning sound when a large, cumbersome vehicle backed up.

George took the seat opposite. Irene sat one seat behind them. George explained, briefly, he intended to sketch a few of the old, historic structures he'd seen the day before. He was going to show her the sketch he'd made the day before but thought it might feel like he was fishing for a compliment, so he kept the sketchpad hidden in his bag.

"Sketching, huh? My second husband was sort of an artist. He said he was, and at first, I didn't have the heart to tell him he wasn't so good. Then I did. But it's what love does to you, George. Love makes you tell lies sometimes."

Lewis watched carefully as Irene spoke, nodding as she did.

She stared back.

"Lewis, I am telling the truth. Sometimes telling a lie is a kind thing to do."

Lewis snorted and shook his head.

"Well, I think it is," Irene said firmly. "Lewis doesn't believe me, George. You tell him. You lied to your wife, I bet. Once or twice. Told her she looked good when she didn't. Or that the meatloaf was good when it tasted like cardboard. You tell him, George. It's what marriage is sometimes."

Lewis looked over at George with a confused look on his face, as if he was not liking, or believing, what Irene was saying.

George tried to think of a time when he'd done so—tell his wife a lie about clothes or food. The bus turned sharply onto the main road. George held onto the seat back, and Lewis leaned into the seat behind him.

"Irene, I can't think of a time."

Lewis wuffed happily and turned back to Irene with a smug look on his face.

Irene laughed. Her laugh was loud and cheery and unforced, and her whole face turned into a broad smile. "Okay, I give. I can tell when I'm outnumbered."

She scooched over on her seat and took Lewis's face in her two hands and pretended to give him a kiss, although she stopped a few inches from the tip of his snout. Lewis appeared relieved.

"Sorry, Lewis. I admit I didn't tell lies often. But it was wrong of me, okay?"

Wuff.

"You ought to rent him out as a lie detector, George. I don't often admit to such things."

The bus crossed the bridge over the river with a metallic hum on the grated roadway and headed into town. Lewis kept an eye on Irene the rest of the short trip, as if making sure her truth and honor were not compromised again.

27

George and Lewis and Irene departed the bus at the same corner, just on the southern edge of the old historic district.

"So where's your first model, George?" Irene asked.

"Over there about four blocks. It's a regular house."

Lewis wuffed a few times, looking at George and then Irene, with a mostly plaintive expression.

"Hey, tell you what, George. You want me to take Lewis while you do your drawing? He and I can walk around. Good exercise. Then you don't have to worry about him. Where can I meet you and when?"

George did not appear to quickly embrace the idea.

I hardly know this person. What if she kidnaps Lewis? What would I tell the Burdens?

But Lewis was gently bouncing on his front paws, looking between the two of them, happily expecting to go on an extended walk.

"You okay with this, Lewis? You don't mind?"

Wuff. Snort. Wuff. Snort.

"Okay, then, I guess it will be okay. I'll meet you in front of the newspaper building at between 11:30 and noon. It's down this street three blocks. Or maybe four. On the west side of the street."

Irene took hold of Lewis's leash as if she had been walking dogs all her life.

"See you in a while, George. Have fun drawing."

And the two of them took off, Lewis high stepping, like a drum major, at the start of his walk, Irene turning to speak to him, and him

130

turning back to wuff in response, like an old couple accustomed to the intimate routines of each other.

George took a deep breath, then set off for the Little house.

I'm sure they don't mind people drawing their house, George thought to himself. *If they didn't like it, I bet they wouldn't have bought the house in the first place.*

George looked at his wristwatch, a venerable Timex, at least three decades old, a gift from his wife and daughter for Father's Day.

Old, but still reliable. A little tarnished, maybe, but so what.

11:25.

George looked up and down the street, but there was no sight of a sprightly older woman being dragged along by a large, furry dog.

Should I pull out my chair? Would it look too pathetic?

He heard him before he saw him. A series of wuffs, each one louder than the one before, echoing down the street. Then he saw them, turning a corner two blocks away. Irene waved enthusiastically, and Lewis nearly jumped when he saw George waving back.

Almost jumped, but not quite. Jumping for joy was not a word, or action, often used in Lewis's nonverbal vocabulary.

"We had the best time," Irene gushed as Lewis did jump, a little, and placed his platter-sized front paws on George's chest. "Everyone loves this dog. If I were running for office, I would have him beside me every day. People stop and talk. Even little children come up to him. Something about this dog, George. Something special."

George gently took Lewis's paws and returned them to the ground.

"Have you had lunch?" George asked. "I know a place two blocks away. Outdoor seating. Lewis likes their hamburgers."

Irene eyed him with a moment's hesitation.

"Well, sure. I'm hungry. I could eat. A hamburger sounds great. I haven't had any meat since breakfast."

George laughed and then quickly replaced his smile with a puzzled look.

"You were being funny, right? I mean, people in VW buses, they are supposed to be sort of . . . vegetarians, right?"

Irene kept hold of Lewis's leash as they made their way to the Firehouse—following George's directions.

"I suppose," Irene replied. "But I'm not one of them."

George had hoped Parker might be on duty, but he was not. The other waiter, the one who looked like Parker, was there, the one who had given Lewis the discarded hamburger.

"No, he's at the library again," the rumpled waiter explained. "Said he got some e-mail from the marines or something and had to send them some more information. I never figured him as one to join the marines, though."

George thought of explaining it all but also figured Parker would be able to do so later.

Irene watched their interaction with curiosity.

"You come here often?"

"Nope. Just yesterday."

Irene looked up from her menu.

"Didn't take you for someone who gets to know people so quickly."

George shrugged.

"I'm not. Lewis is, though."

When the food came, George took his bag and moved it to the empty chair at the table. The flap fell open, revealing the organized interior: a copse of pens, snug in an accordion of tiny sleeves, two notebooks held shut with thick rubber bands, erasers, Wite-Out, all set just so in the interior pockets.

Irene glanced at it and smiled.

"An engineer, right? Did I guess correctly?"

George nodded.

"My first husband was an engineer. He was a methodical man. Precise. Liked everything just so. Loved to organize the kitchen pantry. To him, it was a day well spent. And my shoes . . . don't get me started on how much he loved to organize shoes."

George took a sip of his coffee. Lewis was smiling up at him, anticipating a repeat of yesterday's lunch.

Talk to her, George. You might learn something.

George took another sip, trying not to react to this sudden, unexpected impulse.

If it's a nudge from you, Lewis, you better stop. I can handle things on my own.

"And what are you, Irene?" George asked. "Not an engineer, I suppose."

She stirred three packets of sugar into her iced tea.

"What am I? Me? I'm an old hippie, George. Ex-hippie, perhaps."

"So where is home?" George asked.

"Home? Don't have one anymore. I've never had kids. I've got three dead husbands. I've got a passel of relatives and ex-relative-in-laws and friends all over. I travel. I visit friends. Sometimes I rent a place for a month or two. Mostly in the winter, mostly down South. Three small pensions still add up to a small pension. But I'm frugal these days. I don't need much. But I do get itchy staying still."

George took the ketchup and made sure his hamburger was evenly covered with the condiment—more in the center, less on the edges—so there would be no unexpected drippage.

"So you're on the road all the time? You enjoy it? In a VW bus? It's pretty small."

Irene seemed surprised by his question.

"George, I keep my possessions to a bare minimum. There's no room for excess in the bus, for sure. Traveling this way is an enforced reduced diet of possessions."

She took a bite and continued as she chewed.

"I call it my Ezer wagon."

"Ezer? What's that?" George asked, thinking he misheard through the remnants of a double bacon cheeseburger.

"It's an Old Testament word. You know, like from the Bible. It means warrior. And it also means woman. Eve, you know, from the garden, the Bible calls her an ezer. A warrior and a woman. At least according to my third husband. He was a pastor. He knew Greek and all those other Bible languages like the back of his hand. But he could be a bit of a theological rebel at times."

"So, do you enjoy what you're doing?" George asked again. "Do you enjoy the journey?"

Irene appeared surprised by the question. Even Lewis snorted in response. They both looked at George, almost as if his question was impertinent.

"Well, George, if you don't enjoy life right now—I mean, like right now—today—then when will you enjoy it? When will you find life to be joyful? It has to be now, George. There is no other time than right now. Life will never be perfect. You have to find the joy in this moment, George. Lewis knows. You can see it in his eyes."

George took a bite of his burger, choosing to chew and stay silent.

Lewis, however, was not eating anything at the moment and agreed with Irene with a series of happy but restrained wuffs.

Irene responded by giving him almost a full slice of bacon she took out of her bacon cheeseburger. There was a thin veneer of golden yellow cheese on the bacon—just the perfect balance for a hungry and agreeable St. Bernard.

As he ate, Lewis looked over to George.

George thought he detected a smug, self-satisfied look on his face. He couldn't tell if it was from the cheesy bacon or him finding a philosophy of life he agreed with.

28

The next morning, the "Morning Zoo Crew" at the Bridge radio station loudly bemoaned the fact it was raining.

These people are not farmers, for sure. Rain is a good thing.

George walked Lewis, quickly, because of the drizzle. He had three old beach towels reserved for just this situation, neatly stored in a cubby under the couch. He removed one, hurried back outside, and wiped Lewis down as best he could, making sure he got to each paw, hoping he would not track mud into the RV. Lewis growled as George did his feet—almost a good-natured growl, as if dogs were supposed to growl at this indignity, and Lewis was a dog, of course, and he was simply letting George know if Lewis were any other sort of dog, more mean-spirited, more normal and doglike, then the growls would be more intense and authentic.

"Settle down, Lewis," George cautioned as he wiped his back paws. "You're too big to let in wet and dirty. And I know the growls are just for show. You let little kids yank at your hair, as Irene said you did yesterday, so I know this doesn't bother you."

Once Lewis was mostly dry and mostly not muddy, the two of them hurried inside and George measured out Lewis's breakfast. Lewis wuffed at the scent of it and settled into his long, delicate consumption of the two cups of kibbles. Heaping cups, actually.

George took out the current issue of the local paper, spread it out carefully on the table, smoothed the edges, and sat, reading and drinking his fourth cup of morning coffee. As Lewis finished his leisurely breakfast, they both nearly jumped at the sound of rapping at the RV door.

Irene stood outside, holding a huge golf umbrella, nearly making her invisible.

"My second husband was a golfer. He would play in all sorts of weather. Sleet, hail, hurricanes, whatever. I kept his umbrella."

She stepped inside.

"Do you have any half-and-half? I forgot to get some yesterday, and I hate coffee without it. I could drive into town, but begging off a new neighbor seemed so much easier."

"Sure," George answered.

Lewis listened and then moved to block the door. He sat down heavily, then lay down, sprawling across the entryway. The only way anyone inside could get out would be to crawl over the center console, not an easy or dignified way or egress.

"I think Lewis is trying to keep you here. I could offer you coffee. All I have is instant."

Irene shrugged.

"Okay by me. I'm not a coffee snob. As long as it tastes vaguely like coffee, I'll be okay," she said, then quickly added, "It's not decaf, is it?"

"No. Regular."

"Good. Decaf is an abomination. I'll join you for a cup."

She sat on the other side of the table.

"Anything interesting in the news today?" she asked.

"The city council is asking for bids to repair the roof of city hall."

"I can handle it. I don't pay attention to most of the news. It gets me too frustrated and angry. Life is too short to be irate all the time."

George nodded, feeling awkward and disconnected.

It has been years and years and years since there was a healthy woman opposite me at the breakfast table.

Irene's curious expression made George think she was thinking the same thing.

Lewis looked up and wuffed loudly, breaking the momentary spell of discomfort.

"George, you said you had an itinerary for your trip. Can I see it? I want to be reminded how it feels to be organized and have a real schedule. I'm just a little envious."

George, happy for the interruption, pulled out the "master map" from the cardboard tube in the closet and spread it out on the table. The map was the exact size of the table—something George had calculated before buying it.

"Here's Gloucester—where we started," George explained.

Irene nodded and bent closer, tracing his intended route, marked with yellow highlighter, and each stop marked in green with the name of the campground and the dates he expected to spend there. She traced the route from Towanda to Pittsburgh, and the side trip to Falling Water, and then on into West Virginia. She did not speak while following his journey. It took several minutes until she reached the West Coast and the San Juan Islands near Seattle.

"Impressive, George. Very impressive. Precise. Like an engineer."

"It is what I was. Hard to change stripes. Like a zebra, right?"

"I would allow a few more days in a few of these places. You need to spend at least four or five days to get the feel of a place. Any less and it's like being on a Greyhound bus just passing through. Like the Grand Canyon here. You need three days. You need to see it at sunrise and sunset. And Lewis can have a ball meeting people."

Lewis wuffed twice and stood up and walked to Irene, butting her gently with his head.

"Lewis agrees with me, George. Slow down a little. You have time. Live a little."

George was going to agree with her but then didn't. He wasn't sure why, except he felt some obligation to see things through as planned. To deviate from the original plan would be wrong, somehow.

I made a promise when she died. A promise to myself. It is . . . destiny, right?

"And maybe we'll see each other again," Irene said.

She does sound chipper . . . optimistic.

"Maybe. It's a small world," George said.

"But I wouldn't want to paint it," Irene added.

George almost laughed, but instead only smiled, not knowing if she meant it to be funny or simply profound.

Later in the afternoon, as the rains continued—not heavy, but enough to make outside activities unpleasant—George sat on one side of the couch, and Lewis assumed his normal position on the other.

Every few minutes, Lewis looked over to the campsite next to them. All he could see was the white top of Irene's van. No one came or went since the morning.

"Lewis, we'll go out for a walk in a little bit. Maybe things will clear up soon."

Lewis snorted and looked at George, as intently as he had ever done.

"Lewis, I have a plan. I have a schedule. I know Irene means well, but I can't go changing my plan all willy-nilly, can I?"

No one says willy-nilly *anymore, do they?*

"I made a vow, Lewis. And a vow is not something you can go back on. Maybe you'll understand later. It's what I have to do. To stay honest to myself."

Lewis looked absolutely perplexed and confused

George wondered if it was because Lewis didn't know what he was saying, didn't know what George had vowed to do.

But maybe it's because Lewis knows he gets the truth out of people, but he knows he can't change what is fated. Maybe it's what is making him confused.

Lewis stood on the couch, then jumped down, growled a little, which was not his style, not at all, then he burrowed his head against George's thigh, growling softly, as if repeating some sort of dog mantra to himself, hoping George would somehow understand.

It was almost dark, dreary and dark and rainy. Lewis had moped about the RV in the afternoon, moving from one spot to another, seemingly not able to find a comfortable place. He even crawled over the center console and tried to nap in the passenger seat. It hadn't seemed to be right, either, so he'd crawled back over, and circled the carpeted floor in front of the kitchen sink, and lay down, looking more weary than a dog has a right to appear.

George had napped fitfully as well, in between reading the newspaper and his tablet and listening to the all-news station on the radio. Finally, after Lewis had fallen asleep, which George could tell by his rhythmic breathing and his adenoidal snoring, George carefully laid aside the newspaper.

He looked out the window at the gathering gloom.

"I miss her so much, Lewis," he whispered. "I don't know if I can endure this whole trip. I am so . . . I just miss her so much."

29

When George woke up the following morning, Lewis was already up and perched on the rear sofa, staring out at the campsite next to them.

It was empty. Irene must have left early in the morning.

It's why Lewis looks upset.

George put on his shoes, and Lewis did not appear excited or even look like he noticed the activity. George knew that Lewis knew shoes meant going for a walk, but it did not cause the dog to show any visible signs of excitement.

"Lewis," George said.

Lewis did not move, just kept staring out at the empty spot.

"Lewis, you can't be depressed every time someone you like leaves. If you're going to do this trip, you have to develop a thicker skin."

Lewis turned, then snorted loudly, obviously disagreeing with him.

"Come on, Lewis. She said we would probably run across each other again."

Not likely.

"She said so, Lewis. We'll see her again."

Lewis seemed to narrow his wide eyes, as if expressing disbelief. He looked back over to George, then back at the campsite.

"She said we would meet up somewhere. She said it, Lewis, I didn't."

Lewis slowly turned his head and offered an almost whispery wuff in response.

"And we have to take a walk this morning. You ready for a walk?"

Lewis stood slowly, then rather than jump down off the couch, he sort of climbed down, like a cow taking a step down out of a barn, slowly and reluctantly.

"Okay, Lewis, I know you're sad. How about we try the Skype thing when we get back? Then maybe you can see Mrs. Burden."

He perked up at the sound of her name. George did not say the name *Alex*, because he was certain the young boy would be at school and did not want to add to Lewis's disappointment.

A breeze came in off the river—not cold, but chilled—and the skies remained close and overcast. The Morning Zoo Crew did not mention rain, but they also did not mention the day promised to be dreary and gray.

The weather even dampened Lewis's normal outside exuberance. Today he plodded along, sniffing things in a most perfunctory manner.

Well, I have down days. I suppose Lewis is entitled to a down day as well.

As they climbed back into the RV to begin preparations to depart for Pittsburgh, George was struck by an unsettling thought: *It's why you don't stay anywhere for more than a day or two. It just makes leaving all the more difficult.*

The Skype connection did not work, and George tried not to let on to Lewis there would be no connection with Mrs. Burden this morning.

He doesn't have an understanding of time. And maybe I'll try again this evening. And then, Alex may be home. It will cheer him up.

The drive to Pittsburgh, George had calculated, would take around five hours—in a car. In the RV, probably closer to six. Leaving in the morning, they would arrive in the afternoon.

George did not want to rush when driving.

No sense in driving fast . . . not on these narrow roads.

"Do you think Lewis is having a good time?" Alex asked, looking up from his bowl of Cheerios.

Trudy stopped making his tuna salad sandwich and tilted her head, as if deeply considering the question. The truth of the matter was that she had already determined how to answer the question, even before Lewis had left with Mr. Gibson.

"Of course he is. He loves traveling and meeting people. I bet he's having a ball."

Alex stirred the cereal.

"Do you think he'll forget about me?"

And this answer had already been rehearsed.

"Of course he won't forget you, Alex. You're his best friend, right?"

"I guess so. I do miss him a lot. I just hope he and Mr. Gibson are getting along."

"I'm sure they are. Mr. Gibson is a kind man. They're perfect for each other."

Alex tried not to force a smile in response.

"Yeah, I'm pretty sure Lewis needs to be with Mr. Gibson. You know, to keep him . . ."

Alex wanted to say "alive" but knew it would cause his mother some measure of anxiety, so he instead said, "company."

"You're right, Alex. He needed to have someone with him."

Alex nodded, knowing in his heart his mother was more correct than she knew.

⸺

George did not like driving in congestion—especially congested old cities built along the banks of rivers and streams and ravines, which is all Pittsburgh seemed to consist of. Of course, Gloucester was an old city, too, but compared to the hills and switchbacks and narrow roadways in Pittsburgh, Gloucester was as wide open as Paris, and just about as level.

Never been to Paris. But I've heard they have wide boulevards—not like these roads at all.

George pulled off three times on his trip to Pittsburgh, not including his stop for lunch. He blamed the stops on Lewis and his specific needs. While Lewis enjoyed getting out and stretching and whatnot, he didn't need stops three and four. But he did not complain and happily jumped down and sniffed whenever George stopped.

George used the stops to check his map again and then again, consulting with the GPS system as well as the compass. As far as he could tell, he had remained on the correct, most efficient route to Pittsburgh. He had expected a wider road, more of a thoroughfare, but instead traveled on a two-lane road, most of the time, with dozens of stops signs and red lights pocking the journey.

When he reached the final turn of this leg of the trip, he breathed a sigh of great relief. The RV was not much wider than a wide SUV, but to George, it felt wider and more unwieldy. When encountering a semitruck coming the opposite way on the two-lane road, George hugged his side as close as he could and winced as the truck rushed past.

"I don't know how they do it, Lewis, those truck drivers, I mean."

Lewis looked over, a hint of anxiety in his eyes.

George assumed the dog was mirroring the anxiety he was experiencing.

Or maybe he's anxious and nervous all on his own.

When he arrived at the West View RV Park and Sales, he breathed an even bigger sigh of relief.

This was hard. Harder than I thought.

The park was behind the RV sales lot and almost buffered by a large copse of trees. Down the ravine to the south was a shopping center. To the north was a craggy hillside appearing to be impossible to build on. His campsite this day was closer to the rear of the small park. Only a few sites were taken.

"Not many RV people would pick this as a scenic place to stay, Lewis."

Lewis had his head out the window, sniffing deeply.

A charcoal fire was the predominant scent in the air; perhaps Lewis could tell what was cooking.

George maneuvered the RV into reverse and backed into the site. There was no bus service into Pittsburgh—at least none the park offered, so he would have to drive into Pittsburgh tomorrow to find his first subject. He did not want his first act of the day to be backing out onto a narrow, one-way lane.

The shopping center down the ravine boasted a supermarket and a few other shops, including a restaurant. As George made certain the RV was level and stable, he wondered about leaving Lewis in order to walk down and get a meal.

He would be okay being alone for a few minutes. Not much more than a five-minute walk. And I eat fast.

In the end, after a twenty-minute afternoon nap, George decided to cook in the RV. He could have walked to the restaurant, but it seemed more trouble than it was worth. He grilled a thickness of sausage and made up some rice and beans as a side. Lewis watched him cook, as he had always done, sniffing loudly, as if to let George know he was participating in this meal, if only peripherally. When George delivered the meal to the table, he brought Lewis a medium-sized rawhide bone. Lewis appeared grateful for the snack, took it in his mouth, but did not stop staring at the sausage on George's plate.

"I know, Lewis. But you can't always have what I'm eating. Mrs. Burden said you would try and mooch something at every meal and I was to resist your wily charms."

Lewis hung his head, or at least George thought he hung his head, then slowly lumbered down off the couch and went to the far rear of the RV to gnaw on his bone, his back to George as he ate.

George told himself to eat slowly and enjoy the food. Otherwise, all his efforts would be consumed in five minutes. He switched on the local all-news radio station and let himself get lost in whatever argument over the local political landscape was consuming the host at the time.

After he finished, after he cleaned up, after he straightened up, he took Lewis's leash out of the drawer.

"Ready for a walk?"

Lewis bounced to his feet; whatever slight he had felt before apparently had been forgiven and forgotten.

The park, such as it was, was not large—only a few dozen spots, probably added as an afterthought to the sales lot in front. The few RVs they passed on their walk seemed devoid of outside activity. No one came out to say hello, no one was grilling outside, no one had built a campfire—although the weather was a little on the warm side for sitting around a campfire.

Lewis had not been deterred. At every RV, he stopped and wuffed once or twice, quietly, politely, as if asking if anyone wanted to come out and play.

But there were no takers.

"Maybe because we're near a big city, Lewis. Maybe it's what happens when you're not in the country."

Lewis looked up and appeared to consider the statement, then nodded in agreement.

"You seem like you understand, Lewis. And sometimes it gives me the willies."

Lewis bounced a little at those words, agreeing with them.

"You don't understand everything, do you, Lewis?"

Lewis stopped and looked at George, an earnest look on his face.

"Do you?"

Lewis nodded. Or at least George thought he nodded.

"Do you want to try the Skype thing again? Try to talk with the Burdens?"

At this, Lewis did dance and, for the first time ever, pulled at the leash to get George back to the RV without spending undue time investigating the local flora and fauna.

And no one gets the willies anymore, do they?

∽∽∽

The Skype connection failed. And they must have been in an area causing cell phone reception to be erratic and weak, because his phone call did not go through as well.

Instead, much to Lewis's apparent dismay, George typed an e-mail to the Burden family, explaining where he was, what they had seen, and what was planned for tomorrow. He tried to be chatty and upbeat—all things he had no real practice being.

The e-mail took a long time to register as "sent," but eventually the tablet made its curious whooshing noise, indicating a successful transfer of data.

Lewis took his seat on the couch and closed his eyes. Normally, he slept some during the day, but this drive had them both somewhat agitated, tense, and more tired than normal. George felt much

145

more fatigued than usual as well. He looked at the map of downtown Pittsburgh and noted the street addresses of the three bridges he wanted to sketch the following day. He traced the route he would need to take and took mental notes as to the streets he would cross.

I don't like feeling lost.

As he got ready for bed, George hoped he would be able to get the RV downtown and find a place to park it on the city's narrowed and tangled streets.

It was one thing I had not truly considered, he thought as he climbed up to his bed, trying to be quiet, trying not to disturb Lewis and his loud snoring. *Getting back and forth from RV parks to where I want to go.*

He lay down. The boxlike windows in the front of the unit opened up to a dramatic and darkening sky. He stared up at the few stars that broke through.

If Hazel were here, she would tell me to pray about it. She was always praying about something or someone. Even at the end, she was praying, not even for herself anymore, but for other people. And for me . . .

The sharpness of the memory almost took his breath away, and he closed his eyes tightly, not wanting any tears to come, not wanting to utter a sound.

I couldn't do what she did. I couldn't. I'm not strong. And I never want to put my daughter in the same situation. Never. Never. No one should ever have to watch someone in so much pain. I'll not allow it.

In the stillness of the RV, he heard Lewis stir. He waited, still, and then heard three soft, and comforting, wuffs.

I won't ever ask Tess to pray the horrible prayer I prayed. Never in a million years. It is better this way. It is.

Lewis wuffed again, a soft, warbly wuff, as if he were trying to say, "There, there." At least George assumed his wuffs were meant as comforting because it is how he perceived them.

"Thank you, Lewis," he whispered. "But you don't understand everything."

Wuff.

30

"Did you know Charles Dickens visited Pittsburgh?" George asked as he turned the RV toward the city. Lewis looked back over his shoulder with a slightly bored expression, as if he had heard this story before, which he had not. "Dickens said the city was full of smoke and boorish people."

Lewis snorted in reply.

"Since most of the steel mills are gone, the smoke is gone, too," George continued, feeling the need to explain his choice of a stopping point to his passenger. "I don't know about how the sensibility of the population has changed. I can't imagine they are all still boorish."

No one says boorish *anymore, do they?*

"But did you know Pittsburgh has more bridges than Venice, Lewis? Venice—in Italy."

Lewis tried to look interested. At least, George thought he was trying, even if neither of them were convinced.

The streets were narrow and hilly and roads intersected with each other seemingly at random, not neat and precise blocks like George would have preferred. George had left after rush hour, or what he perceived rush hour would be, and they were on the north banks of the Allegheny River in relatively short order.

"There it is—Pittsburgh."

Lewis looked through the windshield and offered a weak wuff in return.

"See the metal and cable bridge there—just down the block? It's the one I want to see."

George navigated the RV across the span, turning and twisting in his seat when he reached the other side, hoping against hope a large parking place would suddenly open up.

No such space was to be found.

George drove around for fifteen minutes, thinking there must be an open space somewhere.

There was not.

He began to get panicked. It was the return of a familiar feeling he thought had ceased with the passing of . . .

I don't want to think about it right now. I'll leave her out of this.

He felt a bead of sweat on his forehead and quickly wiped it away.

I came all this way. It is such a stupid idea. Like this would somehow make me feel better. As if drawing things will fill this emptiness. And now, I can't find a place to park the stupid RV. I should have thought of it. I should have driven a car. Or I shouldn't even have bothered with this foolish trip. I'm an old man. With no purpose. I'm fooling myself. Just wandering, lost, in a strange place. This is foolish. It is. But I guess I'll have to fake this as long as I can . . .

As he turned the corner on Ninth Street, a parking lot came into view. It was not full, not by any means.

"Can I park the RV here?"

The young man at the booth shrugged.

"Gotta charge you like a truck."

George wanted out of the RV and out of traffic and wanted to sit for a minute without being nervous or anxious or lost.

"Okay. I'll be couple of hours."

"Whatever. Pull over there by the wall. You won't get blocked in."

George gathered up his materials, chair, and bag and snapped the leash to Lewis's collar.

"Some dog you got there," the attendant said as they walked past. "He friendly?"

George was beginning to get used to the question, but it was still a bit peeving.

"Extremely."

The attendant stepped out of his booth and bent down to Lewis, who greeted his approach with a canine, lopsided grin. He wuffed as the young man scratched behind his ears.

"You're not from around here, are you?"

"No. Gloucester."

"Where?"

"In Massachusetts."

The young man still appeared puzzled.

"Sort of by Boston."

Only then did the young man nod, apparently having heard of Boston before, but George was certain he would never be able to point it out on a map.

No one knows anything about geography anymore.

"Well, you two have a good morning. Maybe I'll see you when you get back," the attendant said, with hope in his voice.

"Maybe."

George and Lewis began walking toward the river and toward the bridges.

"They're called the Three Sisters, Lewis," George explained, as if Lewis needed to know why they stopped at this particular place. "The bridges, I mean. They are all alike—pretty much—and all are suspension bridges, all self-anchored. Tremendous design and execution for the time they were built. You'll see, Lewis. They're famous—as bridges go."

They crossed the street and immediately came upon the first of the trio, the one on Ninth Street. The other two identical structures were at Sixth and Seventh streets.

George walked to the bridge, touched the thick metal plating, ran his fingers over the rivets holding the sheets of steel together, tracing the arc of the metal. Walking out a ways, Lewis sniffed and stared out at the fast-flowing Allegheny beneath them.

At least these are solid things . . . real things . . . they last. Nothing else in life does, apparently.

Lewis cowered, a little, edging closer to the inner rail.

"Have you ever been on a bridge before, Lewis?"

Lewis snorted and kept his left shoulder almost touching the interior side of the protected walkway.

"Well, we don't have to walk the whole way across. You don't care much for rivers, do you? Let's go back and I'll start to draw, okay?"

Lewis turned halfway through his sentence and hurried back to the more solid ground. George looked for a moment and found a good vantage point, close to the bridge, with a clear view of the entire structure, off the sidewalk, in a bit of an alcove of sorts.

"This will do," he said, as he opened the chair, sat down, and took out his sketchbook.

Lewis appeared relieved and sat down heavily, his back to the river, his face to the sidewalk.

George looked about. There was little pedestrian traffic but hardly any on the river side of the street.

Good. No interruptions today.

Lewis sighed deeply and offered George a weak smile of encouragement.

"I know, Lewis. But maybe we'll meet someone back at the RV park today."

Hopefully, we won't.

No more than five minutes had passed, and George was discovering drawing a bridge was more difficult than drawing a building.

A lot more parts to a bridge. At least this bridge.

He had the arch of the span drawn, he had the roadway penned in, and now he was starting to draw the supporting cables. He kept working, drawing with care. The time ticked past. It was taking much longer than drawing a house or a building.

A voice from behind him almost surprised him into making an errant line.

Thankfully, it didn't.

"Hey, what are yuns doing?"

George wondered what a "yun" was, but obviously it was a plural, indicating he meant himself and Lewis together.

George turned his head.

A young man wearing white sneakers, white pants, white T-shirt, and a thin windbreaker stood there, holding a white paper bag in his left hand.

"I'm drawing the bridge," George replied.

Why do people ask such obvious questions?

"You're pretty good. Good perspective. It's hard to do freehand."

Lewis stood and wuffed.

"Hey, boy, how are you?" The young man bent down and patted his side. Lewis stopped a moment, then inhaled deeply, as if savoring some aroma. Lewis tended to be obvious when he found a scent he liked.

"He smells the bread, I bet. I work in a bakery. Always come away smelling like cookies or donuts or fresh bread. All the animals love me. Birds and squirrels especially."

George nodded.

You don't have to stop. You know that, right? I can do without the company this morning, okay? I'm in no mood to be personable right now.

"Good dog. Good dog," the young man repeated, as Lewis pushed the top of his furry head against the young man's chest. This level of intimacy was mostly reserved for people he knew well—or those he knew for more than four minutes.

"What's his name?"

"Lewis."

If I give short answers, maybe he'll take the hint.

"Well, Lewis, you are one friendly dog."

Lewis took a deep sniff, poking his nose close to the white bag in the young man's hand.

"Ahh, you smell the pepperoni, don't you? We make the best pepperoni rolls in Pittsburgh." The young man looked over at George. "Could he have a bite of one?"

George shrugged, trying not to answer or involve himself.

Listen, I don't want to talk today. Let me be miserable, okay?

"You can have one small bite." The young man took out a fist-sized roll and tore a third of it. From the corner of his eye, George could see layers of pepperoni, coloring the roll, letting loose a terrific smell of yeast and bread and Italian seasoning.

I'm almost mad I'm in a bad mood.

Lewis gently opened his mouth and slowly moved toward the roll. He gently closed his jaws, making sure there were no errant fingers mixed in with this delicious new taste. He began to chew, and his eyes almost sparkled in response, his head bobbing, as if he was hearing music.

"Wow, you like this, don't you? Want a little bit more? Is it okay?"

"Sure," George grunted, not taking his eyes off his sketchpad. He could tell by the loudness of Lewis's chewing he truly did relish the taste.

The young man hunched on the curb, refolded the bag, and said softly, but firmly, "That's enough," then draped his arm around the dog and turned to watch George draw.

"You're not an architect. It's not an architect's style. I would say an engineer. But I don't think mechanical. They would use small insets to show the placement of the rivets and cables. I would guess some other field of engineering altogether. The precision shows. Maybe chemical?"

Okay. I'll talk. Then will you leave?

"You were right at mechanical. I might do the inserts on a separate page."

The young man in white laughed.

"Hey, I'm Lucius Boziok. And I've met Lewis."

"And I'm George. George Gibson from Gloucester."

"It's right on the ocean, isn't it? What are you doing here? Besides drawing bridges, I mean. On an engineer's busman's holiday? It's what they call it, right? A busman's holiday if you keep doing the work you did when you left on vacation?"

"It is what it's called . . . but I'm retired. I always wanted to do this—take a long road trip and draw the things I saw. Mostly buildings. I'm not real good with scenery. But I might have to . . . like at Mt. Rushmore or the Grand Canyon."

"Wow. This sounds so cool. I'm jealous."

Lucius watched silently for a few minutes as George added details to his drawing.

"They used to call them the Three Sisters—these bridges, I mean."

George turned around.

"They changed the name? The guidebook I used said the Three Sisters."

Lucius waved his hand in the air in a good-natured act of dismissal. "Now they call them the Three Siblings—and named them after some famous Pittsburgh people. I guess it's okay, but I liked the way the Three Sisters sounded. Like a Chekov play or something."

George nodded in agreement. Even Lewis wuffed twice, as if making it unanimous.

Ask questions.

George shook his head. He was almost getting used to this sort of nudge from somewhere . . . but it still went against his innate nature.

"You like being a baker?" George asked. "I admit the roll smelled awfully good."

Lucius kept his hand on Lewis's neck, scratching, as he replied. Lewis watched him speak, watched carefully.

"It's okay. The people are nice. The pay is okay. The hours are horrible. But I'm only doing it to save up money."

"For what?" George asked, although if he had been asked, he didn't care.

"To go back to school."

"College?"

"Yeah. I'm a year shy of graduating."

Ask questions.

"From where . . . in what?"

"You know Carnegie-Mellon? Right next to University of Pittsburgh?"

"I do. A good school, I've heard."

"And expensive. I have one more year to go. And I ran out of money."

"What are you studying?"

Lucius smiled, and only Lewis saw him.

"Well, I suspect you know more about this than most people— mechanical engineering."

At this, George turned around and lowered the sketchpad.

"You are?"

"Actually, I have a little less than a year to go. They said they would hold my spot for another semester. I'm getting close to having enough cash. I'm even selling some stuff to make up the difference."

Lewis wuffed excitedly. Then he stood, walked over to George, and placed one meaty paw on his arm.

George shook his head as if to say no.

Then Lewis half-stood and placed both paws on his arm, looking deeply into George's eyes, pleading as it were.

"Lewis, you can be a real pest, you know?"

Lewis wuffed in agreement.

George felt the nudge full force, especially with Lewis leaning on him. It was not typical behavior for the dog. This was Lewis in his insisting mode, George thought.

I must be growing soft. But . . . maybe Hazel would have done this.

"Where do you live, Lucius? If you don't mind waiting until I finish this, Lewis and I could take you home. Save bus fare, right?"

The young man grinned and pointed.

"It would be great. I live in West View. It's over there about seven miles."

This time, George grinned.

"It's where we're camped . . . or RVed. Sort of on our way home."

"Cool."

So, Lewis settled down, stepped away from George, and wuffed softly as he allowed Lucius to pet him while George finished his drawing of the first of the Three Sisters, or Siblings, bridge.

<hr />

"Right over here. I live in the basement. Small, dark, and cheap."

George maneuvered the RV up a narrow gravel driveway of a ramshackle Victorian house, perched at a seemingly precarious angle to the steep hill behind it.

"How do you manage all these hills in the winter, Lucius? I'm getting the heebie-jeebies now with no snow. And . . . no one says *heebie-jeebies* anymore, do they?"

"Probably not often," Lucius said.

"And these narrow streets. I'm tempted to leave Lewis at home tomorrow and take a bus downtown. It is not easy parking this big thing," George explained.

"I can imagine," Lucius replied. "It takes me two buses to get here, and I get nervous riding in them sometimes. The roads are narrow."

Lewis began jumping and wuffing and bouncing in the rear of the RV. George thought it was because Lucius had his seat for the drive home.

"Okay, Lewis, you can have your seat back now."

It did not settle him down, not at all.

"You need to go out?" George asked.

Lewis snorted and kept on bouncing, a most uncharacteristic behavior for the generally docile animal. Bouncing and wuffing and even turning in circles, like a small, overexcited bear trying to play charades.

Ask questions. Ask questions.

George shook his head.

Lewis, if this is you, you can stop. I'll ask questions.

"You said you were trying to sell things," George said. "Anything I might be interested in? Or Lewis? Like a soundproof cage, perhaps?"

It's when Lewis went even more ballistic, wuffing, standing at the door, whining almost. Lewis was not a dog who whined, nor often needed to.

"Well, maybe. I mean, I don't have a cage, but I might be able to help with your parking problem."

Lewis and George stood in front of a small, square trailer, painted black, well-cared for.

Lucius went to the rear door and grabbed a padlock and unlatched it and lowered the back door, which formed a ramp. Inside the trailer was a motor scooter with an attached sidecar.

Instantly, George felt himself temporarily thrown backward in time, back to when he attended college and when he first met Hazel. They were both poor college students, barely enough cash on hand for a shared milkshake. And George had come squiring this wonderful girl, this young, pretty, funny, vivacious Hazel . . . on his motorcycle.

It wasn't much of a motorcycle—a small BSA model, English, just powerful enough to carry them both, at speeds well within the legal limit.

George found himself smiling.

Hazel had loved the motorcycle. She had laughed as they drove together, her hair lost in the wind, her arms around George's waist, her chin against his shoulder, even in chilly weather, when she would gather her arms even tighter around him.

She had cried when, two years later, the spring of their senior year, the engine seized and the cost of repairing it went well beyond their modest means. George had sold it for parts, bought a used Buick and a thin wedding band, and put down twenty-five dollars as a security deposit on their first apartment.

There was a photograph of the two of them, sitting astride the motorcycle, smiling the smiles of youthful passion and love, each face turned to the other.

George had not thought of the photograph for years.

It is buried in a box back home, he thought. *How she loved the bike. Buried.*

Lucius was in the trailer explaining the workings of the scooter. George had hardly heard a word, so deep and powerful was his first memory.

It has been nearly fifty years since I thought of my motorcycle.

"It's not fast, but you can keep up with traffic. And Lewis can ride in the sidecar. At least around here, it's legal. I asked a cop once. I took a friend's dog for a ride. He seemed to like it. More wind in his face, I guess."

Lewis had climbed in the trailer as well, sniffing, turning back to George, then sniffing again, wuffing quietly to himself.

"It's my last big-ticket possession," Lucius said. "To be honest, I never used it enough, even when I could. Been trying to sell it for months, but it seems as if everyone wants something bigger and faster and more dangerous."

George saw an image of Hazel, sitting on this new machine, and blinked and rubbed his eyes.

It was one powerful rumination.

He took a deep breath.

And no one says ruminations, *do they?*

"What do you think? Your RV already has a trailer hitch. This whole unit hardly weighs anything."

Lewis climbed down the ramp, excited, wuffing loudly, head-butting George's thigh, circling him, looking back to the trailer, then up to George.

Lewis could manufacture a pleading look, and today, his look appeared to be on steroids.

George let his engineering checklist mentality ask the first question. "Can we take it for a ride first?"

"Absolutely. I have a helmet for you, George, and I have this gnarly set of goggles to fit Lewis for sure."

In a few minutes, the scooter and sidecar were out of the trailer, the engine started, helmet on, and dog goggles in position.

Lewis looked like he was wearing a Snoopy costume for Halloween, when Snoopy thought he was a World War I fighter pilot, attacking the Red Baron.

"This is as easy as riding a bike. Twist and go. No shifting. Brakes are here and here. Use the rear one first. No worries about balance, since you've got three wheels. Take corners slow at first."

George felt it all come flooding back to him, all those times from so long ago, out in the open air. It was as if Hazel had found this young man at this one specific moment to talk with him at the bridge.

Lewis looked at the sidecar, a little hesitant at first, then climbed in, looking like a badger trying on a suit of armor.

He turned around and then let his backside drop onto the seat in the sidecar.

"See, there's a lot of room in there, Lewis."

The two of them, George and Lewis, looked over at Lucius. George grinned. And Lewis grinned even more broadly.

And then George puttered off down the driveway, braking to stop at the end, then with a mufflery rattle, turned left and scooted up the hill, Lewis wuffing loudly as they slipped out of view.

Ten minutes later, the pair came back to the drive and the old Victorian. Lucius had been sitting on the front steps. He stood and waved.

George turned off the engine. Lewis, almost laughing his dog laugh, climbed out of the sidecar, the fur on his head swept up like an Elvis pompadour.

"Lewis got such looks on this ride—people stared. I was afraid some of the other drivers were going to crash because of the distraction."

George took off the helmet.

"How much?"

Lucius stroked his chin.

"Three thousand? For everything. Trailer, scooter, helmet, the works."

George thought for a moment.

"How much do you need to get back to school this year? How short will you be after you sell the scooter?"

"I'm like . . . $3,500 would do it. I could work another month or two, and then . . . yeah, it would be enough. I could finish up by the end of the year. Then graduate. And do something I've always wanted to do. Finally."

Lewis walked over and head-butted George again. He was still happily wearing his goggles.

"I know, Lewis. You don't have to nag."

George took out his checkbook.

"I'm paying you $3,500 for the scooter. No complaints, now. I'm not good at doing nice things for people. But you've brought back some dear memories to me—of when I was young and in love. And you're going to be an engineer. If I don't help, Lewis will not let me hear the end of it—right, Lewis?"

Lewis wuffed with gusto, nodding and smiling and obviously thinking he looked quite dapper in his new leather-trimmed goggles.

"And all you have to do, Lucius, is to promise to do the same some-day—when you're in a position to help someone. Okay?"

Lewis again wuffed in agreement.

———

Backing up an RV with a trailer can be a tricky proposition, but George was lucky. Early in his career, he'd helped with company deliveries—using a trailer. Turning the wheel to get the trailer in the right position wasn't child's play, but the memories of the proper procedure quickly came back.

And Lucius was a whiz at hooking up the wires for the brake lights.

"I had like a dozen cars I towed stuff with. After a while, you figure things out."

"Like life, isn't it?" George replied. "After you do something long enough, you get good at it, and then it turns out you don't have to do it anymore."

As he pulled out of the driveway and headed back to the RV park, listening to the new rattle of the trailer, he smiled.

"Well, Lewis, this should prove to everyone I'm not as sclerotic as people think I am."

Lewis wuffed in agreement, though it was obvious that he did not understand the word *sclerotic*.

"Yes, I know, no one says *sclerotic* anymore. But they should. It means rigid and unadaptable, Lewis. I'm not really that way. Most of the time, anyhow."

They turned into the RV park.

"And I wouldn't think there are more than one or two people talking about me—if any. I don't think I'm the topic of anyone's conversation, Lewis. At least not often."

31

The KDKA weatherman pronounced the day to be a perfect late spring day—bright and sunny, temperatures in the low seventies.

"Just the kind of weather for scooters, right, Lewis?"

Lewis appeared to agree, but George could tell the permanence of objects could be confusing to him. He seemed to love riding in the sidecar, but George thought once it was shut back up in the trailer and hidden, it sort of disappeared, at least a little bit, at least in dog consciousness.

Maybe after we've had it for a while . . .

He had mentioned the scooter several times this morning as they got ready for the day, and Lewis did not seem to register any undue excitement.

But when he pulled the goggles out of the drawer, and Lewis got a good look at them, then he did get excited and began his paws back-and-forth dance, up-and-down sort of steps. It wasn't pretty, or particularly graceful, but it seemed to fit the noble Lewis well. He grinned as if he was sure of what was coming next.

George put the goggles on Lewis, and he wuffed happily.

When George unlocked the trailer and Lewis, saw the scooter and sidecar again, he began to wuff happily, a little louder than normal, but still kept his volume to polite early-morning levels. He climbed into the trailer with George, trying to wedge himself into the sidecar.

"Lewis, back off," George said firmly.

Lewis looked up, his left front paw on the sidecar, surprised.

"Sorry, Lewis, but you have to wait. Now get back down and outside."

Lewis appeared confused, obvious even behind the goggles. George had never had to speak firmly before. Lewis shrunk down and backed out of the trailer, looking guilty and sad.

George backed the scooter out and down the ramp.

Lewis sat down and put his head down.

George closed the trailer, locked it, and then returned to the scooter.

"Lewis, it's okay. Now you can get in."

Lewis shook his head.

"Seriously, Lewis. You just shouldn't get in while it's in the trailer. Makes it harder to push out."

Lewis finally looked up, his eyes a bit distant behind the goggles. Then he slowly made his way to the sidecar and climbed in, slowly, as if her were waiting to be scolded again.

"Good dog," George said when he sat down. At this, Lewis smiled. He wuffed once, politely.

George put on the helmet, put the key in the ignition, started the engine, and looked over at Lewis.

"You ready to go to Pittsburgh again?"

Lewis bobbed in his seat.

And smiling, George puttered off, slowly rounding the gravel road of the RV park and carefully entering the main road, south toward downtown.

During the next two days, George drew three more bridges and, taking a suggestion from Lucius, the old Allegheny County Courthouse and Jail, built by the famous Boston architect Henry Richardson.

George and Lewis immediately found a small parking spot for the scooter, right on the street, and walked around the block, just staring.

"See, Lewis, there's Renaissance and Romanesque styles. The arches look Turkish, the tops of the towers are Byzantine, the windows are Gothic—and can you see it?—it all works together. Amazing—and just look at the massive stone work."

George spent an entire afternoon there, setting up on opposite corners in order to do two perspectives of the building. A steady stream of attorneys and defendants and policemen and jury members, and perhaps criminals, filed in and out, down the marble steps, all the while George was drawing.

It felt to George as if everyone stopped to talk to Lewis.

It took him twice as long to draw the building as he anticipated, such was the volume of interruptions. Lewis appeared to love every minute of it.

He refused to allow George to take off his goggles. He did let him slide them down so they rested around his neck. Lewis felt it was appropriate. And because of it, and the fact George carried the scooter helmet with him, even more passersby engaged them in conversation.

There was even a reporter who passed by, saying he was going to call a photographer from the newspaper to come and get a shot—mostly of the dog, and maybe George in the background.

Thankfully, George was finished before any flashbulbs went off.

They took the scooter across the Monongahela River to the south side of downtown and rode one of the two remaining incline railways to the top of Mt. Washington. George had checked the website the night before, and it said the transportation commission allowed for service animals to ride on all public means of transit.

"If anyone asks, Lewis, you're a service dog today. Emotional support, okay? I go a little loony if you're not with me, okay?"

And no one says loony *anymore . . . except Canadians. And it's about their dollar bills, I think.*

Lewis grinned and nodded as if he understood.

Emotional support . . . got it. Therapy dog. Right.

George was pretty sure it was what Lewis was thinking.

No one stopped them, nor even questioned them, as they got on the Duquesne Incline. At first, when the car first lurched into its ascent, George saw Lewis become a bit apprehensive, but then, a young girl asked if she could pet him. George said yes, and the rest of the short ride was most pleasant, even though the young girl's parents kept repeating, "But, honey, look at the view. Don't you want to see the pretty city?"

Once on top, on the visitor's platform, George sat on a bench, Lewis took up his position next to him, and George tried to do justice with a sketch of the city, spread out before him like a miniature train layout. The three rivers, the park at the confluence with the massive fountain of water, the new baseball stadium, the bridges—George tried to wrap it all up in a sketch. He knew he couldn't do it justice, but he tried. It was like trying to envelop a life in a paragraph. It just couldn't be done adequately.

The last night in Pittsburgh, George made hamburgers on the small charcoal grill he had brought with him. Lewis lounged in the grass as George fussed with the coals and aluminum foil. The RV park remained nearly empty, which suited George fine. And even Lewis looked relieved, such was the volume of strangers he had met over the last two days.

The scooter had already proved to be the perfect solution. George did not have to drive an unweildy RV into a congested city. Parking was a simple matter. The scooter, even with a sidecar, could fit in the tightest of spots, and even up onto the sidewalk, if the situation called for it.

And to Lewis, George could see riding in a sidecar seemed even better than riding in the RV. He was closer to outside, closer to people, freer.

George felt the same way. Memories of his first, and only, motorcycle came welling up as he drove. He tried not to dwell on those memories, since they all included Hazel, and it was a place where George did not want to go. But still—the effect, the wind, the openness of it all was a cleansing experience for George.

After the hamburgers, after the cleanup, after a long time, sitting as darkness fell, George felt, for the first time on this trip, if he was being totally honest, at peace.

Or at least, no longer anxious.

Things will work out.

Lewis looked up as if he had heard something.

Things will work out, right, Lewis?

Lewis did not nod, or smile, or wuff in the affirmative. Instead, he looked at George with a most curious look of apprehension and concern and maybe even fear.

Whatever the look was, soon passed, and Lewis stood and insisted on his evening constitutional around the RV park one last time.

Things will work out, Lewis. It is all going according to plan.

The next morning, George woke the dog up early.

"We need to beat the traffic, Lewis. Let's get going."

Reluctantly, the dog rose, stretched, then stretched again, yawning, blinking his eyes, and, even being shown the leash, showed no signs of enthusiasm.

It was as if he was complaining about the early wake-up call.

"Sorry, Lewis. We just have to get on the road. Don't want to be stuck in Pittsburgh traffic. We'll be through the city before you know it. And then, on to Falling Water."

32

George looked up the directions to Falling Water on his tablet. The computer said it was an hour and half drive and gave him the choice of two routes.

He chose the one with more freeways and less small roads. And he doubled the time allotted.

"Those times are for fast drivers, Lewis. And I'm not a fast driver," George explained as the groggy-looking Lewis settled into the passenger seat and leaned against the door, looking like he might nod off at any moment.

George carefully made his way through Pittsburgh and found the freeway heading west. Falling Water was east and south of Pittsburgh, and George was anxious to see it.

Hazel had often mentioned the house and had even bought a book about it once, with the money George had given her for Christmas.

"I don't know what size she is," he had explained when his daughter found out about his "impersonal" gift. "This way she can get exactly what she wants."

George had never understood the problem involved with a gift of cash. But his daughter had continued to roll her eyes and sigh loudly whenever the subject of his gift selections came up.

"It was so long ago, Lewis. She did seem to enjoy the book. I might have kept it. It might still be in one of those boxes in storage. Might be."

Lewis snorted, just a little, as he often did when he was drifting off to sleep.

The distance the computer gave was spot on, and George was spot on about his driving abilities and steady, not fast, pace. They arrived after just under three hours on the road.

George knew reservations were needed to tour the house. Those he had secured months earlier, and for the first tour in.

"It's why we stick to the plan, stick to the schedule," he informed Lewis as they headed into the sparsely filled parking lot.

Lewis still looked sleepy.

"I have to leave you here, Lewis. There are no pets allowed. Not even good dogs like yourself."

If Lewis was hurt by this announcement, he did not show it. On the contrary, he looked grateful to be able to crawl in back and resume his nap.

"I'm parking in the shade. It's only going up to 65 degrees today. And all the windows will be partially open. I know you'll be fine."

Lewis paid scant attention and had already climbed up on the couch and laid his head down on the cushion.

"But I'm going to lock the RV. It won't keep anyone out, but it would slow them down. By then, you'd be on high alert, right, Lewis?"

Lewis only managed a weak wuff in response and did not even open his eyes to do so.

George gathered up his bag and left his chair in the RV.

They probably would not like me banging the chair into walls. And I'm not doing a full drawing—just a couple of quick sketches.

He turned the key in the lock, looked at Lewis, already asleep, and checked his watch.

"Ten minutes early," he said and headed off for the start of the tour.

In less than two hours, George had returned.

There was now a small line at the beginning of the tour. The official tour started on the far side of Bear Run, a smallish stream, about a quarter mile from the house.

I'm glad I picked the early tour. Hardly anyone there.

A few cars were now parked near the RV. He unlocked the door. Only then did Lewis wake up, stretch, yawn, and climb down from the couch to greet him and go outside.

"Over there, Lewis," George whispered. "Out of view, okay?"

Lewis looked up, puzzled, but obediently shambled over to an area of small brush. He plowed his way into it, and whatever he was doing was well hidden from any prying eyes of rangers or dog police or whoever else may be lurking, looking for Falling Water violators.

"They seem to be a fussy group here, Lewis."

If dogs could shrug, it's what Lewis did. Lewis returned, looking for a treat, which George supplied.

"Well, the man was a great architect, I guess, but a lousy engineer. Even the guide admitted it. He said the house cost $155,000 to build—and get this, Lewis, more than $11 million to fix all the problems of leaning concrete."

Lewis looked up at George and tilted his head.

"I know you don't understand money, Lewis. But, boy, oh boy, what a mistake."

From the car on the left side of the RV, George heard a woman's shrill voice—not of pain or complaint, but of . . . maybe discouragement. Lewis perked up immediately and then began to trot around to investigate.

"Lewis," George hissed quietly. "Don't bother anyone."

Lewis did not stop, and George felt obligated to follow him and make sure his appearance didn't cause any panic in small children or large-dog-sensitive adults.

"I can't believe I didn't ask. I am so disappointed, Peter. I knew how much you wanted to see this."

If Peter answered, George could not hear his words.

When he turned the corner of the RV, he saw the woman, standing beside an older model sedan, next to the open passenger door. She looked upset. George could not see anything else.

"I didn't even think to check. And I always check. Now, I've ruined everything."

Lewis wuffed loudly, as if calling for a time-out.

"Oh, goodness, is that a bear?"

The man mumbled something. It might have been followed by a laugh, but George could not make it out either.

"Sorry, sorry," George called out. "He thinks everyone wants to meet him. This is Lewis. He's a gentle dog."

The man said something, and Lewis hurried to his side.

In another three steps, George saw behind the open passenger door—a man in a wheelchair.

The woman, obviously his wife, looked to be near tears.

"They just told me it's not wheelchair-accessible—at least not for the size wheelchair we have."

George nodded. "No. It really isn't. The hallways are almost too small for a full-size person to walk in. There would be no way that wheelchair could fit."

The man looked up, or tried to.

"You go," he said softly.

The woman shook her head.

"No, I don't want to go without you. It's okay, Honey."

"Paid for tickets."

She stopped.

"Well, I guess it's true. Maybe I could sell them back. Get a refund."

"You go," the man mumbled again.

"No, you're the one who always talked about this place," she said, then turned to George and Lewis. "He was a cement contractor. Peter, he's my husband. He liked to build things. He always talked about this place. He said when we had time, we would go."

Lewis spun around to George, as if demanding he do something, staring at him with a most earnest look, the most earnest George had yet noted on Lewis's face.

Okay. Okay.

"Listen," George spoke up, almost interrupting, "No need for both of you to miss it. You go. I'll stay here with Peter."

The woman's expression did not change. It was still confused and angry and sad.

"I can't ask you to. It takes more than an hour for the tour."

"More like two. But it will be fine. I have nowhere to be."

Lewis wuffed.

"And I can make us coffee in the RV."

Lewis wuffed again.

"And I could show him the drawings I made—where all the builder's mistakes are. I was an engineer, so I know."

The woman's face tightened, as if in pain.

"I just couldn't ask anyone . . ."

"Listen, my name is George Gibson. This is Lewis. We're from Gloucester, Massachusetts. We're on a year's tour of the country. I can afford to spend a few hours here."

"But . . ."

Her eyes darted to her husband, and his wheelchair, and his face—slightly tilted, slightly lopsided, slightly twisted—and then back to George. She did not have to say one word about her fears.

"I know," he said, as if he understood everything going through her thoughts right then. "I took care of my wife for more than ten years. She had ALS. I can sit with Peter for a few hours."

Lewis wuffed three times, smiling, wagging his tail.

"And we have Lewis as a bodyguard. Go. Use your ticket, at least. Enjoy the time. Tell him all about it when you get back. It will be okay. One of you should go. Take plenty of pictures."

The woman's hands were twisted together, wringing them as if in pain.

"I don't know . . ."

"Please. Go. It's okay, isn't it, Peter?"

Peter tried to nod. He mumbled out the words, "You go."

The woman took a deep breath.

"All right. I'll go. And thank you."

Lewis wuffed and hurried to her side as if to escort her toward the beginning of the tour.

<hr />

George waited a minute, until he saw the woman enter the line of people, already moving forward, toward the house.

"She's Lucy."

The word came out "Looshy," but George knew what he meant. Hazel, at the end, had suffered the same sort of impairment, as her muscle control left her. The words were there but hard to get out.

"Stroke," Peter said.

George nodded. "I thought so. You want coffee? I have instant."

Peter tried to nod, his head bobbing just slightly.

"Come on, we'll go around to my front door. It'll be easier. Cream or sugar?"

"Boat," Peter mumbled. "Lost of shu-gar."

Lewis sidled up to the man in the wheelchair, sniffing the apparatus thoroughly, then, without being told, found Peter's good side, his slightly mobile side, and sat down, his head at hand level.

Peter, his frame thin and drawn and newly scrawny, George thought, slowly stroked Lewis's head and tried to smile, a thin, pained smile.

"Frustrating."

In a moment, George carried two coffee cups outside. He had practice deciphering badly pronounced words.

"My wife said the same thing. Frustrating. Wanted to talk, but the words got stuck."

Peter nodded. He pointed to a cup holder on the arm of the wheelchair.

"Need a straw? It might be too hot."

"Will wait. Okay."

George inserted a straw he found in the soft drink cup in Peter's car, and carefully set it into the coffee.

"Give it five minutes to cool down," he said. "It's not good enough coffee to risk being burned over."

Shafts of sunlight filtered through the overhanging branches, lighting the three of them in dapples of brightness. The parking area was far from any main road, so birdcalls, cricket chirps, and leaves rustling were the loudest sounds. George could even hear the sound of Peter's white bony hand, slowly smoothing the fur on Lewis's head, a muted, soft, barely audible hiss.

Comfort . . . comfort . . . is what it sounds like.

"She dead?"

George nodded, making sure Peter could see him.

He had talked more about Hazel in these past few minutes than he had in several months.

"Sorry."

George nodded again, and Lewis wuffed softly, not moving away, content to let this stranger pet his head.

"Suffer?"

George nodded again.

I'm sure he understands what it means.

"She prayed a lot. She said it gave her peace."

Peter sort of pointed at himself.

"No more," he said, indicating he must have given up on the practice. "Poor Looshy. Works hard. I make life hard."

Lewis looked over to George. His face—the dog's always expressive face, a face of which George could easily discern the emotions within—was a cipher this morning. It was as if Lewis did not know what to think or how to help.

George felt no nudges to ask questions or to offer some sort of advice. There was nothing. George felt completely on his own with this.

"Maybe she's okay with it," George said. "Maybe she doesn't mind."

I don't think I believe it. It wasn't true of me. I minded. I did. I just could never be honest about it. I could never tell Hazel. I could never tell anyone. Only once did I let my true feelings show . . . and it is a time I never want to think about again. Ever.

"No," Peter replied and shook his head, not shaking it, more like rolling it back and forth, slowly. "Her eyes . . . pain . . . lost dreams."

My dreams . . . they keep coming back to one time. Nightmares . . . not dreams. It's unforgivable, I guess. Hard to make go away

Lewis did not look at George. Instead, he stared up at Peter's face.

"Maybe it's just you, Peter. Maybe she is . . . I don't know . . . maybe she's okay with it."

Peter kept moving his head back and forth. "No. Too much."

He bent down and took a sip of the coffee.

He looked up.

"Good. Sweet."

"Thanks," George replied. "It's just instant."

Peter's face turned up to the sunlight. George could see the tightness of his skin on his cheekbones, as if he had lost a great deal of weight

171

since his stroke, since his body had betrayed him. Slight stubble on his chin glistened in the light. He lifted his hand off Lewis's head and wiped at his mouth. It took a long moment.

Then he spoke again, his voice even softer, somehow more conspiratorial. George had to lean closer to hear.

"I had guns. Would use one. Too hard. But . . . I can . . . I can't."

Lewis appeared alarmed but did not bark or move.

He does understand.

"In Holland . . . they help people die."

Lewis looked up at George.

You have to say something.

"You know, I loved my wife. I tried to tell her it was okay—my helping her."

"She believe?"

"Maybe."

Lewis stood and nervously rocked from left to right, as if trying to decide on a course of action. Then he half-climbed into the wheelchair, getting his front paws on Peter's lap. Peter smiled in response. His good arm went around Lewis's shoulders.

"Lewis, good dog. You run . . . play. Me? No more. Trapped."

George realized this intimate conversation was the conversation between two strangers, two people who understood each other perfectly. It was a conversation which could never be held between friends— one of them would become alarmed, one of them would be ashamed of telling the hard, dirty, painful truth. No, this sort of honesty only existed between souls who would never pass each other again, this side of heaven or this side of whatever forever one believed in. There was no need to hide any flaws. Transparency could be dangerous—but not with strangers. Strangers could not hold judgments.

This honesty, this cut-to-the-bone honesty, was only born of serendipity, of the chance encounter of two people climbing along the same path, nodding at each other in recognition of having endured the jagged rocks and the blistering heat and the abject frigidity.

Only those so purified could participate in this truth.

Lewis looked at Peter, then George, almost pleading, his pleading-for-a-treat face.

I know, Lewis. This is hard. We can help people with a dream, with a future, but this man . . . he has no dreams left. His future does not stretch off forever.

Lewis turned to look at Peter. He wuffed quietly.

"Peter, I could tell you my wife had faith right to the end."

"Help?"

George did not think before he answered.

"Maybe it helped her. Not me."

He took a deep breath.

"I didn't see any comfort in it. Maybe it did help her, but I just didn't see much effect. So for me, no."

Lewis gently stepped away from the wheelchair and sat, wuffed several times, then stared at the ground, as if he were being punished.

"Lewis is a dog who seems to like the truth," George said. "Or maybe he dislikes lies. He gets upset when people lie to him. And I would be lying if I thought her praying did any good at all. She still suffered. She still just gradually wore away. There was always pain. She couldn't walk or talk or even swallow at the end. And she prayed. To what end, I ask you?"

Silence filled the air. George did not even hear the birds chatter.

Lewis wuffed and shook his head and stood up, then barked, loudly, as if to call a halt to this discussion, this painful conversation.

Then he barked again, and one more.

Show him . . .

George took a deep breath. "Peter, let me show you the mistakes Wright made on the house. I made some sketches."

Peter's face remained silent for a bit. Then he offered a smile.

"See here—this is where Wright wanted to use only eight steel bars for reinforcement. Kaufmann's engineers insisted on more. Wright gave in, the guide said, and was quoted as saying, 'Well, it's your house. You can do what you want.'"

"How many?"

"They added eight more. Wasn't nearly enough. The guide said when it was built it was nearly two inches off level. Back in '95, they measured again, and it was a full seven inches off level."

Peter kept nodding, almost smiling. He pointed to the bottom terrace on George's quick sketch.

"Fall into the stream."

"It's what the guide said would have happened. So, they used cables around the concrete beams under the floors and put in hydraulic jacks to tighten them. Said it won't correct the problem, just not let it get worse."

Peter shook his head in happy dismay.

"Architects."

"I know," George replied. "Would you have built it like this?"

Peter became almost animated. "No. Terrible. Never."

Lewis happily followed this conversation, obviously relieved the tone and tenor had changed.

George kept talking, pointing out construction details to Peter, making a few small, quick sketches to illustrate one problem or another.

"And the roof leaks," George concluded. "Twelve million dollars and the roof still leaks."

At this, Peter laughed, a mumbling, rolling sort of laugh, but a laugh, nonetheless.

To which Lewis wuffed happily in response.

Two hours later, Lucy hurried up to the RV.

"It took so much longer than I expected," she said, as if either Peter or George had asked for a reason for her long absence, which they had not.

Lewis stood, wagging his tail, greeting her politely, not standing on his rear paws and trying for a bear hug.

"I have lots of pictures, Peter."

Peter pointed to George.

"We talked . . . construction."

He was still smiling.

"Oh, Honey, I'm glad. I wouldn't know anything about it. So thank you, George."

"My pleasure. You want some help getting the chair into your car?"

There was an expression of palatable relief on her face.

"If you don't mind . . ."

In a few minutes, Peter had been moved to the front seat, seat belt fastened, and the wheelchair manhandled into the sedan. It was not an easy task, even for George. The wheels kept spinning as he tried to pick it up.

Bad engineering . . . bad design.

Lucy walked Lewis and George back to the side door of the RV.

"Again," she said, quietly, not wanting her words to travel far, "thanks so much. It was nice to have a few hours alone. And I did like the house. I couldn't live in it, but the setting . . . oh, my."

"I know the feeling. Not about the house. But about being in charge. About taking care of someone. About taking care of someone totally dependent on you. I do. It never lets up, does it?"

Lucy's eyes were almost glistening, and she quickly wiped away the forming tears. "No. It doesn't. It never stops. But this is my lot in life. I have faith. This is just temporary, right? This is just our lot until we see Jesus, right? Just temporary. This whole world is just temporary."

Lewis wuffed, offering his version of a comforting word.

"I guess so," George replied. "But it sure seems like a long time, though, doesn't it?"

She tried to smile, then nodded.

"If I thought this was it, well . . . I don't know what I would do. Too much pain if this was all there is."

Lucy sort of nodded to herself, then looked to both George and Lewis with a heartfelt smile on her face, not of joy, but of peaceful resignation, perhaps.

"Thanks again. Truly, thanks."

⁂

As George maneuvered the RV and trailer out of the parking area, and back onto the main road, Lewis wuffed at him several times.

"You need an answer?"

175

Wuff.

"I don't think I have one, Lewis. Not for this."

Wuff.

"Because some things can't be answered."

Wuff.

"I know, Lewis. You would like to think the truth will help everyone and everyone will find their dream and everyone will be happy. But it doesn't always happen."

Wuff.

"Maybe there is a limit to what the truth will do."

Lewis did not respond. First, he looked down at his front paws, then slowly raised his head, stared out the passenger window, and remained quiet for the rest of the afternoon.

33

George did not curse, had never been a man given to epithets and swearing, or even harsh words, but tonight, he felt closer to the edge than ever before.

They were somewhere in the middle of Pennsylvania, on their way to Gettysburg, taking a scenic back road, through the Allegheny Mountains, and the sun had set and the road narrowed to a tight two-lane affair. And now, feeling lost in the dark, George realized the RV Park that was supposed to be there, simply wasn't.

George pulled the RV to the side of the road.

"I don't know why I'm bothering pulling over. There isn't any traffic out here. I could just stop in the middle of the road."

But I follow the rules.

As normal for his breed's characteristics, Lewis was not one given to anxiety or nervousness, but this evening, he was exhibiting signs of both.

Maybe it's because of what happened at Falling Water. He encountered a sort of deep-soul sorrow he couldn't make any better.

George took out his cell phone and checked his reception.

"One bar is better than none, Lewis."

He dialed the number he had for the RV park.

He heard static, then a hiss, then an automated voice, explaining the number was no longer in service.

I didn't call them before we left . . . I just assumed they would be open and have space. But they are not where the map said they would be. They must have closed. Or maybe they're somewhere where the GPS doesn't reach.

George looked out into the blackness.

There are such spots, I'm sure. Where even a satellite doesn't reach. Too dark, maybe.

He tapped at the GPS screen, found the setting to decrease the size of the map. He hit the button once and saw nothing other than a road passing through a beige emptiness. He tapped it again. Still nothing but road. One more time, and a town came into view, on the far northeastern side of the map.

"Thirty miles," he said to himself. "Maybe forty."

George had decided to take the back roads to the Gettysburg battlefield and had selected Route 220—the Bedford Valley Parkway.

In the darkness, he saw a few lonely, cold, sodium vapor lights on barns, the illumination frosty and uninviting, opposed to the warm, the intimate glow of lights inside houses, filtered by gauzy curtains. But those he saw only on occasion, miles apart from one another. Other than those isolated points of light, the land was dark and felt uninhabited.

Like life itself. Like people.

To a man who had grown up in a city, had never camped in the wilderness, had never traveled to remote places, the isolation, such as it was, was unnerving. Perhaps his uneasiness had affected Lewis. Lewis whined a bit when George stopped, looking out on the expanse of lonely darkness.

"Bedford. It's not so far. We'll go there. It's a pretty big town, Lewis. An hour or so is all."

Lewis whimpered, softly, almost as if he did not want to show his discomfort.

"You need to go out?"

Lewis looked out the window and saw only dark.

Then he looked back at George with a worried expression.

"Lewis, I'll come out with you. And I'll get my flashlight, okay?"

Lewis seemed to be comforted and stood, waiting to be unhooked from the seat belt.

He hopped down to the gravel at the side of the RV and began sniffing loudly, with great purpose.

Then he heard a gentle chorus of mooing and the crunching rustle of the grass and launched himself back into the RV, tumbling inside, barking and whining and scrambling to find his footing.

George was startled as well. He turned the flashlight toward the sound. A trio of cows stood behind a wooden fence, only a few feet from the side of the road, chewing slowly, looking as if their sleep had been disturbed.

"They're cows, Lewis."

Lewis peeked around the side of the RV door, growling softly, hoping it would scare off those large, dark, ominous, and potentially deadly creatures.

"They're vegetarians, Lewis. They wouldn't eat a dog. Not even a soft one like yourself. Come on down. You need to go out. They won't hurt you."

It took four minutes until Lewis finally climbed down to the side of the road, all the while listening to George's encouragements and entreaties. The soft mooing of the cows offered Lewis a peaceful reception. No screeching or bellowing, just a soft bovine lowing, clear and distinct in the silence of the valley and the absence of traffic.

Lewis accomplished his mission outside, never once letting his eyes off the mooing trio.

"You done? Time to move on, Lewis."

Bravely, Lewis took a step toward the fence, and one of the cows nudged forward as well. Lewis had his nose up to the top of the fence, and one cow leaned its head over the top.

"They must think you're a furry baby cow, Lewis."

The two animals sniffed for a moment, and then Lewis snorted once.

"Hay fever?" George asked.

Lewis backed up to the RV and then hurried inside, wuffing gratefully as George secured the door behind him.

"Cows, Lewis. Just cows."

Lewis took his seat in the front and kept a vigilant look outside.

"They won't come after us, Lewis. They're slow. And mostly gentle."

George put his blinker on, looked in the rearview mirror, and pulled out onto the road.

"We'll find a place near Bedford. Maybe there's a Walmart there. I hear they don't mind if an RV spends the evening in their parking lot."

The night felt as if it wrapped up George and Lewis and the RV in an encompassing bear hug, only a blink of a barn light or isolated farmhouse breaking into the darkness, and not often. The absence of the moon, hidden behind a thick scud of clouds, removed even a possibility of seeing behind the arc of the headlights.

"Makes you think, doesn't it, Lewis? I mean, the darkness. All you can see is the small patch of road in front of us. Everything else is gone. Maybe the world is out there . . . and maybe it isn't."

Lewis turned to George and turned his head sideways. He looked like he wanted to wuff in agreement, but he did not. Instead, he waited and then turned back to the passenger window.

"It's like being adrift from everything else. It's where I'm at. Lewis. I'm not tangled up with anyone . . . except you, and only temporarily . . . and being alone is not a bad thing at all. I don't have anyone else to worry about."

Lewis shook his head. George did not think he was disagreeing with him, although he might have been.

"You know, Lewis, I think I realized something important today."

Wuff.

"I realized a person's last days can be good, or they can be horrible."

Lewis did not reply. He simply looked and listened.

"I suppose I knew it all along. Well, I don't suppose. I did know it. But it wasn't until today the truth finally made a real impression on me. I truly grasped what it means, you know?"

Wuff.

"With Hazel, her last days, her last years, our last years, were simply unbearable. Hard, unforgiving, painful, and horrible. And I bet, with Peter, the days are terrible for him as well now. Having his wife do everything for him. Feeling totally helpless. He's trapped by a broken body."

Wuff.

"But here's the difference between Peter and me, Lewis. I know when the end is coming. We haven't talked about it, you and I. And I'm not going to talk about it with you. Some things are better left unsaid. I think it would just upset you if I said anything more about it."

Lewis snorted.

"Well, some secrets are going to remain hidden and unspoken, regardless of how you feel about it."

Silence filled the RV, other than the low rumble of the tires on the rough macadam road.

"I think Peter hoped he was near the end of things, near to absence of pain, but he couldn't get there. You heard him, Lewis. He would have ended it if he could. He could see a place where he wouldn't suffer and where he wouldn't make his wife suffer alongside of him. But now, all he can do is wait. He has to suffer. His wife has to suffer. Nothing fair about it, if you ask me. Nothing fair at all. This world is just not a fair place."

Lewis shook his head.

"I know what people say—it is part of life and it's what you sign up for when you get married. Okay, maybe so. But what if I get sick, Lewis? Then what? My daughter has to take care of me? She didn't sign up for it. She has a husband. She doesn't need to take care of two people. It wouldn't be fair to her."

Lewis simply stared, a confused look in his eyes.

"So . . . a person in my situation . . . without attachments—well, I have some wonderful liberties, Lewis. I can decide if the last days are good—or bad. And I have decided they will be good. This truth, this realization, is liberating, Lewis. Liberating."

Lewis appeared ready to agree, then stopped and did not utter a sound, as if he were trying to understand George's logic, his argument, what he was saying. Lewis was smart, but he was not versed in every human possibility, in every nuance of the human condition. Some things people did confused Lewis. Some emotions he could not read, could not understand.

"I have spent my life being in control, Lewis. I have been straight-laced and followed the straight and narrow, and I have obeyed all the rules. I didn't speed. I paid my taxes. I went to church with my wife, when I would have rather stayed home. But I did what I had to do. And for the most part, I guess it was okay. I suppose, if I'm being honest, I don't regret any of it, Lewis. I don't."

George slowed down for a narrowing of the road. It was a bridge, and the concrete abutments were no more than an arm's length from the side of the road. The road noise changed, for the short instance, then grew louder, then fell away again, a near silent, hissing rumble.

"Lewis, my life is in my hands. And I say it is time for a change. It is time for me to embrace what time I have left . . . and to enjoy it."

Lewis stared, then after a moment of consideration, he wuffed, twice.

"I'll enjoy this trip, Lewis, instead of treating it as an obligation. We have a long way to go before we sleep, Lewis. A long, long way."

Lewis looked out the front windshield with a worried look.

"Not tonight, Lewis. We don't have a long way to go tonight. Only a few more miles. Then we're done and we'll stop, and I'll make some dinner, okay?"

At the word *dinner*, Lewis brightened and smiled and began to fidget, as only a St. Bernard can, with elegance, solidity, and stately bulk.

George smiled, then something came to mind, something he had not thought of for years and years, even decades.

He was in the eighth grade at Gloucester Junior High school.

Mr. Roescher.

English.

The section was poetry.

George, like many of his eighth-grade friends, had little use for it.

It sounded prissy, if you ask me.

George let the memory wash over him.

And no one says prissy *anymore, do they?*

But each reluctant student, no matter what they thought of iambic pentameter or free verse, each and every one in the class had to pick one poem and commit it to memory.

George picked Robert Frost because he lived in Boston, near Gloucester.

The last stanza of his selection came roaring back to him, the words loud in his mind, and he spoke them aloud, in a deep clarion voice: "But I have promises to keep, and miles to go before I sleep."

Lewis listened intently, to the rhythmic words, and if George could guess an emotion expressed in Lewis's face, it would be a graceful resignation to the unchangeable.

"Do you want to hear the whole poem, Lewis. I think I remember most of it."

Lewis looked over, with a quizzical look, and wuffed.

"I'll take it for a yes. He called it 'Stopping by Woods on a Snowy Evening.'"

34

Trudy heard the thump from upstairs, the quick footfalls on the steps, and the blur of Alex as he slid, on stocking feet, into the kitchen, like a hockey player sliding into the boards.

The computer monitor on the kitchen desk filled with Lewis's smiling face, his nose the width of a man's palm, as he sniffed at the camera on his end of the Skype call.

"Lewis!" Alex shouted, to which Lewis stared, a little perplexed, and then smiled back and wuffed excitedly.

"It's Alex. Your buddy, Alex."

George must have been to the side of the camera and was trying to explain to Lewis, again, Alex was not behind the small tablet computer, but back home in his kitchen.

Lewis looked over his shoulder, then leaned to the right, trying to see what was behind George's tablet device.

"He thinks you're here," George explained. Alex saw George's hand pat Lewis on the head.

"How are you, Lewis? Are you being a good dog?"

Lewis wuffed happily, several times. Alex could tell Lewis was excited because he began shifting his weight from one front paw to the other, rocking his frame back and forth, a few inches at a time.

"Where are you, Lewis?"

Lewis looked off-camera to the still unseen George.

"Williamsburg, Virginia."

Wuff.

"Is it fun there?"

Wuff.

"Lewis saw a horse, and I think the horse was more afraid of Lewis than the other way around."

George narrated their recent travels, with Lewis adding an enthusiastic wuff now and again. Then George moved the camera slightly and showed Alex his recent drawings, holding the sketchpad up close and flipping the pages.

"You draw good, Mr. Gibson."

"Thanks, Alex. And by the way, Lewis has something to show you. I'll have to help him with it."

George's back filled the screen.

"Hold still, Lewis."

In a moment, George moved away and there sat Lewis, wearing his goggles, which Alex had already seen, and now, a helmet, neatly strapped under his chin.

"I found this in Washington, D.C. It's a child's size and fits him perfectly. We got to talking to a woman we met at the Vietnam memorial and she suggested the idea. And now Lewis is much better protected when we use the scooter."

"Mom!" shouted Alex. "Look at Lewis! He's got a helmet."

Trudy hurried over to look, standing behind Alex, peering down at the screen.

She could not help but laugh.

"Mom," Alex complained. "Don't laugh. You'll give Lewis a complex or something."

"Sorry. Sorry. You look absolutely charming, Lewis. And I'm glad you're safer, too."

George put his face into the frame for a moment.

"I never go much above forty miles an hour . . . but still, better safe than sorry. And Lewis enjoys wearing it."

Then Lewis's face returned to the center of the screen.

Alex started to tell Lewis about his day and week and all the things happening at school and how all his friends told him to say hello for them. Lewis appeared to love these talks, and if Trudy had to venture a guess, she would say Lewis definitely recognized Alex and knew exactly what was going on.

I find it hard to believe as well . . . but it certainly seems like it.

Trudy edged away from the vicinity of the computer and went back to dicing green peppers for the evening meal, adding them to a bowl of other chopped and minced ingredients.

Alex and Lewis talked for a long time. Alex told Lewis the desensitizing shots were going well, they didn't hurt, and the doctor said he was making fast progress. And Alex talked about Little League, which he was trying again, and maybe even soccer. They chatted and wuffed.

The Alex looked back to his mother. "Mom, say good-bye!"

Trudy looked up, called out a farewell, and watched as Alex waved and saw the connection go black.

Alex stared at the screen, then slowly turned to his mother.

"He seems to be having a good time."

"He does."

Alex bit his lower lip.

"Does Mr. Gibson seem different to you?"

"Different? How?"

Alex shrugged. It seemed like a shrug was his first response to virtually any question.

Maybe it gives him time to think.

"I dunno. He seems . . . more cheery. More happy."

"Happier. Not more happy."

"Whatever. But he seems different than when he left. Like he's not as serious as he was."

"It's a good thing, right?"

"I guess."

Trudy had noticed the same thing but did not mention it. She had told herself Alex would make up his own mind as to how this George and Lewis arrangement was working out.

"Maybe Lewis has been making George happier. Because he has someone to talk to. Everyone needs to be part of something, don't they? Families are important, and maybe George sees Lewis as part of his family—temporarily."

"I guess."

Alex got up and walked to the kitchen door, heading back upstairs to his room.

"But he wasn't supposed to change, Mom," Alex said. "Mr. Gibson was just fine the way he was."

Trudy put down the knife.

"Are you worried Lewis is going to like him more now? And he won't want to come back home?"

Alex appeared as if insulted, or almost insulted.

"No. He wants to come home. I can see it. It's Mr. Gibson I was worried about. Lewis is fine."

Trudy did not know how to respond, so she put on her best mommy smile.

"Mr. Gibson is fine. He was just excited to show you the new helmet for Lewis. I think it's all there is to it."

Alex nodded.

"Yeah, maybe. I hope so."

And then he was off, back upstairs, back to work on his project for American history.

He was giving a report on the Battle of Gettysburg, using drawings of Little Round Top and the Devil's Den drawn by Mr. Gibson, who had sent photocopies to Alex.

I hope it was just the helmet and not something else.

Trudy went back to chopping, turned the gas on the stove, then stopped.

Why are we so suspicious of people being happy for no reason? It doesn't seem logical, does it? But it is the truth.

35

Lewis barked as George motored the scooter past the small dog park. Several dogs looked up, searching for the barking, and appeared surprised—no, shocked—to see a large dog wearing goggles and a helmet, seated in a sidecar, his front paw up on the rim of the sidecar, the wind blowing back his fur, his jowls slapping as they rolled along.

George had taken to waving to just about everyone who noticed them. He would smile broadly, lift his left hand, and offer a friendly wave of acknowledgment.

"Not every day they see a senior citizen driving a St. Bernard in a sidecar, Lewis. You see people point and stare and smile."

It wasn't like this before. I wasn't like this before. I've changed. The plan hasn't changed, but I have.

"Well, Lewis," George said as they came to a red light. "If you don't want the interaction, or the attention, don't take a dog for a ride in a sidecar, right?"

Wuff.

The pair, George and Lewis, were scootering up Lookout Mountain, just south and west of downtown Chattanooga. George would have described it as "scootering back and forth, up the mountain," because the road switched back on itself many times, the slope being much too steep for a direct, frontal assault.

After more than four months on the road, riding in the scooter had become old hat for Lewis, although the joy he expressed at getting into the sidecar had not yet seemed to dim in intensity.

187

And George felt more and more at ease in piloting the scooter in traffic.

Best purchase I ever made, this scooter. Makes almost every place accessible.

George wanted to escape the afternoon heat of a late summer day in the mid-South and decided going up in elevation would offer some cooling relief.

On account of the recent heat wave that lasted for several weeks, he had even taken Lewis to a professional groomer. Up until then, George brushed the dog with some regularity, a chore that neither of them seemed to enjoy.

But along a back road, south of Knoxville, they had traveled past a large sign pointing to Luella's Dog Spa and Hair Cuttery.

George, in a moment of expansiveness, had pulled in and cajoled a most reluctant and hesitant St. Bernard inside.

It must smell like a vet's office because as soon as we stepped into the parking lot, Lewis got the heebie-jeebies.

Lewis had whimpered the whole way inside. If Lewis had been scared, Luella had calmed him immediately with her honey-thick Southern drawl and kindergarten-teacher patience.

Lewis was treated to a bath, a four-legged pawdicure, and a thorough dethatching. Luella had described the process as stripping out his dense undercoat, but George saw it as dethatching, plain and simple.

Lewis looked twenty-five pounds lighter when she was finished.

"When it gets hot like this," Luella had said, turning the word *hot* into a three-syllable effort, "he should get this treatment every month or so. Y'all from around here? I could sign y'all up for my 'big-dog-double-discount program.'"

George had demurred on the offer, explaining they were on a road trip of America.

Lewis had wuffed and danced as Luella had pronounced him finished. He'd stopped in front of the floor mirror in the spa's entryway and had spent nearly a full minute looking at himself, admiring himself, as it were, turning several times to fully appreciate his new look.

"First time I've seen a dog do this, Mr. Gibson. Lewis looks like he likes it. You got a special dog there."

George had nodded.

"Trouble is, he knows it."

And now the lighter-looking Lewis and same-weight-as-ever George were headed up to the Lookout Mountain Battlefield Park, at the top of the mountain. The last two days had been spent exploring downtown Chattanooga, sketching some old steel-truss bridges and exploring the massive train station.

It's called the Chattanooga Choo Choo Hotel now, but the name feels stupid to say, so I won't.

George had already sketched the incline railway up the eastern face of Lookout Mountain and now wanted to see the city from above.

He puttered the scooter to a stop. The parking lot was sparsely filled with cars and only one tour bus.

George could now determine the crowd-ability of certain attractions by the number of tour busses parked out front. He'd developed the equation in Washington, D.C.

More than ten busses equals moving on to the next site on your list. I don't like being tediously shoved aside by a slow-moving horde of senior citizens from Reading, Pennsylvania, all intent on making it back to the bus before it heads off to an early-bird special.

Lewis did not seem to mind waiting so much. He would sit as a long column of travelers trudged past, a fair percentage of them staring at their feet, looking like prisoners on a death march, and grin up at them, hoping to lure one or two or a dozen to stop and pet him. This stoppage, of course, would disrupt the entire delicate balance and schedule of the Reading Senior Citizen Spring Fling, usually causing the tour leader/cattle drive foreman to shout out, "Stay with the group! Stay with the group! No stopping."

Watching with a critical, yet dispassionate eye this slowly unfolding spectacle was the only way George could enjoy an overcrowded venue.

But Lookout Mountain was not on anyone's top-ten list of must-see sights, nor any bon vivant's bucket list, and as such, it remained blissfully uncrowded.

"Let me get your helmet, Lewis."

This time, Lewis submitted to the unbuckling process without complaint. A few times, he'd adamantly refused to relinquish the protective gear, and had spent all afternoon wearing it, like a first-grader wearing a favorite Halloween costume for days afterward.

George locked the goggles and helmets in the small storage area built into the rear of the sidecar. He retrieved his sketchbook, and they made their way toward the point, to the peak of the mountain, where the Confederate artillery had set up before the Civil War battle in 1863.

"See, Lewis, this looks like no one could ever storm the mountain, but it's what the Union forces did. The Confederates couldn't get their cannons raised up high enough to shoot down the face of the palisades. And even if they could, the cannonballs would simply roll out of the cannon. So if you wanted to storm these positions, all you would have to do is follow the trails leading up here. Not easy, but not impossible, either."

Lewis appeared distracted. He politely listened, George assumed, but his attention was elsewhere.

And now I'm thinking he understands what I'm saying about everything. One of us is losing it.

George found a bench near the promontory and opened his sketchbook. Lewis happily sighed and sat down, looking back toward the park, rather than out and over the city.

"One of the units fighting in this battle was the Twentieth Connecticut Infantry. They fought at Gettysburg, too."

When Lewis heard the word *Gettysburg* he lowered his head for a moment, almost appearing reverential about it.

George reached over and put his hand under Lewis's chin and gently lifted his head.

"Lewis, it's okay. I know you remember Gettysburg. It's okay to be sad."

George scratched at Lewis's chin as he remembered. They'd reached Gettysburg the day after being lost in the Bedford Valley and spending the night in the darkened parking lot of the shuttered Western Acres motel. Across the street had been a twenty-four-hour mini-mart, so George had not felt he was compromising his safety by using an abandoned lot as a campsite.

George had spent the first day sketching monuments on the battlefield. It's where he'd learned Civil War veterans from Connecticut had erected eight monuments around the battlefield. None of them were as ornate and large and impressive as the one erected by the Pennsylvania veterans, but each was moving in its own small, stone way.

The monuments had not seemed to affect Lewis. George had liked them for their precision and their enduring testament to their fallen friends.

But on their third day at Gettysburg—the place they'd visited had seemed to affect Lewis. George had taken the scooter and sidecar and had stopped at the Devil's Den. He knew drawing things of nature was not a strength of his, but on a battlefield, a Civil War battlefield, a lot of the important elements and locations were simply fields and fences and ditches and tree lines.

Devil's Den was a little different. It was a huge outcropping of boulders, just by Little Round Top and Big Round Top. The solid bulk of rock jumbled above the horizon, every bit as intimidating and formidable as any man-made fort.

George had let Lewis off the leash, and Lewis had stayed by his side without complaint. George had rehearsed what he would tell a ranger or a security person if they'd objected to a dog on park grounds.

"He's a service dog," George had rehearsed. "I have to keep him with me to avoid unpleasant outbursts. My psychiatrist recommended I get a therapy dog for use at all times, and it's what Lewis provides—therapy and safety."

George would not volunteer the unpleasant outbursts at being left alone would come from Lewis and not his human companion. And so far, he had not been called on to employ his elaborately constructed ruse. It seemed as if most people were willing to accept a dog, in most places, if the dog was obedient, quiet, and friendly—of which Lewis was all three.

Even though this breaking of the rules was a bit unsettling to George, he justified it by explaining to himself Lewis was a wonderful, well-mannered, well-behaved, and inordinately docile dog, who did not chase or bark or run after squirrels, and if he had any "accidents," George would immediately clean them up.

So George had hiked around to the front of the rocks, the front of Devil's Den, and had come at them from the same direction as the Confederate infantry would have taken in their effort to storm the position.

It's when Lewis had started whimpering.

George had immediately stopped and bent to him.

"What's wrong, Lewis?"

Lewis's eyes had met George's, and then they had moved to focus in on the rocks looming above them, and then to the ground they stood on and then back to George. There had been an immense sadness in Lewis's eyes, as if somehow, after all these years, Lewis could still sense the sacrifice and the immense loss this ground had witnessed.

Lewis had whimpered, then he lay down, with his head between his paws.

For a moment, George had imagined Lewis was trying to pray.

Behind them, a breeze had stirred, coming through where the wheat field and the peach orchard stood. Lewis had lifted his head and sniffed and then whimpered again, a soft noise, coming from deep in his throat.

George had never experienced anything like this with an animal.

But he was there with a purpose, so he'd sat down next to Lewis, put his arm over his shoulder for a moment of comfort, then had taken out his pad and drew what he saw before him—the rocks, the shadows, the clouds, the trees and scrub foliage around the base—and had imagined what it felt like and sounded like all those years ago.

Despite the fact George felt drawing things of nature was difficult, the sketch of Devil's Den might have been his most compelling drawing yet on the trip.

He'd made the sketch in a hurry, but the style was anything but hurried. It looked precise, as were all the drawings George had done, but the ink lines seemed imbued with more emotion than any man-made structure.

Lewis had appeared relieved when George closed the book and said, "Let's go home, Lewis, okay?"

And now, they were on another battlefield, but while this field of combat may have had a more dramatic setting, George had read the night before some historians called it more of a "glorious skirmish than a true battle."

Lewis did not seem upset here, but he also faced away from where most of the fighting had taken place.

Maybe he's just a sensitive animal, George thought.

Instead of drawing right away, he flipped through the pages of his recent drawings and their itinerary stops. There were eleven pages on Gettysburg, then in Philadelphia, he had drawn Independence Hall, the Liberty Bell, and Ben Franklin's simple grave marker. In Washington, D.C., he had done the Washington Monument ("Ridiculously easy to draw"), the Vietnam memorial, the Capitol Building, and both the Lincoln and Jefferson memorials, plus the National Mall from the vantage point of the Lincoln memorial steps. Lewis seemed to have the most empathy with the Vietnam memorial. Visitors still left personal effects at the foot of the wall, and Lewis was most reserved in sniffing at them. In Williamsburg, he had drawn the Governor's Palace, the Capitol building, and a series of small houses and shops. In Annapolis, he'd found a view of the harbor and the Maryland State House in the background. At Kitty Hawk, he'd drawn a series of the high dunes and the sea grass marking the spot of America's first powered plane flight.

He had drawn other places—some famous, some simply visually interesting.

His original intention had been to focus only on famous locations, well-known structures or landmarks, but then, after only a few weeks, he found stopping in small towns, drawing abandoned and empty buildings, was curiously compelling. He found those subjects were every bit as stirring and moving as some well-known, iconic image. He'd drawn an abandoned Chevrolet dealership in Gladstone, Virginia. It seemed to sum up man's desire to achieve greatness as well as man's inability to hold on to the frail human greatness. He'd drawn a shuttered Dairy Mart in Madisonville, Tennessee, which told stories of summer nights and shared malts. He'd drawn an old five-and-ten store, George thought might have been an old Kresge's but could not be sure—though the windows and the stairs and the façade reminded him of a similar store back in his childhood memories of Gloucester. He'd drawn an abandoned farmhouse virtually in the middle of nowhere, somewhere on a back road in Kentucky.

He had already filled four notebooks and run through several dozen pens.

And now the two of them were in Chattanooga, two days away from heading further south, to Atlanta first, then on to the coastal cities of Charleston and Savannah.

In spite of having every stop pre-planned and laid out with great precision, he had been forced to modify his schedule. The first time, he'd agonized over cutting one visit short. The second required staying longer than expected in Williamsburg. And after the third unplanned stop, it became easier and easier for George to follow his original route—in a general sense, and not exactly—but shift days with less emotional trauma and apprehension.

There is a freedom in this. I know where I started and where and when I will finish. What's in the middle . . . well, we'll take it a little easier.

George opened to a blank page and began to draw. He could see the river and part of the city, but not all of it. He drew the trees and the clouds and the cannons, still keeping guard at their assigned position.

His work went faster now, as he had now practiced it for months. The lines flowed easier, and there was less hesitation in his hand. He employed more detail, his trees bore leaves, clouds appeared in the sky. George realized, or began to realize, after all those decades of drawing straight lines and using instruments to carefully make curves and radii and arcs, he could simply look and translate what he saw onto paper. It was a heady achievement to someone trained to execute exacting, millimeteric precision.

The park remained quiet as George drew. A few people wandered past and peered over the edge. The younger the tourist, the closer they came to the rocky edge, leaning over, holding onto the railing with one hand, extending one arm out to get a better vantage point with their camera. Older people stayed away, a few feet from the railing, content to see the city from three feet further back.

"The people who shouldn't take chances," George said quietly to Lewis, "are the ones tempting fate. The old folks, like me, who have much less time left, are the ones who play it safe. It doesn't make logical sense, does it, Lewis?"

Lewis answered with a wuff, this one sounding like a bad starter in a 1967 Ford Fairlane—a car George once owned. It seemed to George that each one of Lewis's wuffs were just a bit different; though his vocabulary was small, his intonation was expansive. We wuffed again, this time more solidly. Then he bent his head forward, peering into the distance.

He wuffed again, then again and then once more, even louder, louder than he normally conversed in polite, private dialogue. These were declarative wuffs, as if he were stating something quite important.

Then Lewis stood up and bounced, front paws up first, then the rear, like doing the wave from front to back.

"Lewis, settle down. What's got you so hepped up?"

And no one says hepped up *anymore, do they?*

George swiveled on the bench, thinking another dog wandered nearby or a pack of surly ground squirrels were plotting, bent on mocking Lewis's slowness by rushing past him in a blur.

But it was none of those things.

He saw the red van before he saw anything else.

Lewis was now dancing in anticipation.

George noticed the driver lean out the window and wave enthusiastically.

It was Irene, and she was piloting her red and white VW bus, and it rattled and squealed to a jerky stop in the parking lot.

36

Irene moved quickly for a senior citizen.

Or so George thought as she jumped from her van and ran—not jogged or trotted or ambled, but ran—toward them.

Must have been on the track team in high school.

Then George smiled at the thought.

Like it would translate into being in shape and speedy a half century later.

"George! Lewis!" she shouted out as she came within hugging distance.

She hugged George first, much to Lewis's obvious annoyance, but she hugged Lewis longer, which appeared to pacify his initial indignant expression.

When the hugging was done—and to Lewis, hugging was never really done, only postponed to be picked up later—Irene stood, put her hands on her hips, and assumed a scolding expression.

"Where have you been? I have crisscrossed your path more times than I want to count these last months."

George looked confused.

Irene glared at him, but in a good way.

"You showed me your itinerary. I took note of where and when you would be at places. I may be old, but my memory is still pretty darn good. And I saw you had all your planned RV stops marked down. And I followed you, sort of. Either I would get there early—probably—or show up four days after you left."

"Well . . ." George said, obviously unsure of how to explain whatever offense Irene thought he had committed.

"You're an engineer, for heaven's sake," Irene blurted out. "If anyone is going to follow a schedule, it would be you. You need to surrender your engineering society membership card."

"I'm a retired engineer, Irene. Maybe I'm losing my need for precision."

Irene snorted, surprising Lewis, who also snorted, as a way of showing canine solidarity with this person whom he had met months earlier and was so happy to see again.

"Malarkey."

George tried not to grin.

"No one says *malarkey* anymore, do they?"

Irene narrowed her eyes, took a critical stance, then softened.

"You do it, too? Hear yourself using words that no one ever uses anymore?"

Lewis wuffed loudly.

"Well, I'll be. I thought I was the only one."

Irene pushed a strand of errant gray hair from her face and tucked it behind her ear. She was wearing some sort of dangling gold and red stone earrings.

"So," Irene said, summing things up. "I found you two. Thank heavens. And now, we need to go to dinner to celebrate. You game, George?"

Lewis answered for him with a series of wuffs and a stately, furry, bulking dance around the pair of them, bobbing up and down, prancing like a short Clydesdale, with none of the grace, but all of the enthusiasm.

Irene looked back to the parking lot.

"So where is the black Maria?"

George grinned.

"No one says that anymore, either. And the RV is back at the RV park."

Irene grew puzzled.

"So . . . did you two walk?"

And that's when Lewis grew excited again and bounded off toward the scooter, eager to show Irene their new mode of transportation.

Tess looked up from the computer on her desk in the kitchen and stared, her face a mask of stark unbelief.

Even Gary, her husband, not one to take much notice of subtle, or even not-so-subtle, clues his wife often used, looked up from the newspaper.

"What's up? You get an e-mail from the Nigerian prince again?"

"No. It's actually more unbelievable."

Gary lowered the paper.

"You won the lottery?"

"Nope."

"Then I give up. You know I'm no good at guessing games."

"I do. And it's one of the things so endearing about you. And it means I can always beat you at twenty-one questions."

"Just because I'm in a little slump . . ."

"Gary, you never once get the answer in just twenty-one questions. Never once. And we've been married for eight years."

"Well, it's sort of true . . . but maybe my luck is changing. I feel it. Let me try this one."

Tess smiled and sighed.

"You'll never get it. Never in a million years."

Gary stroked his chin, pretending to be deep in thought.

"Never in a million years . . . hmmm . . . then I will guess your dad went out on a date. It would never happen in a million years, right?" he said and chuckled softly.

Tess's previous expression of unbelief just amplified by a factor of ten.

"Gary," she all but shouted, "Did you read this e-mail before! Did you cheat?"

Gary stood up and made the sign of an X over his heart.

"I swear I didn't. Cross my heart. Did I guess it right? I won once? A date? I won. I won. I won."

Gary let the paper fall to the floor as he did a most uncharacteristic victory dance in front of his favorite chair. Had Tess the presence of mind to grab her phone and take a video of his small, disjointed, awkward celebration, she knew it would have gone viral, for certain.

But she was still reeling from the e-mail report from her father.

"Read it to me," Gary said. "Let me luxuriate in my triumph."

Tess smiled and shook her head.

"Okay. But no gloating. You got lucky."

"Says you."

> Dear Tess and Gary . . .

"Hey, he remembered my name. Another first, isn't it?"

"He knows your name, Gary. He's just judicious when he uses it."

It had been a good-natured game between them—debating which set of in-laws were more oblivious to the other side of in-laws. Tess was pretty sure her father usually was most obtuse and distant.

"Go on. I'm enjoying this," Gary said, the gloating still obvious in his tone.

> We're in Chattanooga. Almost hot here. Had Lewis
> dethatched by Luella. Looks lighter and cooler.

"He's also judicious when using words, too," Gary said. "He does know he is not paying by the word, doesn't he?"

Tess smiled but ignored her husband.

> Chattanooga is a nice city. Not too big. Wonderful
> scenery. Went up to Lookout Mountain and drew some
> pictures of the site of the Civil War battle.

"I thought he was just drawing buildings. Engineered stuff. Man-made."

Tess shook her head. "No, he started drawing just normal things . . . like outdoor scenes. Might have started back in Gettysburg."

"Oh, yeah, he told us about the dog—how he acted, remember?"

> Did I ever tell you about Irene and her VW bus?
> I met Irene, or should I say, WE met Irene, during the
> first week or so of the trip. In Towanda. She's a widow. I
> think she said three times a widow.

"Think she's some sort of 'black widow' preying on unsuspecting engineers?"

Tess scowled, although part of her was thinking the same thing.
"No. Not with Lewis there."

"Just asking."

She said she's been trying to catch up with us ever since.
I'm not sure why. She said she wanted to see Lewis again.

Maybe that's it.

We went out to dinner last night. The three of us.
Outdoor seating and barbeque—a perfect combination.

We had a nice time.

I said we were headed south and then on to the
coast—Charleston/Savannah—like I told you before.
She said that she has friends who live in the historic part
of Charleston in a four-story house looking over the harbor, and she wanted to know if I would enjoy visiting
them with her. She said they love company. I think the
husband has some sort of condition. She said "crippled,"
but didn't go into detail.

She did say he was an engineer, too, and she thought
he would enjoy talking with me. Since we're headed
there, and Lewis seemed to get excited about it, I said
yes. We won't get there for another week. I have a few
stops to make in Atlanta.

Always wanted to visit the Coke place there. Lewis
won't be able to go. I don't think I can get him in by saying he is a therapy dog.

And maybe the new aquarium. I hear it is an engineering wonder.

This is all the news from the road.

Hope you and Gary are well.

"Twice he used my name. A new record."

"Oh, hush."

I'll try and set the Skype thing up in Charleston—if
the house is as nice as Irene said it was.

She said it could be a museum.

Love, Dad.

"Does he always sign his letters with 'love'?"

Tess pursed her lips in thought.

"I don't think he does. Or did."

"Your dad has a girlfriend," Gary said in a singsong voice, as if he were back in grammar school. "Your dad has a girlfriend."

"Wait," Tess said. "He sent a picture with the e-mail."

She tapped at it, and the screen filled with a picture of two people and a large, happy St. Bernard sitting at a picnic table with hundreds of Christmas lights strung from the trees above. George sat on one side of the table, and Irene, apparently, sat on the other side. Lewis sat on the ground in between them, grinning.

"Tess . . ."

Tess nodded.

"Yes, I see it, too. It's obvious. She looks like my mother."

37

"Well, I'm glad to be out of Atlanta," George said as he piloted the RV past the outer beltway ring and found the two-lane road to eventually get him to Charleston. "Sleepy Southern city, my foot."

Lewis wuffed twice in agreement.

Their RV park, on the outskirts of Atlanta, was situated too far to drive the scooter into the center of town. George had to navigate the thickness of traffic, and it did not seem to matter when he left or returned, the traffic was always the same—thick, fast, and apparently impatient.

And so much for Southern hospitality and gentility.

He did leave the scooter and trailer at the RV park, which made navigation and parking a little less stressful, but not much.

He visited both the Coke museum and the aquarium but did not spend as much time as he might have liked. The weather was hot and muggy, and while he left the air-conditioning on in the RV for Lewis, he also knew anything man-made ran the risk of breaking, at least on occasion, and he did not want to return to a malfunctioning RV—and an overheated dog.

"I didn't mind rushing through, Lewis, honest," George explained when he returned after only a brief absence. "It's hard to enjoy things when you're alone. And even though the aquarium was amazing, there wasn't anything there I felt worthy of drawing. And it was crowded. I don't like crowds."

Lewis seemed to know and wuffed softly again, agreeing with George.

He picked a route out of Atlanta leading to Athens. From there, they would drive to Augusta. And then on to Charleston.

Irene said she would be there well before their arrival, so George had no firm schedule binding him to a specific date.

"I've never driven in the South, Lewis. Might as well take the back roads, right?"

Lewis had his head out the window. He withdrew it, wuffed once, then proceeded to let the wind flutter in his jowls.

While making his original plan, George had not included many stops in the South. There was Atlanta, which they had just left, and which George thought just too big, too not Southern, too congested.

He had included Charleston and Savannah, and he listed St. Augustine. He had decided on visiting Cape Canaveral and the Space Center to see a rocket up close. He had decided to include the old section of New Orleans. And from there, he would leave the Deep South and head west.

"Not many stops in biscuits and grits country, Lewis. I guess we never traveled in the South, so maybe I don't know what I'm missing."

He had explored Athens in a virtual way on his tablet. He grudgingly came to appreciate the wonders of technology. A few places he had heard of and included them among his stops—until he saw them on a virtual tour—and afterward, excluded them.

One of the places was the Morton Theater. It had been billed as one of the surviving relics of the vaudeville age. It intrigued George. He liked relics; he often considered himself a relic of a bygone age. But when he saw the pictures of the theater, he was disappointed. The interiors looked wonderfully rococo and ornate and over-the-top, but the outside was no more exciting or interesting than your run-of-the-mill office building.

And I'm not into interiors.

So he crossed the location off his list but added a few others.

The road to Athens, bucolic and green and smelling of freshly mown kudzu—especially fragrant in comparison to the diesel-scented grating urbanness of Atlanta—and the peaceful drive helped remove the jangled tangle of nerves George felt as he headed out of Atlanta.

"Most of Atlanta looks like it had been built ten years ago. Too many strip malls. Too many Starbucks. Not enough Waffle Houses."

Lewis pulled his head inside the RV when he heard the words "Waffle House."

He had taken a keen—no, actually an obsessive—liking to Waffle House. Every time he saw one of their oddly out-of-date, and perhaps a little ugly, yellow signs with black letters, he would begin to bark and whimper. Of course, he could not go into the restaurant, even under the guise of being a therapy/companion/service animal. George told Lewis he did not feel comfortable taking their innocent deception so far. And if he had gone inside a Waffle House, with its assorted and often widely varied clientele, Lewis would most likely want to stop and say hello to each and every one of the restaurant's patrons. George did not think your standard service animal would be so gregarious or avuncular, and thus Lewis's cover would be blown.

So Lewis would remain in the RV while George would have a quick breakfast. And he would then order a plain waffle to go. It became Lewis's most perfect petit dejeuner—a delicacy he obviously relished.

As they neared Athens, George kept a lookout for the Team RV Park, advertised as "Just behind the Team Biscuits and Burgers building—the big red place on Danielsville Road." Apparently, the park catered to all the fans and alumni who tailgated to the University of Athens football games.

The park billed itself as "family-oriented, well-lighted, close to downtown, and walking distance to grocery and liquor stores."

"Everything we need, Lewis, close at hand."

Lewis smiled, his head still out the window, the fur on his head nearly permanently smooched in one direction, and wuffed loudly, so George could hear over the noise of the wind.

George found the RV park without difficulty, and since football was not in season just yet, George easily found space.

The environment was oddly small-town urban. Landscaping, some in large pots and urns, tall light stanchions, mostly asphalt, with parking spots only an arm's width apart.

"Tailgating here would be fine. Not so much for extended camping, Lewis."

Only three of the several dozen spots were taken, so George had an entire row of vacancies surrounding him.

They arrived mid-afternoon. He unpacked the scooter while Lewis watched patiently.

"Ready?"

Lewis climbed into the sidecar and tilted his head back, ready to have the helmet buckled under his chin.

They puttered out onto the street.

"Just a quick tour of the town, Lewis. We'll get our bearings today and do some drawing tomorrow."

Wuff.

They slowly cruised down the wide boulevards and headed south toward the University of Georgia's Athens campus and the downtown area. George turned on Jackson and could see the lip of the football stadium hovering above the tree line. Since it was summer, there were fewer students, apparently. But there were more than enough Georgia Bulldog fans to take notice of an old man and a St. Bernard in the sidecar of a motor scooter, cruising along at a sedate thirty miles an hour.

A lot of them stopped, mid-step, stared, laughed, waved, gave a thumbs-up, or simply nodded casually as if the dog/man/scooter/sidecar was something they saw every day.

"Maybe they do see things like this every day, Lewis," George said as one more wispy-bearded student in sandals and shorts nodded carefully as they passed.

Lewis wuffed in reply.

"I think they're called hipsters, Lewis."

Lewis turned to look at George, the sun glinting off his goggles.

"I heard it on the news station in Atlanta. I wouldn't have known how to identify them otherwise. Hipsters . . . I think we called them beatniks. Back in the day. When everything still made sense."

Lewis appeared to shrug and went back to leaning to the left, his front paw on the padded lip of the sidecar opening.

"And yes, Lewis, hippies came in between the beatniks and hipsters."

George slowed to a stop in front of a square, two-story brick building with four large white columns in front. A small sign on the front indicated it was the Phi Kappa Literary Society, circa 1836.

"Interesting building, isn't it, Lewis? Common red brick and white columns—an odd pairing for a traditionalist like me."

Lewis appeared not to be paying attention and instead was focused on climbing out of the sidecar to begin his investigations.

"No, Lewis, not yet. We still have a ways to go."

Lewis sat back down, and George reached over and adjusted his helmet. It had a tendency to slide to one side.

As he did the adjusting, a young man, better dressed than most of the people on campus, walked up.

"Sir, do you mind if I take a picture?"

George was almost used to the request.

"Sure. Just tell Lewis to smile. Lewis is the dog, by the way."

The young man did and Lewis did, and George grinned as well, and when the young man raised a large and complicated camera to his eye, George heard the electronic click of a dozen pictures being taken in less than an instant. The young man moved the camera from his face and looked at the back, reviewing his work.

"Back in the day," George said, "you had to wind the film between pictures. And each picture cost money, so you didn't just snap away."

The young man smiled.

"Before my time, sir. Electronic is all I know."

He took another dozen snaps from a different angle, kneeling on the sidewalk.

"It was better back then. People moved slower. And you had to wait a week until you saw what you had on film."

"Again, before my time, sir." The young man pulled out a small notepad. "Do you mind if I ask where you're from?"

George shrugged, gave his name, his hometown, Lewis's name again, and the fact that they were on a cross-country trip and that George was drawing the sights as they traveled.

"On a motorscooter? Pretty wild. You must pack light."

"No, no. I have an RV. We have an RV, I guess. We take the scooter in a trailer. We just use it to get around in towns. Easier than driving an RV. Parking is much easier."

"So tell me, where have you been so far?"

Lewis, you draw all kinds of people to us, you know? Maybe you could take a day off once in a while.

They talked for a few more minutes, and George gave him a thumb-nail sketch of where they had gone, what they had done, and where they were going.

"Well, I hope you have a great trip, sir. Seems like Lewis is ready to get going again."

George started the scooter, waved, and puttered off toward the stadium.

38

Tess almost tripped as she walked toward the Safeway grocery store. She stopped, shook her head, then leaned forward.

"It can't be. It can't."

She hurried to the newspaper box, fished out a handful of coins from her purse, and deposited them, only dropping a quarter once in her haste.

"It is him. And Lewis. My heavens."

She stood still, in the cool shade of the wide overhang in front of the Safeway store on West Osborne, in Phoenix, Arizona, her shopping list containing two dozen items still clenched in her right hand.

On the front page of the current issue of *USA Today*, above the fold, nearly taking up the whole top half of the page, was a picture of a man on a motor scooter accompanied by a smiling St. Bernard in a sidecar, wearing a helmet and goggles and grinning as only a satisfied St. Bernard can grin.

"Dad . . . and Lewis. On the front page."

The newspaper was spread out on the kitchen counter of the Burden house. Trudy stopped to stare at it several dozen times. When she saw it in the rack by the train station, she bought five copies.

And when Alex returned home from school, she called him over to look.

"I don't care what's in the newspaper, Mom. Unless I have to read it for history class or something."

"No, you'll want to read this one."

Alex remained speechless for a long moment.

"Is it really Lewis?"

"It is," replied his mother.

"They're in Athens? I thought that was in Greece somewhere."

"No, there's an Athens in Georgia. The photographer says he snapped the picture while touring the campus there . . . the University of Georgia."

"Wow."

"And this newspaper goes all over the country, all over the world, actually."

"Wow. It means Lewis is sort of famous, doesn't it?"

"Well, I guess he is. At least a little famous. At least for a little while."

"Wow. Wait till I take this to school."

"That's my friend and his dog," Irene said, pointing at the photograph, holding the copy close to Douglas's face. "They are the ones coming here in a few days."

"That's a big dog," he said slowly.

"But gentle as a lamb. You'll love him. And George was an engineer. I told you that, didn't I?"

Douglas nodded. It took some time for his head to rock back and forth.

"You did," he said, almost out of breath. "What kind?"

Irene shrugged.

"Don't know, exactly. Didn't ask. But he seems to like precision. Or at least he did until he got the motor scooter."

Douglas grinned and patted his wheelchair.

"Two wheels will do it. Make you lose all control."

The grounds of the Gospel Pilgrim Cemetery were hushed and still, the heat of the day not yet evident among the thicket of the skinny third- and fourth-generation trees and choking underbrush. Where they stood, not even the noise of the traffic could be heard—just the chirp and twang of the birds, and even those seemed muted, hesitant, and shy.

George and Lewis parked at the gate and walked into the cemetery, the ten acres mostly used by black families in Athens in the late 1800s, and only recently restored and cleaned.

"It's like a haven in here, isn't it, Lewis? Peaceful. Quiet. All these folks here are through with the cares of the world."

I sort of envy them.

Lewis shuffled along the path, strewn with leaves, rustling with each footfall. George wondered if Lewis understood about these things— death and loss and forever and eternity. Lewis seemed affected in a deep way by Gettysburg, and he seemed to be exhibiting the same emotions today. Lewis's good-natured romping was subdued, quiet this morning as they walked along the paths.

George spotted what he would draw this morning: a triptych of three headstones, none bigger than a shoebox, and the identifying carved words worn off by the years, with only the faintest ghosting of letters visible. The headstones were surrounded by a loose fist of shrubs or azaleas or some manner of flowering bush, the scent just hinting in the warming air—not pervasive, but just a wisp filtering in the soft breeze.

George unfolded his chair and opened his sketchpad. Lewis arranged himself so a shaft of sunlight would illuminate his face. He closed his eyes and sat, with a small groan.

George's pen moved slowly this morning, the bushes harder and more detailed than any building. He tried to capture the look of the filtered sunlight as it made its way through the green canopy.

An hour later, he leaned back and held his pad out and tried to be unbiased.

"Not bad, Lewis. Not bad. For someone who doesn't do nature, not bad."

George liked being in this quiet place.

"Lewis, there is a peace here I don't feel anywhere else. A peace from all the troubles of the world. Yes, I know I told you this already, but I like it here. No more pain. Just quiet."

Lewis opened his eyes and snapped his head to the right, cocking his head slightly.

"You're like an owl, Lewis, who has to tilt his head to locate mice by listening to their echoes. It's how they do it, you know. Their ears are slightly uneven. Echo-location. Like animal radar."

But then, George heard the rustle as well. The dry-leaf-crunching steps of someone walking their way. In a moment, a young man in a baseball hat, wearing baggy cargo shorts, carrying a hefty set of binoculars, made his way closer.

He waved at them.

"Don't mind me. Looking for birds. We get some odd bird visitors here on their way to somewhere else, usually. Saw a kestrel here last week and am looking to see if it has nested here. It's a pretty rare sighting for Athens."

He walked up and petted Lewis without asking if he was friendly or not.

Perhaps Lewis's happy grin and generally inviting demeanor helped.

"Hey, this is a good drawing. You like an artist or something?"

George was used to the question. He would have said, "I am an artist, just not a good one," but never did. Instead, he replied, "No. This is just a hobby. I like drawing."

The young man slipped the binoculars around his neck and then stared at George.

"Don't I know you?"

"I don't think so," George replied. "We're not from around here."

The young man peered closer.

"You look so familiar . . ."

George tried to smile. "I look like a lot of people's grandfather, I guess."

The young man waved his objection aside.

"No. It's not it," he said, squinting even harder. "Now I remember. It's where I saw you. And the dog. Lewis, right?"

I didn't mention his name.

"I saw your picture. In the newspaper. This morning. You and Lewis in some sort of scooter and sidecar thing. It was a pretty cool picture. You both looked pretty happy."

Good grief. Our picture is in the local shopper ad paper? Must have been desperate for news.

"Lewis! It's in *USA Today*! He never said he was with a real newspaper!"

Lewis obediently sniffed at the folded paper when George sort of thrust it at his face. He sniffed twice, just to make sure George wasn't hiding a pork chop bone under the paper. George had never done it before, but obviously, Lewis thought there might be a first time for everything.

"This is terrible. I didn't want this. I didn't agree to be put on the front page of anything—let alone *USA Today*."

He sat on the scooter, outside of Horten's Drug store in downtown Athens and wondered just how many copies of the paper are actually produced in a day.

"Maybe it's not so bad. Maybe I could buy a bunch of them up . . ."

Later, back at the RV, he discovered on his tablet, to his great dismay, the daily circulation was in excess of two million copies.

George sat down with a groan, mimicking Lewis's groan when he sat down.

"All I wanted was to do this trip quietly and without fuss. I didn't want any attention. It's not part of my plan."

He stared hard at Lewis.

"See what you've done to me, Lewis. Bad dog. Very bad dog."

And then, Lewis lowered his head and stared at his front paws, unsure of what terrible thing he had just done, but well aware of George's displeasure.

39

The two of them rose early the next morning and got ready to visit a few selected sites in Athens.

"We'll be forgotten, Lewis. Yesterday's news is yesterday's news. Sorry for being upset. Wasn't your fault."

Lewis seemed to smile in accepting the apology.

"And we're not real memorable, right? But let's get on our way early, okay?"

Lewis was fine with early departures—except for when he wasn't. He often napped during the day but was always awake when George climbed down from his sleeping compartment above the cab of the RV.

On their way to George's first stop, they passed the now-familiar yellow and black sign.

Lewis began wiggling and barking immediately.

"But, Lewis, we're in the scooter. I'd have to leave you outside."

Wuff, wuff, wuff, wuff.

For an instant, George thought Lewis might be planning to take matters into his own hands, or rather, in his own paws, and jump from the moving, albeit slowly, sidecar and make his own way to the Waffle House.

"Okay. Okay, Lewis, we'll stop. I'll just order coffee and something small, okay? And a waffle to go. Will you be satisfied?"

Lewis turned to look up at George with a beatific smile on his face, his eyes, even behind the goggles, half shut with the anticipation of pleasure.

George parked right in front of the entrance and made sure he was seated so he could keep an eye on Lewis and his scooter at all times. This was one of the days that Lewis insisted he be allowed to keep his helmet and goggles on. It wasn't so much as if he barked or whimpered, but he would twist and fidget and maneuver, like an interior lineman blocking for a pass play in football, and when he did so, getting the helmet unbuckled was nigh on impossible.

So George sat at the booth, ordered biscuits and gravy and coffee, and watched Lewis in the sidecar as he beamed back at George, knowing his wafflelicious treat was soon to follow.

The waitress, an older woman with a tired smile and a crooked nametag reading "Lilly," brought out his order and refilled his coffee cup, unasked.

"I don't mean to be staring, but you're the guy in the paper yesterday, ain't you?"

George was forced to nod.

"Yep. It was me. And the dog outside."

"Looks like a real nice dog."

"He is, and he's friendly. Enjoys traveling."

Lilly set the half-full coffeepot on the table. Only three other patrons were in the restaurant, so Lilly had time to talk. The cook bent over the grill, and George heard a thick scraping. The scent of fried bacon permeated the small space.

Maybe it's why Lewis likes this place. I always come out smelling like meat.

"Your picture said you been traveling all over."

Lilly pronounced it as "yer pitcher."

"We have been. My wife passed on three years ago. Always wanted to travel."

"Sorry for your loss, there."

"Thanks."

George scooped up a small piece of biscuit covered in white gravy.

"The dog like being cooped up all day in that small thing?"

"Well, actually, we only use the scooter around town. We're traveling in an RV. We're parked behind the Team Biscuit and Burgers."

"Oh, yeah, I know the place. Been there once or twice. And now you mentioned it, I remember it from your picture. You did say you're driving around in a RV. Must be the life."

George chewed, swallowed, took a sip of coffee, then replied.

"It's okay."

Lilly looked like she wanted to sit down, but it was probably prohibited by the Waffle House code of conduct for waitstaff.

"Always wanted to travel. I want to go to Memphis before I die."

George tried to appear sympathetic. "Memphis. What's in Memphis?"

Lilly put her hand on her hip and looked at George as if he had just sprouted an extra head.

"Why, Graceland. Like you didn't know. Everyone knows about The King. I want to see it one day. Before I kick the bucket, anyhow. But getting the money and the time . . . I don't know."

George glanced out to the scooter. Lewis remained in the sidecar, of course, for he was a dog who followed orders well, but he also looked a bit fidgety.

"You know, Lilly, if all you do is save one or two dollars a day and put it in a jar and promise yourself you can't touch it, in a year or so, you'll have enough."

Lilly nodded, as if she had heard the advice before.

"Maybe I'll try it again. Would like to go. I guess if you and a big furry dog can do it, don't see why I couldn't, right?"

George knew she had intended her comment to be inspiring to herself, and not a criticism of George and Lewis.

"Lilly, could you get me a waffle to go? Just plain. It's Lewis's breakfast."

"He likes waffles? My dogs never did."

"Seems to."

"He like bacon?"

George smiled.

"One bacon waffle to go, coming up."

When the waffle came, George paid the bill and went outside to present Lewis his special treat for being so patient.

As Lewis sat, chewing slowly, like a furry Buddha finding his waffle/bacon Nirvana, the morning sun glinting off his goggles, George could see Lilly inside bussing his table. She looked down, quickly looked outside, offered an odd expression of shock and gratitude, then ran outside and embraced George.

George was not a man used to getting hugs from near total strangers, and Lewis wuffed as she hugged him, apparently wanting her to hug him as well.

"Thank you so much. I'll put it aside. I promise I will. And I'll get to Memphis, like I been promising myself. Soon."

She leaned over and gave Lewis a scratch under the chin.

"You got a real nice owner there, Lewis. Real nice."

Lewis kept chewing, but his expression wizened up at the word *owner*.

When Lilly returned to her station, Lewis looked up at George puzzled.

"I gave her fifty dollars, Lewis. She wanted to go to Memphis. Maybe it will help make her dream come closer."

Lewis sort of shook his head, as if to say he knew all along George was a soft and tender-hearted person and he should just let the emotion out, where it could touch people.

At least it's what George thought he was trying to say.

Or it could just be he likes waffles.

⸺◦◦◦⸺

George accomplished two drawings this day: one of the Taylor-Grundy house, a two-story Greek Revival-style home with six massive two-story columns flanking the front porch and another six on each side of the house, and a large open-air agora running the perimeter of the house.

"I like it, Lewis, but a bit too imposing and grand for my tastes."

The second was a quirkier place, the James Sledge House, which offered three tall, narrow, peaked dormers, almost higher than the roofline, with decorative iron stanchions on the porch roof and fussy iron work outlining the front porch area.

"I like it, Lewis, but it calls too much attention to itself."

They made it back to the RV park just before dinner. George busied himself with stowing the scooter and making sure it was securely tied down. George sat on the sidewalk, catching the afternoon sun, positioning himself to be noticed if someone came down the narrow driveway.

No one did, much to Lewis's disappointment.

George reheated a meatloaf he had made two days prior, complete with baked potatoes and corn. He brought out a small folding table and ate outside.

"The weather won't always be this nice, Lewis. Might as well take advantage of it."

Lewis sat at a right angle to George as he ate.

Mrs. Burden had said she seldom, if ever, fed Lewis from the table, but then, the day George and Lewis departed, she had pulled him aside and had whispered to him she fed Lewis from the table all the time—except for chocolate and cheese, she'd said.

I know about chocolate, but cheese?

So far, George had kept both banned substances from Lewis's diet. He did taste a large corner of the meatloaf, which seemed to please him greatly.

Feeling expansive, George made a cup of coffee for himself and sat in his folding chair outside, listening to the steady hum of traffic on the road out front, hearing the chatter and clatter of the restaurant less than fifty yards away.

"Feels like living in a big city, doesn't it, Lewis?"

Lewis appeared to nod.

"I wonder, Lewis, if I'm wrong in attributing all your wuffs and snorts and nods and grins and sad looks as expressions of your true inner emotions. Maybe I'm just projecting my emotions on to you. You ever think about it, Lewis? Maybe I just think you understand, and all you are doing is normal dog things, and I read those as indications you do understand me. Am I making sense? You don't understand everything I say, do you?"

Lewis shook his head and snorted.

"Well, maybe it's true—I'm projecting," George replied calmly. "You remember—there was a movie with a character stranded on a deserted island and he began talking to a volleyball with a bloody handprint as a face. He thought the volleyball was having conversations with him at the end. And now, after a few months, I think I'm having two-way conversations with you, Lewis. I guess we're both sort of delusional, don't you think?"

Lewis scrunched up his face as if he were thinking the argument through. Then he snorted.

"Well, all I'm saying is maybe I put too much humanness on your reactions, Lewis."

Then Lewis stood and butted his head against George's thigh and sat closer to him, peering up at his face, appearing to fully understand everything George was saying—and not agreeing with him—but telling him he didn't agree in the nicest way possible.

After all, Alex did say you would never bite anyone.

The sun lit up the sky behind the Team Biscuits and Burgers, like a giant swath of neon, glowing red and purple.

He reached down and stroked Lewis's head.

"You would purr, if you could, right?"

Lewis bobbed a little.

"I think my life is changing, Lewis, you know? Ever since we bought the scooter. Maybe ever since I bought the RV."

He sighed.

"Maybe ever since Hazel . . . died."

He took a sip of coffee and stretched his legs out.

"I feel a little guilty saying this, but I feel more free now . . . freer. But I'm not sure it's always a good thing. Freedom comes from knowing what's coming, Lewis. And I know what's coming. Maybe it's good. And maybe it isn't. Hazel knew. She knew every day of her last decade on earth. She knew she would die. She knew she would die before me."

Lewis stood and lifted himself up, both front paws on George's thigh.

"You only do this when you want me to tell you the truth, don't you?"

Wuff. Wuff.

"I know you want the truth. But I'm not sure I can handle the truth. Like I told you, Lewis—some things should just be left unsaid. I'm trying to let go, Lewis, but there are some things I simply can't. Some things in a person's life are never to be forgiven. It's all there is to it."

George's voice had gone to a whisper, a confessional whisper. He pushed the one image in his mind further back, further and further, where even he couldn't see it anymore. Lewis butted his head against George's chest. He put his hand on the dog's head and held it there.

"I'm happier now, Lewis. I am. It's the truth. Can I leave it there?"

Lewis leaned back.

"Maybe it's because I'm thinking about the cemetery again. It's our ultimate destination, Lewis. Why is it so wrong to be more in control of our departure date?"

Lewis butted against him again, and this time a little harder.

"Okay, Lewis. I'll think about it."

Lewis did not move.

"I will. Honest. I'll think about it."

Lewis backed off and slowly lowered his front paws back to the ground.

But my mind is still made up. There is no sin in knowing the end of days. I simply want to be in charge of my own destiny. What harm is there? No one will miss us. And it needs to happen this way. It does. After what I did. After what I asked for. After what God did.

40

When George pulled up to the house, he checked his handwritten note again—rather, Irene's handwritten note—and compared the address on the house to the one written down.

All George could do was whistle.

Lewis was busy sniffing. The house . . . more suitably, a mansion, faced the battery, or the Charleston Harbor, the morning sun glistening off the water, the reflections dancing against the three-story, cream-colored structure. Two curved balconies graced the second and third floors, each with a picket of curved balustrades, perhaps done in carved marble, plus a third set of fencing on the roof.

"You must be able to see the ocean from up there," George said as he unbuckled Lewis's seat belt. "It's got to be ten thousand square feet inside if it's an inch."

Next to the curved balconies was a three-story, square entryway, with four two-story pillars holding up a square counterpart to the curved section of the house. Underneath the two-story columns stood the main entrance—double doors, of course, probably mahogany, or ironwood, with wrought iron hinges and a brass lock rail running the width of both doors, with a polished brass strike plate on each door, each the size of a large hardback book.

The metal looked polished, and the wood gleamed as well.

In fact, George surmised the entire house must have been recently painted, the thick, creamy luster of the paint looking like a thin coat of vanilla ice cream.

The plinth block above the doors was engraved with a date: 1856.

"Ye gads," George whispered to himself, "and I know no one says *ye gads* anymore, but this place is spectacular, isn't it, Lewis?"

Lewis did not appear thoroughly impressed. Instead, he intently sniffed his way along the public sidewalk in front of the house, as if he were a detective searching for overlooked clues.

Then Lewis heard it and lifted his head, his ears peaked.

A small dog, from the sound of the shrillness of the bark, had taken notice of Lewis and did not sound overly hospitable.

"Might be from inside, Lewis. Be prepared. And be on your best behavior, okay?"

Lewis appeared not to hear, or at least, not to pay attention.

George drew back on the leash and turned Lewis around, knelt down, and put his face only a few inches from Lewis's own.

"You are on notice, Lewis. Be good!"

Lewis's eyes tried to peer sideways and over his own shoulder, but George had a hand on his jaw and kept him staring straight ahead.

"I mean it, Lewis. They might have a dog. I didn't ask. But I am sure Irene mentioned you to these people. After all, you're hard to overlook. So behave."

Lewis tried his best not to fidget.

"Understand?"

Lewis relaxed some and offered a weak, and not entirely convincing, wuff of agreement, like a small child saying he would behave in the toy store—this time.

"Okay, then. As long as we're clear on your behavior."

George felt like a poseur coming to the door of such a grand residence, in his worn khakis and somewhat wrinkled white shirt. But it was what he was wearing and there was no place to change or alter himself into someone more sophisticated, cultured . . . and moneyed.

He lifted the massive doorknocker and let it fall, only halfway.

"Could use this as a battering ram if we had to."

The bang sounded loud to George, and it seemed to echo throughout the massive home.

He debated whether or not to lift the heavy pineapple-shaped doorknocker again.

"It's probably a couple of hundred years old as well, Lewis. What if I break it? Or knock the door over?"

Instead, he took a breath and waited.

"If I knock again and the door falls over, we make a run for it, okay, Lewis?"

Lewis looked up, grinned, and wuffed.

"I swear you understand every word I say, Lewis. In spite of being a dog."

He wuffed again.

He heard footfalls from inside, then he heard Irene's voice, loud and a little shrill. "Takes somebody forever to get to the door in this place. It's why they had servants. It's why you should still have servants."

The door swung open. Irene stood there, almost breathless, and grinned. Behind her was an entryway filled with antebellum opulence: mirrors, mahogany, carvings, marble, and brass.

"Welcome to the humble abode of Douglas and Eleanor Parker. You can get a map or a GPS system from the butler's table on the way in."

She laughed and her laugh was clear and full-voiced, without any hesitation or reluctance.

"You said museum quality—and you were right," George said. "This place, at least from the outside, is magnificent."

Irene leaned close to him.

"And you ain't seen nothing yet, George. Just wait."

She then bent down to Lewis and gave him a long hug. He enjoyed it yet all the while kept looking over her shoulder. The barking had come from somewhere.

"Lewis, you'll see him soon enough."

She stood, took George's hand, and led him inside.

"I'll introduce you to our host. His lovely wife is out at a charity function. He has been so eager to meet you."

———

Irene led them up a curved flight of stairs winding around an open central core. If one looked up, one could see the whole way to the domed roof, complete with some sort of scene painted on it, but it was too far away for George to discern the subject. The railings and balustrades were done in white marble. The rug on the steps must have been handwoven and had to have been made especially for this house because it followed the curve of the stairway.

Irene saw him looking.

"Turkish. 1860-ish. Handmade. Hand-knotted. Just the rug is worth more than you and me put together, George."

On the third floor, she led them down a wide, sunny hallway—more like a salon, as the French would label it—and through two, full-length French doors, into a huge circular room.

"Welcome to the solarium, George. Come meet our host, Douglas Parker."

In the far side of the room, bathed in the early morning sunshine, was a small man in a large wheelchair. Over his knees was a tartan blanket.

Probably an authentic Scottish pattern, too, George thought to himself.

Douglas was rail thin, balding, with piercing blue eyes. He slowly raised his right hand—very slowly, as if it took a great effort to do so. His smile was broad and appeared genuine.

"Welcome, George. And Lewis."

Lewis walked carefully to the wheelchair, sniffing and smiling and wuffing, offering his caregiver's wuff this time, a solicitous wuff, as if he were trying to ask how the patient felt.

Douglas lowered his hand to Lewis, and Lewis accepted it with grace.

From behind them came a ratcheting sound of nails on a marble floor, scrabbling to gain traction, a sliding, raspy, clattery noise.

At the same time, George and Irene turned to look.

Into the room flew a small gray and white blur, sliding first to the left and then to the right, barking, almost squealing, as he made his grand, excited entrance.

Lewis spun about, quick for a dog his size, and the grey and black blur screeched to a sliding halt, several yards distant.

"This is Burby . . . a good Scottish name . . . for a bad Scottish dog."

Burby's eyes grew wide, taking in the vast enormity of Lewis. Lewis wuffed hopefully and lowered his head and spread his front paws in a playful posture.

Burby was frozen to the spot where he'd stopped.

"Burby's never seen a dog this large," Douglas said slowly, drawing in breath halfway through. "And he's not much of a fighter."

Lewis wuffed and wagged his rump back and forth.

"In fact," Douglas added, "he's intimidated by most anything larger than a wren. Not a Scottish warrior, in any fashion."

Burby must have decided discretion is the better part of valor. He turned and ran out of the room, his nails scrabbling to gain purchase on the slick floor, turning his head to look over his shoulder, making sure the behemoth was not giving chase.

Lewis looked up at Douglas with a most puzzled look.

"Lewis, he will be back. In time."

Douglas pressed on the control of the wheelchair, and it turned slightly, an electric whirr loud in the quiet of the large room.

"Come in. Sit down. I will call for coffee."

He motored over to a grouping of a coffee table, settee, and chairs, all bathed in the sun from the curved window George had seen from the street. Even from the third floor, he could make out the shimmer of the ocean beyond the harbor.

"This is a most magnificent house," George said as he took a seat.

"Thank you," Douglas rasped in reply. "Helps if one has filthy rich great-grandparents. Amassed a fortune. Early in life, according to family history. Spent most of the rest of their lives spending it."

Douglas waved his arm carefully in the air.

"On this, mostly."

"Well, it is truly spectacular. I can't say I've been inside any place this grand."

Douglas offered a wan smile.

"Yet Irene said you were scheduled to visit Falling Water. Did you?"

"I did."

"And is it not more grand than this?"

The coffee arrived, and George accepted a cup of coffee in a delicate bone china cup.

"Perhaps more dramatic. Not more grand. Not at all. It was obvious to me Wright didn't like people much. Nothing seemed comfortable. Dramatic does not mean homey."

Douglas coughed some.

"It is a complaint I have heard. Pity I can't make the trip."

"I could show you the drawings I made. As an engineer, you might appreciate them."

Douglas smiled broadly.

"It would be wonderful. But not this morning. I leave for therapy in a few minutes. Perhaps after dinner."

"I would love to."

And then, a young man in a white coat arrived and stood behind the wheelchair.

"Ready, Mr. Parker?"

"No, I am not. But it won't stop you, will it?"

"No. Not today, sir. Just like it hasn't stopped me all the other days."

"Such is the life of an invalid," Douglas said. "Then I shall see you both anon."

George watched as the young man lifted Douglas out of the chair and carried him down the steps.

"He has a chair on every floor. He claims the house would be ruined with the addition of an elevator," Irene said in a whisper. "Instead of an elevator, he simply hires burly young men to be his legs up and down the stairs."

Lewis walked with him to the stairs and watched him being carried. Then he turned back to George with a puzzled look on his face and wuffed softly, as if asking for an explanation.

"Lewis, there are some questions I cannot answer."

41

By the by," Irene said after they had nearly finished their coffee, "Douglas asked me if you would mind parking the RV behind the house. They have a large garage and parking area away from the street."

"Sure," George replied.

"Douglas wouldn't mind where you park, but he claims all his neighbors are real estate OCD impaired."

"Moving the RV is not a problem. It's not."

Irene stood and looked down at the street below, watching Douglas being taken in a van to a special rehabilitation center on the west side of town.

"Douglas has said, on occasion, his neighbors wouldn't mind having him replaced, if they could, because of his handicap. He says they would prefer someone young, a bon vivant. Someone who could host the right sort of lavish parties a house like this deserves, he said."

George could not tell if Irene was joking, so he smiled, just a little.

"I say he is simply being paranoid," Irene said.

"Is he?"

She shrugged.

"Maybe a little. But not without reason, I guess. He says they used to have company all the time. Now, only a few people stop by. Myself, for one. Now you and Lewis. I think we might be the first real guests in several months."

Lewis circled the large room, sniffing slowly and quite carefully, wuffing to himself as he made the circuit.

"I don't want to assume, but Douglas . . . what does he have? It must be relatively recent, since you said things have changed since . . ."

"ALS."

"I thought so," George said. Lewis came over and pushed his head against his thigh. "My wife . . ."

Irene's faced showed a marked difference; a cloud of sympathy passed over her expression, but at the same time, a reluctance to let herself wallow in the moment by providing unnecessary or, worse, unwanted pity.

"Sorry to hear it. Terrible condition."

George just nodded.

"And Douglas wanted me to tell you . . . and Lewis, of course . . . you have complete freedom to come and go while you're here. His wife will be back this afternoon. You'll like her."

"Good. I think Lewis needs to go outside. And I'll move the RV, if you show me where. And then I'd like to take a walk around the neighborhood."

"Follow me downstairs, you two. If you want, I can show you around the historic district a little. Been here often enough to know some of the tour guide spiel."

Lewis wuffed in agreement.

"Well, sign us up, then."

Mid-afternoon found George and Lewis in what was obviously the library, a huge room with a massive stone fireplace, lined with what George surmised were mahogany bookcases, floor to ceiling, filled with what George surmised were rare first editions.

He carefully set his bag down on a chair—the chair looked old, but not museum old, George hoped. Even Lewis seemed cowed by the scope and grandeur and understated history of the room.

Lewis sniffed and snorted.

"I know. It smells like a library, doesn't it?"

Lewis turned to look at him.

"I guess you've never been in a library before, have you, Lewis? But trust me, this is what it smells like. Good books have a particular aroma about them. Leather and ink and ideas."

He slid one volume off the shelf.

It was a biography of Benjamin Wright, the "father of American civil engineering." George thumbed through a few pages. Apparently Wright engineered both the Erie Canal and the Chesapeake and Ohio Canal.

The book, leather-bound and large, looked to be a first edition. George carefully replaced it in the exact spot. He noticed not a single speck of dust on the shelves.

"Good afternoon. You must be George Gibson."

Lewis spun around and wuffed.

"And Lewis, of course. I am Eleanor Parker, Douglas's wife."

Eleanor, a tall woman, with elegant features, straight dark hair and dark eyes, stood in the library entrance, a double string of pearls around her neck, resting on what must have been a cashmere sweater, with a matching skirt.

George seldom noticed what a woman wore, but Eleanor's outfit just seemed to fit exactly the tone and the scent and the ambiance of this house. It appeared as if everything inside, including her clothing, was carefully and masterfully coordinated just perfectly.

"I am," George replied. "It is so nice to meet you. And to be able to thank you for inviting me as a guest. And Lewis."

Eleanor walked into the room, or perhaps strode into the room, the way a confident person enters, with grace and precision and not a wasted, unnecessary movement of leg or arm or head.

"It is our pleasure, Mr. Gibson."

"George."

Eleanor smiled, demurely.

"Mr. Gibson, I was raised in a most traditional home in the Deep South. Mississippi. On a soon-to-be-derelict plantation. But what we did not have in material things, we had in the richness of tradition and heritage. From the time we could talk and curtsey, we were firmly instructed to greet and converse with anyone older than ourselves using the titles Mister and Sir and Missus and Ma'am, if we weren't sure. It is an ingrained habit and not one I wish to break. So you must please forgive me if I call you Mr. Gibson."

George shrugged and immediately wished he had some other gesture not as classless and inadequate. "It will be fine, Mrs. Parker."

"But I shall call Lewis, Lewis. I think any other name would confuse him."

"You might be surprised, Mrs. Parker."

She bent down and looked into Lewis's face.

"Well, I might be, Mr. Gibson."

She stood up.

"Shall I call for tea? Would you like tea? Or coffee."

George did not answer for a moment.

"I can tell you want coffee, Mr. Gibson, by your hesitation. You do not want to upset your hostess, but you don't like tea, and you're wondering if by asking for coffee you will somehow expose yourself as being ungrateful."

George held his hands open, palms out.

"You would be a good detective, Mrs. Parker."

"I simply pay attention, Mr. Gibson. I will call for tea—and coffee."

The silver tea set, plus a silver coffeepot, glistened in the pale afternoon sun, only a few shafts of direct sunlight coming through the south-facing windows. The service appeared old and, most likely, valuable—very valuable.

Eleanor busied herself with pouring and serving and then offering a delicate tea cookie to Lewis.

George took a seat on the leather couch just by the coffee table. Lewis took up his position between his hostess and George, staring at them with hungry but polite eyes.

They all heard the snaffling sound of a dog carefully approaching the room, paws sounding and clacking on the polished hardwood.

"Oh, please, do come in, Burby. I have already fed Lewis. He will not eat you."

Burby peered around the end of the couch. Keeping his eyes fixed on Lewis, in case of sudden attack moves, he slunk toward Mrs. Parker and then jumped into her lap.

"Good Burby," she said, petting him. "I understand from Irene that their first meeting did not go smoothly."

George looked over to Lewis and gave him a stern look, tempered with a smile.

"I think the juxtaposition of large and small was intimidating."

"Completely understandable. Burby was supposed to be . . . well, he is a miniature schnauzer. But he is a most miniature, miniature schnauzer. The breeder said he was destined to be the runt of the litter, and even she was surprised to see how small he has remained. But he is a tender soul. Just not the feisty dog Douglas assumed him destined to be."

Eleanor took a sip of tea, from a bone-white china cup, delicate and antique. George must have been watching.

"Yes, the cup is old, Mr. Gibson. Produced in England just after the war, actually," she said. "The great war of secession, you know."

George smiled.

"I have never traveled in the South, Mrs. Parker, but I can see history is more alive in some places than others."

"And I have found living among old things is a dead experience, unless you make use of them. No sense in storing the 'good china' away. But please, if you run across my mother-in-law, you must not tell her I am serving cookies to dogs from her wedding china."

They both laughed, but George wasn't sure if he was in on the joke.

Lewis stood up and walked carefully to Mrs. Parker. Burby noticed immediately and stood, adjusting himself to the unevenness of Eleanor's lap. Lewis stopped a few inches short and sniffed and appeared to be smiling, in a most calm, conciliatory manner. Burby leaned back, then slowly forward, his front paws trembling just a little. After a moment, Lewis snorted, Burby almost fell off Eleanor's lap, and Lewis, now satisfied, sat back down and stared up at Eleanor, since George was not forthcoming with any cookies at all.

"I know, Lewis. I am the soft touch in the room. It has always been this way."

She broke a cookie in half and gave the slightly smaller half to Lewis, the other to Burby. Lewis simply swallowed. Burby chewed for a long time.

Obviously, both enjoyed the treat.

"Irene tells me you are drawing your way across America, Mr. Gibson."

"I am, sort of," George replied and explained a little of what he and Lewis had been doing for the last several months.

"It sounds so delightful. It is something Douglas would have loved to do. If he could draw. Which he could not."

George sipped at his coffee. He reminded himself again to ask whoever was responsible for the coffee for the brand or the process. It was among the two or three most delicious cups of coffee he had ever tasted.

"Irene said Douglas was an engineer. Most engineers have some drawing in them. Straight lines, anyhow."

Eleanor smiled.

"Douglas was a chemical engineer. Less drawing there, than most. And soon enough, he started his own consulting firm. Then, no drawing at all, just managing and selling."

Lewis and Burby busied themselves with staring intently at Eleanor and then to the neatly stacked cookies on the silver tray on the coffee table.

"And then, well, he was diagnosed, and any chance of drawing . . . or traveling . . . vanished."

"I am sorry, Mrs. Parker. My wife . . . she passed on several years ago. She shared the same diagnosis as your husband."

"Irene let me know. So I would not be surprised, I think. A Southern gentlewoman attempts never to be surprised. And Mr. Gibson, I do feel sympathy for your loss—as well as your long travail."

Outside, in the harbor, a ship, a large container ship, slowly headed out to sea. George heard the horns and bells as it slipped closer to the open waters.

"It is an active harbor. But a ship laden with trailers simply does not have the same mystery, or panache, of a traditional sailing vessel, don't you think, Mr. Gibson?"

"I do. Living in Gloucester since I was a child, I still remember the mystery of a closed ship steaming into port. When a ship still looked like a ship."

Each dog got another half of a tea cookie. Burby appeared nearly sated. Lewis, well, Lewis—not so much.

"Mrs. Parker, I do not want to appear inquisitive."

Eleanor smiled.

"Irene said you were related. I think it's what she said. I guess I'm curious as to how."

"Then it is not inquisitive, Mr. Gibson. Inquisitive is asking about a lady's age or weight. Relatives . . . should be an open book. And Irene is my sister-in-law. Or was. I'm not sure of the etiquette and proper terminology involved."

George nodded.

"My younger brother was her first husband. Many years ago."

George held his coffee cup and wondered if he should pour a third cup of coffee.

"He perished from the results of a car accident."

George did pour his third cup.

"They had been drinking. Irene and my baby brother."

George sipped quietly. He did not ask for the information, he did not solicit it, but also he did not want to interrupt his hostess. She seemed to want to open this page of this book.

It is the intimacy of strangers. The mystery of sharing without foreknowledge.

"He crashed the car into a utility pole. And was paralyzed from the neck down. A tragedy for all concerned."

George watched as Lewis ate another half cookie.

"Irene gave everything up to care for him. He lived for two more years. She was with him every moment of every day. She had to do everything for him. Everything."

Eleanor put down her teacup and looked out toward the harbor. The ship had slipped from view.

"Now, we see her every year or so."

Eleanor picked up a cookie crumb from her lap and placed it on the tray.

"You are on a journey, just like Irene, it seems. She feels guilty, after all these years, after us offering complete forgiveness to her, yet she still harbors guilt. I can see it in her eyes, Mr. Gibson."

She reached over and patted Lewis on the head. He offered a soft wuff in response.

"Lewis wants to hear the truth, doesn't he, Mr. Gibson?"

"He seems to."

"Dogs and I seem to have a bond."

She drew in a deep breath.

"Irene appears to be on a journey to find forgiveness. To find peace. I have told her what she seeks is not on the road. It is inside."

Eleanor tapped at her heart.

"It is inside, Mr. Gibson. Only through faith can you find forgiveness."

Lewis wuffed and stood and placed his right paw on her arm. Burby snarled softly, theatrically, but remained on Eleanor's lap.

"Only through faith, Mr. Gibson."

Lewis looked up at Eleanor, then over to George, with a look approaching pleading.

Then Eleanor stroked his head.

"Lewis, I must change for dinner. We will dine at six, Mr. Gibson. And I am not dressing up—I am slipping into a comfortable pair of old jeans. The setting may be formal, Mr. Gibson, but it does not mean I must be."

42

Nearly two weeks had passed, and George had filled an entire sketchbook with drawings using Charleston and the city environs as his models. He and Lewis took the scooter up and along the waterfront, sketching ships and smaller pleasure craft. He and Lewis walked in the historic district and sketched out dozens of the old stately homes dotting the area. The two of them scootered outside the city and sketched the view from Patriot's Point and Fort Moultrie and the *USS Yorktown* and the seashore on the Isle of Palms and dozens of other small and large sites. Lewis seemed to love the salt tang in the air and would hold his mouth open as George piloted the scooter, as if to consume the scent and aroma of the nearby sea.

Wherever the pair of them went, people would stop and talk and pet Lewis and tell George details of the lives—more details than George wanted to hear, but details nonetheless.

While staying in Charleston, while in the Parkers' massive guest bedroom—one of several, which was at least twice as large than their entire RV—George's troubling dreams seemed to have abated. Even Lewis slept better as a result of George's calmer sleep habits.

Both Eleanor and Douglas appeared to thrive on having company. Some of their evenings were spent playing board games or bridge while Burby pretended to stalk his elusive prey, the lumbering Lewis.

Lewis, with his genial nature, played along with the small dog and did not even seem to mind the high-pitched yapping as he mock-attacked.

One afternoon, Irene made a special request of George.

"The park down the street. The small one with the fountain. The one on the water . . . could you do a drawing of it? For me?"

George quickly agreed.

"But . . . I want to be in the drawing. With Lewis. Could you do it?"

George wanted to say no but did not.

"I can. I'm not good with people. And I'm not sure if I can do justice to Lewis, either. But if you want, I'll try."

Irene beamed.

"I would like for you to."

So in the afternoon, the three of them walked the few blocks to the park. Irene arranged herself in a bench near the fountain. George instructed Lewis to sit beside her. He set up his chair several dozen feet away and began sketching. Lewis got up several times and hurried to George's side, and each time, George would walk him back to Irene and instruct him again to stay put.

Obviously, Lewis was unsure of the meaning of "stay put."

As he drew both Lewis and Irene, George surprised himself with the fluidity of their drawn images.

I never thought I could do this. I never thought I could draw people.

When he showed his finished work to Irene, she examined it closely, then looked up at George, obviously touched by his work.

"Thank you," she said, her voice almost cracking. "It has been a long time since someone caught who I was. Inside."

Lewis sniffed at the drawing and looked up at George, a bit confused.

In the picture, with just a few pen strokes, George had captured her facial expression—something between hope and despair, something between joy and sorrow, an emotion on the cusp, as it were, with neither the positive nor the negative dominating.

The following morning, at breakfast, usually served in the bright solarium on the third floor, Douglas set down his coffee cup, his hands only shaking a little this day. He carefully used his napkin and then turned to face George.

"I have a favor to ask you, George."

"Whatever, Douglas. I owe you for letting Lewis and I stay with you. I never would have captured so much of this city had we been here on our own."

"Then I am glad. This morning, I think my favor is a simple matter."

Douglas drew in a deep breath. George had estimated the stage of Douglas's disease by recalling the progression of labored breaths during the last days of his wife's life. As her end grew near, each breath became a harder and harder commodity to purchase. Douglas had appeared to steel himself before breathing in—especially when he chose to speak above a whisper.

George surmised he had months, rather than years.

"I would like to go for a scooter ride, George."

George responded with a quizzical look.

"A scooter ride?"

"Yes," Douglas said, his voice soft again. "In your scooter. I see Lewis sit there and . . . enjoy himself. I want to feel the wind again."

George knew the pain Douglas must face and knew how hard it was to simply move from one room to another. Again, he had experienced all of the pain and watched all of the pain reflected in his wife's face all those years ago. *Once you see it*, George said to himself, *the feeling never leaves you.*

"Are you sure, Douglas? Are you up to it?"

George wanted no part of adding to anyone's pain or discomfort.

Douglas looked over at his wife, then to George.

"If it kills me, would it be so bad?"

George's face must have shown his surprise, or shock, or dismay.

"I am joking, George. I assure you I do not have a death wish."

George struggled to find a cogent reply.

Douglas drew in a deep breath.

"George, if I wanted to end things, pitching myself off a third-floor balcony would do it nicely. And even I could accomplish it. Slowly, perhaps, but it could be done. Yet it is something I would not do. So take courage, my friend. Take courage."

He slumped a bit after finishing the statement.

"But this is true: I am closer to contentment than I have ever been."

Eleanor remained silent, then stood. She looked every bit as elegant as always, even wearing jeans and a starched white blouse.

"Would it be acceptable with you, George? To take Douglas for a ride? He has spoken of little else for the last several days."

"Sure. I mean . . . I guess so. If it's okay with the both of you . . ."

Eleanor brightened.

"Splendid. I shall call for Tony. He will assist Douglas in getting into the sidecar."

Lewis wuffed softly from behind them. Burby growled whenever Lewis spoke.

"Lewis," George said. "You will have to stay here and guard the house, okay?"

Lewis appeared perplexed. George had never taken the scooter without taking Lewis.

It took some delicate maneuvering on Tony's part, but soon enough, Douglas was seated in the sidecar.

"No helmet, George. I want to feel the wind."

George started the scooter and carefully pulled away from the curb. He could hear Lewis inside the house, at the large windows on the first floor, wuffing and yelping, calling George back to pick up his regular passenger.

"A devoted dog you have there, George."

George nodded. He had not told them much of how he and Lewis had come to travel together, and like the Southern aristocrats of old, they refrained from asking a single additional question about the subject, sensing their guest's reluctance.

There is no reason not to tell them . . . but somehow, I wanted to keep it private. I want them to think I wanted to travel with Lewis—not as though he was thrust upon me. It does not sound noble.

George drove along the waterfront and headed toward the easternmost point of the city—the White Point Gardens, framed by the Ashley and Cooper rivers. He continued on Murray Boulevard and then returned into the historic district.

All the while, Douglas held on the padded edge of the sidecar and grinned. George could see he wanted to wave at people he passed but was too weak to let go and raise his hand in greeting.

After thirty minutes of touring the downtown area, George pulled over.

"Where else?"

"Back to the gardens at the bottom of town," Douglas said. George had to lean close to hear him. "If you have the time."

George headed toward the point and stopped at the edge of the park, the greenery and flowers, full and lush, almost glistening in the afternoon humidity.

"I love this town, George. Despite the heat and oppressive humidity, I still love it."

"I can understand why. It is a remarkably beautiful place."

Douglas stared out toward the water.

"I am having a wonderful time, Douglas."

George turned the motor off. The engine clicked and popped as it cooled.

"You seem to always be happy, Douglas. How do you do it?"

"What is the alternative, George? To be miserable? I had a wise uncle, who drank himself to an early grave, but no matter, and he said if you spend your days complaining, you will get the miserable life you deserve."

Douglas slumped an inch or two after speaking for so long. But the color in his cheeks was good, more pink and robust than George had noticed during the last two weeks.

"George, we all wear masks sometimes. But this is not a mask. I am happy."

George got off the scooter and walked to the other side so he could sit on the curb and more easily talk to his passenger.

"But why? You are living with a death sentence. What you have killed my wife."

"I heard, George, and you have my deepest sympathies. It must have been a trial to endure it with her."

"It was, but what makes your experience different?"

"Did your wife have faith?"

George looked away.

"She did. But can anyone be totally sure?"

"With faith, yes. I know where I shall spend eternity. Makes this pain simply a temporary thing."

George stood up. His knees popped in protest.

"But aren't . . . you know . . . aren't 'His followers' supposed to be spared pain? Doesn't the Bible say so? Maybe not the no-pain part, but the no-sadness part? 'I will give you rest.' Right? I'm right, aren't I?"

Douglas worked at screwing his face into a lemon.

"George, life cannot be easy. The Bible promises us we will suffer. And even without faith, a man's life without care . . . would be boring and stagnant. One cannot have contentment and peace without having tasted pain and defeat."

George turned away and stared out through the trees to the water beyond.

"But so much pain for such a good person. It doesn't make sense. Never did. My wife was a wonderful person. She never hurt anyone. She cared for people. She was my opposite, actually. Why her—and not me? I would be the one deserving of punishment. Not her. She was blameless."

"George, we are to expect troubles," Douglas said, pulling in air after each word, nearly, fighting for the ability to talk. "And none of us are blameless. Trust me. Every man has a dark heart. It is a broken world in which we live. Faith does not mean not having pain—it means having hope. I am closer to my God and to Eleanor than I have ever been."

George knelt by him, on the street.

"Even with what you have? Even in your condition?"

Douglas tried to shrug.

"I am content. God will take me in his time. And in the meantime, I shall have faith and I shall enjoy this world as best I can."

George stared into his eyes.

"I am telling the truth, George. It is what I can do."

George looked away, and back to the sea.

"My uncle—another uncle, not the drunkard, but this one sober as a deacon," Douglas said, as he took a deep breath, "he was a pious man, a man who knew God, and he often said the one thing that gives the devil the worst heartburn, and shows God's power most plainly, is a believer who suffers through tribulations with joy."

Douglas coughed, then tried to raise himself up. George helped him as best he could.

"Now, shall we take one more lap around the waterfront? And this time, let's see how fast we can go. And please, do not worry about tickets. The chief of police in this wonderful town happens to be my first cousin on my mother's side. And he owes me a considerable number of favors."

43

Later in the day, when the evening was spread out against the sky—George, with Lewis by his side, sat in the RV, alone. George fiddled with his electronic tablet and the Skype application.

"Something about the 150-year-old, foot-thick walls doesn't make for a good connection, Lewis."

Lewis sniffed at the tablet and wuffed. He appeared to know what was coming: Alex.

Eventually, George managed to make the two machines talk to each other and Alex's face popped up in the frame.

"Hello, Mr. Gibson."

"Hello, Alex."

Lewis began to wuff and dance and act uncharacteristically impatient. He smooshed his head against George's thigh and climbed halfway up his lap, grinning and wuffing and whimpering.

"Hey, Lewis!" Alex called out.

Lewis sniffed at the screen, tried to peer around it to see where Alex was hiding, then proceeded to wuff and whimper and snort and whirr with gusto.

"How are you? Are you being good? Do you like Charleston?"

George would let a handful of questions pile up and then try to answer the group of them as Lewis would prefer them answered.

"He loves Charleston, Alex. He says you should visit here. There are forts and old houses and ships and the ocean."

Lewis danced in place as Alex spoke, wuffing at the end of each sentence. Alex told Lewis all about his class and their recent field trip to Cape Ann Museum, and his book report and his decision to go out for the basketball team, and how each and every one of his friends asks about Lewis every day, and how Alex always tells them he's having a great time, and how the doctor says he is doing so well the treatments may only take nine months, instead of all year, and how much he can't wait to be able to play with Lewis again.

After nearly five minutes of steady chatter, Alex drew a deep breath and stayed silent for a moment.

George reached over and tapped at the tablet, thinking perhaps a slight tap would encourage it to work a little better.

But Alex was silent for a reason.

"Mr. Gibson?"

"Yes, Alex?"

"I've been thinking."

"About?"

"Well, not just me, but my friends as well. We've been thinking about Lewis."

Lewis grinned, wuffed, and looked up at George.

"What about Lewis?"

"Well, remember when you left with Lewis? Remember I told you that Lewis really likes hearing the truth?"

"I do. And you were right. Lewis is a truth-seeker."

"Yeah, but it's what we've been talking about. I'm not sure it's the truth Lewis is after."

"What is it, Alex?" George replied, and he scratched his chin in obvious puzzlement. "It sure looks like it to me. And to the people we've met."

"Yeah, I guess. But Emma, she's a friend who knows Lewis, she said Lewis isn't after the truth. It's just he likes to fix people. And she said the truth—or telling the truth—sometimes fixes people."

George looked at Alex closely, drawing his face close to the screen. Alex looked like he might be blushing, just a little.

"So . . . Alex . . ." George said, and waited.

"Yes?"

"So . . . you like this Emma?"

Now Alex did blush.

"I don't know. Maybe a little. But she's right about Lewis. He just wants people to stop being broken. And I think people stay broken if they don't tell the truth."

George rested his arm around Lewis's shoulder.

"Lewis, do you think Alex is right about this . . . and you?"

Wuff. Wuff.

And Lewis looked at the screen and offered his widest, most lopsided grin he could muster.

"See, he said so," Alex said and laughed. "He knows."

George grinned as he watched.

"And it's what it says in the Bible. And Emma should know. Her dad's a preacher. She said it was in the Bible."

"What was in the Bible?"

"She said it was something like . . . 'If you know what's true, then the truth will set you free.' Or something like it."

Then, Lewis stood and wuffed loudly, several times.

"I have to tell you, Alex, it sure seems Lewis understands English."

"Yeah, it does seem like it sometimes."

The three of them sat for a moment, still and silent.

"Remember back before I got sick with allergies? I told the truth, Mr. Gibson. To my mom. About being sick. Lewis wanted me to do it. To tell my mom the truth. And now I'm getting better. And see, like Emma said, me telling the truth will get me and Lewis back together again. It's what Lewis wants. He wants things to be fixed."

George took a deep breath.

"Tell Emma she's smart. And maybe she's right."

"Okay, I will."

George leaned close to the screen and whispered, "Is she cute, Alex?"

And this time, Alex did blush, full and scarlet, and Lewis grinned and wuffed his approval.

That night, George sat up in bed, the luxurious, nearly huge bed in the guest room of the Parkers' mansion. He listened. From the harbor came a soft moan of a ship's horn as it navigated the narrowing waterway. He heard a distant siren. The historic district, for the most part, remained quiet after dark. Lewis, at the foot of the bed, sleeping on a soft and thick towel—his preferred bedding material as of late—snored softly.

George wiped his face and tried to clear the remnants of the recurring dream from his mind. Recurring, but no less traumatic—the dream had interrupted his sleep for the past several years.

Ever since the day . . . and ever since she died.

He usually lay back, stared at the ceiling, until sleep found him again.

To sleep, perchance to dream . . . or not dream.

He sighed and remained sitting.

I know it is supposed to knit up the reveling ends of the day . . . but this isn't it.

He stared out the window. A freighter slipped past his sight, its red and green lights flickering in the thick humidity, on its way out to sea.

George closed his eyes, and the words came back to him . . . words from his eleventh-grade English class, one of several Shakespearean soliloquies they could choose to memorize.

George had picked this one, for no other reason than it was shorter than all the rest by a few lines. The words stayed with him all these years.

> To be, or not to be?—That is the question—
> Whether 'tis nobler in the mind to suffer
> The slings and arrows of outrageous fortune,
> Or to take arms against a sea of troubles,
> And by opposing, end them?
> To die: to sleep—
> No more—and by a sleep to say we end
> The heartache and the thousand natural shocks
> That flesh is heir to— 'tis a consummation
> Devoutly to be wish'd!
> To die, to sleep.
> To sleep: perchance to dream—ay, there's the rub.

When George had memorized those words, less than one hundred, he'd had no idea of what poor Hamlet was talking about. It was only after Mrs. Sexton explained it to the class it had made any modicum of sense.

"He's talking about the ultimate sin," she'd said, "of taking one's own life. It appears Hamlet suffered from guilt-induced insomnia."

The first time the words had come back to George was at Hazel's funeral. And they had seldom left him, nor diminished over the intervening years.

"Just tell the truth and the truth shall set you free . . . my foot," George said aloud. Lewis snorted, and George saw the crown of his head as he rose up to investigate the sound.

"It's nothing, Lewis. Just me muttering. Go back to sleep."

He heard Lewis sniff a few times, then heard an audible thud as he let his head drop back to the toweled bed on the floor.

After a moment, George lay back as well and stared at the ceiling.

Sleep will come.

He closed his eyes.

To sleep, perchance to dream; ay, there's the rub.

44

Rain filled the day, a humid, almost horizontal rain, warm as bath water, thick as fog.

In mid-afternoon, George took Lewis for a reluctant walk. The St. Bernard knew what lay in wait for him on his return: a thick, vigorous toweling—an activity Lewis saw no purpose in doing, and one only succeeding in aggravating both he and George.

But George would not allow a wet Lewis into his RV, let alone back into a multi-million-dollar historic house. Even though both Eleanor and Douglas said a wet dog was of not great concern to them, George could not allow it.

"I'm an engineer," George repeated. "And engineers are keen on establishing and obeying rules. And this is one of the rules: no wet dogs in the house."

Eleanor had smiled at him the first time he'd insisted on drying Lewis off.

"With our wet autumn this year, you will only succeed in provoking Lewis. Although I fail to see much of a difference between a provoked Lewis and the typical, genial Lewis," Eleanor had stated.

The only problem George found is the Parkers did not possess any "old" towels. Every towel, every absorbent fabric in the house, appeared either brand new or terribly historic.

"But using a new towel is better than Lewis drenching a million-dollar Persian rug," George explained.

George had spent the morning playing three-handed bridge with Douglas and Eleanor, and the afternoon in the library, reading a biography of the Confederate General William Dorsey Pender—a devout Episcopalian, baptized before taking command and "my quest for glory in both the heavenly and earthly realms."

Before dinner, George packed up his few things and carried them into the RV. He planned on leaving in the morning. He and Lewis had been guests for more than two weeks, and even though, every day, both Douglas and Eleanor had said how much they were enjoying his company and how much fun Burby was having with Lewis, George knew it was soon time to leave. His original itinerary was already in shambles, and with Alex coming off his allergy treatment schedule early and ahead of the anticipated time, George would have to skip many of his original destinations and head, more or less, in a straight line toward the West Coast. It meant leaving the South and leaving the warmer weather, but not heading so far north they would actually encounter real winter.

"I don't mind a bit of cold, but I don't want to drive in a deep freeze, either."

He did not inform anyone yet of his intentions. He found it difficult to disappoint people, and he was pretty sure his hosts might be disappointed with his departure. He was certain Irene would be disappointed.

During these weeks, he and Irene had spent some time together, and George realized it was the longest he had been with any woman since the death of his wife.

The growing intimacy, even if it was only a friendship-based intimacy, a conversational intimacy, made George grow nervous, anxious. Since Hazel's death, he imagined himself as remaining alone for the rest of his life. He could not imagine trying to figure out the intricacies of another human being—especially another female human being.

Once was hard enough, he thought to himself. I don't think I would be up for a second time.

The rain of the morning and afternoon had dissipated, leaving behind a thick veil of humidity, almost like rain itself, save for its downward movement.

Irene stood from the dinner table.

"George, let's you and Lewis and I take a walk," she said, her tone almost a command rather than an invitation, and everyone recognized as more bravado than shrill. Lewis obediently rose, stretched, and grinning, hurried toward the front door.

George took the leash from the butler's closet in the entryway where he stored it.

I have to remember to get this before I leave tomorrow.

"He doesn't need a leash, does he, George? We've taken walks, you know, when you were napping, without a leash, and never once did he leave my side."

"I wasn't napping. Just resting my eyes."

"Of course," Irene said, smiling. "Napping is for senior citizens, right?"

"Right," George replied firmly.

"So why is it you get the free senior citizen's coffee at McDonald's?"

George pretended to glare at her and then grinned.

"Because it's free. And because I'm eligible. A quirk in the law. But those are the rules, Irene. I didn't make them up. I just obey them."

The trio stepped out into the warm dark of the evening. George drew in a deep breath.

"I love the smell of salt in the air. Reminds me of home."

And I will miss it when I leave.

"Me, too," Irene said, and Lewis wuffed in happy agreement.

"Let's walk toward the park," Irene suggested, "so we can keep the water by our side."

The three of them walked slowly, from pool of light to pool of light, offered by the gas lanterns dotting the historic district. If one squinted, George thought, and ignored the cars, one could easily imagine being here after the war, when life was slower, less frenzied.

Lewis walked a few feet in front of them, sniffing first to the left, then to the right, like a sailboat tacking into the wind. Except there was no wind this evening, not even a wisp. The sounds in the air became muted by the thick humidity, much like a snowfall mutes the sounds in a northern environment.

Lewis tacked back to George and more or less ran into his thigh, almost causing him to stumble.

Speak the truth, is what George heard, or rather, what he felt when he made contact with the large, intrusive canine.

I sometimes grow weary of his instructions . . .

Lewis bumped him again, and again George felt the call to truth.

It will set you free.

In the span of a quarter hour of slow strolling, they came to the White Point Gardens at the point of the triangular piece of land Charleston lay on, mostly surrounded by water and river.

Lewis walked over to a bench and sat down next to it.

"Looks likes one of us wants to take a breather," Irene said.

They sat and looked out over the black water, only a few navigation lights visible on the route to the open sea.

Lewis edged closer.

Tell the truth.

"Are you enjoying your stay in Charleston?" Irene asked. She was not one to appreciate silence and often just chattered along, as if narrating the activity.

"I am," George replied. "I have never been in such a wonderful house or had such gracious hosts. It has been a nice few weeks."

"I'm glad. I was pretty sure you and Douglas would hit it off. He needs companionship."

George was willing to let it be the end of the conversation.

Irene was not.

Neither was Lewis, apparently.

Tell the truth.

"So . . . is anything bothering you, George?" Irene asked. "Sometimes you seem . . . I don't know . . . distant, I guess. Like you're not exactly present. Like you're thinking of something else. Something troubling."

I could say the same about you, Irene . . . but it's none of my business now, is it?

Lewis stood up and fidgeted some. Then he pushed his head against George's leg, again.

Tell the truth.

George bent down and almost pushed his head away.

"I thought maybe . . . you know . . . Douglas having ALS and me not knowing it's what your wife had . . . I thought maybe you were in some way . . . maybe you were mad at me and maybe, you know, maybe you blamed me for bringing you . . . and maybe the memories came back and . . . I don't know . . . maybe it made you feel bad. Dredged up something unpleasant. It's not, is it, George? If it is, let me apologize for it."

George began shaking his head no, well before she was finished.

"No, it's not."

"So no bad memories?"

"Not exactly. I mean, there are bad memories, but seeing Douglas, and watching him struggle . . . well, it didn't do anything to make my memories come back to me. I mean . . . I remember well what happened to my wife . . . and I remember it often, so I don't need any triggers. It wasn't, Irene. Trust me."

Irene took his hand and squeezed it.

"Well, good. I mean, not your unpleasant memories . . . but I'm glad I wasn't the cause of them."

George tried not to stare at her hand around his. This would be the first time in years and years he'd felt a woman's touch on his hand, or anywhere on his body, other than the nurses at the health clinic back home.

It was not an entirely unpleasant touch, not an unwelcome feeling.

But then George drew back and gently pulled his hand away.

I can't let this go on. I can't have her think I'm . . . a regular, nice person. When I'm not. When I know it's a lie.

Lewis whined, softly.

Tell the truth.

George sat up straight and bowed his head for a moment. And during this silence, Irene did not intrude, and George was grateful. He was trying to untangle a convoluted, twisted rope of emotions and thoughts and guilt and pain and memories—a veritable Gordian knot, all knitted and kinked and tight and locked inside of him.

"Are you a praying woman, Irene?" he said after a long period of silence, only broken by the baleful call of the lighthouse, miles into the harbor.

"No, not much," she replied, without hesitation. "My second husband, the pastor, now he was a person who prayed. He prayed all the time. I used to joke he prayed more than enough for the both of us. And I guess I could say I pray sometimes. When I'm confused. Or in serious trouble. But praying every day? No, I don't. It would seem . . . I don't know . . . hypocritical. Or dishonest."

She looked at George, examined him, tried to decipher his tight expression. She looked at his hands clasped together in his lap. She looked at Lewis, and even in the darkness, she could see a most serious, somber expression on the dog's face—an unusual expression, to say the least.

"George, why do you ask? Are you a praying person? Do you see some hurdle . . . you know . . . for our . . . friendship?"

"No. I mean . . . I don't know."

Our friendship . . . ? This had not been on my radar. Other things have been there, but not a friendship with a woman. The other things are bigger things. Terrible things. Nightmare sort of things.

Lewis stood up and whined.

Tell the truth.

Lewis put his chin on George's knee and looked up into his eyes. The dog, apparently, had no idea of what secret George might be concealing. He had no idea if the "truth" would do his companion good or harm. Lewis was a simple creature, and as a simple creature, with simple wants, he simply wanted to help George lighten his burdens.

"I was not a praying man," George said, his words almost inaudible. Irene leaned closer to him, not wanting to interrupt by asking him to repeat things. She would listen carefully.

"Before we were married, Hazel and I, well, we went to church, on occasion. It was the thing to do back then. People went to church, some church, any church, on Sunday. You went to church, then came home and had lunch or dinner and read the paper and maybe watched the ball game or listened to it on the radio. It's what I did when I was younger. Before Hazel and I could afford a TV, it was the newspaper and the radio. But going to church did not make me a praying man. Maybe I didn't listen closely. But I didn't pray."

Irene lifted her arm, slightly, as if she wanted to speak or wanted to touch him, to offer some comfort, but she stopped herself. She remained still, and silent, as did Lewis.

"Now, Hazel, at first, the two of us . . . we were pretty much alike. We went to church, and we were good people, or at least, we thought we were. I slipped a ten or twenty into the collection plate when I could. Not always. But Hazel said it was okay. We gave what we could. And we always dressed up for church. I always wore a suit and tie. It was important. To look like you're going to church, you know what I mean?"

George looked away from both of them, both Irene and Lewis, and stared upwards, upwards into the overcast, into the thickness of humidity, into the blanketing clouds of vapor protecting them, hiding them from the heavens.

"But later on, years later, Hazel started to take it seriously. Church. Like it was a special place. She started going to some women's thing at church. I thought it was like my mother had done when I was small— where the women got together and made bandages and things. But this must have been different, what Hazel was going to, because she never talked about bandages. She did talk about the Bible. What it said. What she had learned. I listened like a good husband. I nodded. I agreed with her. It all seemed to make her happy, and if she was happy, I was happy."

He took a deep breath.

"I loved her, Irene. I loved Hazel."

Irene spoke this time.

"I know, George. It's obvious. I think we all see it. We can tell. From the way you talk about her."

Lewis backed up a step, and George stood, his hands at his side, formed into loose fists, as if he wanted to let go, to release something long hidden, but was simply not sure of what to do, or to say next, to provide the release.

Lewis wuffed several times, his tone low and friendly, as if offering George encouragement to go on. At least, it's how George heard it, for he cleared his throat and turned back to face them both.

"So Hazel began to pray. A lot. For lots of things. For the church. For missionaries. For people she had never met but appeared to be in trouble. She was often asking people, sometimes complete strangers she met in the supermarket, if there was anything she could pray about for them. And what was so surprising to me, is those complete strangers often took her up on her offer. They would share all sorts of deeply personal matters—just so my wife, a complete stranger to them, could pray about it. People said she had a sense about her—something seemed to glow inside of her—and people reacted to her. I didn't see it. Maybe I was too close."

"Like Lewis?" Irene asked softly.

"Exactly. People tell Lewis things. Scary, private things. But with Lewis, I see it. I get it. I see what he has causes people to respond to him. Something in his eyes. His expression. Makes you want to tell him the truth. A seriousness. Solemnity. Maybe even a sense of peace humans don't normally see in a dog. Like he knows things we don't. Secrets. And something about him tells people he would never judge them. Not like people. Lewis just listens. Never judges."

Irene nodded. Lewis looked almost embarrassed, if dogs could know what embarrassment was.

George sat back on the bench. Lewis could see George was anxious this evening, agitated almost, unsettled, and not at peace. Lewis stepped closer, so his jaw rested again on George's knee.

"When she got sick, when Hazel was diagnosed . . . she still prayed. Sometimes for herself. But mostly for others. Always for others. People in the church prayed for her. A group of her lady friends came in twice a month, like clockwork, with a meal for me, and sat around her and prayed."

"George, you have nothing to be troubled about. What you're describing sounds so normal. Sad, but normal."

George held up his hand, indicating she should stop—he had much more to say.

"Toward the end, the last few years, she would ask me to pray with her. In her room. While she would lay there—with the oxygen hooked up and everything, just the small wheeze of clean, powerful air being pumped into her lungs, it was the only sound in the room. I would sit in the chair by the bed and hold her hand, and she would pray. Mostly out loud. I told her I was self-conscious praying out loud and she said it was okay and I said I prayed silently. She said God would hear it regardless. Loud or soft or unspoken. God would hear. And he would listen. And he would answer prayers. She was certain God, the God she believed in, would answer prayers."

"It was nice of you, George. It is what people do who love someone."

"No. No. Not me. I said I prayed silently. But I didn't. I didn't tell her the truth. I didn't say the words. I didn't think the words. I didn't even want to know the words. So while she thought I was praying, I wasn't. I was thinking about something else or making up a shopping list in my head or thinking about when I needed to change the filters on the furnace or change the oil in the car or whatever. And after a while, after I sat there pretending for a while, well, then I would squeeze her hand and she would think it was a sign I was through praying and she would smile and I would kiss her forehead and then slip out of the room, so she could get some sleep. Toward the end, she did not sleep much at all."

"George . . ."

George waved his hand, this time with some quickness, as if he did not want to be interrupted again, as if he did not want her sympathy or her understanding.

"She got sicker and sicker and more and more weak, and we knew she did not have time on her side. No one held out any real hope for any sort of real recovery. ALS has no hope. It is always downhill."

"I know . . ."

George just ignored Irene and kept talking, like he had to continue, as if he were to stop, all momentum would be lost and perhaps, perhaps he would not be able to ever release whatever demon he had imprisoned all these years.

"She grew weaker, and as she grew weaker, she prayed all the harder. Her friends remained faithful. She prayed with them. The pastors from the church would show up. Sometimes church people I did not know would show up. Ten minutes. Twenty minutes. Short prayers. Long prayers. They would all pray. I would make coffee for them in the kitchen, and afterward we would sit and talk about the weather while we all drank coffee."

He drew in a deep breath.

"All of them prayed . . . all except me. I never prayed. Never once in all those years, watching the disease slowly rob me of my best friend, my wife, the woman I wanted to spend all my days with, the woman I wanted to die next to. I never prayed once."

"George . . ."

"So at the end . . . though neither of us thought it was the end, is when it happened. She had actually gotten a little stronger. Not much. She could sit up for a bit. It was a major achievement. Maybe it was some sort of plateau. It's what I hoped it was. So she could find some rest."

"George . . ."

"So one evening, she grew limp and tired and sad and scared and she asked me again to pray for her. Whispered, I guess. She couldn't speak loudly then. She whispered her request to me, and I said I would, just like all the other times I said I would pray."

From the distance, in the darkness of the water of the outer harbor, a bell sounded, then a horn. A ship was coming into the port, looking for a safe harbor, a secure anchorage.

"But this time I actually prayed. It was the first and maybe the only time I prayed. I was angry. I was angry—at God mostly. I wondered why I should pray to a God who let this happen to Hazel. Why? But this time, I had a request for this God of diseases and separation. I had something to pray about. Finally, I had a reason to pray. I said to Him, to God, I am tired of watching my wife waste away. I was tired of seeing her die just by fractions of an inch each day. I was tired of watching her wither and pass away, all without dying. So I asked if He was God, and He was this all-powerful, all-compassionate, all wonderful God, then why doesn't He just let her die? Why would He make anyone, or allow anyone to suffer for nearly a decade with a death sentence?"

George drew in another deep breath and sniffed. Lewis looked up at him with some dismay. He had never seen George shed a tear or grow hoarse with emotion, and it was obvious Lewis was not comfortable with the sight.

"I was so exhausted and spent and . . . just done with it all—I asked Him to let her die."

"George . . ."

"All these years, I never once prayed. Other people, prayed all the time for healing, for peace, for grace, for joy, if you can believe it. Not me. I prayed for death."

George wiped his face with his hand.

"I prayed for her death."

He coughed just a little, perhaps holding back a sob.

"Two days later, in the middle of the night, I heard a slight wavering from her bed. The nurse was asleep. And I rushed to Hazel's side to see her die, in front of me, just stop breathing, close her eyes, and cease to be."

Irene did not speak. Lewis remained silent.

"The one time I prayed—and it was for her death—and it is the prayer God chose to answer."

"George . . ."

"I can't forgive myself for it. Ever. It is the unforgivable prayer."

Irene reached over to him and tried to take his hand, but he did not respond to her gesture, so she drew her hand back.

"George, God did not answer your prayer. He did not let her die because of what you said or thought. God is not in the killing business. You did not kill your wife, George."

George was quick to reply.

"And how are you so sure?"

Irene looked hard at his face, trying to read through the anger and pain.

"Because He wouldn't, that's all."

"It's just your faith, or how you think God should act. I don't believe it at all. Not for a moment. I think she's dead because I asked for her to be dead. It's how an engineer thinks. On or off. Black or white. Up or down. Alive or dead."

"George," Irene said, struggling to find the words, "There is no proof of what you just said."

"Exactly," George snapped back. "Exactly. It's why I can't be forgiven."

A small trail of tears marked Irene's cheek.

"George . . ."

"It's why I can hardly live with myself most days."

Irene sniffed loudly.

"George, you didn't do anything different than probably everyone in your situation has done. Pray for release. Pray for mercy. Pray God takes them home and makes their suffering stop."

George acted as if he didn't even hear her.

"It's why I can't let my daughter be put in the same situation. I cannot let her find herself in a situation where she has to pray for my death. No one should have such pain and guilt and shame. No one. Ever."

And then Lewis lifted his head, stared at the clouds above, and began to howl, softly at first, then growing into a howl of pain and release and fear and anger and loneliness.

Only when they both stood, and they both urged Lewis to stop, he did.

He looked at them with the saddest eyes either of them had ever seen. Then he shook his head a bit and started off toward home, not waiting to see if either of them followed him.

But they did. They followed him home—no one speaking, just the sound of their footsteps damply echoing in the stillness of the night.

45

The humidity, the oppressive humidity of the night before had vanished, leaving behind a clear sky and breathable air.

George and Lewis slipped out early for their morning constitutional—very early—around 5 a.m. The sky remained dark, and the streets remained deserted.

Southern gentility does not rise before dawn, George thought. At least not in the rich section of town.

They saw no one; they passed no one on the streets.

And when they returned, the house remained quiet and dark. George quietly picked up his small satchel and left the handwritten note on the breakfast table where someone was sure to see it. They slipped out the rear door and quietly got into the RV. George tried to start it with the minimum of noise. He had already positioned it so he would not have to worry about backing up with a trailer attached; instead, he simply pulled out onto the main street and headed north, through the historic district, and out toward the freeway pointing west.

The note, left on the table, read:

Dear Eleanor, Irene, and Douglas—

Thank you so much for your gracious hospitality these past weeks. I have never met people as kind and as inviting as you. You are truly admirable in all respects.

I dislike good-byes, so I have chosen to ignore proper etiquette—just this once—and make my farewells from the emotional safety of a thank-you note. I hope you will forgive me.

And I know Lewis would have had a hard time saying good-bye to Burby. This spares them all the confusion.

Again, my deepest regards and heartfelt thanks,

George Gibson . . . and Lewis

By the time the noon hour arrived, George was cruising into Jacksonville, Florida. They had only stopped twice, for comfort reasons and for coffee, on their morning trip.

Lewis actually appeared confused at not finding Burby lurking behind some potted plant or couch or floor-length drapery, and having him charge out, full of barks and squeaks, in his effort to intimidate the much larger animal.

Lewis had never once been intimidated.

And he also seemed to enjoy the game immensely.

And sitting in the passenger seat, Lewis did not ask for the window to be lowered. He simply lay down, curled in a semi-circle on the seat, and slept.

He might not have been sleeping. George glanced over, every few miles, and Lewis's eyelids never appeared totally shut—not sleep shut, just closed enough to prevent people from talking to him.

And if George had been talkative in the morning, which he was not, Lewis would have been able to travel in silence.

As he watched for the signs for Interstate 10, a thought came to George.

Funny how we get things we don't think we will, and then not realize it . . . like Lewis wanting silence.

The junction for Interstate 10 West was five miles ahead.

Or maybe I'm simply projecting. Anthropomorphism is alive and well in the Gibson RV.

George would have smiled at the thought a week ago. But today he did not feel like smiling, not at all. He and Lewis seemed to share the same withdrawn, almost sullen mood.

Irene got to the note first. It was addressed to all three, so she did not hesitate to open it. As she read it, she hurried to the rear window of the solarium, thinking perhaps she might see George pulling away, and if she did, she would run downstairs, jump into her van, and give chase.

But there was no RV lumbering out of the sheltered drive.

There was no hint of him or Lewis having been there, save for Burby sniffing frantically, thinking, perhaps, Lewis had somehow hidden himself behind a chair or under the rug.

"Burby . . ." Irene said, and the dog looked up at her, "Lewis is gone. Your playmate is gone."

Irene would later tell the others Burby understood every word she had just said and his face fell, and he lay down on the corner of the rug, in the morning sun, where Lewis liked to lay, and put his head between his front paws and whimpered softly to himself.

"I know where he's headed. I saw his final destination on his map. Remember? When I met him for the first time. I told you how organized he was. Just like an engineer, Douglas. Precise. But I'm afraid his schedule has changed," Irene explained to Douglas and Eleanor. "I'm sure it has. But what I don't get is why he wouldn't want to tell us good-bye in person."

Douglas seemed to understand George's reasons for a silent, unbidden departure better than did Irene or Eleanor.

"I get it," Douglas said. "Good-byes can be difficult."

Eleanor appeared peeved, but in a genial way.

"It's the big difference between men and women, Douglas. Men can just leave. They figure everyone will be fine with it. Women would like to know why you're leaving. A woman wants a reason. An explanation."

"Maybe . . ." Douglas wheezed, "maybe he doesn't know himself."

Eleanor's expression softened, then grew puzzled.

"He might be right, Irene. We both liked George. And we loved Lewis. But something about George puzzled me. Nothing frightening or anti-social, I assure you. Yet, sometimes, I got the feeling he was holding something back, something painful, perhaps. I didn't need to know his secrets, of course, but it appeared to me he was uncomfortable with the secrets. I would have thought if he talked about them, he might feel better. But it is hard for some people, I am sure. The truth can be most painful."

Eleanor then arched her right eyebrow, just a little, just the hint of question, without actually asking a question. Irene knew it was part of the Southern gentility and grace—maneuvering emotions without appearing to be Machiavellian about it.

Irene did not mention their conversation from the night before. It would require lots of explanation and nuance—and Irene knew everyone would start drawing parallels between George's life and her own. And it was obvious from the worried look on Irene's face she did not want it discussed.

"You might be right," Irene replied. "Some men just find it hard to unburden themselves."

After a moment, Douglas looked up.

"Do you know how to get in touch with him? An e-mail address, perhaps? A next of kin?"

Irene brightened, then the smile vanished.

"I do have an e-mail . . . but, for it to work, he has to answer it. He does have a daughter. In Arizona. I think he said Arizona. Out west. I don't know if she's married or not."

Eleanor sat back at the table and lifted up a delicate coffee cup to her lips.

"If you know where a man will end up, then you will be able to find him."

Irene was never sure of just what to read into her sister-in-law's comments. This one, it was obvious to Irene, was meant to be helpful.

"True. I could head out west and intercept him."

Irene looked like she was in the process of making a decision.

"If I decide to follow him. Of course, I have no real reason to."

Eleanor gave her another slightly arched eyebrow.

"And, I suppose, no reason not to, either."

Later, after breakfast, after much more discussion, Irene, back in her bedroom, paced back and forth, wringing her hands, a familiar gesture when she felt troubled. She had almost decided to simply take off, to head west, to see if she could cross paths with George and Lewis again. She would aim her journey's end at his intended end.

If the young boy . . . Alex, I think his name was . . . if he is getting better quicker—it's what George said—then maybe he'll head straight to the West Coast. Maybe he won't make as many stops. I could pursue him, and given a worst-case scenario, I could wait for him at the end of his route. I could do it.

Irene sat on the bed and, without thinking about it, folded a pair of socks, rolling them for easy, space-saving packing.

Maybe finding him will be like me offering some sort of penance. Maybe it's what I've been looking for all these years. A way to get past this guilt. My guilt. Eleanor knows all about it. I know it. I can see it in her eyes. Maybe it will give me the peace Eleanor and Douglas talk about. Maybe it could work for the both of us. Maybe.

She slipped the socks into her battered leather valise, purchased in a resale shop in Pocatello, Idaho, some years earlier.

I have already lost three people I loved. I'm not giving up on this one.

She started to fold her blouses.

I care for him. I do.

She stopped and smiled.

Or maybe it's just his dog.

Maybe.

She stopped moving and closed her eyes and tried to recall Lewis's welcoming, all-encompassing smile.

It is all because of Lewis.

Irene did not explain everything to Eleanor and Douglas—just enough to let them know she was worried about George and she felt she should try and find him.

"Do you think he might . . ." Eleanor said tentatively, "bring harm to himself. Guilt can do it, as I understand it."

Irene knew she was referencing the crash that took her brother's life and impaired Irene's for all these years.

"No. Not George."

Douglas turned in his wheelchair, the tires squealing slightly in the wooden floor.

"No one can be sure, Irene," Douglas said, his words just a whisper. He seemed to have weakened in the past few days. "One must let go of the past to be free. I had felt, when talking with George, there was something in his history he had not let go of . . . something in regard to his wife, I am sure. The sort of pain I understand well. But I did not take it upon myself to ask. Perhaps I should have."

Irene shook her head.

"No. I mean . . . no, I'm sure he was fine. Is fine. I think he just felt the need to move on."

Eleanor nodded and looked at Irene with a serene, forgiving smile on her face. She looked, for a moment, like there was a thought needing to be said aloud and she was holding it back. Then she nodded to herself and spoke. "A portion of a Psalm came to my mind when he and I spoke. I think it is number 32. And perhaps I am paraphrasing a little, 'I confessed my sins and stopped trying to hide my guilt. And you forgave me. All my guilt is gone.'"

Irene listened to her words, was always polite whenever either of them spoke of the Bible and of faith, and never insulted them by saying such words were nice, but simply not for her, not now, perhaps not ever.

But this time, this moment, Irene listened and closed her eyes and appeared to be holding back tears.

"You have nothing to confess to us, Irene. You never have. Any confession is to God. And for whatever has happened in the past, well, it remains in the past and it is forgotten and forgiven. By us and by God. But one is required to ask for it."

It became obvious Irene was trying not to cry.

"It's not . . ."

"Perhaps it is not," Eleanor said. "But we love you. Have always loved you. And now, if you think you can help guide George, help him find peace, then it is what you should do. You have the freedom. And you have our love, regardless."

Irene stood, attempted to speak, but simply could not. Then she turned and hurried out of the room and hurried downstairs to her bedroom and hurried to again start her journey.

46

George stopped at an RV park just north of Tallahassee, Florida.

It was the longest single-day drive he had yet attempted. Over four hundred miles with only short stops for coffee, comfort, and gas. If Lewis acted upset or concerned, George did not pay him any attention. He simply wanted to put as much distance between him and Charleston as possible, as quickly as possible.

Every mile he traveled, all on freeways, all relatively fast, he felt fractionally better. The greater the distance, he thought, the less his confession would echo in his thoughts; the loudness, the clanging and reverberations of his words, he felt, would diminish with each mile traveled.

When he pulled into his spot and switched off the engine, he just sat, for a long moment. Lewis had stood up in his seat, knowing this was a signal for him to be released from his seat belt and allowed to go outside to investigate.

But George simply sat, his hands still on the wheel, his eyes focused on the foreground. Presently he closed his eyes and slowly relaxed his death grip on the steering wheel.

Lewis gave out a series of concerned wuffs, like a lawnmower running over a thick patch of grass.

"Okay, Lewis. Just give me a minute."

Lewis sat back down and stared at George with a definite look of concern on his face.

After another few moments, George leaned over and unsnapped the harness. He got out of his side of the RV, walked slowly around to Lewis, and opened his door.

"You okay without a leash tonight?"

Lewis had always been okay without a leash, and he climbed down to the ground, sniffing.

The two of them walked down to the end of the lane without talking, without wuffing, without trying to meet and greet other campers, without paying much attention to their surroundings.

"Hungry?"

At this, Lewis wuffed.

George simply filled his bowl with kibbles and set a kettle on for making coffee.

Lewis ate his kibbles, without sniffing at them first, and George dank his coffee without truly tasting it.

And they both stared out the RV window and watched the night come over Tallahassee.

Lewis . . . I suppose I should tell you these things . . . but you would just be confused. I told the truth. I explained what happened as honestly as I could. And it has not set me free. The truth shall set you free? Malarkey.

And no one says malarkey *anymore.*

I know. I am a living anachronism.

The truth has not provided freedom. It has simply reinforced what I had thought about myself. I am the epitome of a man haunted by an unforgivable offense.

And it's the truth of the matter.

Sorry, Lewis. But this is a truth and a mistake and simply cannot be fixed.

George put his coffee cup in the sink, without washing it.

There is only one way out of this. Only one way.

Irene pulled into the gas station just beyond the city limits of Charleston. Normally, she would drive several hundred miles, to get between metropolitan areas, where she felt the gas would be less expensive.

Today she did not care. Whatever the price was, the price was. She filled up the tank, paid for it with a credit card, did not take the receipt the machine offered, got back inside the van, and headed west on 17, aiming to pick up Interstate 95 and head south.

"He said he was stopping in Savannah," Irene explained to Eleanor just before she departed, later in the day, after George and Lewis had left. "But I don't think he'll go there. Not now. It's too close. And too similar to Charleston."

"Too close?" Eleanor asked.

"Just a feeling," Irene replied. "I think he wants to put some distance between here and where he's going."

Eleanor sat on the guest bed as Irene packed up her few belongings.

"So . . . he did tell you more than you let on this morning."

Irene stopped folding a faded pair of jeans.

"He did."

She held the jeans close to her chest for a moment, thinking, considering her thoughts, then laid the jeans carefully in her battered leather bag.

"You were right, Eleanor. He does carry a tremendous amount of guilt—over the death of his wife."

Eleanor did not appear surprised. She did not smile, nor frown, nor nod, but it was as if she simply willed Irene to expand a bit more. And Irene did.

"He prayed for her death. The only time he prayed and it was for her to die. And he blames himself now for praying it and it being the only prayer God answered."

Eleanor nodded, ever so slightly, a mature, knowing nod.

"It is what I thought."

First, Eleanor looked down at her hands, elegantly folded in her lap. Then she looked up to Irene with a kind, forgiving expression—a smile, but not a smile—an expression of acceptance and empathy.

"I understand him, Irene. I can understand how a person gets to such a dark, hurtful place. If we were people, Douglas and I, if we were people of more limited means . . . where help was not so readily and easily available, I would imagine my pain and frustration might be amplified. If he could not afford the best therapy, if I could not have the time away to find some strength and peace through being alone, if we did not have our faith, then I'm sure I would be where George was. The thought has crossed my mind as well, Irene. It is the way darkness works. It seduces you into the blackness. You must always be wary of such a seduction."

Eleanor shook her head just a bit.

"Don't be shocked, Irene. I am prey to the same sort of slings and arrows of outrageous fortune as anyone else."

Irene sat next to her on the bed. She appeared to be near tears but also appeared to be steeling herself from showing her emotions.

"But you and Douglas seem so . . . happy."

"It is only by faith we can be so, Irene. Only through faith."

Irene looked away.

"And through forgiveness, Irene. Through forgiveness."

Irene downshifted as the van entered the freeway. A small engine, a four-speed transmission, did not allow for speedy takeoffs. She gunned the engine as best she could to get to the speed of traffic and nudged her way to the far right lane, just ahead of a looming semitruck. With her foot completely to the floor, the van shimmied just a bit but slowly made headway away from being overshadowed.

And he won't go to Cape Canaveral either. I told him I had been there and it was full of tourists and Mickey Mouse hats and foam fingers. I would bet it soured him on drawing any rocket ships. The only place he might be headed for is . . . New Orleans. It might have been Vicksburg on the Mississippi . . . he did say he liked Civil War battlefields. But it's far north and if he has to get to the coast in short order, he would cross it off his list. I think it has to be New Orleans. And the only things to draw in New Orleans . . . the only things I think he would like would be the Superdome, the French Quarter, and maybe the Garden District.

She pulled out into the middle lane of three lanes and held the wheel tight, the eddies and swirls and backdrafts from a slower tandem trailer buffeting the small van like a one-man ketch in a hurricane. She clenched her jaw tight and pushed her reedy van past the truck into clear, less turbulent air.

"So you don't mind making adjustments to your trip, Mr. Gibson? We could meet you anywhere. Then you could stay on track with your itinerary."

George and Lewis sat side-by-side on the couch, with the camera facing them, and watched Mrs. Burden in the small screen of the tablet on the table.

"No, it will be fine. I only have to skip a few places. Since you can't get away until next month with school vacations and all, I still have some time."

"Now you're absolutely certain? You have been such a godsend to us, Mr. Gibson. I cannot tell you how much we appreciate the gift you have given to us—and to Alex. He is simply beside himself."

George nodded and Lewis wuffed again as she mentioned Alex's name.

"The doctor said his progress has been wonderful—in terms of getting through the regime of shots. And we tried it out with a neighbor's dog. We offered to dogsit for a week—and this dog was a super-shedder. The dog appeared to consist mainly of loose hair and a bark. It's some sort of retriever mix who left hair all over everything—and I mean everything. And Alex did not have a single sniffle or cough. The allergist says all of his skin tests for animal dander and fur have all been almost to the point of zero. So . . . basically, with routine follow-ups, Alex is cured."

"Again, Mrs. Burden. It is good news. Isn't it, Lewis? You want to see Alex again, don't you?"

Wuff. Wuff. Wuff.

"Well, then, we'll plan to leave on the fifteenth of next month. Unless the weather is terrible up here."

"And you don't mind risking winter driving?" George asked.

"Not at all. This summer, we bought a big four-wheel drive behemoth. It's bigger than our first house. I think it has six-wheel drive, actually. And we can show Alex some of America this way—and the winter will definitely keep the crowds down."

George laughed with Mrs. Burden. She seemed bright and happy and . . . well, joyful.

"So, you're in New Orleans now, right?"

"I am," George affirmed. "We are. Lewis doesn't seem to like it much. The humidity here is like taking a twenty-four-hour shower. But still, an interesting place."

"And I thought you were headed up river . . . the Mississippi, right?"

"I was. But I have made a lot of adjustments. I'm going to drive straight through Texas. I'll do the Grand Canyon and maybe Monument Valley. And maybe Zion. Then on to California and San Francisco and up the coast. With more than a month left, it is doable. And I won't have to rush any of it."

"Honestly?"

"Honestly," George replied. "And I'm getting to the end of the trip. It's time to call it quits and get off the road for a while. I'm looking forward to finding a routine again."

"As long as you're okay with it, Mr. Gibson."

"I am. And so is Lewis."

Mrs. Burden beamed.

"Alex will be so excited. We didn't tell him we may be traveling so soon. Originally, he figured we might use next year's spring break. But this way, it will be our family Christmas present."

"It sounds great, Mrs. Burden. I'm happy for you."

"Well, then, we'll talk soon—okay, Mr. Gibson? And thank you so much. I mean it." George clicked off the Skype connection and sat still. Lewis seemed to be lost in thought as well.

Christmas . . . I guess I did not take it into consideration.

Lewis climbed off the couch, then climbed back on the couch opposite. He smooshed the seat a bit, then lay down and rolled to his side, his back to the back of the couch. He let his head fall to the cushion.

He's happy. I can see it in his eyes. Happy . . . and probably glad to see this long trip come to an end.

Christmas . . .

I guess no time is a better time than others. What will have to be will have to be.

Fate . . . right?

We're all fated to follow what has been pre-ordained.

47

Irene closed in on New Orleans. The problem of driving an older van—a much older van, an actual antique vehicle in some states—was the lack of air-conditioning. Irene claimed she carried enough hippie-like genes to not require such a creature comfort, a soft necessity for the soft middle class. But driving into a maelstrom of heat and humidity, not altogether abnormal for fall along the Gulf of Mexico, Irene had both front windows wide open, and the resulting winds offered scant comfort. The road rumble and the growling of the trucks and the hypnotic whine of tires added up to make a long-distance trip almost completely uncomfortable.

All these years of me traveling around the country, I don't think I ever went more than a few hundred miles in a day, at most. Now I'm driving eight hours straight. I can see why people get bigger, faster, quieter, more comfortable vehicles.

Irene actually considered pulling off the freeway somewhere around Pensacola and looking for the nearest used car lot and buying the biggest Hummer she could find. But while Irene's retirement finances were not perilous, neither were they overly substantial. She had the freeway exit in view, the one she would take and search for a new, bigger, softer-riding car—but at the last quarter mile, she talked herself out of it.

If I don't find him . . . then I'll have a huge car or bus or monster truck I don't really want and can't afford.

She gritted her teeth and rolled past the exit, wiping at her forehead with a bandana she kept in the front shelf, since the van did not have a glove compartment—just an open shelf under the dashboard.

"I'll find him in this old van. Somehow. Somewhere. Hot or not."

George slowed as he approached the Superdome.

"There it is, Lewis. What do you think?"

The humidity seemed to sap the dog's attention. He simply lifted his head from the seat and glanced upwards.

"The Mercedes-Benz Superdome, I should say. Doesn't look German in the least."

Lewis laid his head back down and smooshed around on the seat a bit, in an effort to find a comfortable position. The hotter and more humid it became, the more readjustments Lewis made per hour. Even though the RV possessed an efficient air-conditioning system, the heat and humidity apparently seeped in through the cracks and joints in the vehicle, infiltrating the interior with its strength-sapping ability.

George pulled into one of the access roads leading to one of the many parking lots surrounding the arena.

"Looks like a mushroom, Lewis," George said. "A giant mushroom, but a mushroom, nonetheless."

He pulled over to the curb. There appeared to be no activities or events inside the dome, so all the parking lots remained empty. He stepped out of the van and walked a few steps.

"I don't know. I can't decide if I should draw this or not."

He turned back to the RV. Usually, if he left the van and left Lewis inside, Lewis was at the window, nose to glass, following his every move with unbridled interest.

Today, not so much. Lewis's head did not appear at all.

"Well, Lewis isn't interested, for sure."

George was outside for all of four minutes, and already he was wet through and through, the sweat from his body escaping, and humidity in the air invading.

"I don't know how people down here survive," he said and climbed back into the cooler RV. "I know they said it was unseasonably warm today, but to me, it is simply hot. Regardless of the calendar." Even though it was cooler inside the RV, by many degrees, George did not feel much more comfortable. It was as if a person carried the heat and humidity with them and remained surrounded by it, despite the interior temperature.

George had left the scooter in the trailer.

And he did not seek out an RV park in the city.

"I could never run the air-conditioning at a high enough setting to stay comfortable all night." Instead, he found an all-suites hotel a few miles out of the city center, in what looked to be on the cusp of a nice residential area.

It was the first time George had to defend his assertion, his false assertion, Lewis was indeed a "service animal."

"Ummm . . . sir, I am sorry, but we do not allow pets in this hotel."

The young lady behind the chest-high counter at the Cajun All Suites Hotel and Convention Center peered over at Lewis, who sat placidly on the cool tile floor, panting softly. She looked uneasy, as if not accustomed to presenting unpleasant regulations to paying guests.

George did a well-timed double take. He had not rehearsed the move, but it did look as if it had been preplanned.

"Oh, him," George replied, nodding toward Lewis.

"Yes, sir. We don't allow dogs in our guest rooms. I am so sorry."

"Oh. I see. But he's not a pet, miss."

The young lady, no older than twenty, tightened her smile.

"But he is a dog."

Lewis stared up at her, or at least stared up at the crown of her head. He offered her the most genial St. Bernard grin he could muster.

"Oh, yes. He is," George said, stammering a little, not sure of what he needed to say to explain his ruse.

"He's . . . he's a service dog, miss."

The young lady, Chrissy according to her nametag, tilted her head slightly and looked back. "But you're not blind, sir."

George nodded in agreement.

"No. He is not a Seeing Eye dog. He is a service animal. A therapy animal, miss. He helps me . . . helps me avoid unpleasant outbursts."

A lie, but a small, inconsequential lie. Maybe.

The young lady—Chrissy—appeared to give credence to the statement.

"Ohhh . . . you mean like those dogs who know when their owners are getting . . . like a seizure or something? I've seen those on television."

"Yes, exactly. I have to keep him with me."

Chrissy seemed flustered and a bit embarrassed.

"Oh, I am sorry. I did not realize. Of course, then. We have a room we set aside for people with service animals. It is a nice room on the ground floor."

She leaned closer to George, standing on tiptoe probably.

"Some of our guests . . . have said service dogs don't like using the elevator. It's why the room is on the ground floor."

"Well, thank you," George replied. "Lewis is okay on elevators. But the ground floor is fine."

Lewis wuffed softly as George took the key, sounding like a handful of marbles rolling down a cardboard tube.

When they entered the room, George turned to Lewis.

"You just keep quiet, Lewis. And don't tell anyone, okay? It is our secret, right? And you need a cool environment. I do, too."

Lewis, happy to be in a room the temperature of a meat locker, nodded and grinned again.

George did not draw the Superdome.

"It's big. It's impressive. But it just looks like a big mushroom. There's no charm. And if I put it on paper, it will still look like a mushroom. Hard to get it into a human-sized perspective."

Instead, the following day, he and Lewis took the RV downtown and stopped at the Café Du Monde. George had read about their famous beignets and wanted to see what the fuss was all about. And the café, at least the one near the historic district, had tables outside. He tied Lewis to one of them and told him to stay put.

"I can see you from inside, Lewis," he said. "So, no funny business while I pick these up."

George came back out with a coffee and a bag of six hot beignets, thick with powdered sugar.

"I don't think sugar is good for dogs," he said as he dusted one of them off, getting most of it removed.

Lewis was delighted, of course. And when he was delighted with food, he sometimes ate it quickly, which is what he did, and soon he was looking up, with pleading eyes for another.

"Grease and the trace of sugar, right? Ambrosia, right?"

George sipped at the coffee.

"This is the second or third best cup of coffee I have ever had," he said to Lewis, who kept his eyes focused on the white paper bag.

George ate through two of them, dusted one more off for Lewis, and decided to keep the last two as a snack for later.

"Won't be as good as they are now—nice and hot and crispy—but this is all I can eat right now."

Lewis wuffed loudly.

"I know you could eat more, Lewis. But not right now. Maybe later."

George took out his sketchpad and drew a quick rendering of the Café Du Monde. The building was not inspiring or significant in the least, but the green-and-white-striped awnings over the outdoor eating area were interesting, as well as the curious mix of people sitting there, chatting, eating, and drinking coffee.

This day, while still warm, especially for the late fall—actually hot, if the truth be told—was less humid than the previous day. George was still sweating as he drew but less so than before. Lewis happily panted away, his fur coat in need of serious dethatching.

George added a few people to his drawing: the woman with the huge flowering hat, the man with a tie-dyed T-shirt and feather boa, the young couple, entwined and in love, the older gentleman sporting a wild beehive sort of beard, wearing spats.

He leaned over to Lewis.

"A curious mix of people, Lewis."

Even Lewis, who normally drew a small crowd, was all but overlooked by the steady stream of locals and tourists who traveled past.

After the beignets, Lewis and George drove into the Garden district, filled with wonderful old vintage homes: Victorians, Gothic, Neoclassical mansions, faux Southern plantation homes. All manner of architectural styles were represented.

"It's like Charleston—only thicker and more Southern and much more eclectic and diverse, Lewis," George explained as they drove along slowly.

He did not stop at any house. He slowed a number of times, however.

"Maybe I'm done drawing old houses, Lewis. And maybe I'm too hot to care."

During one of his slowdowns, Lewis whined a bit and looked backward at his seat belt attachment.

"You want to go out?"

Lewis remained silent.

"You want to lay down in the back?"

At this, Lewis wuffed loudly.

George unfastened him, and Lewis slowly clambered over the center console and into the back. George watched him circle three times and flop to his side, laying his head down and closing his eyes.

I get it, Lewis. The heat makes me tired, too.

And I am so tired. So very, very tired.

And I want this to be over so very, very much.

48

Irene arrived at the city limits of New Orleans in the middle of the afternoon rush hour in a downpour of blood-warm rain. It meant she had to roll up the windows and rely on the VW's anemic air circulation system to keep the windshield unfogged and the sweat on her forehead at bay.

The system did neither task effectively.

Irene used the already damp bandana to smear around the condensation on the windshield, the wipers trying to keep up with the dense rain.

"I need to get off the road soon," Irene said aloud, to herself. She had been driving all day, the trip from Tallahassee taking much longer than she anticipated. She did veer off for nearly several hours into Pensacola, driving through the historic Pensacola Village, filled with historic homes and churches and buildings, hoping to see a black RV or a scooter cruising by—but she did not.

Pensacola was on his map. I'm sure of it.

By the time she'd found her way back to the freeway, the sky had grown dark and she had grown tired, so she'd found a Super 8 Hotel for the night.

And now, nearly a full day later, she was lost and tired and frustrated in the thickening outskirts of downtown New Orleans.

"I am sure he would stop here. Draw the Superdome, at least. Wouldn't he?"

She found the exit pointing to the Superdome, scooted down the ramp, and circled the massive structure three times, searching for the black RV. She saw nothing coming close to resembling it.

The rain had stopped, replaced by humidity, just as thick and oppressive as the rain, and in some ways, more intrusive.

She stopped the van, hopped out, and stood, staring at the huge arena.

"Nope. He would never draw this. Too symmetrical. Too uninteresting. And other than it being large and otherworldly, he would not find it interesting."

Maybe.

She drove down into the Mardi Gras party district—Bourbon Street and the few streets around it.

George would never come here. And while the architecture is interesting, he probably couldn't see past the tawdry bars and tourists.

Irene smiled to herself.

And no one says tawdry *anymore, do they?*

She drove past the St. Louis Cathedral at the far edge of Bourbon Street.

"Wow. Looks like it was designed by the people who built Cinderella's Castle in Disney World."

She looked for a parking place and did not find one.

What would I do inside anyhow?

She drove back toward the Superdome. On a side street a few blocks off the main tourist route, thinking it would be a quicker route to the Garden District, she came to a stop behind a moving truck that was trying to maneuver, backward, up a very narrow driveway, making turns and stops every few inches.

"This will take forever," she said to herself and put the van into reverse and found herself on Bourbon Street again.

"This will take me forever."

She again was stopped by a construction crew digging up the street.

I'm tired and thirsty and I want to get out of here.

She pulled to the side, parked the van, and walked down the block to a coffee shop.

Maybe a jolt of espresso will help.

With coffee in hand, she felt a bit more at peace.

I'll find him. With luck, I'll find him. It's all I need—some good luck—for a change.

As the thought came to mind, she slowly walked past a storefront painted entirely in black: Marie Laveau's House of Voodoo.

Now . . . this is different. Something you don't see in Omaha, for sure.

She stopped and peered into the window, filled with books and talismans and charms and masks and small, faceless cloth dolls and bottles of green and amber liquid and a scattering of rings and beads and candles and incense burners.

A sign in the back of the window, white chalk on a small blackboard, read: "Spells Cast. People Found. Love Assured."

Underneath was a small skull, smiling, with hollow eyes.

And just then, a young woman dressed in black, with a black smock and dark, smoldery eye shadow, stepped out of the store and nearly bowed to Irene.

"I sense you are lost, friend."

Irene looked up, surprised.

"Me?"

"Yes, my friend," the young woman said, her voice syrupy, slow. "Your aura. I sense confusion. You're looking for someone."

Irene did not reply but stared at her, shocked.

"I sense I am correct."

"Maybe," Irene mumbled. "Sort of."

"You know, this is a place of peace and calm," the young woman said. "And of knowledge. I can help. The spirits can help. What is lost can be found."

Irene swayed on her feet, just an inch, as if she were being drawn in by some unseen, magnetic force.

"The world is much more than we can see with our eyes. I can help you, friend. I can help find what was lost and restore what was damaged."

Irene was about to take a step closer. Then she opened her eyes wide, shook her head, just a little, like a person waking from a thirty-second catnap, and all she could see, all around the young woman dressed in black, was more black, like the humidity of the city had taken on a color, or absence of color, and the air and the clouds all slowly lost their natural hue and assumed the color of midnight. Irene blinked several times, and the black disappeared, in an instant, as if a veil had been wrenched away from her eyes.

"Umm . . . thank you. But no. I have . . . I have . . . I have an appointment to keep. Yeah . . . an appointment."

The young woman stepped toward her.

"Whoever, or whatever, can wait a moment or two. It is all it will take. Come in. Browse for just a moment. You will find what you desire inside. We have everything you might possibly want. Answers. Peace. And more, perhaps."

Irene shook her head again.

"No . . . I don't think . . . I mean . . . they won't wait. The people I need to find. I have to be there."

And so saying, she turned and walked away, as quickly as she could, without resorting to running, step-step-step-step, faster and faster, until she reached her van, breathing deeply, her coffee all but forgotten.

She fumbled for her keys, managed to get the door open and the engine started, and she drove away as fast as the speed limit allowed, not knowing where she was going, except knowing she was running from the blackness she saw.

I have to find him. I have to find him.

She turned away from the Superdome and headed north.

He's not here. He must have moved on. Away from the blackness.

She tried to calm her jangled nerves by breathing deeply.

At least, I hope so.

Two miles later, another thought came to her.

Maybe this is something I need to pray about.

Maybe.

49

At the same time Irene was running from the voodoo shop on Bourbon Street, George and Lewis were driving west on Interstate 10.

"There is nothing I want to see until we hit San Antonio. Okay, Lewis?"

After leaving New Orleans, Lewis appeared to perk up. Maybe it had to do with the temperature and humidity, George thought, or maybe it had to do with something else altogether.

"We're going to San Antonio, Lewis. The Alamo. Know what the Alamo is?"

Lewis looked over to George and wuffed.

"Just the symbol of Texas, is all. And it was a great movie with John Wayne."

Lewis remained silent.

"Yes, I know. No one knows who John Wayne is anymore. Used to be all kinds of old movies shown on TV to fill up the empty spaces between real programs. Now everyone watches what they want, anytime they want. Hardly any old movies on anywhere."

Lewis must have heard this opinion before because as George was speaking, he simply lay down on the front seat and closed his eyes.

"So, today, we'll get to the west side of Houston and stop. If it is still as hot as it was, we'll go to a hotel. If it cools down, we'll look for an RV park. Okay?"

Lewis almost wuffed but instead offered a most muffled reply, like a wuff passing through a pillow.

George opted again for a hotel, an all-suites hotel again, with a powerful air-conditioning unit.

This time he was proactive in presenting Lewis. When George got to the front desk, he announced to the young man behind the counter he was traveling with his service dog—a therapy dog—and inquired if they had a designated room for such arrangements.

"We do, sir. And we are happy to accommodate our guests with special needs."

In the evening, in the cool of the hotel room, after bringing in dinner from a fast food restaurant, George also brought in all his sketchbooks—fifteen in total, so far.

Using a white paint pen, he marked the cover of each one with the cities and locations included inside and added the dates they were visited and then numbered the books, starting with number one from Towanda, Pennsylvania.

He tucked them all into a box he had brought along to fit them exactly. He figured he had room for one, perhaps two more books.

"It will be plenty," George said as he slipped them into the wooden box carefully and in order. "The Alamo. Maybe the River Walk there. A cable car in San Francisco. Maybe the street always photographed with the row of Victorians. Maybe Alcatraz. And the Golden Gate Bridge, for sure. And a couple of spots along the coast. And then I'll be done."

Lewis had not been paying attention. He had eaten his kibble plus a plain hamburger patty from Smashburger and was now nodding off on the floor, snoring quietly.

"These will be something for Tess to remember me by."

He closed the lid and latched it.

"It will have to be enough."

George stood on the street in front of the Alamo.

"Looks just like the one in the movie."

Lewis looked at the building, then up at George, and wuffed politely, as if he felt the need to respond but was not sure of exactly what he was responding to.

A low scud of clouds hovered above, and the weatherman had promised afternoon rain, but the morning had been predicted to be dry. A chilled wind blew in from the west, causing small eddies and swirls of dust to dance in the streets and along the sidewalks.

George found a bench a short distance from the entrance, and Lewis knew the drill. He found a spot to sit and began watching the few people who passed by, as George took out his pens and pad.

"Over 250 years ago, Lewis, is when the battle was," George said as he began sketching. The building was not ornate or large or architecturally significant, but few other structures in America held as much mystique and history as did this one mission.

George shaded the sky gray above and drew the few trees bent slightly because of the wind. After all these months, he felt more and more confident with his ability and technique.

"I think it is odd, Lewis, we are sitting here, in peace and quiet, at the exact spot where perhaps one thousand men perished. Makes you think, doesn't it?"

Lewis wuffed softly. Like Gettysburg, this location brought Lewis to a more somber, quiet place. Normally, he would dance and smile and wuff as people came by, asking, in his own way, to be paid attention to. He did none of it this morning. He sat, quietly and solidly, just by George.

As they both pondered the solemnity of this place, the front doors of the mission opened and a small group of young men came out, all wearing long brown frocks and some sort of rope belt, with hoods on the robe left folded to their backs.

Lewis looked over and then back to George. He did it often when he was confused.

"They're monks, Lewis. I think they're monks. Like a priest or pastor. Only more strict. I think."

They smiled and talked among themselves and walked down the sidewalk toward George and Lewis, and when they got to Lewis, they all stopped as a group, and two of them knelt down near Lewis.

"Good dog," one of them said.

"His name is Lewis."

"Lewis, you are a good dog," the other said, his words carrying a definite Texas twang to them.

Ask questions . . .

"I take it you are monks," George said. "Forgive me if I'm wrong . . . but I don't think I have ever met a monk before."

"Novice monks," the one with the Texas accent stated.

"From up at the Holy Archangel Monastery in Spring Branch," the other said. "A bunch of us—well, the rest of this group here—had never been to the Alamo before. As loyal Texans we felt obligated to show them the true Shrine of Texas."

The rest of the group murmured a bit, none of which George understood.

"Foreigners, mostly," the first said. "Me and Brother Thomas are the only Texans in the entire novice class. I say if you're here to serve mankind, you have to understand where you are now. And what better place to start than the Alamo—if you're in Texas."

George thought by now he would be used to meeting the odd and curious people, drawn to him because of Lewis, but it was apparent he was not.

"What's the inside like?" George asked. "Inside the mission. Dogs aren't allowed."

"Well, then, let us serve you a little today. You go inside. I noticed you drawing. Please, take your time and draw the inside of the mission. Your good dog Lewis will be in the capable hands of seven novice monks—two of whom are Texas-born and bred and know something about big—in dogs, as well as states."

George had become accustomed to the curious help he often received from strangers.

"Are you sure you don't mind? You sure you have the time?"

"A monk's time is God's time. If we can serve you in some small way, it is our pleasure, and God's pleasure, to do so. Now go in and draw, y'all."

George looked at Lewis.

"Lewis—no trying to convert these nice young men, okay?"

Lewis wuffed, obviously enjoying the attention.

And George hurried inside the dark and close interior of the mission.

"He'll stop at San Antonio. I would. The Alamo. He would have to draw it. It was on his list."

Irene was piloting her van along the interstate, growing tired of having to struggle against a persistent westerly wind.

"Other vans are bigger," she said once, "but this one is lighter than most. The wind just shoves it around."

The more miles Irene placed between her and the blackness she had felt out front of the voodoo shop in New Orleans, the better she felt.

"Never experienced anything like it before," she said to herself. "All my years. Never. It was as real as this wind. Maybe you can't see it, but I sure as heck felt it."

She gripped the steering wheel harder than needed.

"Maybe all the God stuff Eleanor and Douglas always talk about is playing tricks on me."

And two miles down the road and she thought, "No, maybe I'm just ready to hear what they have been saying."

She saw the sign reading SAN ANTONIO 225 miles.

"And maybe the Alamo will lead me to the truth they always talk about."

And she wanted to add, "But I doubt it," but she did not.

Inside the Alamo was dark and quiet and somber, plain, unadorned, and simple.

Subdued light filtered through two large windows on the south side. George slowly walked in the dim light, trying to see if there was a vantage point to present a good spot for a sketch. But the simple nature of the inside of the mission did not present many opportunities. A brace of flags flew at one end, representing the countries from which the defenders had hailed.

George stopped and stood and closed his eyes for a moment.

People died here—for what they believed in—for what they saw as the truth. It was a fool's mission. They knew their fate. They had to.

283

In the end, after a long while, George decided against drawing anything in the interior.

The space is too sacred for me trying to capture it.

He came out and saw several people surrounding the group of monks, chatting away, Lewis in the center of it all, as usually occurred.

When George came up, the Texas monk called to him.

"We have to get one of these Lewis dogs. We have never talked to so many people before. Lewis is the best introducer I have ever seen."

"He does have a talent," George said. "And I appreciate you watching over him while I was inside."

"It was our pleasure, sir. You should enjoy this life. It's all we have here on earth. Enjoy what God gave us. Live our lives to the fullest. And serve God by serving man. Simple, right?"

George waved to them as they departed, their robes sweeping along the dusty sidewalk. Lewis wuffed at them as they departed, then looked up at George and wuffed again.

"I know, Lewis. I know. You want me to 'get' it. But I don't think I can."

50

In the late afternoon, Irene saw the first sign indicating her distance from San Antonio.

"Only some two hundred miles. I can do it by dark."

He has to stop there for sure. And I'm sure I'm not far behind him. I know this is a fool's mission—trying to catch him on the road. A needle in a haystack, for certain.

She snapped off the radio, which only received AM frequencies, because she had grown tired of tuning and retuning to keep a station clear. Her efforts only seemed to last ten miles or so before the static began to build and the words became unintelligible.

I'll spend the night in San Antonio and get to the Alamo at first light. If he's there, he would be there early.

George looked on his tablet, querying sites around San Antonio. There were many, but none of them intrigued him enough to stay an extra day.

"We'll leave tomorrow morning, Lewis. Okay with you?"

Wuff.

"And then we'll head straight for the Grand Canyon. Since it is so far off-season, maybe it won't be crowded."

Wuff.

"I know you like crowds, Lewis. But I don't."

Wuff.

"It will be a long drive, Lewis. You okay with it?"

Wuff. Wuff.

"The tablet says it will take twenty-two hours. A long drive. Probably three days. We'll stop a few times. If the weather stays warm, we'll do RV parks. If it gets cold, we may do hotels. You mind hotels, Lewis?"

Wuff.

"Good. Just don't blow our therapy dog cover."

Wuff.

The skies remained dark and overcast as Irene puttered into a parking lot just a block from the Alamo.

"I'm not even sure if the Denny's are open now, it's early."

She locked the car and walked over to the front of the Alamo.

"9:00? What am I going to do for . . ."

She looked at her wristwatch.

". . . for two hours?"

She looked around, trying to get her bearings. She walked west, toward a group of tall buildings. She saw a Marriot sign on one of them.

"I can get coffee there for sure and wait in the lobby."

Two blocks west, she did indeed find the hotel and the lobby coffee shop open for business. She ordered a large coffee with extra cream and sugar and found an empty corner of the lobby and sat and began her two-hour vigil.

George found the route through Texas on the interstate a bit boring, as is the case with most interstates.

"You think they could find something interesting out here, Lewis."

Today, Lewis was asleep in the back of the RV, on the floor. He tried sleeping on the couch once, but a sudden stop rolled him to the floor with an embarrassing thud, and he would not climb back up while the RV was in motion. George listened for Lewis's wuff of agreement but instead only heard his soft adenoidal snoring.

"I suppose the civil engineers planned it this way. Interesting views are probably more expensive, so why not build the road where no one is and no one wants to go—except through it."

Before leaving, he penciled out his route, with stops in Lubbock, Albuquerque, and somewhere around the Grand Canyon. He would still have to drive some eight hours a day, not his preferred mode of traveling, but if he wanted to get to San Juan Island on time, there would be no drawing stops, other than the few he had planned for on the West Coast.

"So, we'll just have to drive harder, Lewis."

Oh, I forgot. He's sleeping.

He looked out at the vast, empty plains.

And perchance to dream.

<hr>

At 8:45, Irene stood up, took her now empty coffee cup back to the coffee shop, and headed back to the Alamo. The sky remained overcast and gloomy, the sun barely apparent through the thickness of cloud.

"Fits my mood, just fine," Irene muttered to herself.

She arrived at the western side of the mission just as a park ranger was unlocking the massive wooden door.

"Good morning, ma'am. You're our first visitor today."

She offered him a weak smile in return.

She had not noticed any black RVs in the area, nor had seen George or Lewis camped outside, drawing.

Maybe I missed them again. No. I did miss them again.

She walked inside, her footsteps echoing in the empty space, echoing against the simple masonry and stucco-covered walls.

"There's not much to see in here, is there?"

She saw a bench on one side, and since she was the only person inside, she sat down and looked up.

"Where's the cross? Isn't there supposed to be a cross in here?"

I'll bet Eleanor and Douglas would expect a cross in a church building.

The door opened and a single person came in—an old man, with a cane, walking slowly.

Maybe since it was a fort back then, in the Alamo days, maybe they didn't have a cross back then.

The man walked past her and smiled and nodded his head.

"Sacred spaces . . ." was all he said and continued walking.

Sacred spaces?

Irene tried to calm her inner voices. Her tension had been building inside, ever since she left Charleston, ever since Eleanor had spoken of forgiveness and guilt, ever since some sort of near-cold spark had been rekindled. She realized now she was searching. And she was not sure exactly what she was searching for. George and Lewis, for one—for sure—but there was something else now. Perhaps it had always been, Irene thought, but the spark had now become a flame—an uncomfortable flame.

A flame she wanted extinguished—one way or the other.

What do you want from me, God? What do you want?

She looked around, as if her thoughts had somehow been sounded out loud and had filled the quiet space. The old man did not stop or turn back to her.

What do you want?

She closed her eyes.

Okay. I admit I am lost. I can do it. It's obvious, right? Is this what you want? Eleanor said admitting one's weakness was the start. Is this it?

All the words that Eleanor and Douglas had shared with her over the years came bubbling back into her consciousness.

Okay. I'm lost. It's easy.

She took a deep breath.

Maybe this is the question I need to ask.

She held her breath.

Can you find me? Even now? After all this time?

From outside, from the dark sky, from above, came a soft roll of thunder, slowly building upon itself until it filled the entire sky, as it were, like a freight train moving fast across the universe above.

Okay, okay, I hear you.

Then a strike of lightning lit up the southern sky, and the flash ghosted against the windows of the mission.

Can you forgive me? It's the question I don't want to ask because I am afraid of the answer.

Another roll of thunder twisted across the area.

Under her heart, deep inside, came a gentle uncoiling, a gentle rebirthing. She gasped at the feeling, like a fish coming into the air for the first time—only this fish found it could actually live in the land of the air-breathers. She opened her eyes.

You don't do things in a small way, do you?

And as she sat there, with the sound of rain pattering on the roof, she felt the weight slowly edge off her shoulders and edge off her heart.

It has been decades since she had felt totally unburdened.

And now, it was happening, life a flower opening, like a butterfly unfurling its wings, like a woman waking from a deep sleep, blinking her eyes to a new reality . . .

Is this what forgiveness feels like?

A lightning strike flashed again, with a roll of thunder as an echo.

She looked up and, perhaps for the first time in years, smiled, an honest smile.

Okay. Okay. Please forgive me.

Please.

51

In Lubbock, they stayed at an all-suites hotel again. The larger room sizes suited Lewis well.

"I don't want to make my bed in the morning, okay? Simple."

Lewis liked sleeping on the other side of a big, soft hotel bed.

A few hours and a few hundred miles west of Albuquerque, they did the same thing, finding the same brand of hotel within a stone's throw off the interstate. Lewis appeared to be getting in practice sitting in front of the reception desk, looking genial and mildly therapeutic. No one seemed to register any note of concern or asked if St. Bernards were often used as therapy dogs.

"It's like at the movies or McDonald's: no one wants to ask impertinent questions—like asking to see your ID to prove you're a senior citizen. Besides, Lewis, every hotel staff we have met so far were no older than twenty, and to them, everyone my age looks ancient. And I guess I have a trustworthy face."

Lewis would smile at this—having heard it before, several times— and wuff appreciatively.

From west of Albuquerque, George set a course to the Grand Canyon, directly. He thought about stopping in Phoenix and seeing his daughter but was afraid that might weaken his resolve. He did not want that to happen.

"Only eight hours, Lewis. And then we're there."

Lewis snorted, just a little.

"Okay. Eight hours to the hotel. But it claimed it was only forty-five minutes from the canyon. Not too bad."

Wuff.

George woke feeling fairly miserable. His head hurt and his sinuses hurt, and he wondered if he were coming down with something potent.

"Maybe it's the dry heat in these places. Back home, in Gloucester, it is always sort of damp. Not like out here in the desert. Maybe it's just—too dry."

Lewis snorted, then he did it again, three more times.

"Maybe we both have it, Lewis. Wonder if there is a human and animal urgent care place combination around here."

Lewis looked up, a hopeful expression on his face.

"Lewis, I don't think such a thing exists."

George took three aspirin at breakfast and left the bottle out in the front of the RV, just in case. He only managed two cups of coffee and a single piece of toast.

"Maybe I'll feel better when we get to the actual canyon."

Irene looked at the road atlas she'd purchased at a Shell station on the outskirts of San Antonio. Up until this moment, she had never once used a map; instead, relying on road signs and directions given to her by friends.

Now she needed knowledge of the most direct route.

She found San Antonio, then had to flip to several pages.

"Good grief, that's far. I forgot about New Mexico being there."

She went back inside to get a fresh cup of coffee.

"Ever drive to the Grand Canyon?" she asked the older woman who sat on a tall bar stool behind the counter.

"Nope. Not much of a nature lover, I'm afraid. But it's a pretty far poke. Couple of days, anyhow."

"Ye gads. I thought I was closer."

"Gotta remember only the south side of the canyon is open. My son went a couple of years back. He liked it. But then he likes lots of strange things. The south side is where the Indians built the glass bridge out over the edge. I saw pitchers of it. Wouldn't set foot on it for all the oil in Texas, I tell you."

"Well, thanks."

Irene puttered out of the station.

A couple of days. I wonder if I could do what I did when I was in college and just do a straight drive with no stops.

She considered the effort for a moment.

Naw. I couldn't. Not anymore. But maybe two days instead of three. Maybe.

George felt no better when he pulled into the parking area of the Grand Canyon. He looked out and saw more than twenty tour buses.

"I don't know, Lewis. I don't have a good feeling about this."

Lewis stared outside.

"And I don't feel up to drawing anything today."

He pulled to the side of the road. He could see the rim of the canyon from where he sat.

"It is overcast. And it looks like rain."

George put the flashers on in the RV and walked quickly to the path along the southern rim of the canyon. He looked out for a moment or two, then hurried back to the RV.

"Lewis, it is impressive, but I don't think I feel up to drawing anything today. And there are just too many buses here."

Lewis all but shrugged in reply.

"Let's just head to California. It will be warmer there. And sunny."

Wuff.

Irene had never felt so bedraggled as she did when she pulled into the vast parking lot of the Grand Canyon visitor center. The signs had encouraged everyone to park further away and take the complimentary shuttle bus to the rim, but traffic was light, and Irene figured she would be able to find a parking spot.

She cruised through several lots, looking for George's black RV. Then she parked in a lot close to the center, switched off the engine and let out a huge breath.

"I am so tired of driving. How do truck drivers do it?"

She got out, stretched several times, bending to the left and right, hearing the muscles or the joints or the ligaments in her back snapping and cracking and complaining.

"He's not here."

She walked toward the center, toward the facilities and coffee and maybe a couple of candy bars.

"I've eaten more terrible food the last four days than I have in the last four years."

She sat with a cup of coffee and stared out at the groups of people following their tour guides, like sheep following a shepherd.

I know the odds of finding him on the road were so remote. I know. But I had to try. And I had to go this direction anyhow. To get to San Juan. Maybe I'll get to California and simply head north through the center of the state. It would be faster and then I could rest and recuperate on the island—and wait for him there.

As she pondered her next move, she slowly unwrapped a value-sized Snickers bar and chewed it thoughtfully, not tasting its innate goodness nor feeling the slogan written on the wrapper: "Snickers. Satisfies."

George pulled into the parking lot of the Hotel del Coronado. Usually, while parking, or getting close, George would explain to Lewis why the specific spot was noteworthy or historic. Today, he did not. He simply drove in and parked.

Lewis got out, sniffed at the air.

"Salt in the air, Lewis. Like back home. Where Alex lives. Remember?"

Then, Lewis seemed to become much more animated, aware. He looked to the west, then offered his sedate St. Bernard dance, back and forth, left and right.

"Yes, the ocean over there, Lewis. But first, I'm going to draw the main building. Then we'll look at the beach, okay?"

Lewis wuffed happily.

George set up his chair on the far side of the circular drive by the main building, with its famous conical roof and windows circling the cone, and topped with a circular widow's walk. It was a complex building, with lots of intricate detail. In the sun, in the sea air, with the desert behind them, George felt much better. His sinuses, if they had been the problem, seemed to be functioning as designed. His headache had left somewhere in the middle of the drive to California.

Meant to live at sea level, I guess.

It took George nearly two hours to finish the drawing. Of course, the palm trees and the various additions and wings to the original structure added time and complexity.

He sighed deeply when it was finished.

He stowed the drawing back in the RV and took Lewis toward the beach. When he got closer, he could see that the majority of the area by the hotel had been fenced off. The signs on the fences read: BEACH ACCESS FOR HOTEL GUESTS ONLY.

In small print, underneath the warning were the following words: Public Access at Coronado Central Beach. Violators will be prosecuted.

"Well, Lewis. I guess no walking in the surf today. Maybe later, okay?"

Lewis appeared confused.

"I know, Lewis. It doesn't make sense. But we'll get you to a beach soon enough."

Irene took out the map for California and attempted to get her bearings.

Too many freeways and way too many numbers.

She traced the route with her finger.

There. Up the middle of the state. Interstate 5. It will get me north as fast as anything else.

She pulled back into traffic and began her watch for road signs bearing the number five.

I'm tired of thinking I just missed him. This way I can simply wait for him.

She pulled even with a Mack truck, the van shuddering just a little from the turbulence.

If he is still going to where he said he was going. The island is sixty square miles with a half dozen campgrounds and RV parks and just about as many hotels and B&Bs. I can do a circle every day if I have to. Or wait by the ferry docks. I'll find him. I will.

52

George found an RV park near Candlestick stadium. It was a longish drive into town on the scooter, but it was as close as George could get.

"Hotels in a big city are very expensive, Lewis. And I bet they are fussier about therapy dogs. This will work out fine. We'll drive in on the side streets. Okay?"

Lewis seemed to understand they were settling in one place for a couple of nights, and it appeared to make him happy.

Driving the scooter around San Francisco proved not to be the novelty it was in other locales. It appeared as if the local population were more than used to St. Bernards in sidecars, wearing helmet and goggles or not. As they scootered toward downtown, hardly a soul turned to give them a second glance.

A few did, and it made Lewis happy. If someone yelled "Hello" or waved, Lewis took it upon himself to wuff back, in return, smiling as best he could with his headwear in place.

George found several locations he deemed sketch worthy: Alcatraz from Fisherman's Wharf, a pier laden with sunning sea lions, a cable car, Coit Tower, the Painted Ladies (the series of colorful side-by-side Victorians), the Palace of the Legion of Honor, Lombard Street, and the Transamerica Pyramid Building (which he did not like but found worthy of a quick sketch, nonetheless).

Of all of them, Lewis appeared to enjoy the sea lions the most. The aquatic animals barked and wuffed as they flopped and lounged on the piers, and Lewis felt obligated to wuff back at them. A few of them looked up, perhaps weary at being shouted at by tourists and, apparently seeing no threat in Lewis, promptly fell back to a prone position.

"No, Lewis, you cannot go out there and play with them. They are protected animals. It's why the boat owners can't get rid of them. But if I had a boat there, I could see why they're frustrated."

After nearly a week in town, George had one more spot to draw: the Golden Gate Bridge. He wanted to catch it in the early light, so he and Lewis rose early and made it into town and to a small parking area at the south and east side of the bridge, looking up at the massive, yet delicate structure.

George pulled the scooter to a stop and adjusted it just so. He did not have room on the scooter for his chair, so he used the scooter seat to sit and draw. Lewis usually lumbered out of the sidecar, walked around a bit, stretching and yawning, then sat down on the ground next to George and the scooter, apparently waiting for people to stop and chat.

The early sun lit the bridge, making the orange hue of the structure glow red and gold.

George smiled as he drew.

"Magnificent bridge, isn't it, Lewis? Makes the bridges in Pittsburgh look like Erector Sets, doesn't it?"

George was certain Lewis had no idea of what an Erector Set was.

Do they still make Erector Sets?

He drew a few more lines.

I'm sure they do. Maybe they do it with plastic parts now.

Lewis stood up and shook, then stared back down the parking lot.

A young man, carrying a set of binoculars, was walking toward them. He stopped by Lewis.

"I bet he's friendly, right? A dog this big doesn't need to bite anyone to be intimidating."

"He is friendly. He's Lewis."

The young man bent down and scratched at Lewis.

"It's good, sir. Your drawing, I mean. If you don't mind me saying. I see a lot of people down here painting or drawing this view. I would put yours up in the top five I've seen so far."

George stopped sketching.

"Thank you. You come here often?"

"A couple of times a week. For the last two years."

George turned to the young man. He was of average height, average looks, brown hair, cut short, brown eyes, a rounder, pleasant face, and wore a zippered sweatshirt with UCLA stitched across the front.

"Are you . . . studying bridges? Or an architect?"

"No. Nothing so good. I work at a Starbucks, actually. Don't all post-graduate students in psychology work at Starbucks?"

George smiled, not sure if it was a joke or if he meant it as a serious commentary on his economic situation.

A smile seemed to be the appropriate response.

George felt the urge, the nudge.

Wait. He will tell you.

"I'm Amos. Amos Nescot."

"I'm George. And you met Lewis."

Wait. And he will tell you.

George, by now, was accustomed to these nudges. He still could not be sure if he was simply projecting or if Lewis had some sort of power. He had pretty much decided he was simply an old man who projected his feelings onto a dog who had no special power or ability—other than to encourage people to stop and chat.

"I'm sort of on a mission, I guess. It's why I come down here so often."

"A mission? Here? I don't see any homeless people. Or anyone in need."

Amos shook his head.

"Not down here. Up on the bridge."

George looked up. His drawing was half completed. He had the cables to add and perhaps the morning clouds to the west.

"On the bridge? I don't understand."

Amos appeared uneasy.

"You know, I've never told anyone why I'm here. Your dog made me stop. He seemed to want to know why."

"And now, so do I, Amos. Who's on the bridge? Who needs help from down here?"

Amos took a deep breath, then stared off into the distance, before looking back at George.

"You know over fifteen hundred people have jumped off the bridge since it was built? Every week, they say, one or two people jump."

"I had no idea."

Lewis snorted and stared up at them both.

"There's an allure to the bridge. Something hypnotic about it, they tell me. People, the ones who come out ready to jump, they stand in the middle of the span. Sometimes they pace back and forth. Sometimes they seem to be rehearsing what they're going to do. Sometimes, they take off their backpack and set it down. Or a purse. That's when you know they're getting serious."

George was stunned into silence.

"Two years ago . . . my brother jumped. He's gone, of course. They never found his body. That often happens. The water is cold and the current is strong."

"But . . . what . . ."

Amos nodded as if he anticipated the question.

"I sit over there on the bench. Gives me a clear view of the walkway. On this side. Most people use this side. So they can see the city, I guess. I watch. If I see someone just standing there. Or walking back and forth . . . I call the police, I read about one police officer—Briggs, I think his name is—who has talked, like, a hundred people out of jumping. So I call the police, and they send someone out to try and talk them down. It doesn't happen all the time. But in two years, I've been part of getting twenty people off the edge. One I didn't. And it . . . well, it still haunts me."

George could only stare.

"I know. They should do something about it. The people who run the bridge. Make it harder to get over the ledge. But, George, well, it wouldn't matter. People . . . desperate people would find a way. I guess I can only hope to save those I can save. Who are ready to be saved. Who want to be saved."

"Amos . . . I am astounded. I don't have the words to express . . ."

"You know . . . the way I figure it, if someone had seen my brother, if someone had talked to him, just listened to his pain, well, maybe he would still be here. There is always something to live for. There is."

"This is simply amazing. I am stunned."

Amos looked a bit embarrassed.

"You know, I've never told anyone this. Makes me feel a little . . . weird, I guess."

Lewis wuffed.

"Amos, we won't say a word. And besides, after I'm done here, we're traveling north."

"Well, it was nice meeting you both. Hope you have a good trip. And you draw well. I mean it. A gift."

Amos turned.

"I need to get over there, okay?"

"Sure. Good luck . . . I guess."

And Amos walked off, leaving Lewis to stare hard at George, wuffing softly, as if to say he needed to listen to the young man and hear there was always something to live for.

George closed his sketchbook without finishing the drawing. He motioned for Lewis to get back into the sidecar.

"Nice try, Lewis. Nice try."

But it won't work. I have made up my mind.

53

"Bejeebers . . . and I know no one says *bejeebers* anymore, but is it chilly here or what?"

George and Lewis sat in the RV as it was ferried toward the Friday Harbor on San Juan Island. The rain in Washington turned cloudy, rainy, and cold.

"Typical for this time of year," the ticket taker at the ferry said. "Though they're predicting some fine breaks tomorrow."

"Fine breaks?"

The man stared and smiled.

"You're not from around here, I take it. Fine breaks—when the sun comes out. We expect to see it tomorrow. Occasionally. Hopefully."

Despite the fact George knew the date of the end of his days, he had known it all along, he acted no differently today than he had acted on any other day.

Knowing is power. And power brings peace. Peace from guilt.

Breakfast of toast and coffee. He stopped at a small convenience store and bought a container of half-and-half. He made sure he had enough bread and kibbles for two more days. He checked the oil in the RV. He filled it with gas before they boarded the ferry.

"Gas has to be pricier on the island, Lewis. Might as well save a few pennies where I can."

Once they motored off the ferry at Friday Harbor, he drove south to a small RV park on the water. The website said whale sightings were common from the beach. George did not take note of what season would be best for watching for whales, but he thought he would like to see one, to see one before . . .

And then he changed the subject in his thoughts.

George and Lewis found the RV park and it was indeed perched above the shoreline. A path from the park led to the beach.

"If the sun comes out, maybe we'll walk down, Lewis. But not in this drizzle."

Lewis had hurried his functions outside and returned to the RV, waiting his toweled rubdown.

George set up the tablet and sent a quick e-mail to the Burdens, who were en route.

Mrs. Burden had written two days earlier:

> We are making great progress. As a person who seldom traveled, I am amazed at the beauty of this country— even in winter. The three-thousand-mile trip has been a wonderful event in the Burden family. Such memories. We have listened to books on tape, we have played games, we have visited Niagara Falls and Chicago and Wall Drug. Alex loves this trip. Of course, he is super excited about seeing Lewis again. No distance would be too great for Alex. And since this SUV is so big, my husband and I can change driving chores and the other can lie down, full-out flat in the back and take a nap. I recommend buying this sort of armored tank for any-one who does serious traveling. I will send you an e-mail tomorrow and let you know where we are. If the weather holds, and they say it will, we should be right on sched-ule and meet you in Friday Harbor as planned. Again, your gift to us has been wonderful. Thank you. Thank you. Thank you. Trudy Burden.

Lewis appeared to realize something of importance was nigh at hand. He paced about the small RV with more eagerness. He whined at the door. He did not eat all his food in the morning. He went from window to window, looking out, searching for something. He bumped his head into George's thigh or arm and leg several dozen times a day, as if asking "what's up?"

George did not want to mention Alex's name very often.

No need to get the dog any more anxious and excited than he already is. I don't think dogs understand what delayed gratification means. We'll wait until . . . well, he'll wait until they show up.

"Lewis, tomorrow, if the sun comes out at all, we'll walk to the beach and see if we can see a whale."

As he mentioned the beach, a snippet of a poem came back to him. Often, in the past few years, George's distant past appeared more real and more accessible than his more current memories. He began remembering classmates from elementary school and teachers and field trips and assignments turned in decades earlier—all while forgetting where he put his keys.

His memory included poetry—again.

Maybe the rhyming makes it easier to recall.

"Did I tell you, Lewis, Mr. Roescher was big on memorizing? This is the end of a poem . . . by . . . now, I forget the name. The poet's name, I mean. But I remember the poem."

> I grow old . . . I grow old . . .
> I shall wear the bottoms of my trousers rolled.
>
> Shall I part my hair from behind? Do I dare eat a peach?
> I shall wear white flannel trousers, and walk upon the
>   beach.
> I have heard the mermaids singing, each to each.
>
> I do not think they will sing to me.
>
> I have seen them riding seaward on the waves
> Combing the white hair of the waves blown back
> When the wind blows the water white and black.
>
> We have lingered in the chambers of the sea
> By sea-girls wreathed with seaweed red and brown
> Till human voices wakes us, and we drown.

George repeated it out loud to Lewis, who sat and watched, staring up at him, staring at his eyes, with a puzzled, near-worried expression on his wide face, no smile visible, no joy, just concern.

He remained silent after George had finished, as if to say he did not like the poem, no, not at all.

⸎

There were no whales in the water. Or if there were, they had decided to remain under the water and not show themselves to an old man, bent into the wind, and a large shaggy dog whose fur, tousled by the wind, appeared kinetic and alive.

Lewis wuffed several times, wuffed out to the waves, as if calling to them.

They did not answer.

In the evening, after a dinner of ramen noodle soup with added peas and ham, George set out to work on the three letters he had to write. One was to his daughter. One was to the Burdens. One was to the local law enforcement.

Of course, George would wait until they left—Lewis and Alex and the Burdens. He would not trouble them now. Afterward, he would mail the letters, then call the police and let them know what was about to happen. The Burdens would be home before they got the letter. The space, the geographical space would help shield them from having to discover . . . the situation and his solution.

George decided no other plan was viable.

The letter to the Burdens was brief. He thanked them for the time he had with Lewis and how he hated to have it end in this manner, but there was no other option.

The letter to his daughter was more complicated and much longer. And harder to write. He told her that he loved her deeply and that he loved her mother deeply, but there was too much pain in his heart to go on. "I would never want to have you placed in the position I was with your mother—life and death in your hands. The power of God. It is too much for a human to bear and too much for me to live with." He explained all the details of the wills and estate and which attorney to contact and how to dispose of any remaining effects.

In two pages, he summed it all up. And he signed it simply, "Love, your father."

The letter to the local authorities was the quickest. It simply informed them of what to do with the RV and the remains.

He placed all three in plain white envelopes and addressed each one with bold, distinct letters.

All the while he was writing, Lewis whined and paced and whimpered. George had offered to let him go outside three times, but each time, Lewis simply refused to go out. And if Lewis did not want to do something, it was a difficult matter to make him do something. So George was forced to let him stay inside and tried to tune out all Lewis's tics and outbursts.

As he sealed the last envelope, his tablet chirped loudly. George woke up the device and that saw that an e-mail had come in.

> Mr. Gibson, We have made splendid progress. We will be in Seattle this evening and plan on catching the early ferry to Friday Harbor. The man at the hotel said tourist traffic is almost nonexistent now, so we should have no trouble in getting on. He did say in summer, you might have to wait for two or three sailings. Alex is beside himself with happiness. We can't wait.
>
> Love, Trudy Burden.

George read the e-mail twice, then switched the tablet off. He reached over and put his hand on Lewis's head. It did nothing to calm the animal.

Plan your work. Work your plan. I will wait until they are gone. It will be for the best.

Lewis almost pushed George's hand away and snorted loudly.

Or something like that.

54

Lewis stepped away and stood apart from George. And for the first time during their many months together, Lewis growled. Not just a play growl, like when he growled and glared at squirrels, or when he played with another dog. No—this growl was real and authentic and could not be interpreted in any other way than to say Lewis was angry and upset and had to resort to more drastic measures than a simple whimper or whine.

And then he showed his teeth.

Just a little.

Just enough to let George know he still possessed teeth.

"Enough, Lewis. Don't show off. Alex said you would never bite anyone."

Lewis continued to growl.

George boosted himself up on the counter and reached under the small wooden panel and felt for the cold, plastic handle of the gun case. He found it, grabbed it, and slid back down to the ground.

Lewis began to bark. Not his usual wuffs and whines, but full-throated, full-voiced, loud, actual dog barks, barks of alarm and anger.

"Lewis, shut up," George barked back.

Lewis did not retreat. Not one inch. He lunged, and his jaws snapped and closed on the fabric of George's khakis, not coming close to skin, but showing he could affect damage, if he chose to.

"I said stop it, Lewis. I mean it. I could tie you up outside. And don't think I wouldn't do it. This is what I have to do and you're not going to interfere with it. It is the best for all. I just want to make sure everything is ready. You won't see it. You won't be here. So stop worrying."

Lewis stopped barking, backed up, and began nervously whining, pacing, in a tight back-and-forth pattern, never once letting his eyes slip off of George or the black case he had magically made appear.

Lewis sniffed and snorted and whined.

George sat down on his side of the couch. He had tried to estimate which position in the RV would provide the least damage, show the least carnage. He chose his usual spot but sat a bit closer to the wood-paneled wall. He unzipped the case and extracted the pistol. He slipped a single cartridge into the chamber. He made sure the safety was still on—and would be until he needed it to be off.

George wanted to rehearse things, so nothing would be a surprise. That is what engineers do—avoid surprises.

Lewis could not stop moving. He could not stop growling and wuffing and whirring. His eyes appeared frantic. His body appeared frantic.

"Lewis, settle down. It is almost over. It will all be okay. Honest. You'll be going home tomorrow and we'll never see each other again."

Then Lewis jumped up onto George's side of the couch, a spot he had never once occupied. His head and George's head were at the same level.

"Lewis, please. It will be okay. It's time. I'm just . . . I'm just done."

Lewis whined and lifted his right paw as if in supplication.

"I know what they said, Lewis, Eleanor, and Douglas. I know. But they don't know what I did. They wouldn't have been so kind to me and so understanding if they had known. And I know if there is a God anymore, which I don't know if there is, all I know is He could never forgive me. Not my sin. Not the blackness. Not the evil. He just couldn't—because I know I couldn't. I know I can't."

Lewis edged closer, as close as he could, and stared, deep into George's eyes.

"Lewis, please. This is what has to be done. And I'm ready. It is time. And I am so very tired, Lewis. So tired of living with this broken heart. I can't take it anymore."

Then Lewis did something most unexpected.

Instead of barking or biting or whining, all of which Lewis had already tried, the dog instead moved closer and closer, like a puppy, and burrowed his head into George's neck. He made a soft wurring sound in his throat, as if he were trying to calm a snappy, overly tired, overly rambunctious puppy.

Then he maneuvered himself to almost be facing George and then sort of stood and sort of crouched and lifted his front paws and placed each one on George's shoulders and then moved his body closer and embraced George in the closest thing to a hug as a dog could do. All the while he was trying to hug, he was making a soft, almost purring sound in his throat. It was a sound George had never once heard him utter. But it was calming, a calming puppy sound.

"I know, Lewis. You might be sad. But only for a while. You'll be fine without me. Alex is coming tomorrow. Everything will be better. It will be."

Lewis hugged harder and almost more fiercely, as if this were the only way he could show George how deep his feelings were, how deeply he shared George's pain, how deeply he wanted to help fix his pain. His claws caught on the back of George's shirt.

"I know, Lewis, I know," George said, his voice catching in his throat, his words becoming thicker, the obvious emotion of the dog playing heavy upon his own emotions.

I can do this. I can do this.

George felt the nudge, the unmistakable nudge, the nudge he had grown to accept as from himself—or Lewis. It didn't matter, he supposed. But it was there, nearly audible, definitely there.

Call out to Him. Call out to Him.

George tried to take a breath. His throat was tight, constricted. He had shut his eyes, unwilling to look into the pain in Lewis's face, the horror and the fear and the desperation.

Call out to Him.

George drew in a deep breath, finally.

Then his right hand, the hand holding the pistol, wavered, just an inch, maybe less.

Lewis must have felt the movement because he redoubled his efforts and his dog-purring and his hugs and his nudges.

George let his right hand fall. He placed the pistol on the table. Then he reached up and returned Lewis's embrace. Even though he would not use it until tomorrow, the rehearsal felt as real as anything as George had ever experienced. And to Lewis, well, Lewis did not understand the word *rehearsal*. To Lewis, what George was rehearsing felt as real as the dawn.

Lewis hugged him back, purring, wuffing, whimpering.

After a long moment, Lewis backed off, just a bit, to give George just enough room to speak.

"I miss her so much, Lewis. Not a day goes by I don't see her face or hear her voice. We tried everything, Lewis. All the doctors. All the treatments. And in the end, Lewis, what did I do? I prayed—just once—for her to die."

George sat back a little.

"It was because of me, Lewis. It was because of me she's dead."

Lewis pulled back and snorted, staring at his face, his eyes showing deep and total disagreement. Lewis then leaned forward and hugged him again.

And George simply broke and began to weep.

And wept into the tender paws of Lewis, until he could weep no longer.

The walls George had constructed around himself, around his heart, were, he thought, built of sturdy brick, built by an engineer, and whose only purpose was to keep the darkness inside and to keep the light from entering.

George had added layers to those walls over time, each day adding another thin veneer to the wall, each day of silence adding more to keep the pain inside and keeping people who loved him outside.

He'd worked hard at building those walls.

But it took a dog to show him no wall could stand before the truth.

No wall could stand before forgiveness—and the walls George had considered strong, built of heavy brick and mortar, were, in reality, only a mere shell, scrabbled together of tin and scraps and cardboard and held in place with guilt.

If the guilt could be dissolved . . .

And Lewis proved to be the solution, and the walls tumbled away, letting the light in and overcoming the darkness.

⸺❦⸺

Sometime, around midnight, George woke. He had fallen asleep on the couch, sitting up. It had never happened before. Except it happened tonight. High emotions were absolutely draining.

The pistol was still on the table.

The letters he'd left on the table were gone.

He blinked his eyes and rubbed his face. Like it had snowed inside the RV, the letters had been shredded into tiny, dog-sized bits and scattered all over the floor.

In the midst of this small snowdrift of nibbled letters, lay Lewis, snoring deeply.

They had both been near the precipice, they had both teetered on the edge, and now they both were exhausted.

Yet Lewis had one last task to accomplish.

Destroy the evidence.

As quietly as he could, George picked up the pistol, looked at it for a long, longing moment . . .

To sleep, perchance to dream . . .

Then he blinked again, withdrew the cartridge from the chamber, placed the pistol in the cavity of the case, and zippered it closed. As quietly as he could.

⸺❦⸺

Lewis blinked when he heard the soft ratcheting of the zipper. His eyebrows shifted, and one could tell he was looking at George, searching his face.

Then Lewis lumbered to a standing position. He looked down at the blizzard of paper bits on the floor and then looked back to George with a guilty look on his face.

"I know, Lewis. You chewed up the letters."

Lewis hung his head, as if in shame.

"Lewis, don't be sad. It's okay. It's okay that you chewed them up. Honest."

Lewis slowly lifted his head and his eyes, as if somehow he expected this to be a trick and he would be blamed for the mess nonetheless.

"Really, Lewis. It is okay. They had to be torn up."

Lewis's eyes went from shame to puzzlement, then to a more solid expression—an expression that conveyed much more than a dog's expression should ever have to convey. He walked over to George, placed his paws on his knees, lifted himself to be face-to-face. Then he wuffed so very softly and with so much understanding.

"Can He forgive me, Lewis?"

Lewis all but nodded and wuffed with firmness.

"Are you sure, Lewis? God can forgive what I did?"

Wuff. Wuff.

Then Lewis pushed his head against George's shoulder and against his heart and whirred softly.

"You're sure?"

Wuff.

"For now . . . for now, I'll just have to accept it, won't I, Lewis?"

And Lewis leaned back and did something he had never once done, in all their time together. He leaned forward and licked George's face.

Lewis made a face after doing so, but he still appeared happy.

"Lewis, you and I . . . we are quite the pair, aren't we?"

Wuff.

Wuff. Wuff.

55

As dawn broke over the island, and the sun made an early and unexpected appearance, George was sipping on his fourth cup of coffee, watching out toward the harbor, watching for the splash of a dark fin or the curved back of a whale.

Instead, he heard the rattle and clank of an old vehicle pulling up, at full speed, requiring a screeching halt, stopping just outside his front door.

He heard the other door open and slam shut, and by the time he reached his door, it was already being yanked open.

"You're alive. Thank God. You're alive."

Lewis, roused unexpectedly from a deep, emotionally drained sleep, rose with a clatter as well, barking and wuffing in surprise, trying to focus on what was happening.

"Lewis, look. It's Irene."

And the three of them were locked into a long, furry, sloppy, welcoming, joyous embrace.

And had they been looking, they would have seen the fluke of a whale's tail slap at the placid water of the bay, sending a shower of sparkling drops to be illuminated by the rising sun.

But none of the three saw it, and none of the three cared they had missed it.

56

The reunion at eleven was much more predictable, but no less joyous.

"They'll get the early ferry. Unless the ferry hits a whale or something, they'll be here before lunch."

Before Irene had appeared, George had already tidied up the RV, sweeping all the bits of letter and burning them outside, hiding the pistol, and putting away all he could put away.

George thought about taking the gun and pitching it into the dark waters of the Pacific, to be swallowed up by the cold depths. But he did not.

"I could sell it when I get back home. Waste not, want not."

He zippered the case and reinstalled the small padlock and then hid it again under the small panel of wood above the cabinets.

"It is what an engineer does, I guess."

When Irene showed up, Lewis was too overjoyed to go back to sleep, so the three of them hiked down to the water's edge and sat, watching the sun rise over the bay. Lewis never got close to the water, not being an aquatic canine, but was content to chase the gulls when they swooped too close for his comfort.

Just before the time came for the Burdens to arrive, George took a brush to Lewis and tried to make him as presentable as possible.

As he combed him through, George whispered to his friend, "I'm going to miss you, Lewis. You were . . . the best friend, ever. Ever and ever."

Lewis stood back and stared into George's eyes, telling him, in his own nonverbal way, George meant the same to Lewis, he was the best friend a dog could ever have . . . except for, maybe, a small boy named Alex. But after him, he would be number two, for sure.

When the Burden's SUV pulled up to the RV park and came to a stop, it was very difficult to tell dog apart from boy, such an intimate tangle of flesh and fur, of smiles and yelps of joy, of pure, unbridled elation and happiness.

Irene and George stood to one side, and the Burdens, Trudy and Lyle, stood to the other, watching Lewis attempt to envelop Alex and Alex attempt to envelop Lewis.

George introduced Irene to the Burdens, and her introduction only warranted a slightly arched eyebrow from Trudy, but the eyebrow was coupled with a welcoming smile. Later, after the celebration diminished, only slightly though, George asked everyone in for coffee.

"Alex looks taller," George said.

"He is. And Lewis looks lighter."

"He is," George replied. "He was dethatched in San Francisco. They put a bow on him and wanted to do his nails in pink. But I had to draw the line somewhere."

Alex and Lewis stayed outside while the adults sat inside and drank George's instant coffee and told of their specific adventures of traversing America.

When Alex finally popped in, breathless, cheeks red, eyes bright, followed by Lewis, of course, he sat next to his mom and looked up at her and asked, "Did you ask him yet?"

"No, Alex. Maybe you should ask him."

George was puzzled.

"Ask me what?"

Alex leaned forward, appearing quite earnest.

"Well, Mr. Gibson, you know I don't have any grandfathers . . ."

"No, I didn't know."

"Well, it's true. And lots of other kids have them. And when we have Grandparents' Day at school, I never have anyone to bring."

George nodded.

"So . . . would you like . . . want to be my grandfather? You wouldn't have to do anything. But you could come to my school and stuff. And you know Lewis. You could be both our grandfathers. Sort of."

George waited for a moment to reply. He swallowed several times before speaking.

"Alex, I would love to be your grandfather . . . for school and stuff."

"Swell, Mr. Gibson. It would be swell."

And no one says swell *anymore, do they?*

Epilogue

The old red VW van led the way into Pocatello, Idaho. Irene used her turn signals religiously, so George was well aware of her intentions to depart the interstate, nearly a half mile before the actual exit ramp appeared. They had taken turns leading and following since leaving San Juan Island two days prior.

"You're sure you want a slow VW bus to be part of your caravan? It is a long drive, you know," Irene said.

"Only three thousand miles or so," George replied. "We'll get to know each other as we go. In small chunks. At rest stops and lunch."

"And dinner?"

"Okay. Maybe dinner, too."

Irene smiled.

"No sense in being overwhelmed right away."

"Exactly."

As they both parked and walked toward Elmer's Restaurant, Irene took a chance and reached out and took George's hand in hers. She felt a momentary hesitation, or confusion, then he allowed his fingers to relax and intertwine with hers.

"Swell," she said.

"You know no one says *swell* anymore, don't you?"

She nodded.

"I do. I do indeed."

Group Discussion Guide

1. Let's start with the big question that drives the book: Did God answer George's prayer to allow his wife to die?

2. Does God hear the prayers of a person who does not claim to have faith?

3. We know that God uses all sorts of things to draw the lost to Himself. Do you think that God used Lewis, the St. Bernard, to reach George where no one else could have?

4. We all know, or have known, people who have suffered, or who are suffering. George's daughter, Tess, saw that her father was troubled. Should she have done more for him? And what might that be? (She did, after all, get George connected with the Burdens—and with Lewis.)

5. There is a lot of movement in the book—people on the move—as if running away from something, rather than running toward something. Does this mirror any of your own experiences with pain and loneliness?

6. Alex seemed very mature for his age—and at peace with events in his life, such as losing Lewis for a long period. Why do you think Alex was so composed? Do you think his early medical problems had anything to do with his maturity?

7. Trudy Burden recognizes early on that Lewis has a special bond with people—that he listens intently and subtly nudges people toward the truth. There is no clear indication that Trudy has faith, but do you think this experience will draw her closer to God?

8. Why do you think George was so intent on drawing—and leaving something behind for his daughter? Might he feel guilty over not being involved in her life—or upbringing? It does seem that he deferred a lot to his wife.

9. There are characters in this book who seem to be crippled—or at least hobbled—by guilt. And some of that guilt was decades

and decades old. What advice do you think might have saved them all those years of being weighed down by guilt?

10. Lewis leads a life without much carryover from his past—and seems to have little concern with the future. He lives in the present, as much as possible. Is there a lesson humans can take from living in the "now" and not worrying about what might happen?

11. If Lewis was not with George, do you think George would have followed through with his initial plan of ending his life?

12. What advice would you give to George and Irene about facing their future together—seeing as how they have been damaged by long-term guilt and repressed secrets?

13. Do you think God uses animals—or even a dog like Lewis—to reach people who may shun "religion" in any other form?

14. People tend to give animals human emotions. Are any characters in the book guilty of that? If so, does it affect the outcome of the story?

15. Do you think Irene or the Burdens or George's daughter, Tess, will ever know how close George came to committing that "ultimate act of anger"?

Want to learn more about Jim Kraus
and check out other great fiction from
Abingdon Press?

Check out our website at
www.AbingdonFiction.com
to read interviews with your favorite authors,
find tips for starting a reading group,
and stay posted on what new titles are on the horizon.

Be sure to visit Jim online!

www.jimkraus.com
www.facebook.com/james.kraus.18

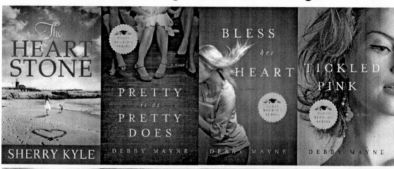
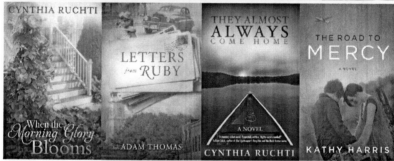

CPSIA information can be obtained at www.ICGtesting.com
Printed in the USA
BVOW04*0848040615

402934BV00001B/1/P